SORROW DRAW

TIM BRUMBAUGH

Copyright © 2024 by Tim Brumbaugh

All rights reserved.

No part of this publication may be reproduced, distributed, or transmitted in any form or by any means, including photocopying, recording, or other electronic or mechanical methods, without the prior written permission of the publisher, except as permitted by U.S. copyright law.

The story, all names, characters, and incidents portrayed in this production are fictitious. No identification with actual persons (living or deceased), places, buildings, and products is intended or should be inferred.

Original Cover and Inside Title Art by Yaroslav Gerzhedovich

1s Paperback Edition

ISBN: 979-8218396152

www.timothybrumbaugh.com

First edition 2024

For Dawn,
my first reader and my biggest fan.

And for Cyndi.
You would have loved this book.

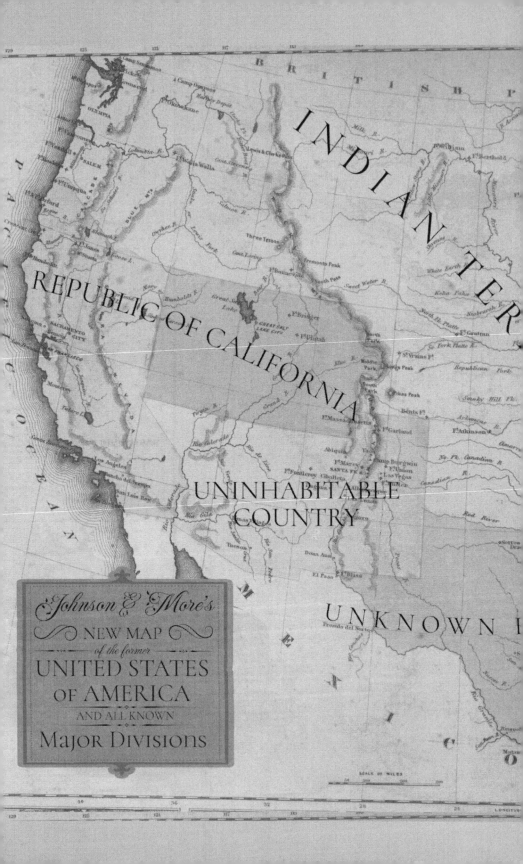

Chapter 1

Uncontested Lands, Old Mississippi (July, 1881)

Eudora Becker

She gripped his hand as a mother would hold the hand of a child on a scavenging run. A hardened grip, like stone, to yank the boy this way and that. But the palm she clutched was not that of a child, but of a man. A man who didn't move with the practiced skill of someone used to being on the run. They left an easy trail for their pursuers to follow, at a time when a single mistake could mean a bullet in the back, or a neck stretched by a rope.

The pair had made many mistakes in the week since they had escaped Memphis. In many ways, it was remarkable that they had gotten this far into the dusty and windswept southern corridor. The Uncontested Lands had taken more capable people than them, and the girl worried that her blind luck would only last so long.

But she *was* lucky. She always had been, and she was always content to let that luck conduct her through life but now that fear tightened her throat, she felt that providence had abandoned her. Fitting, she thought, that it would leave her now, in Mississippi, the land of the dead, when what passed for justice in the barren Wastelands was right behind them and gaining fast.

Through her exhaustion and fear, she had decided to keep to the river as much as possible. The underbrush in the dead woods beyond the banks of the Mississippi was thick and dry from the summer drought and nearly deafening to run through. The damp earth near the flowing waters muffled their steps, but it also left deep impressions of their bootprints.

"No help for it now," the woman said. "And no, we can't stop. They're nearly right on top of us." She knew what the man was thinking and she answered before he could speak it. It wasn't the first time she had done it, and he had once remarked that she could read his mind so easily she must be a witch. Truth be told, his mind was simple and required no witchcraft or divination to know.

"We pushed ourselves too far, Eudora." He stumbled but managed to stay upright. "We should never have left. Jesus Christ, I'm going to die."

"Not if we keep running," she said. "We ain't gonna die if we keep running."

"Oh, you'll be fine, no doubt. I don't think they're going to kill the daughter of Samuel Becker. I think I'm the one who's going to die," he said, his voice thick with fear.

"Fine, Jeremiah. We run or you die, if it's all the same to you."

The air was cold and dry and her sweat chilled her skin. She didn't know how much farther they could run, but they couldn't stop now. Men chased them. At least two bounty hunters, maybe more. They were closing in, and almost certainly on horseback. Horses were rare, but what they had stolen was rarer still and worth sending mounted men after.

They needed a miracle, but Eudora didn't put any confidence in those. Instead, she ran through the Wastelands like a fool who had lost her mind, driven mad by the choking dust that obscured the face of the sun so only a soft red glow burned in the sky to the east.

The river grew wide and shallow, and the bed underneath the muddy water hinted at underlying rocks, rather than silt. Perfect for concealing boot prints.

"This way." Eudora pulled hard to the right and took Jeremiah with her. They jumped from the bank into the icy waters of the Mississippi, but splashing through the river made almost as much noise as running through the underbrush. Up ahead, the river widened into swift-moving shallows. Flattened granite slabs, worn smooth under the current, emerged from the surface like the backs of great whales. "There. We can cross at those rocks and give them the slip."

Jeremiah, driven by panic, jumped from the bank and lost his footing on the slick rocks. Both feet kicked up, and he lost his grip on Eudora and fell. He threw his hands down to catch himself, but landed hard on his side, his left hand twisted underneath and made a sound like the popping of thick roots. His head hit the rocks with a crack and he cried out in pain, writhing in the shallows like a fish.

"Worthless son of a whore, get up." Eudora fell to her knees beside him. The river roared in her ears and the cold water stung her skin and weighed down her clothes. She grabbed his collar and rolled him onto his stomach, still cursing him.

She cursed herself as well. The most foolish thing she had done since escaping Memphis was to choose Jeremiah to run away with. In the weeks since they left, she had nearly forgotten what she had seen in the man in the first place. She had known right away that he was a fraud. The people of Memphis might have been fooled by his vestments and the well-worn Bible he carried, but Eudora had spent her life being different things for different people and so she had no trouble rooting out a counterfeit. When she cornered him in the back of the old church and turned on her charm, he made no effort at all to keep his hands off of her. Not for God or Damnation, and she knew right then that he wasn't, nor had he ever been, a holy man.

She helped him to his knees, careful to avoid touching his already swollen left hand. He got to his feet, unsteady as a newborn calf, and picked up the canvas bag he carried and slung it back over his shoulder, wincing in pain.

"I hope this shit can dry out proper," he said. "I ain't old enough to remember paper money too well."

"Well you ought to know about it, cause I sure don't. I swear Jeremiah Preacher, I'm really starting to wonder why I brought you along."

Eudora was much younger than him, born just before the Calamity hit eighteen years ago. She had seen paper money before, used it to roll tobacco, or start fires, but her father told her that people used to kill each other over it. They could buy anything they wanted with it—clothes, jewelry, even the love of a woman. She didn't understand the appeal at first. All of those things were free now, if you could find them. The world had no shortage of dresses and baubles, and Memphis had flesh almost to spare. But the banknotes in that canvas bag, were different than any she had ever seen. They belonged to the Republic of California and they promised wealth and luxury and power and as soon as she laid eyes on them, she had to have them.

The cry of a horse interrupted her thoughts. Through the haze of the morning dust, two figures on horseback trotted slowly up the bank of the river. The horses looked healthy and strong, not like the thin beasts Eudora typically saw around Memphis. These were well-cared-for, muscular animals. Her father's animals and his men sent to collect her.

The two men themselves mirrored the horses they rode. Both of them solidly built and sturdy. Men not of the Wastelands, but born and bred to dominate it.

"Oh thank the Lord, you've arrived just in time," she cried. "I don't know what this man wants with me, I just want to go home." Now that they were caught, there was no reason not to play the fool. It did no one any good for them both to swing and if Jeremiah cared a lick for her at all, he'd want her to live.

"Ma'am." The lead man tipped his hat to her and reigned in his horse. He was older than Jeremiah but had a handsome, rugged face and he bore himself like a man who is used to being in control. He pulled aside his long coat to reveal a pair of silver revolvers. "Are you alright?"

"Just tolerable." She smiled and looked up at him from under her eyelashes. As soon as she learned that she could trick men into doing whatever she wanted, she made a study of it. Powerful men like this, she had learned, don't often want powerful women. This one would like her meek and docile, and so she played the part to get what she wanted. When he smiled behind his thick brown mustache and his eyes lingered on her, she knew she played the part right. Men were, if nothing else, very predictable.

Sweat glistened on his forehead and he turned to Jeremiah who sat shivering in the muddy water, confusion etched on his face. "Mornin' preacher," the bounty hunter said.

Jeremiah said nothing but swayed back and forth on unsteady legs, the fog of concussion still in his eyes.

"Now c'mon, preacher," the bounty hunter said after a moment. "Not going to greet me today? I ain't never seen a man of God with nothing to say before."

"He don't look like much of a preacher to me, Ira." The second man pulled his horse up beside his partner. Unlike the hardened and rough man who rode next to him, this one was young with soft, delicate features. "Fact, he looks like nothing but an ol' nibbler to me." He spat a brown stream of tobacco, a rare commodity in the Wastelands. The dust choked out most living things and growing tobacco had become somewhat of an art, a delicate operation that turned to disaster more often than not.

A slow smile spread across his smooth face. His voice was unnaturally high pitched, an affection that many young people adopted in the Northeast Territories, and it had spread all the way down to Memphis, too. It was a way for the young people to separate themselves from the old Calamity survivors. High-pitched voices and beardless faces they plucked every morning—in their world, youth was a virtue. He took his revolver from its holster and laughed a childish laugh.

The sound of it made the hairs on Eudora's neck stand on end. Young as she was, she still preferred the rough faces and calloused hands of men who didn't try to pretend they were still boys.

"Shut up, Boone," Ira, said. He locked his eyes on Jeremiah. "We're here to take you in, preacher. And to bring back Becker's daughter. I can't imagine what the devil got into your head to do something so damn foolish."

Jeremiah laughed, then flinched in pain. After that, he remained silent, made dumb by the hit he took to the head. With any luck, he would keep his mouth shut and the bounty hunters would string him up or put a bullet in his head. If they took him back to Memphis alive, he might talk. He might tell them that it was all her idea, and some people might start to believe him. Her father would protect her, but her reputation would be tarnished and it would take her quite some time before the people would see her as an innocent again, if ever at all. Some people had physical strength, others had willpower or sheer charisma to help them navigate their way through life. Eudora survived on her appearance of innocence. It was only with someone like Jeremiah that she could really be herself, or what she thought was herself. Maybe that's what she liked about him in the first place. She didn't have to play a part to control him. The man could be as dumb as a prairie dog, but he was smart enough to listen to her.

"We can always just gut him right here, Ira," said Boone. "We can tell Becker he drew on us and we had no choice." The young man fingered the gun in his holster. He wore a shirt with oversized sleeves that billowed in the wind, dyed yellow from the bark of the barberry shrub. It was gaudy and expensive, but impressive. Everything else about his appearance was strictly utility. Not enough wealth and fame to be entirely fashionable, but a few more bounties to his name, and Eudora reckoned he'd be an imposing sight.

His partner, Ira, was older and like Jeremiah, a Calamity survivor. Most survivors Eudora knew forged a kinship with each other. For many, their shared hardship had created a bond that superseded all others—race, religion, even family allegiances were second to that extraordinary experience of living through the end of the world. "God Himself couldn't kill us, try as he might," they'd say and clap one another on the back. In truth, it wasn't a bond so much as bondage. Like wretched convicts in iron shackles, they were fettered to each other, to the life they had before the world ended, unable to move on and unable to escape.

"Please," Jeremiah said. He fell to his knees. "I didn't survive Calamity and Hellfire to die like this." It was a coward's voice and it sickened Eudora. Her cheeks burned with shame. Not for the first time she wondered what she had seen in him a week ago when she prodded him to take the money, to take her, and to run away.

"Hobble your lip, preacher," Ira said in a slow, smooth drawl. "Surviving didn't make you special, we're all survivors, even the kid, here. He survived Becker's purge of Memphis, the cholera plague, hell just being born nowdays is surviving something. Ain't that right, Boone?"

"You ain't wrong about that."

"So I ain't in your debt none because Calamity didn't do you in. But I sure as hell don't cotton to killing a preacher, though. Even a gump such as yourself. Something about it don't sit right with me. Now I reckon once you stole from Becker and took his kid, whatever you had between yourself and

God was finished business, so I ain't gonna hold it a sin to take you in. Now get up, before I have to skin my shooting irons."

Jeremiah, still on his knees, nodded his head slowly. "Wait," he said, wide-eyed. "The bag. Look! The bag!" He held the canvas bag out to them. The canvas bag that contained the very reason Eudora had come this far. "Take it. Take all of it. Just tell Becker you found the girl and the money but you didn't find me—or, or tell him that you found me dead. Tell him I hanged myself on account of my sorrow at being a no-good bastardly thief and kidnapper. You can keep the money, please, just let me go. Ain't gonna do nothing to just let me go."

The two bounty hunters turned toward each other and a surprised look passed between them. "Is that what you stole?" Ira paused, his hand steady on his revolver at his side. "Money?"

The younger man let out a confused grunt. "Now why the fuck should Becker care if you took off with some money?" he asked. His tone was that of a man struggling to comprehend some mystery. "What kind of money?"

"Paper bills. Bank notes. Lots of them." Jeremiah turned from one man to the other. He was a cornered hare who spied some hope of escape from the fox. "From the Republic of California."

Ira spurred his horse forward and waded out into the river. "California?" He repeated the word as if he couldn't grasp its meaning. "How much of it you got?" He turned his horse sideways and inched closer to the cowering thief.

"I—I don't know."

"Bullshit." Boone spat his tobacco again.

"Hear that, preacher?" Ira rested a hand on his thigh. "Boone here thinks that's bullshit. I'm inclined to agree. You've been gone a fortnight and never once bothered to count it all?"

"I've been busy running from the likes of you gentlemen. Besides, I didn't feel the need to count it. It's a lot." He loosened the drawstrings with his good hand and fished out a small stack of brightly colored notes banded tight together. He held it up. His breath came in ragged gasps, louder than even the din of the river. "I've got ten of these. They're yours. I shouldn't have taken it, I know that. I know that now. It was foolish. But—now I'm no prophet you understand—but, maybe, maybe I was meant to take it, so's I could give it to you?"

"Sorry preacher," Ira said, though truth be told, he looked like he gave it some consideration. "Whatever you took is between you and Becker. I want no part of it, tempting as it is."

Ira spurred his horse forward again, rope in hand. The dun-colored mare stepped onto the sunken granite slab in front of Jeremiah, its step loud and hollow. In an instant, the horse lost its footing, another victim of the slick rock. The animal let out a panicked cry and fell with a crack on top of its rider. Whether that crack came from man or beast, Eudora didn't know.

The mare struggled to right itself. It kicked its legs furiously, water erupted all around like the mouth of a geyser. Its black eyes, like polished obsidian stones, shone wide with fear and confusion and it looked to Eudora like some great fish that had found itself floundering in the shallows. In another circumstance, she might have laughed. When the beast finally righted itself, it bolted for the woods and left Ira on his back in the middle of the river, the brown frigid water flowing around his stiff body.

The situation changed fast and Eudora struggled to keep up with all the possibilities. There was a different Eudora for every possibility, a different role to play, and until she knew how this would end, she had to be quiet Eudora, the one who hid in the shadows and watched, too innocent and brainless to be of any consequence.

Boone dismounted and walked across the river towards Ira. He took his steps slow and deliberate, careful not to lose his footing. Head cocked to the side and the ghost of a smile on his lips, he stopped and stood at Ira's feet. His fingers caressed the ivory handles of his revolvers.

"Goddamnit." Ira moaned and rolled his head to the side. He raised a trembling hand to Boone. "My leg's busted, for sure. We need to get that horse back. I don't know where it ran off to. I'll keep an eye on the preacher, you fetch my horse. I think I can stand if you help me up."

"Oh, no, now I don't think that I will," Boone said, his voice barely above a whisper.

Ira's eyes turned hard.

"Cocksucker," he said through clenched teeth. "I should have known better than to put my trust in a catstick."

Boone licked his lips and flashed a pair of dimples that only enhanced his child-like features. "I ain't got no love for a survivor, old man, you of all people should know that." He drew, spun his revolver once, and leveled it at Ira. "And there ain't no way in Hell I'm taking that California money back to Becker."

"The fuck you want some California money for? That place ain't no paradise, it's a goddamn myth. Hell, you got everything you could possibly want in Memphis. You got the best food, second scavenger picks, your choice of women to bed. What good is California to you?"

"Not every man likes Becker's rules, Ira. In fact, I don't much care for anyone's rules but my own. Piss on Becker and his fucking city. I'll be my own man now, not his dog."

Ira laughed a dead man's laugh. "He'll find you. You know it, Boone. No matter where you run, he'll catch up to you. I ain't even the best he's got. He'll send his best after you and when they bring you back to Memphis, Becker'll put you to bed good. He'll peel that pretty face right off your fucking head. And if Becker don't do it, Longstreet will."

"I'll be halfway to California by the time he even begins to suspect something's amiss. I'll be well above his bend. His arm ain't that long." Boone cocked the hammer of his revolver back. "No one's arm is that long. Not Becker's and not Longstreet's."

The flesh on Eudora's neck prickled at the mention of Longstreet. Her father may have been the governor of the Memphis Territories, but even he answered to a higher power, and there was no higher power in all the territories in the East as Longstreet. He controlled the land from the upper reaches of New England, where the ice and wind could freeze a man in minutes, all the way down to Memphis, the southernmost reaches of the warlord's domain. Politics never held much interest for her, but she knew enough of Longstreet to fear even the barest mention of his name.

"You don't think so?" asked Ira. "Then you're an even bigger fool than I thought. Longstreet will make you wish you'd never been born before he's done with you." He kicked, knocking Boone off his feet just as the young man pulled the trigger. Ira's head exploded, a bright red spray erupted from the top of his skull and blood flowed from his nose like a fountain. His body sunk down into the earth and water filled the fresh hole in his head. Boone hit the rock hard, the river was too shallow to cushion his fall, and Eudora saw her chance. She could run, take Boone's horse and be gone before the young bounty hunter could get back up. But he would get back up, and that would still leave a capable killer on her trail.

She picked up a stone, dark gray and smooth, slightly larger than her own fist, and she sat in the water next to Boone, her dress fanned out around her like a parasol. She ignored everything, shut out Jeremiah who only stood and looked at her, cradling his broken hand. Even contorted in pain, Boone's face was beautiful. A catstick with a face carved from wax like his must have been very popular back in the Memphis Territories. The boy's yellow shirt, darker now from the muddy waters, fluttered in the current.

Eudora lifted the rock in the air with both hands. She had never killed a man before, but now was not the time for hesitation. Drawing on all her strength, she brought it down on the boy's head. She shut her eyes. Shut her eyes to Boone, to Jeremiah, to the sound of rock cracking bone again, and again, and again until she could no longer hear the splintering of the skull, but only the wet thud of rock hitting raw flesh, like a butcher pounding meat.

When she finally stopped, she sat in silence for several long minutes without a sound passing between the two fugitives. Finally, fear subsided. At last, her hands stopped shaking and her tears disappeared into the running waters of the rust-colored river. She was alive, and so was Jeremiah. Somehow they were alive and their pursuers were not.

"Well, ain't you about the luckiest dumb son of a bitch in all the Wastes?" Her voice had an edge to it that she hoped he didn't miss. It wasn't fair that she had to kill the man called Boone, and Jeremiah got to do nothing but stand there and watch.

"You're about as useless as tits on a nun, you know that? Jesus, was you just fixing to stand there all day? I ain't the killing type, Jeremiah. It shouldn't have been me. Isn't that the man's job? Do I gotta be the man for the both of us? I don't want to be the man, that's not my part. I'm the good girl, I'm the innocent one and now look at me. Look what you've done to me."

He stared at her, his mouth open. "I'm sorry—"

Her tears came despite her best efforts to hold them back and she couldn't stop her lip from trembling, but hopefully Jeremiah would chalk that up to the fact that she sat in the middle of a near-freezing river. She washed away bits of bone and hair from her hand, but no matter how much she scrubbed she couldn't get it clean.

"Dora. Dora. Shhh, stop. Stop." Jeremiah pulled her to him and pressed her head to his chest. "It's all right, girl. It's all right. He would have killed you, you know. You did what you had to do."

"Never you mind me. Here, let me see that." She took his hand. It was red and swollen and looked as if it might need a splint, but nursing wasn't an art she had been trained in. "Let's get to shore and out of these wet clothes before we get sick."

"Wait." Jeremiah picked up Boone's revolvers one at a time and handed them to Eudora. She didn't know much about gunplay, but she did know that a properly loaded revolver could still fire after getting wet. Boone seemed like the kind of man who would do right by his six-shooters. If he took half as good care of them as he did his own appearance, those guns would shoot.

"One more thing." Eudora ran her fingers over Boone's yellow shirt. It was finely woven and, having been almost completely submerged when its owner met his end, bloodless. "You want this? I think you'd really cut a dash in it." She pulled the shirt off Boone's corpse, careful not to let it touch the ruin of his face, the mass of pulp—a crater of meat and bone—that she had made.

Once they were out of the water, they stripped and wrapped themselves in wool blankets they got from Boone's horse. Eudora sat down on the dusty bank, needles stabbed her feet and hands as the warmth returned to her body.

"We did it," Jeremiah said. He threw his wet vestments into the river.

She snorted. "We? We did what? Escaped capture? Murdered a man?"

"We're free. That's what we did, we won our freedom. We've been on the run for days trying to get away, but now we're free. Nothing can stop us now. Boone was right. By the time your father finds out that his men ain't coming back, we'll be long gone. He'll be too late. Only, it won't be Boone over there that's halfway to California, it'll be us. With a sack full of money. We'll be set and living in paradise."

"Paradise... I hope it's true. I hope California is a paradise like they say."

"Of course it is."

He found a bottle of whiskey and pulled the stopper out with his teeth. He took a long pull and offered the rest to Eudora. "You want some, daisy? Dora? What devilry are you up to, woman?"

She ignored him and rummaged through Boone's pack. "Well now, look at what our young friend was indulging in." She held up a tincture of laudanum. The ruddy liquid set her heart racing. The end of the world was a dull thing and opium made her feel. It excited her entire body and took away her pain. Jeremiah had told her that he got the same feeling from having sex, but Eudora didn't believe him. Sex was almost as boring as the rest of life.

The orange glow of the sun rose higher across the sky and the pair of fugitives drank to their freedom. They drank to their future. They drank to disremember the dead world around them, and when their drink was gone and the opium flowed in their veins and their skin burned with the fires of ecstasy, they felt, for a moment, at peace.

Chapter 2

Memphis, Old Tennessee (August, 1881)

Cornelius White

They beat the Morgan boy to death with his own lucky horseshoe. He lay in a bundle in the street outside the Gayoso House; a thin layer of dust covered his body like a russet veil. A single eyeball lay beside him, black in the sanguinary mud. The Fisher brothers had set him up with the girl Adeline who had recently lost her child and was ready for bedding again, but they couldn't get the boy to buckle to, despite Adeline's best efforts. Henry Fisher, the elder brother, said he knew that Morgan boy wouldn't be up to it. Said he couldn't teach a hen to cluck and likely couldn't get his cock to crow either. They laughed, and stripped him bare right then, at least this is the story they would tell later to the men at the bar. They forced the Morgan boy to mount the girl, but he could do nothing except hang there limp between his legs and wail.

"A useless pecker ain't even fit to shoot," Henry said and they dragged him into the street. Then they beat him to death there in the road with the boy's own lucky horseshoe and left his naked body to God and the dust.

Hours later, the man named Cornelius White woke up, hungover. He leaned against the balcony railing and squinted up at a rust-colored sky. There wasn't enough sun to warrant shutting his eyes to it, but it was the first time Cornelius—Conny to whatever friends he had left—had been outside his room at the Gayoso House in almost two weeks. Last night he ran out of whiskey vouchers and Purdy, the old man who ran the saloon for Governor Becker, set him out. He didn't hold it against Purdy, the barkeep was a good man, so Conny didn't trouble him over it. So this morning he was stone cold sober when saw the body of the Morgan boy lying naked in the street.

Conny closed his eyes slowly. A weariness washed over him, not wholly connected to his new and unwelcomed sobriety. He turned his back to the ruined body of the boy in the road and sighed. He would have to bury the kid. No one else would. He would have to tell the boy's father, unless he could get the preacher to do that. That was the job of a preacher, he reckoned, and was high time that preacher went back to doing his job.

But first, he would need to wake up.

Conny pulled a small pocket Bible out of his coat and tore out the first page. He knew an old junkmonger from South Carolina, Edith Mansfield, who told him once that she could tell a man his fortune by reading random lines from the Bible. She called the practice bibliomancy, and for a pinch of tobacco, she'd tell you your future. Conny didn't put much stock in those unnatural ways that had become so common since the Calamity, but still, he figured it couldn't hurt to try it himself. He had made a habit of reading a verse from his Bible before using the page to smoke his tobacco.

The Lord shall make the rain of thy land powder and dust: from Heaven shall it come down upon thee, until thou be destroyed.

A childish fear gripped his heart and he had to chide himself for his foolishness. He had seen men gone mad in the Calamity, afraid of their own shadows, gripped with a fear that drove them to end their own lives, and he could not allow himself to come to that end.

The Lord shall make the rain of thy land powder and dust...

The trouble with bibliomancy is that it only makes sense after the fact. This prophecy, he told himself, had already come true. The land had long ago turned to powder and dust. Dust carpeted the sky and all but blocked out the sun. It fell like snow, suffocated the earth, choked out life, muted everything so land and sky bled together into one.

And it was still slowly falling, covering the Morgan boy lying in the street below.

In the eighteen years since the dust first arrived, there was never a time that Conny didn't taste it in his throat or feel the grit in his mouth. He spat. If the world wasn't a ghost town before the dust came, it certainly was now. Many who survived the Calamity died soon after when the dust came and brought famine with it.

With the dust and famine also came the winds. Or rather, as Conny reckoned, it was likely the winds that brought the dust. When the dust storms came, life outdoors stopped. The people of Memphis were skilled at keeping the dust out of the houses, hotels, and saloons, but the dust was cleverer still and seemed to always find a crack in the mortar or a space under a windowpane to steal itself inside, keeping the occupants eternally busy sealing gaps, filling cracks, and stuffing holes.

Conny took a large pinch of tobacco from his pouch and rolled it up. He preferred using the bible to roll his cigarettes. The pages were thinner than other books, and there were so many Bibles in Memphis, and as far as Conny could tell, the whole of what used to be the United States, that no one paid him no account for tearing pages out, and no preacher or god-fearer dared speak up against them anymore for the sacrilege of it.

He smoked his tobacco alone and listened to the wind and the quiet sounds of the dead town. His temperance brought back memories. The solitude made them impossible to ignore. His thoughts intruded. Visions of men, women, and children either dead by his hand or dead because he did nothing to stop it. Faces flashed in his mind like echoes. Even good memories were turned tragic by time. The woman he loved and the children she bore him, lost in the Calamity. Those memories were too much. He would need to be on the next scavenging run. He needed laudanum or a bottle of whiskey and Becker wasn't hiring him for jobs lately, so he'd have to go to the source. That meant a scavenging raid through the Wasteland. He stretched and spit over the railing.

"Son of a bitch. Watch it, Conny." A familiar voice called from the street. Abe stood below, near the body of the Morgan boy. He wore an old Confederate long coat and a wool blanket thrown over his shoulders to protect himself from the biting cold. That was another thing the Calamity of '63 brought with it—a perpetual cold that the obscured sun could do nothing to alter.

A young boy stood behind Abe. He wore a purple shirt and white pants that he had somehow managed to keep clean in the midst of all the dust and ruin. The Memphis youth loved their flashy clothes and finery and found all kinds of ways to dye old shirts and trousers all manner of loud colors. Conny should have known the boy's name, but he couldn't remember it. James? John? He didn't care.

"What do you want, Abe?"

"There's only one thing I ever want when I pay you a visit." The old man pulled a note from inside his coat and held it up. Abe ran errands for Becker, who kept himself locked up in his manor, always sending his runners out to do his business. He was hiding. Hiding from the people of Memphis, afraid to look at the faces of the people they had conquered. Conny understood because he was hiding, too. Only he hid himself in a bottle of whiskey.

"Not a chance," Conny stood up straight. For Becker to be coming to him now after passing him over for months, means the work can't be good. He would just have to go without whiskey if the alternative was to go on shakedown runs against the scavengers, or to bring in a family for failure to pay their share, or to force a woman to bed a man she didn't want to bed. That was where Conny found the line he had drawn, and that was where he had fallen out of favor with Becker.

Abe shrugged. "That's on you. I could give a goddamn, I'm just here to deliver it."

"Well I told you I don't want it, so take it straight back to Becker, if you don't mind."

"What do you want me to tell him?"

"Tell him he can take that summons and use it to wipe his ass for all I care."

"On another spree, eh crowbait?" the boy asked. His teeth flashed white against his dark brown face.

Abe laughed.

"As a matter of fact, no. Just coming off of one." Conny took a drag from his quirley. "And I reckon I'm not in the right state of mind for that." He jerked his head at the note.

"That's up to you," Abe said. "Like I told you, I'm just here to deliver it. Nothing else. If you want to make Becker angry, that's on you. I warn you though—that devil's full of piss this morning. I almost hope you don't. You ain't half bad. I don't hold things against you like most, you know."

"Hurry up and get down here," the boy said. "My trousers are getting dusty."

Conny's legs were stiff and his knees ached and he had no desire to walk down the steps. "Come up here and give it to me. It's your job to deliver, not mine to fetch."

"Gimme some tobacco and I'll bring it up," Abe said. Steam shot from his mouth with each word and he pulled his blanket tighter around his shoulders.

"Fine." He had a pinch to spare.

A moment later Abe and the boy joined him on the balcony. The old man grinned and waited. The boy eyed Conny with what the man suspected was a smirk.

He was suspicious of young people. They always seemed to him to be smiling and whispering, as if they were party to some inside joke that he was either ignorant to, or the brunt of. He wasn't sure how the youth behaved in other parts of the world, assuming there were still people left in other parts of the world, but here in Memphis, they mistrusted Calamity survivors as much as the survivors mistrusted them.

"Well?" Abe said. "My tobacco."

"Right, hold your horses." Conny tore out the other half of the page from his Bible and handed it to the old man, then he pinched some tobacco from his pouch—a fair bit less than he had earlier pinched for himself.

"What's it say?"

Abe held the paper out, eager. "What does what say?" he asked.

"The paper. What's it say?"

"I told you, that's between you and Becker. Read it yourself. After you give me the pinch. And don't be close-fisted with it."

"Not the summons. The Bible paper."

The man looked confused. "The Bible says a lot of shit, Conny. I ain't reading the whole damn thing."

"Just pick one verse and read it to me."

"I says I ain't reading it. What's the point of it anyway, just let me smoke the toby and be done with it."

"He can't read," the boy said.

"Shut up, George." Abe cuffed the boy in the back of the head. "I can read, it's just my eyes ain't no good no more."

"Sure old man, sure." George turned to Conny, that same expression on his face, unchanged. "I'll read it. I dabble a bit in bibliomancy."

"Superstitious bosh." Abe spat. "Just read your Bible like a good Christian and you'll be fine. No need to fret over the future, it's all in the Lord's hands."

George laughed. "Sure old man, sure," he said again. He snatched the paper from Abe and lifted it up to catch the dim light of the sun. "*Let's see. And thou shalt grope at noonday, as the blind gropeth in darkness, and thou shalt not prosper in thy ways: and thou shalt be only oppressed and spoiled evermore, and no man shall save thee.*"

George stared at the page for a breath, one black eyebrow cocked. "That's grim," he said.

"Fortunate for me I don't put much stock in bibliomancy neither," Conny said, putting the pinch of tobacco in Abe's paper. "Else that's like to be an ill omen."

"That's right," the old man said. "Providence don't issue heralds, bounty hunter."

"Sure she does," George said. "She's a cruel enough bitch, don't you think?"

Conny frowned. It wasn't that he disagreed with the boy—whatever faith he once had in anything divine was long gone, carried away on the winds of the Calamity. "What do you mean by that?" he asked.

"I read that somewhere. But it's true. Fate loves to show you what's coming, Conny. It ain't no warning. She loves to dangle it in front of your face because she knows you can't do nothing to avoid it. She's a cruel bitch like that."

Abe lit his paper off of Conny's and took a deep puff. "Don't mess with none of that shit, Con. It's evil nonsense. Young people these days are being led astray and you don't want to get caught up in it neither."

George laughed again. "Be significant Abe, and let me have a draw of that."

"Significant?"

"Of course."

"I don't follow."

"Jesus, do I have to explain everything to you?"

"Stop using words where they don't belong and then you won't have to."

"Look, you wouldn't want to be common and base, right? You want to be important. Like a significant woman, you know? Pregnant women are better. So be better. Be significant and let me have some of that tobacco."

The young folks in Memphis almost had their own language and the older Conny got, the harder it was for him to understand them.

"Git your own goddamn tobacco," Abe said. "This is mine."

Conny handed the boy the rest of his quirley.

"Thanks, old timer. You ain't half bad." The boy sat on the railing and smoked.

"Alright," Abe said. "Here's your orders. I'm tired of holding on to them. I did my job, the rest is on you now. But just a friendly warning, Becker's got the jitters fierce. Always looking over his shoulder and jumping at shadows. And it's worse today. Something big has gone down, mark my words."

"Like what?"

Abe lowered his voice. "I don't know, but the man's scared shitless of something. Something more substantial than just his shadow this time."

"Thanks for the warning."

"See if you can take care of the Morgan boy, too, won't you?"

Conny nodded. "Planned to."

Abe and the boy left, and Conny felt the sudden weight of years pull him down. Down through the dried and decaying wooden balcony, through the years of dust, and into the once fertile soil. He closed his eyes and tried to imagine his body, withered and decayed, mummified by the parched and arid land, blanketed in that all-consuming rust-colored powder.

When he opened his eyes, he was staring at the body of the Morgan boy. He still had that to contend with. But again, he would have to hold off on that for the moment. Becker shouldn't be kept waiting too long. The two of them may have a complicated history, and if anyone could get away with trying

Becker's patience it was Conny, but Becker was still governor of Memphis and that meant he was the law. As much as he would have loved to ignore the summons, he would end up in a bad way if he did.

Conny pulled on his boots and walked gingerly down the stairs of the hotel. He didn't quite remember much of the last two weeks, but he felt like he had taken a beating or two, and he had to take each step slower than he would have liked.

The bottom floor of the hotel was the saloon. There were no windows, and the doors that had once swung free and open were covered in reclaimed boards, stripped from now-empty homes, nailed up in a hopeless, slipshod pattern by men desperate to keep the strangling dust at bay.

He waited while his eyes adjusted to the dark. The saloon was dimly lit by candles scavenged from the outlying cities. They had long used up the supply of candles and oil within Memphis, and when teams had to make periodic raids on the surrounding towns for supplies, candles and oil were priorities. Purdy's saloon wasn't important enough to get the oil and he rationed his stock of candles carefully, never lighting more than necessary. Purdy was, if nothing else, a very practical man.

Conny crossed the main floor, looking at the candlelight on the wall, transfixed by the dust that drifted across the flame in rivers and eddies. The light illuminated the truth. Conny could ignore the dust in the dark. He could ignore it when the whiskey flowed free and he turned up a tincture of laudanum or morphine from a scavenging raid. But in the light, he was forced to face it, to look at it and acknowledge that it was present every moment of his life. Every breath he took he drew it in. It invaded his body, clouded his vision, and muted every stench so he no longer smelled anything else.

He shivered and hurried out the door. He pushed on down the road to the old city hall building. Becker had taken up residence there when Longstreet promoted him to Governor. While Longstreet was busy securing his power by installing loyalists to governor positions in an attempt to look legitimate, Becker was consolidating power of his own on the fringes of the Domain in the Uncontested Lands, which now included most of lower Tennessee. Becker rode into town nearly ten years ago with twenty men, all of them former soldiers. Most of them Confederates, but a few, Conny included, had been Yankees. They rode in like legends with Samuel Becker himself leading the charge along with Edward Crowkiller, a Comanche from Texas who was exiled from the Indian Confederacy, Farhad, the only Arab man Conny had ever known, or was like to ever know, and Cornelius White. They were the four horsemen told of in Revelations when they brought the law back to Memphis. And it was the law they brought. At least at first, it was.

The old city hall building loomed in front of him, the upper floor obscured by the dust in the air. Becker had chosen this building as his base and as his home. Most of the folk in Memphis lived on the outskirts, away from the town square. Though there hadn't been an execution in some time, the gallows were still up in front of the courthouse steps. When Becker and his gang first arrived in Memphis, there was some resistance to their rule of law. They were swift in putting down anyone who openly fought against them. No one broke the law here now. What little defiance the people once had was completely beaten out of them.

While he understood why Becker lived so remote from the rest of the townsfolk, Conny needed the noise of the saloon, the piano, the singing, *Down by the River Liv'd a Maiden*, *The Cottage by the Sea*, and *Into the Barren Lands I Go*. He needed the occasional hushed sounds of laughter followed by the frightened silence of a people who were too afraid to be happy for too long as if happiness were a currency they had long ago spent and what little they had now in poverty, they must expend in secret. He needed the boots on the floor, the sounds of vouchers stacked high at the Faro tables, the cards shuffling, and the whiskey glasses slamming down. He needed noise to drown out his own thoughts.

The silence of the Becker manor was everywhere. As he opened the door, the oppressive emptiness pressed in on Conny, like the weight of the boundless dead had gathered here, in this building, to crush him, to drag him down to the deep places of the Wastes. He quickened his pace.

The city courthouse was grand, but, like everything else now, it was empty. It wasn't empty of things—eighteen years since the Calamity and they still weren't in danger of scavenging the remains of society bare. No, it wasn't empty of things but of people.

Becker's office sat in the back of the building, the hallway leading up to it dark, lit only by a few small oil lamps. The office itself was well lit and Conny, relieved, let out a sigh when he walked in. A large window faced east towards the rising sun, though you couldn't see it most days. Oil lamps dotted the walls, and candles flared on his desk. In one corner of the room stood an old Confederate flag, "The Stainless Banner" they called it. Most of the folk that Conny knew had forgotten the war. It was a relic of the past, of a time when, even though things had been grim, they somehow now seemed simpler, easier, and they would lament how they didn't realize how good they had it in those days. But Conny remembered the bone saws, the piles of limbs, the screams of men as the saw cut through their flesh. He remembered the gangrene, the smell of rotting meat that used to be men's arms and legs. Not everyone, he reckoned, had it better back then. At least the Calamity killed most quickly. The hunger after the Calamity though, killed slow.

When the old timers did talk of the old war, it was usually in the taverns and saloons after a few rounds of whiskey had been traded, and then it was mostly old veteran talk. They wanted to know what unit you served in, who you fought under, what battles you were in. Sometimes they would debate—who would have won the war if the Calamity hadn't come and put a stop to it? There was no anger in those quiet conversations. No accusations, no mistrust. Only talk of what-was and what-ifs.

Becker, however, was one of those men who clung a little tighter to the tattered remnants of the old ways. Or perhaps it was more a feeling of pride the old man had in who he used to be. The flag was important to him, yet Conny's time in the Union army during the war didn't seem to darken Becker's feelings towards the man. Conny's rather vocal impertinence after their sacking of Memphis was the reason their relationship had soured. Conny refused Becker's offer to be his personal bodyguard and leader of his gang. He didn't want to be a Law Man, if being a Law Man meant terrorizing innocents, hanging women and children, or worse. Conny saw all that in the sacking of Memphis and wanted no further part in it.

The Governor looked up from his desk. He was a tall man, a full half-head taller than Conny, but thin. His gray officer's frock coat—the same one he wore twenty years before when he served the Confederate army as a colonel—hung loose, the body inside more bent and withered than it used to be. A large map of the United States lay in front of him, and he had been wholly absorbed in the study of it. When Conny approached, he leaned back in his chair. "I see my boy managed to pry the bottle out of your hand long enough for you to drag your arse out here," he said, his voice deep and rich, almost musical.

Abe had spoken true. Becker was full of piss this morning. "I'm sober," Conny replied. "Don't you worry none about that."

"I will worry about whatever I goddamn please," he said, "and right now I'm worried about your ability to perform your contract duties. I have a bit of a delicate situation that requires your... talents... but only if you're fit to use them. If you aren't, then we need to discuss other arrangements."

"I said I'm sober, didn't I?" Conny smiled ruefully. "Ran out of whiskey slips."

Becker nodded. He looked the man up and down and Conny felt as if he were being appraised at an auction. He didn't appreciate Becker giving him the once over like he was some wet-behind-the-ears catstick. Drunk or sober, he was good for a fight and Becker knew this better than almost anyone. Finally, Becker sighed. "I have a situation," he said. "I needed you for a job a month ago but I knew you were on one of your little indulgences, so I left you to it. Now the situation has gotten away from us and I can't wait for you to pull your dead-alive head out of your arse."

"If it's that bad, why not send Ira? He's more than capable—"

"I did send Ira. He should have been back from the job two weeks ago. So I sent two runners out to find him and they came back this morning with news. They tracked Ira and that bloody catstick he kept with him all the way to Friar's Point." He wrinkled his nose. "Nothing but blacks there; it belongs to the Coloreds, with the rest of Mississippi, at least for now. Longstreet has his eye on it, for what it's worth. He says we're going to take it back once all this dust finally settles. Regardless, my runners found what was left of Ira and his boy. Found their bloated, stinking corpses washed up on a riverbank. Ira had a hole in his head the size of a fucking apple and that catstick had been beaten so bad the devil didn't even have a face left."

Conny listened, intent. He needed a lot more information, and he was sure Becker had it. "Any ideas who did this? Who was the mark?"

"That goddamned preacher," Becker said.

"Jeremiah?" Conny asked incredulous. "I heard he hadn't been seen in a while. I think we all just figured he was taking some time to himself." Conny frowned. "He doesn't seem the cold-blooded type. Maybe they came up on some loners. There's plenty of strange folk out in the Uncontested Lands. The ones who learned to survive out in that are a special breed, for sure."

"No. The preacher left his vestments at the scene. Seemed to take off in a hurry. Somehow, he got some sand in him, for sure. Ira was a good man, a copperhead from way back." Becker slid back into his seat; his eyes darted everywhere. Conny watched him closely. He's terrified of something, he thought. Becker had been increasingly paranoid over the last few years, but that's what happens when a man does a lot of killing. The killing comes back for you. Just a matter of time. He looked like a man facing death, like the people he had sent to the gallows when they culled Memphis of its undesirables.

"What did he do?" Conny asked. Best to just get straight to the point.

"He took my little girl." Becker's voice was thick.

"Jesus, Sam."

"Eudora's coming up to womanhood soon, but she still has the virtue of a saint. That preacher stole off with her like a coyote with a hen. I should've know'd it, too. I should've paid more mind to her. I'd been distracted with a matter of some urgency. I let my guard down for a moment and that's when that fucking snake struck."

"Alright, so you want me to track them down and bring them back? You want the preacher dead or alive?"

"We'll get to that. There's some more you need to know, first." Becker gestured to a chair. "Have a seat."

Conny pulled up a chair and sat. A small cloud of dust boiled out and whirled along the invisible eddies and currents in the air.

"The preacher, he also stole money from me. A great deal of money." Becker lowered his voice. "He stole it from me, which means he stole it from Longstreet."

"Money?" Conny frowned. Money hadn't been used since the Calamity hit, and it certainly wasn't rare. Coins were sometimes melted down and made into things, but there was plenty of coin money still left, even in Memphis. They usually passed over any money they saw in scavenging raids. Paper money was even more worthless, although most of it in the Memphis area had been collected and used to roll cigarettes.

"That's right. Money." He kept his voice low. "I had come into the possession of a certain amount of paper bills from the Republic of California."

Conny's eyebrows shot up and his jaw went slack. "New money?"

Becker nodded. "Dated 1876. Seems California is setting up a right prosperous government. Longstreet's runners have been hearing stories about it. I'm sure those stories have come to the regular folk, too. It's supposed to be some kind of paradise. Sun shines bright, the air is clean, you can see stars at night, the women all swollen with babes and fat tits. Oceans of grain, green growing things, harvests like we used to have. Mountains of food. I even heard that ships have started sailing again from ports."

Conny didn't believe it. People had been talking about California as if it were some Heaven on Earth since right after the Calamity, but no one could prove it.

"California's a fairy tale. The world is dead." Conny said this with the finality of a man who has accepted his fate, like a man awaiting the gallows. There would be no help or pardon for mankind.

"I saw the money for myself, Con. It's real, make no mistake. But I wasn't sure what to do with it. Keep it? Burn it? Forget I ever saw it? I sent a few bills up north to Longstreet to see what he thought about it. Now he's obsessed with it. Wants to go to California and live like a king."

"So why haven't we gone, then? If California really is this paradise, why don't we ride for it? We can take the women and children, load up the wagons, and ride out. The whole damn town can go. Hell, the whole Domain can go. We don't need their money. We can ride in there and settle where we want. There's got to be plenty of land for the taking, no matter how much of a paradise it is."

"We can't. Even if we could load everyone up for the trip across the entire continent, the Indian Confederacy keeps expanding its borders. They control the entire Midwest and Great Plains now. See this?" He gestured to the large map on his desk. "As far we know, everything that sits north of the Red River in Texas and between the Mississippi and the Rockies now belongs to Sanguin Corvus. He calls himself The Prophet, now. No white or colored man that's crossed his borders has ever come out again. Least not in possession of all his original body parts."

"So we go south."

"Sure, there's a narrow corridor through Louisiana, but a company the size of this town can't stay hidden long, even all this dust couldn't conceal us. We'd draw the attention of Lukango and Taylor, and those bloody Negroes would love nothing more than to massacre a pilgrimage of whites." Becker wrung his hands. "No, Longstreet wants to see California for himself before making any decisions. And he wants to make a goddamn impression when he arrives, flashing money, buying expensive things."

"So Longstreet wants to travel west with a small group…and he intends to stay there?"

"That's the impression I got."

"Where did you get the money?"

"Scavengers found a wagon about thirty miles south. The fellow who was driving it appeared to have met an unfortunate end, but they brought back his supplies. Five bags of rancid flour, but stuffed inside one of those bags was thirty thousand dollars in California bills."

"And the preacher took it…"

"He came right in this very office to give last rites to Mabel's babe. The bloody thing couldn't never really breathe right. It didn't live but a fortnight. The preacher must have read my letter to Longstreet about the money. And I was the damn fool for leaving it on my desk. Mabel was distraught on account of the babe. She's been losing them all and she figured that one was her last chance. I didn't even notice the money was gone until the next morning.

"Abe sent out the letter with a runner before I knew the money was gone. I sent some men after him, but they never could catch up. Longstreet's runners are good. I can't be sore at the boy, it ain't his fault. The preacher, though, I will boil his entrails right inside his stomach before he dies."

"Careful, Becker. I ain't no religious man, but some folks might not be too keen to see you boil a priest from the inside out."

"I'll boil whoever I goddamned like," Becker said. "That cocksucker just may be the end of me."

The prospect of watching Becker grovel in front of Longstreet was enticing. The old man had a lot to answer for and this seemed like a bit of backhanded justice. Still, Becker was once his friend and the man he used to be didn't deserve the justice Longstreet would visit on him.

"So you want me to ride out and bring back the preacher and your money, that it?" Conny asked.

"Not quite. Problem is, you'll never make it back before Longstreet gets here. Make no mistake, I can't be in Memphis when he arrives. What I'm asking is that you help me get my little girl back. After that, we can split the money and go to California ourselves."

"Leave Memphis? For good? That's a hell of a thing to ask, Sam."

"It's the only way I can see myself living past next week. If I stay here, I'm a dead man."

"I'm still waiting for the part where you tell me how this is any of my concern." Conny stood up.

Becker stood up too, and pressed his fists into his desk. "You help me get that preacher, Conny. You help me get that preacher or I'll hang you with the other turncoats. You want to make a stand here? Is that it? You finally find your conscience and your nerve? We both know what you've done in Longstreet's name. This town won't shed one tear for you when I gut you right in Union Square in front of God and man and hang your corpse from the Tenth Street bridge."

Conny's face tightened. "You've got a lot more to answer to here than I do, Butcher."

"They don't call me Butcher no more, from what I've heard. I've been soft on the townsfolk lately. They might not love me but they're doing better here than they would be with the marauders outside the walls," Becker said. He clenched his fists and dropped his voice low like a man ready to be done with talking and get on with fighting. "I've made my peace with them."

"It ain't easy making peace when you've got blood on your hands," Conny said. He stood rigid; his hand conscious of the empty holster where his gun should be.

"Your hands are just as red as mine, Conny. Don't you forget." The old man sat back down. He bent his head and sighed. "Do this for me, Conny. Longstreet's on his way. I have to leave. Even if I found the money and came back here with it, Longstreet would crucify me for losing it in the first place. He'll already be here in Memphis long before I've caught up to the preacher, if I even could reach him on my own. Help me get my little girl back. Help me get her back and take us to California and you can have the money. You can be the one living like a king in California. For our old friendship's sake."

Conny thought it over. The truth of the matter was he'd been looking for a reason to escape Memphis. A way to start over fresh, but he hadn't believed such a thing was possible. Taking Memphis ten years ago had given him purpose and, for a time, made him feel as if the world could be reborn. Since then, he had been nothing better than a prisoner, the pride and glory of Longstreet's reign had faded, and the old battle cry of a new hope for mankind had given way to the brutal reality that there was no hope. The Age of Man was over.

But if this money was genuine, if people in California were living well enough to print money again, then it was worth any risk to get there. "I'll need my guns and a lot of lead."

Becker handed him a note. "I've already signed your requisition with the quartermaster."

"I'll need some time to get my things. I'll see if Crowkiller wants to come along."

Becker nodded. "That's a good idea. I don't think he ever really liked it here anyhow. What about Farhad?"

"No, I think he needs to stay here. His consumption is bad enough as it is, a trip like this would be the death of him. I will need to see him before we leave, though. You know, to say my goodbyes."

"Better make it quick, Con. A dust storm's on the way."

"A dust storm on our heels don't bode well. What about Mabel?"

"What about her?"

"You just gonna leave her here, or are we taking her with us?"

"Mabel will be fine here. I don't think she cared none for me, not like my Anne, God rest her soul. Besides, Mabel don't have the constitution to survive out in the Wastelands."

"Give me a few hours to get everything ready."

"Six o'clock. I want to be out before midnight. We'll be traveling in the dark until we can put some distance between us and Memphis."

Conny put on his hat and walked back down the dark hallway. His old footprints, still visible in the dust, headed back towards Becker's office. Stretched out before him like the endless expanse of the Wastelands themselves, lay fear and uncertainty. Behind the veiling dust, an ember of something resembling hope.

Chapter 3

Memphis, Old Tennessee (August, 1881)

Farhad

Farhad stretched out his hand and touched Isabella's naked belly. Her skin was taut and stretched, hot under his palm. Her child would not come for many more months, but she was thin, and even so early in her pregnancy, her stomach swelled. He traced the dark line that ran down her stomach. His mother believed it was a sign of a healthy child. She told him that when that line appeared on a woman's belly it meant Allah was pleased and the baby would be blessed.

"Look at the sky, Farhad," she had told him. "You see the line of stars stretching from end to end? That same line will show on Maryam's belly if she is worthy. It is an omen from God that He should show the universe in the belly of a woman."

Farhad believed her once, as he had believed many things as a child that proved untrue. He had seen too many children born lifeless or monstrous from women who were blessed with the black line. The world, it seemed, had fallen out of favor with God.

"Did you feel it?" Isabella whispered.

Farhad nodded to her. He didn't really feel it, but he knew it made women happy when he shared in their excitement, and so he smiled under his curled mustache.

Isabella sighed. "Maybe this one'll live." She laid back down and turned to Gussie, the other woman Farhad shared his bed with that night. "Wanna feel?"

Gussie shook her head. "I cain't bear it, Izzy. I just cain't. Your last baby—"

"Wasn't no baby at all, Gussie. Don't call it that. Never was no baby at all."

Gussie flinched. "Least you can have them, I guess."

"Never you mind, Gussie. You gots time. Far as I can reckon, we both evens. You ain't had one, I ain't had one that's lived. So we both dead evens."

Gussie put a pale hand to Isabella's dark face. "Sorry, Izzy. I didn't mean to make you take on so. Jealousy don't look so good, I know."

Farhad rolled onto his side and propped himself up on his elbow. They shared a large and comfortable bed that had once belonged to a wealthy banker, and when Farhad had decided to stay in Memphis after riding in with Conny ten years ago, he found that the banker's house had yet to be liberated of its property. The bed, along with most everything else, hadn't been touched. So the house, and all its possessions, had been something of a reward from Becker for his service. Here, at the end of the world, he lived like a king.

The fire had died down, and the chill of the evening air crept in and settled on his skin. The gooseflesh rose on Farhad's naked body. Despite the chill, his face burned from whiskey and laudanum, and sweat fell from under his thick black hair.

"How many is this for you, darling?" Farhad asked.

"Four."

"Four? In one so young? And none of them lived?"

Isabella stole a glance at Gussie. "No. Last one was nearly whole, though. Least, that's what my mama said. They ain't let me look on none of them. They said I don't have the nerve for it."

"Probably for the best, Izzy," Gussie said, emotion thick in her voice.

Farhad pulled a bottle of whiskey from under the bed. He held up the hazy glass and the amber liquid caught the candlelight. "Well, may this one breathe in the dust and shit of this world and ask the devil himself for more." He took a long draft and handed the bottle to Isabella, who took a drink and made a sour face.

Gussie laughed and snatched the bottle. She put it up to her lips but didn't drink. Instead, she licked the rim of the mouth slowly and peered at Farhad from under her thick eyelashes. She held him in her eyes for a moment, then she laughed and took a deep pull. Shadows danced across her naked body and Farhad felt his blood rush.

"I'm surprised you can even get that pecker up with all the whiskey you drink." Isabella stared at him between his legs.

"Darling, I do everything better drunk. Including this."

"You must have been born with a bottle in your hand." She pulled her legs up as much as her swollen belly would allow.

"Not at all. Alcohol is haram in the religion of my father. I never touched the stuff before the Calamity."

"Haram? What's that?" Gussie asked. She had attempted to imitate the sound of the word but tripped on the unfamiliar tongue.

"Forbidden."

"To who?"

"Everyone."

"So no one drinks?"

"No one drank, no. No one that I knew, anyway." Farhad took another long drink and then wiped his chin with the back of his hand. "I got a late start, so I suppose I have a lot of catching up to do." He kissed them both, and they kissed each other.

"How old were you when you came to America?" Isabella asked. Her question caught him off guard, nearly startled him. He spoke often of his life in the desert of Arabia and Syria before he came to New York as boy, before the Calamity took everything from him, only to give it back tenfold. When bedding women, he would seduce them with tales of scheming djinn, sorcerers who summoned efreeti, and women with eyes that could see the future. But he wasn't sure how much he could answer tonight, sometimes the demons of the Calamity whirled in his mind and threatened to overwhelm him and he couldn't shake the memories of Maryam, or his mother, his family, all gone. It wasn't often that they intruded on his thoughts, but when they did, he was a boy again, and he saw them as clearly as if their very ghosts stood in front of him. He pushed them away, but his thoughts were no longer on the naked women in his bed, and he lost his vigor.

"I was twelve years old." His tone was matter-of-fact. A tone that invited no more questions.

"Did you have a girl back home?" Isabella pressed on.

"Her name...was Maryam." He closed his eyes and pictured her face. The vision contorted in his mind, one moment she appeared as he remembered, then the next her features became muddy and indistinct. "Some of my first memories are of her. I knew her all my life. She was the daughter of my father's sister."

"What was she like?"

"She was beautiful. Small. Delicate. Tender. Her skin was dark...darker than mine even though she never worked outside in the sun, but still her skin was so dark and smelled of oud and her black hair of perfumed amber. She wasn't even promised to me. She was meant to wed my brother, Hassan, until he was killed by an Ottoman captain. They had come to recruit men from my tribe for military service in their war and my father refused to give them anyone. He was our sheik, my father. He spit on the captain and for that the captain ran Hassan through with his sabre. How my mother wailed... But I... I never mourned him."

"You didn't like your brother?" It was Gussie who asked this time.

"I loved my brother. I thought that Allah had sent those Ottomans to our camp because He was saving Maryam for me. I thought it was Allah Himself who guided that sword through my brother's chest so that I could have the woman who was supposed to be his wife for myself. Isn't that something? That a boy could be so heartless? I loved Hassan. I did. So how could a boy find so much joy and happiness in the death of his own brother? But I did."

"Your accent changed just now," Gussie said. "It sounded strange and foreign."

"Well, I suppose that's because I am strange and foreign." Farhad laughed.

"Well, yes, but you never sounded foreign before until now. You always sounded like a Southerner to me."

Isabella poured a measure of whiskey into a glass along with several drops of murky liquid from a small black bottle. She stirred the drink with a dark slender finger and handed the glass to Farhad. The Bedouin drank it back and closed his eyes. When he opened them again the room was a blur, the air hot and thick. A noise sounded in his head like a waterfall and the room twisted and convulsed. He shut his eyes and reeled. His body floated and he was back on a ship loaded with camels and headed to New York City. He traveled with his father, uncles, and cousins across the Atlantic Ocean to deliver seventy camels to the US Army. They were to train the Americans to care for them, to breed them, and to ride them so they could fight their war against themselves, and also kill Mexicans and Apaches. He didn't want to leave home, he wanted to stay with his mother, with Maryam. And now he was angry his father brought him on this ship where he had to sleep in the hold with the animals and where his nose burned with the stench of piss and dung.

"How many children do you reckon you've fathered here?" a voice asked.

Farhad opened his eyes. He willed himself back into his room, back into the bed he liberated from the money lender, the bed he now shared with two women, one as dark as midnight with raven black hair, the other pale as the dust-shrouded moon. "Oh true apothecary, thy drugs are quick," he whispered.

"Farhad?" The dark-skinned girl asked. "I said, 'do you think you have any children here?'" Isabella. That was her name.

Farhad raised his eyebrows and smiled. "Thousands," he said. He grabbed her thigh and she shrieked and pulled away. She leaned into him and kissed him, hard and rough, her tongue cold and wet. They tasted each other, then she pulled away again.

The door swung open, and Farhad's hand went instinctively to the revolver at his bedside. He looked down the barrel of his gun and saw the face of Conny White. What devilry brought Cornelius White to him, he couldn't guess, but the man was clean-shaven and dressed for the road. He wore a thick long coat and headscarf worn in the way of the Bedu, the way that Farhad had taught him to keep the dust out of his face when travel was necessary.

"Why Conny, this must be terribly embarrassing for you. As you can see, I have company," Farhad said.

"You always have women," Conny said.

"Yes, and while you are tolerably good company, as you can see, I am otherwise engaged at the moment. Oh, don't worry ladies, Conny here won't hurt you none. He may be uglier than a new-sheared sheep, but he's harmless. Wouldn't you say, Isabella? Isabella? My girl, you're a bit forward with all your gawking, you're like to turn me to jealousy."

Isabella laughed but continued to stare at Conny.

"I need you," Conny said. "Get dressed." He turned to the naked Isabella and nodded his head. "Ma'am,"

Isabella laughed again.

"That's a hell of a way to enter a man's room when he's trying to bed down a couple of women, Con." Farhad coughed. There was a chill in the air, but the sweat beaded on his forehead and his face flushed.

"How are you doing with...all of that?" Conny waved a hand in the air, gesturing at nothing, a look of intolerable concern marred his face.

"I'll live. Izzy, be a dove and hand me that bottle." Farhad dropped some laudanum onto his tongue. He stood up and bent over. He coughed and spasmed and coughed again. His lungs burned and the muscles in his chest felt as if they had been torn away. With every breath he drowned and gasped for air, he spit and gasped again. When it was finally over, he sat on the edge of the bed with his head in his hands. The iron tang of blood was in his mouth.

"Ladies, if you could give us a few moments alone." Conny gestured towards the door.

"Izzy, Gussie...begging your pardons, I do believe our time together has concluded. Though I have appreciated your company immensely and I certainly hope we can continue our little adventure another time." Farhad wiped his mouth with the back of his hand.

The women got dressed in a hurry. Isabella let Conny know just how much she disapproved of his intrusion before she left. For his part, Conny took the tongue-lashing with a quiet patience. Farhad knew he should be upset, but the night had already gone to hell, and he had long since lost his mood. He could have rallied his strength and finished the job, but he was almost grateful to Conny for the intrusion and the excuse to cut his bedding short.

After the girls left, the silence was palpable. The only sound was the rasping of Farhad's lungs.

"How have you been?" Conny asked at last.

"Tolerable fair, can't you tell?"

"You sound in pretty bad shape."

"Dying will do that to you. But you'd know that if you hadn't made yourself a stranger."

"Sorry. It's hard seeing you like this is all."

Farhad waved him away. "What's this all about, Con?" he asked.

"You know Becker's little girl?"

"Eudora? I'm not sure if you were aware of this, Con, but she's hardly little anymore. She grew a pair of tits and got half of Memphis fired up over them."

"Yeah, I suppose you're right."

"She dead?"

"Dead? No. Missing. Becker wants me to find her." Conny had a way of talking that summed up a lot but left as many questions as what he answered.

"Alright, is that all we know?"

"No. Seems one of those men she got fired up was the preacher. He ran off with her."

"The preacher? Jeremiah? That wiry little shit? Never did like him."

"That's the one. They've been gone about a month now and Becker's afraid the trail's gonna go cold soon. When the sandstorm kicks up, it'll be a hell of a lot harder to follow them."

"Why the devil did he wait so long before sending someone out?"

"He didn't. He sent Ira and that catstick of his to fetch 'em awhile back but the preacher killed them."

"Well shit, I'd have never would have thought that preacher had it in him. Ira's a pretty capable fellow. A bit too serious for my tastes, reminds me too much of you and one of you is more than enough. So what's the plan, Con?"

"Becker wants to sneak out tonight so we're plenty far from here before daybreak."

"Why is Becker going? He's a bit too old to be chasing after people himself, that's what we're for. What do you know that you ain't telling me, Con?"

There was hesitation in the man standing in front of him, and it burned Farhad in the pit of his stomach. "You don't keep secrets from me, Con." He stood up, his long black hair clung to his shoulders, damp with sweat. The air bit at his naked skin, but he could not back down. He had known Conny since he was a boy who didn't speak a word of English, wandering lost and alone in the ruins of New York. Conny White didn't get to lie to him.

Conny looked abashed. "You're right. You're right. The preacher stole something from Becker. Something that Longstreet's after. And when he finds out that Becker lost it..." Conny let the implication hang in the air between them.

"What did the preacher steal?"

"Money."

"Money? Who gives a shit about money?"

"This money's different. It's from California."

"California?" The West was on everyone's lips lately. The more the dust consumed everything, the stronger the people held on to the hope that somewhere there was a paradise waiting for them. "Our very own Shangri-la. Christ Con, you can't believe that nonsense, right?"

"You know me, Farhad. I believe in what I see right in front of me. Nothing else is real. But Longstreet believes it. Whether that makes it more true to you, I don't know. I don't right know your mind."

"So, Becker needs to leave right now to put distance between himself and Memphis before anyone realizes he's gone?"

"Yep. And it looks like a sandstorm's coming. With any luck, we can keep ahead of it, and it'll cover our tracks so Longstreet can't follow."

"You do realize that we will never be able to show our faces anywhere near Memphis again? Hell, anywhere in the Northeast Territories."

"You're not coming," Conny said.

Farhad started. He almost couldn't believe what he had just heard, though it had been clear as day.

"The Hell I ain't. What are you on about?"

"I'm only here to say goodbye."

"You got some fucking nerve coming here to tell me I ain't going, Cornelius White. You think you're going to drag me to Memphis and then leave so I can die here alone? Have you lost your mind?"

"Farhad, you're sick. You can't make it out in the Wastelands. I ain't gonna be responsible for you dying out there."

The Bedouin's anger subsided. "No secrets, Con. It's true, I ain't got too much longer. Doc said a year at most. But what the fuck does he know? I am having more bad days than good days lately, though. A trip like this is like to make my time shorter still. But one thing I don't want to do is die in this fucking town. And I sure as shit don't want to die slowly in this bed. Consumption takes its time. I want to die like a man, Con. On my feet with a bullet in my chest. You know it ain't my fate to die here. Not in this town, not like this. So let's stop pretending like I ain't fixing to go with you. You ain't never had a say in that and you know it."

Conny stared at the floor for a breath. "Alright," he said. "Get dressed and meet me at the quartermaster's in half an hour."

"Quartermaster's? What for? That might tip someone off that we're leaving."

"We need our guns."

"Wait. You don't have your guns?"

"You've got at least one of your revolvers, I see."

"I got both. And my rifle."

Conny frowned. "Becker didn't take them?"

"Becker tried. Found out real quick he wasn't getting them. You let him take yours? I'm positively beside myself with shock, Conny." Fewer things in life gave Farhad more joy than needling Conny, though his love for the man ran deep. Conny was a father to him, and his greatest friend.

"He managed to nibble them from me when I had a little too much whiskey."

"No such thing. Really, Conny, you have to learn the first rule of being a gunfighter—never allow yourself to be disarmed."

"I know, I taught you that."

"And now the student has become the teacher."

"Get dressed. You look ridiculous."

"Ridiculously good, you mean."

Conny turned to leave but stopped in the doorway. "Farhad," he said, looking over his shoulder. "You're right. I wouldn't do this without you."

"You couldn't do this without me, more like."

"I mean it. If you don't want to go, just give me the word. I'll tell Becker to do this by his damn self."

"You want to get out of Memphis just as bad as I do. And if you're going, someone has to be there to make sure you don't shoot yourself in the foot."

Conny's mouth twisted in what Farhad assumed passed for a smile with the gruff man. "I suppose I might need some practice along the way."

"It's a little like making love. You might never be as good as you once were, but you'll never forget how to do it."

After Conny left, he put his clothes on and packed his things. A tin of pomade. A bottle of perfume. An extra pair of trousers and a shirt. A razor and a small round mirror. He gathered all the whiskey and laudanum he could find.

He hefted his pack onto his shoulders. Though he had done well in Memphis, he couldn't help but feel it had all been for nothing. His worth, his entire legacy, everything he had accomplished and accumulated in his life fit into this small pack that he slung over his shoulders.

He had more than most, yet it wasn't enough.

Chapter 4

Sorrow Draw, North Texas (August, 1881)

Hattie Mothershed

The reverend was thin, almost hollow, and he appeared to all who looked on him as an apparition, a ghoulish wisp of a man. It always seemed to Hattie that a strong breeze could take him apart, undo him as if he were made of ash. But the old man had a strength of mind harder and sharper than any in Sorrow Draw. He could command a room like no other. And make no mistake, the church was his room. When he looked upon his congregation, they all shrank, if only inwardly, from his stare. There was a severity to him that the people could only attribute to his closeness to God.

Hattie learned a long time ago how to navigate life with a man as severe as Reverend John Mothershed for a father, and yet she still felt the intensity of his gaze. It was a feeling that no amount of familiarity could undo.

"We stand here today," the Reverend said, his voice as thin as his skeletal frame, harsh and acetic. He didn't speak in more than a whisper. He didn't need to—no one dared make a sound while he spoke. "In the very midst of the most troubled of times. Some of us wonder what offenses we've committed against our Savior Jesus Christ to suffer under the evil of this pestilence, this plague of dust and sand that conceals the very sun, that withers our crops, and sees our children die before they've tasted the first breath of life."

Hattie elbowed Erasmus in the ribs. He had been scanning the crowd for Lupe. Though her brother was two years older, Erasmus didn't have the cunning for the game that she had. He played it terribly poor. He never should have let her see him looking for Lupe. At the very least, he should have been much more discreet about it. What fun would there be now in revealing that she saw him pining for his lover if it was something he made no effort to try to conceal? She made a mental note to remind him to be more clandestine about his forbidden affairs in the future.

Though she loved nothing more than to lord it over her brother that she knew of his secret lover, if she were to be honest, she would say it worried her more than anything. Not only was Lupe a man—a sin her father could never forgive should he find out—but he was also an Indian, a wicked heathen in the preacher's eyes.

"He's only half Indian if that would make father feel better," Erasmus had told her once. "I'm sure he'd only be half as upset if he were to find out."

"And you'd only be half as dead?" She had thrown the question at him as if it were an insult. Her brother had the irritating habit of not taking anything seriously, least of all his own well-being. Which left it up to Hattie to worry about. Most people had the decency to fret for their safety so she didn't have to, but not Erasmus.

When she turned her attention back to the sermon, she felt the full and sudden power of Reverend Mothershed's gaze. He's like a little gargoyle, she thought, nothing but a gremlin. Why should I fear that look? But she did fear her father. She had always feared him. The only living soul she had ever seen her father show any semblance of tenderness towards was her mother. He doted on her still, yet the Calamity had turned him harsh towards everyone else. If he wasn't an evil man before disaster struck, he certainly became so after. At least in Hattie's eyes, he was. Not that it was necessarily a bad thing. The way she figured it, you need a devil as a guide when you're living in Hell.

"We stand," the Reverend continued, "on the very edge of calamity. Yes, that's right. The edge of calamity. On the precipice of chaos and destruction. We haven't fallen completely into it yet. By the grace of the almighty God, we're still here. We still survive. The storm outside rages and yet here we abide. We are the chosen few, the vanguard, who have been fortunate enough to endure these trials. And good fortune it is. A blessing it is to suffer under the will and warrant of the everlasting Jesus Christ. So what is the Christian duty in times of tribulation?"

Hattie squeezed her brother's hand and dug her nails into his flesh, but Erasmus made no sound, nor did he pull his hand away. Her father's sermons sometimes followed certain patterns. This one was building up to something. A message. The Reverend was using his sermon to deliver orders to the Paluxy Boys.

Hattie's stomach turned. If there was a rational driving force behind her hatred of the town of Sorrow Draw, it was the Paluxy Boys. Her father's personal army here in the Wastes. Nearly every able-bodied white man in Sorrow Draw was a member of the gang, and they were led by Hiram Eisenhardt, a deeply pockmarked German who was as cruel as he was ugly. But most of Hattie's hatred was laid entirely at the feet of his son, Ransom. He had shown an interest in her when she was a young girl, but Hattie ignored him. Unlike other girls her age, she had that luxury. Her father never had to sell her out to men for food or supplies. Instead, he sold out the church. Tithes brought in enough food and supplies. He was the flesh-monger, and the church his soiled dove.

Six months ago, her father promised her to Ransom to shore up the support of the Paluxy Boys for his various "crusades," and so he had used the only non-divine leverage he had—Hattie—to secure them as his holy order. When her marriage to Ransom is complete, her father's control of the town will be absolute.

From that moment on, Hattie had been a thorn in the side of both the Paluxy Boys and her father. It wasn't that Ransom was a bad-looking fellow. Hattie was sure he was right handsome enough. It was the fact that her father had ordered her to marry him that Hattie couldn't abide.

"I have prayed, brethren." Reverend Mothershed bowed his head for a moment. "I have prayed and communed with God. I have walked with Jesus Christ, me in the flesh and He in the spirit. I've prayed earnestly and fervently as to what actions we can take to remedy our situation, to right ourselves, to correct the course of our ship before it's too late. What can I do as captain of this vessel? What can I do to shepherd my people? What must be done to herald in the Kingdom of Jesus Christ on this Earth? As his harbingers, it falls on us to prepare the way. To prepare His way. It must be plain to see by all but the heathens and marauders of the desert and the savages in the plains that this tempest is directed by the Lord Himself. It is He who sends the dust; it is He who commands the wind; it is He who snuffs the life from the babes in the womb. How strange to me that there should be any doubt about this."

Reverend Mothershed continued. He read from his Bible. He called upon the angels and the heavenly hosts to guide him and, through him, the people of Sorrow Draw. Hattie's thoughts drifted to tonight. Tonight was her turn to care for her mother. What that usually meant was she would sit in her mother's room and watch her slowly die. She would listen to her moans, her soft whimpers, and her ragged breathing. She would smell the bile on her breath and the shit in the bed. She would clean and scrub her mother's naked body, wash the linen, and keep watch over a woman who had been a mother to her in name only.

"No one here proposes, least of all me, that this will be an easy thing," the Reverend continued. "The heathen and the savage alike will not be subjugated. They will not relent to be ruled over and they cannot be converted. This has been tried in the past and it does not work. They are born of demon seed and cannot glorify the Lord. And, though it is a lamentable thing, an Indian child will, in time, grow to be a savage man or woman, ignorant of God no matter how they were raised. Now listen to me well." He paused and looked around the room. "The Lord has confided in me that the savage is the reason for our present troubles."

Someone shouted "Amen." It was followed by another "Amen," this time by Ransom Eisenhardt, who stood by the door, a rifle cradled in his arms. The sound of his voice made Hattie's hair stand on end.

"Good Christians here today, I ask you to harden your heart. Harden your hearts as God hardened Pharaoh's heart. Relocation of the Indian is no longer a sufficient recourse. Relocate the Indian and he will still call upon his strength to make you wretched, blasphemous, and immoral. Ladies and Gentlemen, I have traveled to the Red River. I have seen the grotesque effigies constructed by the Indian savage. Figures fashioned in the likenesses of men, abominations created from the flesh and bone of the white man whose only mistake… was to wander too close to the river that the Savages have claimed for themselves."

Erasmus clenched his fist. If he realized he was still holding Hattie's hand, he didn't show it. It hurt, but Hattie made no move to uncouple her hand from his. He was afraid. And she was afraid for him. Lupe's father was an Apache who had left for the Indian Territories years ago. She scanned the room but didn't see Lupe. Maybe the boy had the good sense to leave before her father worked the crowd into a frenzy. He would have Lupe gelded and nailed to the steeple before the closing benediction. She had no love for Lupe, but she hoped the boy was already far away from here. For her brother's sake, at least. Erasmus promised to take her away from Sorrow Draw someday, and she intended to hold him to that. She needed him clear-headed because their time was coming.

Reverend Mothershed led them in prayer. He prayed for the town. He prayed for strength. Not for himself, he pleaded, but for the people of Sorrow Draw. Strength to do what must be done when the time comes. He prayed for the sinners who fornicated with the Negroes of Serpent Bluffs, for if they could not be brought back into the fold, they would suffer the same fate, the same wrath of God as the Indians, for when the Lord returns, he would also return the Negro to his rightful place as servant of the white race.

Hattie squirmed in her seat. There was a time when she believed him. For years she hung on every word he said from the pulpit. She did her duty as a daughter and would have gladly wed Ransom for a chance to play a part in the ushering in of the new reign of Christ on Earth. And sometimes when she listened to him preach, she wondered if it was true. She wondered if she should give in, and marry Ransom like her father wanted. But try as she might, she couldn't force herself to believe it. No, there was no Second Coming of Christ on the horizon. They weren't God's chosen people. Whatever separated the races before the Calamity made everyone equal had been buried in the Wastes with the numberless dead. Or at least, it should have been, if not for her father who's raised it up like Lazarus. No, she would leave Sorrow Draw. Strike out west. She would find a place that wasn't a barren wasteland. Someplace new.

The congregation filed out of the church. The sun was a warm orange glow that burned through the dust. Ransom and about a dozen Paluxy Boys were already mounted, some loading rifles, others covering their faces with scarves to keep out the dust, all of them ready to go hunting.

A silent look passed between Hiram Eisenhardt and Reverend Mothershed. The men milled about, checking buckles, adjusting straps, some kissing their women and sending them home. A few hurried off to home.

"Looks like we may have a few too many who won't pull their weight around here," said Ransom whose eyes followed the men who scurried into the haze. "You fucking cowards are going to get what's coming to you, too."

"Not everyone's fit for fighting Indians, Ransom," Mason said. Once her father's right-hand man, he had fallen out of favor with the reverend years ago. Hattie wasn't sure what had happened for him to lose that status, but she suspected he had questioned her father's ambitions that kept them in constant conflict with the Indians, the blacks in Serpent's Bluff, and even the bands of roving scavengers. He scratched at the deep scar on his neck, a wound he got fighting a group of Comanche that raided the town a few years after the Calamity, before the prophet Sanguin Corvus took over and the Indians became reclusive.

"If a man ain't fit to fight Indians, he ain't fit to be called a man." Ransom spun his horse around to face Mason.

"I'm just saying, a man can support us but not be a gunfighter. It ain't in everyone's blood. Some don't got the nerve, and that's alright."

"I agree with Ransom," Judson said. Hattie didn't have to turn around to tell it was him. His voice was too high and it didn't fit his tall frame. Hattie found him intolerably ugly. She hated his patchwork beard, his small chin, and the way his lip always curled up as if he were perpetually confused by everything he saw.

"What a fucking surprise," Mason said. "You always agree with Ransom. You ain't had an original thought in your head in years, dog."

Judson took out his revolver and leveled it at Mason. "I could blow the top of your skull off. How's that for an original thought?"

"Try again. You ain't the first to want to do that."

"Boys, boys. Put away your pistols und save them for the Indians, yes?" Hiram said, his German accent still thick despite having lived here for as long as Hattie's been alive.

"Of course, Hiram." Judson slid his revolver back in its holster, though he never took his eyes off of Mason.

"Und you, Mason?"

"I ain't skinned my irons, chief. But I'll only murder Indians today if that's what you want."

"Why use this horrible word, 'murder'? It's not murder to kill an animal, or to slay a demon, is it?"

"No, you are right about that, Hiram."

"Goot. Now we ride." He addressed the rest of the men. "Your preacher has heard the word and will of God. This business is not for the weak. But life is not for the weak. The kingdom of God is not for the weak. The weak among us had better find their strength quickly because we will not suffer them much longer."

The Paluxy Boys rode off in a whirl of dust and war cries. Hattie and Erasmus walked back home. Hattie put her arm in her brother's and they made their way in silence. She took comfort in his presence, though she knew he had no real ability to protect her, should the need arise. Erasmus wasn't a killer. He was soft and delicate, something midway between a man's body and a woman's.

"What are you going to tell Lupe?"

"That he needs to leave. Sooner rather than later."

"Where will he go?"

"I don't know."

"The Indian Territories? He's half Indian, he could go there?"

"No. They won't take his mother. She's not Indian, she's Mexican. He won't go without her."

"They won't survive out in the Wastes by themselves."

"No."

"What about Serpent's Bluff? You all go to Hill Lodge there to gamble and drink and do whatever fornicating you all do, maybe he could go there."

"Maybe. I might be able to convince Deliverance Hill to let him stay. But it'll cost me."

"Convince who?" Sometimes it amazed her how many people her brother knew. With how few there were left in the world, she really ought to know more of them, yet she couldn't find the inclination to care about the comings and goings of others.

"Deliverance Hill. She runs Hill Lodge. And the Freemen. Well, I guess the Freemen belong to Sovereign, but I hear he's hen-pecked enough that it's Deliverance who's making all the decisions. I guess I'll find out when I talk to her."

Hattie knew that some women held power over the men in their lives. How they were able to do that, she couldn't say. She imagined herself domineering, lording over Ransom Eisenhardt, making him cower, forcing him to bend to her will, but even in her mind, it didn't work. She would end up as yet another thing for him to control. He would take her brother from her, he would take away her drink and her pills, she would exist only to serve him and after a time, she would no longer know herself. She would live in constant fear of him from the day she becomes his bride. Her chest tightened. She wouldn't—couldn't—allow that to be her future.

"How does she do it?" she asked. "I've heard that Sovereign is a frightfully large man. Is this Deliverance big, too?"

He laughed. "Oh no, she's a good deal shorter even than you."

"Then how—"

"Some women are perfectly ignorant of the importance of size. So ignorant of it that their short stature seems to have absolutely no effect on them at all."

"But how?"

"Because, dear sister, they know that real power over men lies between their legs, not in how high above the ground they stand."

"There has to be more to it than that."

"Oh, I'm grossly simplifying it, of course. You have to be confident and carry yourself with that confidence. You have to be sharp and full of wit. You have to know when to be a harlot, and when to be demure. In short, Hattie, you have to be perfect. Be perfect, and you might rule the world someday."

For a moment she thought she could, but the feeling passed. It flew away from her on the winds, lost somewhere in the shifting sands.

Chapter 5

Somewhere Outside Memphis, Old Tennessee (August, 1881)

Cornelius White

When the dust storm made moving forward impossible, the four men took shelter in the first house they came across that looked as if it could still stand up to the gale. The winds were a chorus outside, not a single sound, but an army of shrieks, whistles, howls, and moans, all playing in concert like a demonic choir. Conny couldn't shake the idea that the wind knew where he hid and had come for him. It beat against the door, threatened to push the windows in and rip the boards from the walls, desperate to pull him down into the earth and cover him with dust. He pushed the thought back and shook off his scarf. It left a cloud the color of terracotta.

Becker lit some candles and Conny was able to get a good look at the house. It wasn't much, but he hadn't suspected it would be. Like most houses around the outskirts of Memphis, this one had been stripped of anything useful. Small and barren on the inside. Soon even the walls would be stripped of wood and the frame torn down. Someday he reckoned, after the people of Memphis had burned all the wood in town, they would find their way down here, to this house that is going to shelter them for the night, and they'll raze it to the ground. Everything would eventually get consumed.

Farhad came from another room, candle in hand, his boots clacked against the wooden floor as loud as the wind outside. He sat on his bedroll and pulled out a can of wax, warmed a chunk between his fingers, and then twisted it through his mustache. "Nothing here," he said.

"Of course there's nothing here," Becker said. "We're still too close to town. Scavengers and runners have picked through all this shit years ago." Becker peered out of a window at the far end of the room. There was nothing to see. The dust obscured everything. The storm had come on much quicker than they had anticipated and the mood in the house was sour. The wind would bury every last trace of their quarry.

"No harm in checking, is all. From my own experience, scavengers and runners ain't exactly the smartest men. Sometimes they overlook a good thing," Farhad said. He put his hands behind his head and leaned back on his bedroll.

"They ain't stupid enough to leave anything at all in a place so goddamned close to town." Becker turned to Farhad. There was a look in his eyes, as hard as flint. Becker might have been a good man once, Conny could hardly reckon the good from the bad anymore, but the old governor always had a short fuse and this was one of his warning signs. Conny signaled to Farhad to pull in his horns. Farhad only smiled wider.

"Why Becker," he said, "if I ain't mistaken, I'd think you were cross at me."

"And if I didn't know any better, I'd think you were goading me into a quarrel."

"Quarrel sir? No, sir."

"Why in God's name did I bring you along? I forgot how insufferable you are."

"Because you're all a bunch of old-timers who couldn't fight your way out of an orphanage. Or fuck your way out of a whorehouse. Someone's gotta do the killing here."

Becker let it drop. He sat on his bedroll, his back to the two men. Farhad turned to Conny and winked.

After what seemed to Conny like an intolerably long stretch of silence between the men, Farhad asked where Crowkiller had gotten himself to. He had been gone a long time.

"He went to hitch up the horses. There was a barn out back. I guess he's staying out there with them tonight. Might be he prefers the company of them to this lot." Conny waved his hand at both Farhad and Becker. He tried to put the storm out of his mind, but it sounded like a battlefield in his head. They hadn't been on the road long, and Farhad seemed determined to get under Becker's skin. The two didn't get on well together, and should it ever come down to it, Conny would take sides with the Bedouin. He loved Farhad like a son and a brother. He hoped it wouldn't come to that.

"Or maybe," said Farhad, "maybe he's sweet on that Betty he was riding and the poor thing keeps givin' him the mittens?"

Becker laughed, though it looked to Conny as if he tried not to. The wind gusted hard, and the house groaned and shook. If emptiness had a sound, this would be it. He imagined himself on a vast plain of dirt and dust. The sky and the ground a single color and as far as he could see there was only the barren, infertile earth, a lifeless void from which he could run but never escape.

"Con?" asked Farhad. "You alright?"

"I just remembered...I forgot to bury the Morgan boy."

"The Morgan boy? The one they call Cotton on account of that's all he's got between his ears?"

"That's the one."

"What happened to him?"

"They killed him."

"Who killed him?"

"They. Does it matter? Does any of it matter anymore? What are we even doing?"

"I believe, right now, we are attempting to shelter from a fairly substantial dust storm."

"No. What are we doing? People, I mean? What are we doing? We're dying, you know that? The whole human race. We ain't gonna make it. I mean, what's the point of all this? Look at it outside. Listen to it. This world ain't gonna let us make it. It's comin' for us. We're just gonna be the last to die is all."

"Now Conny, you aren't gettin' all melancholy on us again, are you?" Farhad threw his whiskey flask at him. "You need a drink. You get morose when you're sober."

"Might be so. But I am speaking truthfully."

"I think you give humanity too little credit. We've made it this far. And we're gonna outlive this, too. This'll come to an end someday and we'll still be around to take back what's ours when it do."

Conny wished he had the optimism of Farhad. He wanted to believe, as the young man did. But try as he might, he couldn't shake the idea that humanity was on its last leg. It was a dying beast, struggling to hold on to its last few moments of life. He pulled up the stopper on Farhad's flask and took a long pull. The firewater burned as it went down.

"You ever think back to when we first came to Memphis? How the four of us rode in?" he asked.

"We rode in like kings. Like the four bloody horsemen."

"Sure. An' we brought all that plague and war, too."

"We did. But we did what needed doing, that's all."

"I don't know about that anymore. I've been thinking a lot on it. Seems to me we did a whole lot that didn't need done. Seems we killed a whole lot more than needed killing."

"Maybe some of us did."

"Some of us that didn't still turned a blind eye to those of us that did. And we still do."

"Life is harder now than it was, Con. We can't change that. Much as we'd like, there are things we can't change. Then there's things we can. We can't change that life is harder now. We can't change the children born dead and deformed. We can't change the dust storms. We can't change the fucking hunger. But if hangin' a few people and stringin' 'em up outside the walls brought order and peace to our little corner of the Wasteland, I'm good with it."

"It'd be one thing if it had been only a few." Conny lowered his voice. "Now Becker has the nerve to want to save his own child? It don't sit right with me." The howling wind outside was loud enough to muffle his voice, even with Becker in the same room.

"No, it don't. Maybe Crowkiller was right." The two sat in silence for a moment. "What's this all about, Con?"

"I don't know. I've been thinking. Shit, I'm getting old, Farhad. I always thought things would be back to normal by now. Or at least, somewhat normal. But it ain't. It's getting worse. I need to find something good still left in the world. If there ain't nothing good left, how are we gonna go on?"

"There's plenty of good, Conny, you just don't know it when you see it. A strong drink. Winning at Faro. Strong tobacco. And there's always the feel of a woman's thighs wrapped around you."

"Plenty of people looking for good in the world, Conny. But no one willing to be the good that others are looking for." It was Crowkiller. It always startled Conny how silently the man could enter a room. He was an imposing figure. Taller even than Becker and he wore a heavy canvas duster and a Spencer carbine in a sling on his back. He always wore his long black hair in three braids. Because he was an Indian, he held a reputation in Memphis for being a cheat, a liar, and drunk, though he was none of those things. At least, no more than anyone else. He carried in with him a bundle of wood, scavenged boards from some shed or outhouse on the property. He walked across the room to the fireplace and threw the boards in. Within minutes he had a roaring fire.

They ate a meal of scorpions that Crowkiller caught and a handful of hickory nuts. Conny spent the next few hours to himself. He cleaned and oiled his revolvers, something to do to pass the time. Crowkiller sang quietly, barely audible above the din of the bellowing wind. Several times Farhad had coughing fits. He would lay on his side, doubled-over from the pain and exertion, face so deep a red that it looked almost purple. When it was over, he'd apologize and smile and Conny would give him water. He was getting worse, and Conny feared the young man wouldn't last much longer. He hoped this journey would bring them closer to the old southern border with Mexico and Texas where he reasoned the air might be cleaner. Conny watched his mother die from consumption when he was a boy, and later his daughter Bess, when she had just turned two, had wasted away and he was helpless to stop it. Although it pained him to think of sending Farhad away, he wasn't sure if he had the strength to watch another person he loved die from the White Plague.

They passed a somber night, each man subdued, each lost in his own thoughts. Becker retired early to his bedroll. Crowkiller took the loft and smoked and hummed to himself, yet even he seemed to catch the mood of the night and finished his smoke in quiet solitude. Farhad read from his book by the light of a candle. When Crowkiller broke the silence and asked what he was reading, Farhad said it was a book of poems by an Englishman. Said they were called sonnets and they were about love. Well, mostly about love, he said. Some were about sex, and others about beauty or the pain of loss.

"So, they are all about love, then," Crowkiller said. It was not a question.

"Yes, I suppose they are. And what song was it that you were humming just now?"

"It's a Lakota song. About a woman named Black Feather."

"Is it a story about love, too?"

"Of a kind, yes. Black Feather loves all her people but she believes that they hate her. She feels they can't see the love and beauty that's in her heart."

"Let me guess. It's on account of she's ugly as a mud fence."

"No. She was very beautiful. But she didn't feel beautiful."

"So what happens to her?"

"She takes her own life."

"What? That's it? That's the song?"

"No. In the end, she is given her life back when she discovers that the hatred she thought she experienced from the people was only a reflection of the hatred she had for herself. She had to learn to love herself first. Then she understood that her family and her people did indeed love her."

Farhad took out his tobacco pouch and asked if anyone had any paper. Conny tore a page from his Bible and handed it to his friend. "Read a verse. Just pick the first one your eyes land on and read it to me."

"Sure." He took the paper and held it up to the light of the fire. "These words are exceedingly small, Con. No wonder you asked me to read it to you. Your old eyes would never be able to read this."

"That's enough, Farhad."

"You know, we could've asked Cooper for some reading glasses for you before we left. Now I'm gonna have to go out of my way to look for some for you."

"I said that'll do, Farhad."

"Might improve your aim, to boot."

"Would you just read the God-blasted paper?"

"Alright, no need to be ornery with me, old man. Let's see... '*Yet thou shalt see the land before thee, but thou shalt not go thither unto the land which I give the children of Israel.*' You happy? It's nonsense."

"I knows it."

The fire cracked in the hearth, but it couldn't overcome the chill in the air and it offered Conny little comfort. He pulled his wool blanket tighter around his shoulders. He thought of the verse that Farhad read. Could it mean something? He knew in his mind it was nonsense, as his friend said, but it was something to think about, to keep the demons of the Calamity at bay. Thou shalt not go thither unto the land.

Conny grew restless. He wanted to take a walk, but the wind had not yet died down and even still, walking alone outside the city walls could be dangerous, even for a gunfighter. He emptied a tincture of laudanum into his whiskey bottle and drank deeply. He put his head back and listened to the sound of the driving wind and the spray of dirt and sand on the house. He thought of his wife, Elizabeth. In the haze of the laudanum, he could sometimes almost remember her face and the sound of her voice. He could recall the feel of her skin, soft and warm in his hands. He tried to think about her smile when she told him she thought she might be with child. He thought of her tears when he told her he had to leave for war.

It was the nights alone when he couldn't find sleep that were the worst. Conny feared nothing in life more than being alone with his thoughts. They would always drift back to before the Calamity. To his wife and children, his little Bess most of all. In the bitter cold of the small, empty house, Conny despaired. He wished he had been home to comfort his family in their final moments. He wished he had died with them in the Calamity. He rested his head on his pack and took comfort in his regrets. Like a familiar lover, he knew their movements, their proclivities, their shapes and contours. They hurt him, but they hurt him in a way he knew and could predict, and they promised always to be there, to never abandon him.

He listened to the shriek of the wind and drifted off to a dreamless sleep.

Chapter 6

Sorrow Draw, North Texas (August, 1881)

Erasmus Mothershed

Erasmus Mothershed knew the dust storm was coming. Guadalupe and his crew scavenge as far east as the ruins of Dallas on occasion, and they said it was headed right for Sorrow Draw.

"You saw it, Lupe?" Erasmus had asked.

"Not really saw, no," the boy answered. "More like, I don't know…sensed it? Felt it?"

"So you didn't see it? Just felt it?"

"It's just as good," he had said.

It was just as good. From his place on the porch of his family home, he could see it now with his own eyes. The lightning flashed blue and white across the top of the colossal wall of dust. It boiled and seethed, but slow, as if time moved differently for it than it did for the rest of the world.

Erasmus took a deep breath and sighed. By this time Sunday, the winds would be fierce, the dust nearly intolerable, and his father would have the town in the chapel, captive to his sermon. During a dust storm, the chapel would stay open, and he would be expected to be there to help his father—supply water to the congregation, hand out what food they had to spare, administer ointments and medications, and anything else he was told to do. Reverend Mothershed did none of this out of a sense of good Christian charity. He suffered the people because he could use them. He demanded loyalty from the people of Sorrow Draw, and in return, he fed them and eased their suffering. And they were always suffering.

And they would continue suffering. The last time a dust storm this big came through, it was the summer of his twentieth year. During the summer months, the ground didn't freeze every morning and growing things was still possible. Tobacco, turnips, barley, and oats could often survive the cold drought. But that year, nothing survived. The dust blocked out what little sun they did get, and there was no escape from the frost, even in July and August when he should have been able to walk outside and not see his breath. But it was November, and their meager crops had already been harvested.

The cold air stung his arms, and he considered going back inside for his coat but thought better of it. He could make the trek to Lupe's without it, and Lupe's mother, Maria, always kept their home warm. If nothing else, it will be warm under Lupe's blanket.

He smoothed the front of his paisley waistcoat. There was still a day or two before the storm hit. It would do no good for his friends to see him moping about. Appearances had to be kept.

He tucked his sandy hair underneath his top hat. He dressed in gray tonight, to match his mood. His clothes fit surprisingly well. He found the waistcoat and trousers on a scavenging run with Lupe and his friends a few months back. They were in a trunk in the back of an overturned wagon on the old road leading to Dallas. His hope that it had been abandoned fell apart when they found the bodies, mummified in the cold and scalped.

He polished his black shoes to a mirror shine. Three years ago, he had traded a pocket watch for them and he still felt he got the better of the bargain. The watch he carried now stopped telling time ages ago, but its purpose was not to tell time, but to simply look as if it told time.

He stepped onto the road, his feet light and a knot in his stomach. He would see Lupe and he would forget about the dust storm, about his father, and about the end of the world for a time.

"You're leaving? And without your coat?"

Erasmus spun around. There was an unmistakable sharp edge to his sister's voice. "Well, yes. I suppose I am," he said. He kept his voice light and playful.

"I find this weather perfectly suits me, and perfectly suits the operation for which I aim."

Hattie stood on the porch with her hands on her hips. Her golden hair framed a face that retained a perpetual frown, undoubtedly meant strictly to express her ongoing disappointment in him.

"And where are you going?" she asked.

"Little sister," he said, "I'm off to see Guadalupe and his mother. She's having a bout of thrush, so I thought I'd bring some tincture to her to help with the pain."

"Erasmus Mothershed, I don't know who you think that little lie is going to work on, but it certainly ain't me. Not when I know you get your supply of drugs from her."

"Yes, I suppose it wasn't a very good lie was it?" He held out his arm. "Walk with me awhile? At least to the end of the road?"

She took his arm. Lightning flashed, bright and searing, and in the light, he was exposed and vulnerable and unable to hide from her. From his father, Reverend Mothershed. From his mother, and her suffering... And then, just as quickly, the feeling was gone. It left behind only the ghost of the thought, like an image momentarily burned into his vision that fades away.

"How is Lupe?" Hattie asked. "Have you talked to him about leaving yet? I haven't seen him since the spring scavenger harvest. Those Indians always seem to find the best things. You know those glasses I got for ma? I got them from Elijah, but he said that old squaw found them."

Erasmus winced at the crude word, but he stayed silent.

Hattie's smile deepened. "Yes, those Indians sure do find the nicest things."

"Scavenging." He rolled his eyes. "The problem with scavengers is they only find the most useful things. The best things in life have no practical value."

"I never understood why he stayed around here as long as he did," Hattie said. "I mean, he should have seen this coming. We all know it was only a matter of time before Father really started this crusade of his in earnest."

"I didn't think it would really happen."

"Really? The Paluxy Boys have killed Indians before. And Mexicans. And they only get worse about it."

"I suppose I always thought they needed Lupe and Maria. Those two are the best scavengers around. He needs them, so he pretends like he doesn't know they're here. Maybe he'll just keep pretending. Maybe this is more of his talk."

"Not this time. I don't think he cares anymore about scavengers and trinkets and supplies. There's less and less of that stuff every year. Soon there'll be nothing left at all."

"Someday, but that's how he keeps control. He provides for the people. Without that, he loses their loyalty. So, he leaves Lupe alone and he gets his stuff."

"How long do you think he'll keep that up? He's getting worse, you know. He's riling people up more and more. I'm afraid that soon he'll go after Hill Lodge."

Erasmus laughed. "He wouldn't. It would be a massacre. Besides, the folks in town won't support it. I see half of Sorrow Draw at Hill Lodge when I visit."

Her shoulders fell. "I don't suppose there's any way I could talk you into staying here with me tonight?"

"You know I need to see Lupe. And then I have to prepare for a trip across the Flats to Hill Lodge. I'll make it up to you, I promise."

"You're going to leave me with...her. Again."

It wasn't fair, he knew. "For that, I apologize, little sister. Mother is dreadful company, isn't she? I'm not sure that dying has improved her disposition or not."

"I hate it, Rasmus. I hate it. She's awful, I can't stand the sight of her anymore. I know it's a terrible thing to say, I know she's suffering. Sometimes I'm glad she's suffering, but most of the time I wish it would all just be over."

"Oh, I'm sure it will be soon enough. She's getting worse by the day. Enjoy it while you can, I doubt it will be much longer."

"It ain't just her neither. Ransom was here this morning, eying me up something fierce. Asking father about me. Rasmus, I'd see my own neck stretched before I let that man give me to the likes of Ransom Eisenhardt."

"They would have to contend with me, first." Erasmus gave her hand a gentle, reassuring squeeze. Hattie was past the age that many young girls in town were given away by Reverend Mothershed as gifts, mostly to members of his gang, the Paluxy Boys, as rewards for loyalty, or for carrying out particularly unpleasant orders.

"Well, I don't think it would bother father a bit if they did." She took both of his hands in hers. "Look. I think that it's going to happen, and soon. Only reason he's kept me pure this long is to strengthen his hold on the Paluxy Boys. Now that Ransom is in charge, all he needs is to make me his bride."

"He wouldn't."

"He would. And he is." Lightning flashed in her eyes. Though she was, in many ways, still childlike, she had an iron resolve when she needed it. There was a strength below the surface that he admired. When they were young, she had once stolen a handful of dried meat from William Young who, to his credit, had insisted that he would have given her the meats had she asked for them. But Ma was furious and stripped her down to her bare skin and lashed her naked back right in front of William's house. She made no noise, only held her breath until her face turned a red so deep it looked almost black until their father stepped in and stayed Ma's hand for fear of the damage she might do.

She put her arm in his and they walked on. They walked past the stables, still untouched after eighteen years. They were empty, of course. Back in the early days of the Calamity, there were too few survivors and too many horses. So the people gorged themselves on horse meat, believing the Calamity to be a fleeting thing. But the Calamity persisted. Now only a few horses remained in all of Sorrow Draw. His family had two that they kept in a shed built into their house, so the horses didn't freeze to death in the stables. The Paluxy boys likely had ten or twelve between all the gang members. He also reckoned the Freemen clan and the Bandeleros had a few as well.

"How long do you think before the dust storm hits?" Hattie asked. Two long curls of flaxen hair framed her soft face. Her voice was small and light in the cold night air.

"I don't know," he said softly. The great beast marched closer, illuminated in the flashes of lightning. "I wouldn't count on having another night before it's here. And, Hattie, this one looks bad. Real bad. That's why I have to leave. I have to make sure Lupe and Maria have everything they need to ride this out." He put a gloved hand on her shoulder. She put her hand on his and held it momentarily, then she shrugged it off.

"Go," she said.

"Come," he replied.

"No."

"And why not?"

"Someone needs to take care of Mother."

"I'll be back in the morning. And that storm will be around for a week—at least—and you'll see so much of me that you'll be right sick of the sight."

"Maybe I already am." She turned on her heel, her brown dress spun like a wagon wheel about her waist.

"I love you, dear sister," he called after her.

Hattie looked back and spat. "Fuck off with you," she yelled.

"Hattie, how perfectly scandalous. I should think you would be very much disappointed in anything of that nature, I'm afraid. By the by, I left a little gift for you next to Mother's bed. It's the one in the black bottle. I think it'll help you get through the night."

She disappeared into the darkness.

Erasmus returned to the road and quickened his pace, careful not to kick up too much dust. The wind picked up and brought new misery. The cold bit at him, stabbed him everywhere it could. Not for the last time he wished, above all else, that he had brought a walking cane.

Chapter 7

Old Tennessee (August, 1881)

Farhad

By morning, the howl of the wind had died down enough for the four men to attempt to set out again. No man among them wanted to admit the truth. They wouldn't find any trace of the preacher, or the girl. Farhad searched his pack for one of his tinctures. He found relief from his consumption in whiskey and laudanum, and where those weren't to be found, it was opium—powder, pills, rolled into tobacco, it mattered little what form it came in, as long as he had them. Without whiskey or opium, his coughing fits would hit with all the fury of a sandstorm, and last nearly as long. He managed to survive in a perpetual state of drunkenness, though truth be told, most who saw him couldn't tell. He was never one to stumble or lose his wits, his senses remained keen, and he was quicker on the draw with two pints of whiskey down his throat than anyone else stone-cold sober.

When he found his bottle, he carefully measured out twenty-five drops into his tin drinking cup. Back in Memphis, he would think nothing of taking forty or more, then, a few hours later, take another forty. But Laudanum was easy to come by in Memphis. Scavengers would often bring boxes of it back from runs and raids. Opium pills were even more common. Both the old Confederate and Union armies kept their surgeons well supplied and the area around Memphis had been teeming with war when the Calamity hit. Most people wanted to take the opium pills, but Farhad preferred Laudanum. The bitter flavor, the immediacy of its effect, the ritual—it meant relief. It kept the White Plague at bay. It also meant an ecstasy beyond anything else. Not tobacco, not gambling, and not the company of the bawds in town with their painted lips and sweat-stained corsets could match the lovemaking of opium.

Farhad poured a small dram of whiskey into the cup and drank the mixture down. He waited a moment for the drug to take effect. The warmth rose first in his chest and then the hair on his arms stood erect, but it was muted, subdued. He wanted more, but the thought of running out terrified him, so he tried to be satisfied.

He finished and stepped outside. Crowkiller had the horses saddled and waiting. It was as bright a morning as the Bedouin could remember. The dust that normally lingers for days after a storm was nowhere to be seen, and an orange patch burned in the east, glowing like parchment held up to a candle, a faint suggestion of the long-absent sun.

"Storm must have come from far off, brought the sand all the way from Africa, even." Becker rubbed the back of his neck. "It travels on the winds across the ocean and drops it down here. Least that's what that German says."

"The one from Bamberg? Engel?" said Conny.

"That's the one. Harelipped bastard. Can't stand the sight of him. Pretty good naturalist, though. He knows the weather." Becker pulled at the straps on his saddle bag.

"So what's our plan now?" Crowkiller asked, scrapping his teeth with a chokeberry twig. "No tracks."

"No need for tracks yet. We know they made it down to Friar's Point, that's where we found Ira and his catstick. We keep heading south. Follow the river."

"And when we get to Friar's Point, huh?" Crowkiller spat. "What then? Still no tracks."

"We figure that out when we get there."

"We have some ideas," Conny said. "We know they can't go west right away. They won't make it ten feet into Indian territory. They won't go east, either. With the dust storms and Taylor's bandits marauding up and down the southeast coast, they'll steer clear."

Conny was a good man, but he sometimes still didn't understand that, much like Becker, he clung to some old ways himself, though perhaps not intentionally. Taylor's men were called bandits or animals for what they'd done, though when white men do the same it's in the name of "reclaiming civilization."

"They ain't fixing to turn around and head back to Memphis either," Becker said.

"Only one way for them to go. They'll head south at least until they hit Louisiana, then they'll cut across the Miss and head west for California," Conny finished.

"You think the two of them can make it all the way to California?" asked Crowkiller.

"To be frank, I am surprised the two of them made it out of Memphis without that preacher shooting himself in the foot. But what I do think is they're fool enough to believe they can make it to California."

"Listen. All of you." Becker looked at each man in turn. "I'm going south. My daughter is south, that's where I'm going. Not one of you is obligated. You can take your chances back in Memphis with Longstreet, I'm sure he'll be there soon enough." Becker held his hands up in a gesture that said, this isn't the choice I would make, but I won't stop you.

Farhad wiped the sweat from his forehead. It ran down his back like a ghostly finger, soft and caressing. "Becker, I don't think any one of us wants to do what you're suggesting. I prefer my innards to remain on my insides, if you please. I'm sure we all do. I believe what we're looking for is a little guidance, is all. None of us like to feel as if we don't have some level of control. Makes us feel all warm inside."

"We aren't in Memphis anymore, Sam," Conny said. "Out here we're all masters of ourselves. We're here out of friendship, mostly. So how's about you come to and share what you know?"

Becker nodded slowly, hesitating. "Eudora and that preacher have been missing since Lammas Day. It was two days before I found out. After those two Mexicans came back with word of Ira, it had already been nearly a month since they left."

"We know most of that," said Crowkiller.

Farhad took a pull from his flask. "What are you not telling us, Becker? Conny?"

The two exchanged a glance and Becker nodded, something unspoken passed between them. Farhad didn't like the secrecy, didn't like being kept out of the confidence, especially when Conny knew something. The man had raised him since he was a boy, alone in New York, his entire family dead, and couldn't speak a lick of the American's tongue. What else has Conny kept from him?

"Told you about all there is to tell. About two months ago, a group of scavengers operating out of Grayson came through Memphis with a haul. A wagon load full of shit, mostly, but in with all the shit was an old bag we nearly passed up, truth be told. Looked like something an Irishman or Chinaman might carry. Now I wish we had looked it over. It brought nothing but trouble. Inside the bag was thirty thousand dollars from the Republic of California."

"Something I've been thinking about," Farhad said. "We don't even know how much thirty thousand is. If I remember, money from different places had different values, is that right?"

Conny nodded. "Yeah, that's right."

"So, what if thirty thousand ain't shit?"

"Well, I guess then we'll have walked all the way to paradise for nothing." Becker raised his voice. Farhad suspected he wasn't used to people challenging him. Ten years as governor of Memphis had made him soft, too weak to accept the ideas of others. "I know as much about that money as you do now. But I ain't fixing to get my hopes up none. Hope's a goddamn dangerous thing and the letdown will bring a man straight to his knees. Might be the money's fake and all those bills ain't worth a copper cent. Might be there's no California left at all."

"Now now," Farhad said. "Now now. If there ain't no more California, then where'd that money come from?"

"Don't you get your head full of a bunch of nonsense, son. We're here to find Eudora, and if that money turns out to be genuine, then you got your payment. But don't expect it to be."

"I agree with Farhad." Crowkiller drew himself up. Once again Farhad could count on the big Indian to back him up. "I bet that Longstreet didn't think it was nonsense, eh? That's why you needed to come along. Not to play leader, not because it was your daughter, but because Longstreet wants that money, doesn't he?"

Becker looked to Conny for support but found none. "Yeah. Yeah, that's right. Look, I want my little girl back. I do. And I'm gonna skin that dirty preacher for taking her from me when I find him, not for stealing the money. For taking Eudora. But you're right, Longstreet knows about the money and he wants it."

"He's already left New York. He'll be in Memphis by Sunday." Conny let the gravity of what he said settle before continuing. "That's why we have got to get as far away from here as possible, as soon as possible. The more distance we put between ourselves and Longstreet's irons, the better."

"So he must believe the rumors, then? Why else would he make the trip himself all the way to Memphis?" Crowkiller asked.

"He believes," said Conny, "or he sees it as a way to tighten his control. Promise the people paradise...that's more powerful than ruling by fear. Rule by hope."

Farhad nodded. "Problem with that is, unless he delivers, hope will eventually run out. The world ain't in short supply of fear." He noted that Crowkiller hadn't taken his eyes off of Becker for some time.

"You should have told us this, Becker," Crowkiller said. His tone was calm, but there was an edge to it, a warning. "We had a right to know we'd be facing Longstreet's wrath."

"What do you care about Longstreet? In ten years I ain't never seen you give one moment's thought about him, why now?"

"I never did anything to anger him enough to make him want to hang me with my own entrails before. Maybe I had business still in Memphis and now I can never go back?"

"Your business in Memphis is done, best get used to that. This talk is over."

"I don't take orders from you, old man." Crowkiller pointed a finger at Becker. "You don't get to tell me when I can't speak."

Farhad made a mental check of his revolvers. One on each hip, butts out. Pull aside coat with the right hand, cross over with the left and draw, then—whose face would he see over the irons if it came to it?

"Stand down, Crowkiller." Conny said. "Let's rein it in. No cause to get all hot about something no one can change now."

"I don't like feeling like a cornered animal. The lands I'm welcomed in grow smaller."

Conny's hand moved closer to his hip, a movement not many others would have noticed, but Farhad picked up on it, just as he saw Conny shift his weight nearly imperceptibly, his body angled for the draw. You're getting slow, my friend.

But it was for nothing. Becker straightened up and ran a hand down his thick white mustache. "Alright. You can have it out with me on the road if that's how you want it, but we ain't fixing to draw irons here. Unless you want to find yourself crucified in front of the Union Hotel, we need to put some miles between us and Memphis right quick."

"We'll have words soon, old man." Crowkiller climbed onto his saddle. "I'll ride ahead and scout, watch for scavengers and banditos."

Crowkiller disappeared into the dust and the other men mounted up. Farhad, though quiet, was not angry like his friend. There was no point in wasting energy being irate. Consumption had stolen much of his vigor, and what he had left, he cherished. The possibilities that this bounty promised were nearly as intoxicating as the opium whose phantom fingers even now stroked his skin like an ethereal lover, the Poppy Whore, the bride of the multitude, her silver tongue danced across his body.

Crowkiller returned from his early scout about an hour before noon. He was nearly on top of Farhad before the Bedouin sensed his approach. The clear atmosphere of the morning had given way to a slow and gradual thickening of the dust and the three men were forced to walk single file and close behind for fear of getting separated. A man divided from his traveling companions would be apt to remain lost, wandering the Wastes until his body and spirit give up and surrendered to the dust.

Becker passed a rope behind to Conny, who tied it to his saddle and, in his turn, passed it back to Farhad. Crowkiller pulled up alongside the man and took the remaining slack.

"I was hoping to see some banditos. Sometimes a good fight is all one needs to see clearly," he said.

"Edward Crowkiller, you almost gave me a fright, sneaking up on me like that. A man as large as you really ought to make more noise when he trots around."

Crowkiller smiled. "No good hunting banditos if they can hear you coming."

"Ain't no banditos this far north. Not yet, leastwise. Wait until spring and you might catch a few who risk venturing up here. Besides, why go out of your way? We really should conserve our lead in case we need it."

"I don't waste bullets on Mexicans. Mexicans I kill with rocks. I save my bullets for white soldiers."

"Comforting," Farhad said dryly. "And what do you kill my kind with?"

"You, my friend, may be the last of your kind. I wouldn't rob the earth of her last Bedouin. You are a very rare thing, I think. I would count it as a sin to kill you, if such a thing as sin exists."

"Did you see anything else out there?"

"Dust and sand. A river of mud. A fresh corpse."

A fresh corpse out in this? Corpses themselves are not a rarity. The shifting sands and dust dunes perpetually bury bodies, only for the wind to reveal them later. But a fresh corpse is unexpected, and that made it interesting.

"Well, who was the unlucky fellow?"

"A woman. At least, I think it was. Her clothes were a white woman's clothes."

"And how did this unfortunate woman meet her untimely end?"

"Devoured, I think." Crowkiller lowered his voice. "Pieces of her all over."

"Dogs?"

Crowkiller nodded.

Farhad hated dogs. The devotion the men of this country had towards that animal bordered on religious and now, with men gone, they left in their wake a horde of dogs, turned feral with their self-governance, marauders who hunt the countrysides and suffer little from fear. "Not entirely unexpected, I suppose."

"No, but keep your sidearms close and your eyes keen."

"Always."

"You don't look so good. Best take some of your drug, lunger. We may need you in fighting spirits."

Crowkiller rode ahead to warn the other men of what he found. Becker had them press on. There was no use in circling up. They kept closer to the river on their right and kept a sharp eye on their left flank as they rode on. Farhad took his friend's advice and measured out forty drops of laudanum into his tin, and swallowed the bitter liquid straight. Forty drops this time. He fully intended to be in his right mind if anything should happen.

Conny dropped back and came in beside Farhad. He was glancing about, trying to peer through the haze. "Two more bodies floating down the river up ahead, pretty fresh."

"Well then, I reckon we may be up for a fight soon enough."

"How're you doing? How's your breathing, I mean? The dust's getting a bit thick here."

"I'm fair to middlin' I s'pose."

Conny's eyes narrowed and Farhad turned away.

"You take some more of that opium?" It was not a question.

Farhad was grateful for Conny. The Bedouin had come to America at the age of twelve and didn't speak a word of English. A week later, the End of the World descended on all of mankind and Farhad was left alone. His *hamula*, his father and grandfather, his father's brother Muhammad, and five cousins—all sons of his mother's sister, Salome—all dead. Farhad had been separated from his family when the waters began to recede. When the ocean rushed back in to swallow the city, Farhad lived. Most didn't. He wandered the wastes and ruins of the once mighty city for days until he was found by Conny. Over the years, the quiet man became like a father to him. Conny's concern was genuine, and there was no selfishness or agenda behind it.

"Like you say, the dust is getting thick. And I need to be ready for a fight."

Conny put his hand on Farhad's shoulder. There was a tenderness in the gesture and pain in his countenance. Conny, for all his skill at gunplay, was powerless to stop the consumption that was eating away at Farhad's lungs.

Farhad returned Conny's grip. "I'm alright. For now, I'm alright."

Conny nodded and straightened up in his saddle. They rode alongside each other in silence, the ghost of all their unspoken words rode between them.

The dogs attacked sometime after noon. They weren't stealthy hunters, and the four men heard their barks and cries long before they saw the first of them. They walked through a shallow corridor against the banks of the Mississippi, the river on one side, and a low ridge on the other. At the top, a large shadow moved quickly past them, barely discernible through the haze.

Crowkiller lifted his carbine and fired in a smooth, practiced motion. The animal bolted a few yards and dropped, unmoving. Two more appeared above the ridge, loping past their dead packmate. What the creatures lacked in stealth, they made up for in fearlessness. Becker and Conny each took out one and the familiar smell of gunfire ignited Farhad's spirit. He heard less but saw everything. His revolvers found their way into his hands and he spun on his saddle, turned to face a horde coming up behind them. He fired, alternating hands, each bullet hitting their mark. Through the chorus of the baying hounds, he heard Becker urging them to a gallop. He spun back around, revolvers empty, ten dead hounds behind him.

He kicked his horse to a run and pulled his repeater out of its saddle holster. The dogs gained quickly, snapping at the heels and flanks of the mounts whose eyes were now wide with terror.

Farhad laughed and kicked the hound at his side. His foot caught its jaw and sent it tumbling back. Up ahead, Crowkiller used his carbine as a club, taking swings at the dogs. Conny and Becker were too far ahead to make out.

The rope connecting their horses grew taut. Farhad snapped at the reigns and his mount snorted and foam flew from its mouth in long tendrils.

They were now in the thick of the pack, a horde of fifty strong at least as Farhad could reckon. What kind they were, he didn't know and the dust colored them all the same. They followed the men, biting and tearing at the horses, barking and howling. Farhad stood up his stirrups, laughing and shooting, pausing only long enough to reload his rifle, and then he was firing into the beasts again.

Crowkiller's mount broke to the river in a wild-eyed panic. The big man cut the rope that tethered them together before his mount could drag them all down. His horse splashed through the river's edge and then disappeared into the dust.

Farhad was tempted to go after him, but he knew the Indian was better off on his own than any of the rest of them. He snapped his reins, urging his beast to go faster, but to what end? They couldn't outrun the dogs, and they were soon to run out of lead.

Through the din of howling and barking, Becker's voice rang out. "A ferry! I see a ferry up ahead! Hurry!"

Farhad followed their phantom silhouettes through the haze. Now that he was unbound, he had fallen behind. Again, he snapped the reins and the animal grunted, his trust in his rider still holding out over his fear. Conny slowed up, coming in beside Farhad. He pointed his revolver down at a massive hound running between them and fired. In a cloud of smoke, the dog's head erupted, baptizing Farhad's horse in blood and bone.

"We're almost there. Ride hard and follow me."

Farhad rode hard, as he was told. Up ahead, a long dock came into view with Becker's horse running down its length. At the end, a small wooden ferry with an equally small cabin. Large enough for the men and their mounts, but not by much. Riding on a ferry down the Mississippi was a poor alternative to the pack of dogs still at their heels. Indians were known to patrol the waters of the muddy river aggressively. The thick dust could keep them concealed, for a time.

An unfamiliar voice broke through the clamor of dogs and gunfire. A man's voice, shouting at them in Spanish. "Apuro! Date prisa, hombres!

Apuro!" He laughed and clapped his hands as Farhad, last in line, galloped onto the ferry. Becker was already off his horse, pushing the barge away from the dock with a long oar. Two of the hounds jumped into the water at the end of the dock, teeth bared. Farhad and Conny stood at the edge of the boat, leveled their rifles, and fired.

The dogs on shore barked and howled. In their madness, they ran up and down the bank. They bit at the air, they bit at each other. Becker and the ferryman pushed the boat out until the shoreline disappeared.

The men were breathing heavily, weariness quickly replaced the rush and ecstasy of gunplay. Farhad sat down hard to catch his breath.

"Por suerte para ti yo estaba aquí!" The ferryman was a Mexican, short, and his skin was dark. Darker, Farhad noted, than even his own. He was stout and appeared well-fed, a difficult accomplishment for a man in the Wastelands. Farhad guessed at the source of the man's diet, and his suspicions were confirmed when the Mexican grabbed a boat hook and pulled in a floating dog corpse.

"No hay razón para dejar que esto se desperdicie." He pulled the body up onto the boat.

"Thank you," Becker exhaled the words between labored breaths. The man waved his hands in a gesture that meant *don't worry about it, it was nothing*.

"We need to find Crowkiller." Farhad's breath came in ragged gasps, his lungs burned as if he breathed in fire. He scanned the bank, hoping to catch a glimpse of his friend, but he saw nothing but the undulating mass of hounds.

"What the devil happened to him?"

"Horse spooked. He cut himself free so his beast didn't take us all down with him," Conny answered.

"I lost him. He disappeared," Farhad said. The excitement of the fight had begun to wear off and was replaced instead with a seed of dread.

"Was he swamped?" Becker asked the men. "If he fell, he'd have been torn apart in seconds."

"Tu amigo se escapó de regreso al norte," the Mexican gestured back the way they had come. "Los perros lo soltaron y te siguieron."

Becker shook his head. "We don't speak Spanish, amigo."

"He said our friend took off to the north," Farhad said. "The dogs didn't follow him. Least not while we was still on dry land. Might be that they picked up his sent again now that we're out of their reach."

"How'd you know what he said?" Becker asked. "I ain't never heard you speak anything other than English. Though, I guess you'd speak your mother tongue, still."

"I know'd it." Conny said. "The kid's slick as a whistle with foreign words."

Languages had always come easy to Farhad. Foreign tongues were beautiful and alluring and yet each one passed his lips like a familiar lover, one whose tastes he knew, whose needs he anticipated, and whose pleasures were always shared. When he was a boy, he could speak the language of the Ottoman Turks, as well as the Persians and the Jews, and as many dialects of the Arabs and the Bedu as were known to him. It was the reason his father insisted on bringing him to America. He knew that Farhad would, in a matter of a few days, speak the language well enough to be his interpreter.

What Farhad hadn't known was just how many languages were spoken in America. Though most of the official business with the Army was conducted in English, New York was full of many different people speaking with many different tongues. Dutch, Italian, Spanish, Basque, German, Yiddish, Russian—he loved them all. In America, he had found a harem of language.

"Alright then, Farhad." Becker shook his head. Sweat fell in great drops off his beard. "Tell the ferryman we're right grateful for the ride on his scow. Then ask him how far he's willing to take us."

Farhad spoke with the man and asked Becker's questions. "He said don't worry none about the help. And he can take us as far as Commerce. Said there's plenty of scows around there for the taking. Might even find one that'll stay afloat. If we want to risk Indian attack, that is."

"I don't think so," Becker said, scratching his beard. "I say once we're clear of these dogs, we stick to land. Least until we get to Louisiana."

"What about Crowkiller?" Farhad didn't think Becker to be the kind to leave a man behind, but the two had words earlier and Becker might see this as his opportunity to rid himself of the Indian. "We're going after him, right?"

Conny nodded a silent agreement.

Becker stomped on the decking, knocking mud from his boot. "Fine. Ask him if he'll take us back upriver so we can look for our man."

Farhad turned back to the ferryman.

"Can you take us back upriver to look for our friend?" he asked in Spanish.

The big Indian? I suppose so. How about something for my trouble?

What do you want that we have?

I want one of the gringo's pistols.

Farhad laughed. If the Mexican thought that Conny would part with one of his pistols while he still drew breath, he was very mistaken.

He won't part with those pistols, friend. They were a gift from a general in the Union army. The father of his wife. But here. Farhad pulled his repeater from his saddle bag, *It's a Henry. I've kept it in great condition. Help us find our friend and take us to Commerce.*

The ferryman took the rifle from Farhad and appraised it. *Very nice*, he said. *Tell your men to grab an oar. If we're going upriver, we all have to row.*

Chapter 8

Uncontested Lands, Old Mississippi (August, 1881)

Eudora Becker

JEREMIAH TOOK THE LARGEST piece of hardtack for himself.

Eudora often heard her pa use the expression 'the last straw will break the camel's back.' She wasn't quite sure what a camel was, but the meaning was clear. This had pushed her over the edge, and she vowed to rid herself of the false preacher at the first opportunity.

She could put up with a lot from a man. Especially if he was fair to look at, and Jeremiah was fair to look at, if nothing else. He had taken almost twenty minutes, by her own reckoning, to build the fire up enough that she could take her boots off and warm her feet. They had been on the run for days and her left boot pinched her toes and she had developed a blister on the heel of the right. She had asked him for a salve, but of course, he had forgotten to bring any. Why he didn't scavenge for any in the last dead town they passed through, God only knows. He knew she had sensitive feet.

He had made two tins of brine with a bit of sage. It was only tolerable, but still, she allowed him to think that she enjoyed it, though he certainly did nothing to deserve the thinking of it. Sometimes all a man needed was to feel like he's done a fine job, and making a man feel like he's done a fine job is generally an easy thing to do.

But then he cracked their last piece of hardtack in two with a rock, picked up the biggest half, and dropped it in his brine. He sat across from her on the far side of his small fire, swirling his tin cup and refusing to look at her. She had dealt well with his inability to provide for her on this trip. She turned a blind eye to his complete lack of survival skills. She had even excused him when he couldn't think for himself in life-or-death situations. How he managed to make it all the way from Virginia to Memphis on his own, she'll never know. She secretly suspected he had a woman with him the whole way, one he likely abandoned as soon as they reached the city walls. The man simply could not persist in this world without the care of a woman.

So for the past few weeks, she had looked past all of that, because she believed that he could take her away from Memphis, from her father, from a life of perpetual dreariness. This was a man who had lacked scruples. A man who would think nothing of stealing from the most powerful warlord on the east coast. As soon as she discovered that he wasn't a real preacher, she knew he was the man who could take her to California. He was just the type of man to get done what she needed to get done.

He had been unsure at first. He told her that many people he knew claimed the paradise of California was a myth. A fairy tale, he called it. He even laughed at her for believing in it. Well, it wasn't as if she believed it to be true, she said. She believed it was a possibility. Those are two very different things. It never really mattered that he didn't believe. She won him over with her feminine ways, not with logic or the threadbare promises of paradise. She learned from a very young age how to get what she wanted from men. Men were simple. They wanted to see her bat her eyelashes and smile. They wanted to see a bit of her skin, even just a little shoulder or length of her leg. Those were tangible promises of flesh and pleasure. With most men, she had only to flip her hair to one side and show her white neck and they would get her what she wanted. Opium, tobacco, sweetmeats, or coffee. Men rarely refused her. Jeremiah was no different.

She could forgive a lot, but she was the camel, and this was the last straw. She didn't care how, but she would cast him aside as soon as the dust blew in something better. So, she sat on her bedroll and stared at him. She bored into his face as if, through sheer force of will, she could end his very life.

She analyzed every little thing he did, committing to memory how much his existence troubled her. He breathed wrong. Disgusting. He sat on one foot with his other stretched out in front of him. Unseemly. And what did I ever see in his hair? His long blond hair which she once considered beautiful, clung to his face in thick ropes. Unbecoming.

"What?" He noticed her watching him.

Eudora raised her eyebrows. "Nothing," she said. If he couldn't figure out what bothered her, she was not about to tell him.

He turned his attention back to his cup, his expression confused.

Confused? It was apparent that he was going to need her help in figuring out exactly what he did wrong. Children had more common sense than this junkmonger. He wasn't about to get away with his dull-witted act and continue to go about his business without knowing he had angered her.

"You're still looking at me like that," he said in his ignorant Virginia accent. "What did I do wrong?"

"I said nothing," she replied, a bit harsher than she intended, but he had made her furious.

"Now I ain't that dumb, I know when a woman is mad, and you're mad. So out with it, darling. What did I do wrong this time?"

Darling? Her face burned like she had stayed too close to the fire for too long.

Of course, that would take an adequate fire, and for that, I'd need a better man than this.

"You took the biggest piece of hardtack," she said.

"What?"

"You took the biggest piece of hardtack. For yourself."

"No, I didn't." Jeremiah spit into the fire.

"You did. I watched. That was very selfish of you, Jeremiah Preacher. I thought, seeing as I was your girl and all, I thought you'd at least try to be a little sweet on me and let me have it since I am exhausted from taking care of you all day."

Jeremiah looked as if he had been slapped in the face. Good.

"Jesus Christ, are you being honest right now?"

"Yes, I'm being honest right now. I think I deserved the bigger half."

He just looked at her from over the fire, his expression bewildered, but Eudora could not understand why he didn't get it.

"Why are we gettin' in a blow up over it?" he asked. "Even if I did take the bigger piece, I'm almost twice your size. I need more food than you do. That's just common sense, darling." She did not like the way he spoke to her, as if she were a child and he had to use small words and speak slowly for her to understand.

"I'm hungry. You know something, Jeremiah? I'm starting to wonder if I didn't make the right decision in bringing you along."

"In bringing me along?" He laughed. "You'd have been dead a hundred times over if not for me. Who do you think makes your food? Whose coat do you wear when you're too cold? Who builds your fires? You can't do any of these things. You'd never make it out here without me."

"So, what you're telling me is I can easily replace you with hardtack, some matches, and the coat off your corpse? Boy, you make a poor case for your value in this situation."

"Yeah, and who's gonna make the hardtack? You?"

"We've got enough to last us until we get nearly to New Mexico, you said so yourself. If it's only me eating it, it's bound to get me all the way to California."

"And what happens when some bandits find you? You gonna nag them to death?"

"I have ways of protecting myself. Been doing that my whole life."

"No, you ain't. You've always had Daddy to protect you. You think you've been taking care of yourself? No one had the nerve to cross you, or take advantage of you, or bed you against your will on account of you being Becker's little girl."

He wasn't wrong. She had used her father's influence to her advantage for as long as she could remember, but she always used all the tools she had at her disposal. Her father was a useful tool at times. Anyone else in her position would have done the same thing, but that didn't mean she couldn't take care of herself. "You think I only got my nerve on account of who my daddy is?"

"Let me tell you how it is, girl. I'm getting tired of you runnin' that mouth of yours. Now I've played nice, but you know what? There ain't no one out here but us. Your pa ain't here to protect you and you can't run to the next man you see now that I ain't gonna give you what you want. Now I'm not the kind of man to put his hands on a woman when she don't earn it, but I swear by God you're about to see the back of my fist."

He said those words in a tone he had never used on her before, a voice that she never knew he even possessed. She stood up and walked around the fire, bent over and looked him in the eyes. "Don't you ever speak to me in that tone again Jeremiah Preacher. You'll see the back of my fist. You'll see the bottom of my boot." She hiked her dress up and kicked him square in the jaw. It had more force behind it than she intended, but she didn't feel bad about that. It was less than he deserved for the way he had spoken to her. He fell over and she kicked him again.

"Alright, alright, stop." He cried. "I'm sorry. I'm sorry, alright? Damn, woman. The devil take me, I'm sorry."

He lay in the dust on his side, his arms covering his face. He looked pathetic, but there was no need to berate him anymore. With luck, he had learned his lesson. But Eudora knew she needed a different plan. She needed a stronger man than Jeremiah. Someone who didn't threaten to hit her. A man who knew her value and didn't need her boot like he was a child. "Put up the tent. I want to go to sleep."

Jeremiah grumbled, softer than he usually did, but he put up the tent. Eudora slept that night in fits, her back to him. The cold bit at her savagely, but she kept her distance. She didn't care about his body heat, in fact, the thought of the warmth of his body repulsed her. She didn't want to touch him. She didn't want to face him. She shivered under her blanket and fought against her loneliness, hoping sleep would overtake her before despair.

"Dora," Jeremiah whispered in the cold.

"Yes?"

"I'm sorry, Dora. You know I'd never hit you. I don't know why I said that."

"I know. But I ain't sorry I hit you. You needed it."

"Yeah, I suppose I did. I love you, you know."

"I know it."

"You don't have to say it back. You and me, we got something real special, you know? We're gonna live the good life when we get to California. The two of us, can you imagine? Living like the goddamn king and queen."

"I hope so."

"Good night, Dora."

"Good night, Jeremiah."

Needles of cold air pierced her skin. She moved closer to Jeremiah for warmth. He wasn't so bad, though she didn't think she wanted to face the rest of her life as his queen in California. She would let him take her to paradise, but once there, she would have to find her own way. And he would be fine. Some doe-eyed innocent girl would find herself taken in by him and he would have the kind of wife he wanted. The one he thought she was when they met. The one she had pretended to be.

Chapter 9

Serpent's Bluff, North Texas (August, 1881)

Deliverance Hill

Hill Lodge was busy. Deliverance had never seen this many white people in one place at the same time, and their faces tense, their hands jittery. She had sent a few of her listeners into the crowd to see if they could ferret out a cause for what had gotten the people of Sorrow Draw all worked up but no one had reported back to her yet. If she was a betting lady, and she certainly was, she would bet that old Reverend Mothershed had gotten them riled up over something, and Deliverance aimed to find out what it was.

She pushed it out of her mind for the moment. What concerned her now were the pair of threes in her hand. She kept her Jack of Spades but laid down a six and a two and picked up two more cards. Three of Hearts and Jack of Diamonds. Full House. She tightened her lips. Of course, she smiled on the inside, but she had to play the game. And in the game of Poker, she had to always appear to have her dander up. Anything less would give her away.

This hand was practice, of course. Meant to keep her skills sharp. There was no chance that Jack Hawker and Solomon Cagg were likely to beat her at her own game. But Deliverance hated to lose. She hated to fold, too, when playing against dregs like these.

Since Hill Lodge was hers, she had considered banishing the two to the Faro tables, a game much more suited to their empty brains than Poker. Poker was a thinking man's game, and playing against these two was almost heresy. But no one else was game for thinking tonight.

Jack threw a morphine tablet into the pot. Deliverance nearly raised an eyebrow. Jack's love of morphine had gotten him in trouble plenty of times in the past, so he must be very confident in his hand to make that wager. Or very foolish. Which one it was this time, she couldn't tell.

Solomon threw his cards down. "I fold." He leaned back in his chair, his expression said he was eager to see how this would play out.

Deliverance took a morphine tablet out of a pocket she had sewed into the bust of her dress. She had cut the bust of the dress low to show off her dark brown cleavage. Distracted men make terrible Poker players. She rolled the pill around her slender fingers. She watched Jack for a sign, any hint that he had nothing until...there it was. He pursed his lips. His tell. Deliverance knew he had nothing. A pair of twos, seven high if he was lucky. She laid the pill next to his.

"I call," she said in her most sultry voice.

Jack didn't take his eyes off the pills but slowly laid down his hand. He did better than she thought. Two pair, sixes and eights, queen high. But it wasn't good enough.

Deliverance slapped her cards on the table and snatched the tablets, downing both of them with a shot of whiskey before the man could raise an argument. "Better luck next time, Hawker," she said. She gathered up the rest of her winnings—junk mostly. A few lead balls, some powder, and a handful of roasted acorns. Most patrons had to trade for chips, but Deliverance preferred to play with tangible bets. Chips were meaningless to her, something she would bet without thinking, their value immaterial. But real things in front of her she understood. Those things had value she could comprehend. She knew what a morphine pill meant to her. A clay chip held no excitement, no urgency.

"Get out of here *mzee*, you two bore the fuck out of me."

They both looked like they were about to protest, but Hill Lodge belonged to Deliverance Hill, and when she told a man to leave a table, he left.

When she was alone, she leaned her chair back against the wall and closed her eyes. There had been an unspoken truce between her people and Sorrow

Draw for the last few years, but she knew the Reverend was stirring up shit and she wanted to know what it was. And she wanted to know now. Were all these people here so they could enjoy one last night before the Paluxy Boys raided Serpent's Bluff? She didn't think so. The reverend didn't know their defenses, or their numbers, but if there was to be a fight, she needed to prepare.

The Freemen of Serpent's Bluff didn't have the numbers that the Paluxy Boys did, but the gang was hardened. They were made up of mostly former slaves and the children of former slaves. Deliverance was the daughter of two former slaves of Herr Eisenhardt. Hiram Eisenhardt, along with his son Ransom, head the Paluxy Boys gang.

Her father had been a troublemaker in his youth, and Deliverance always admired that in him. He worked as an apprentice to a tailor, a coachman, and once as a ferry operator. He had been involved in a small rebellion once where he and a few of his friends tried to escape to Mexico. They didn't make it. When he was caught, some of his friends were hanged, the rest beaten and sent back to their masters. Her father, Jacob Hill, was sold because he said his master was tired of the look of him. That's when he went to work for Hiram Eisenhardt and met her mother. They were instant lovers. Deliverance was pretty sure that the thrill of getting caught was what drove her father's passion more than anything else. It was his way of still rebelling.

A few years later, the Calamity struck, and her parents survived. Some of the local slaves gathered together in what would one day become Hill Lodge and declared themselves then—and forever after—free men and women. Over the next eighteen years, those men and women defended Hill Lodge, and the surrounding community of Serpent's Bluff, sometimes with their lives.

Deliverance was born one year to the day after the disaster hit. Jacob and Hope named her Deliverance. For them, the Calamity wasn't the end of the world. Her father saw it as a cleansing. As a divine equalizer. Sure, their lives were hard, he said. The Wastes were not an easy land to survive in. Every day was life and death. But every day was a day lived as a free man. And his daughter was born never knowing the shackles of a life of bondage.

Most of the conflict, in the beginning, centered around Mothershed and his Paluxy Boys. Always outnumbered, the Hill Lodge Freemen had to rely on their knowledge of their land and raw determination. Before long, even the women and children trained to fight. In the defense of home and their right to exist as free people, everyone was a soldier. Soon, the Paluxy Boys gave up the raids and for several years they lived with no contact between the two.

Until Deliverance turned Hill Lodge into a fully functional gambling saloon. What started as a pet project to stave off boredom, turned into a sizable operation. After a time, even white folk from Sorrow Draw would make the trek across ten miles of Wasteland to come spend a night drinking and gambling, singing and whoring. For many, it was the Great Escape, and it firmly established Deliverance as a powerful leader of the Freemen. By all accounts, the face of leadership was Sovereign, her favorite lover. But her influence with him was, as far as she knew, nearly absolute.

Her parents had been eager to step aside. They were old and spent most of their days sitting by the fire and talking about old times. It was the fate of all the mzee, the elderly, as far as Deliverance could tell, and she didn't cotton to that easy life. She planned on going out someday in a hail of gunfire.

"Good evening, Deliverance." A man's voice shook her out of her thoughts.

"Well look at what the dust blew in." Deliverance was a bit surprised to see Erasmus Mothershed standing at her table. The two of them never really spoke more than a few words to each other before. "Have a seat."

Erasmus pulled a chair out and sat down. He took off his dust-stained poncho and laid it on the table in front of her. He wore a white and black striped waistcoat cut and grey trousers. In the middle of the end of the world, this man somehow managed to look dashing. She hadn't seen the Reverend's son in quite some time. He was beautiful and had a slender, delicate manner about him.

"You here for a good time? You're certainly dressed like you are."

Erasmus shook his head no, then hesitated, and nodded a "yes."

"Well, which is it? Yes or no?"

"Both, I suppose. My principal reason for being here is business, but afterwards I'm not opposed to a little pleasure, should someone give me occasion."

"Can you not take the occasion yourself, or does it need to be given?"

He smiled. His white teeth dazzled Deliverance and she wondered how he managed to keep them so pure in the Wastelands where most people were struggling to survive and their teeth gave them little concern, as long as they had some left in their mouth to chew.

"I can take the occasion myself, when I'm moved to. But sometimes I like to be moved, carried away by the occasion, and not have to seek it out."

"I understand. It's sometimes fate, right?" Deliverance said. "Sometimes we just sit here and let things fall into our lap. But that's not why you're here to see me, is it? I mean, if it is, then speak up because, make no mistake, you are the prime article in this room."

Erasmus nearly flushed. "Well, I'm sure I had never considered before, but I certainly appreciate you saying so. I'm not opposed to trying new things, you understand. But that's not the nature of my little intrusion here."

"Pity." Deliverance picked up the cards and shuffled. "You play?"

"No, not Poker I'm afraid. I play Faro sometimes."

"Poker's a much better game. Faro's for simpletons. Liars and cheats play Faro. Poker is a game of cunning. It's a game of deception and misdirection. You can play with a large group, but I find that playing with a single opponent adds a whole other thrill to the game."

"Faro is a game of chance where everyone is equal. There is no advantage and fate holds all the cards. I live for pleasure, Deliverance. The game you play is too duplicitous, too tangled. It's positively Byzantine. It loses all delight for me."

"I live for the game. My mind needs to turn, to labor. If I'm not thinking I'm not enjoying myself."

"That's sounds dreadful."

"It's intoxicating."

"Deliverance, I wanted to warn you about my father." Erasmus closed his eyes when he said it as if he didn't want to see the words come out of his mouth, like his betrayal would be a visible thing.

"Well, this night got a lot more interesting. What's the old codger plotting?"

"I don't…I don't know exactly. Nothing with you yet, I just worry that he's going to come for your Freemen next."

"Next? Who's he coming for now?"

"The Indians."

"The Indians?" Mothershed was cracked, Deliverance was sure of it. She laughed. The pained expression on Erasmus' face made her regret it. "Look, If Mothershed wants to send the Paluxy Boys out to pick fights in the Indian Territories, they won't be a problem for me for long. Nobody—and I mean nobody, Erasmus—fucks with the Indians. Those fucking Paluxy Boys will make such pretty little scarecrows lining the Red River."

"My father is many things, Deliverance. Many awful things, I admit that. But he isn't stupid. I'm sure he has some kind of plan. I don't know what it is, but I thought I'd come and warn you. And maybe you're right. Maybe he just believes he can do this because he thinks God told him it's his duty to kill the savages and maybe he'll fail. But if he does, if he fails, he'll come after you with a vengeance to save face and score a victory."

Erasmus could be right. It's more than likely, an almost certainty, that he would fail in any attempt to fight the Indians, So when he and his boys lose, they'll need a victory. That leaves only the town of Serpent's Bluff—he'd come for Hill Lodge and the Freemen. Unless he wanted to send a raiding party all the way down to Houston, see if there's anyone left down there worth fighting, but those disorganized Highwaymen would be a hollow victory. "And how would the people of Sorrow Draw feel about that? Every night I see more and more of your white people in here, making the journey across the miles of Wasteland to taste a bit of the excitement I offer here. How would they feel about losing this place?"

"Honestly, I think their fear of my father and the Paluxy Boys would silence their tongues. Or they'd just decide that they'll take over Hill Lodge and run it themselves."

"Run it into the ground is all they'd do. This place wouldn't last without me. I am Hill Lodge."

"I know it. But he has them convinced that they're God's chosen people. The one's who'll usher in the Second Coming of Christ."

"You was raised by this preacher. How is it that you don't believe that?"

"He's my father. I see a side of him that they don't. For all his posturing and pleading on the pulpit, I know one thing for sure. All the death and violence he incites because he says it's God's will is nothing more than his own desire to inflict pain on people. His own desire to go back to the way things used to be."

"Well, Erasmus, what do I owe you for this information? I'm quite positive you didn't give it freely."

"Well, I do need someone like you to perform a service for me. I can't do it myself, and no one in Sorrow Draw would dare." He rolled some tobacco and lit it with the candle on the table. "I want you to help me kill someone."

"And what makes you think I'm into cold-blooded murder?"

"I was hoping it would be a target you'd find acceptable."

"Who?"

"Ransom Eisenhardt."

Was this man mad? This dandified soft-skin better have a good reason for wasting her time. "You're more foolish than I thought. Or you think me more foolish than I am. If I kill—or help you kill—Ransom Eisenhardt, it would mean guaranteed war with the Paluxy Boys. Why in the world would I risk that?"

"They won't know it was us. I can't risk them knowing it was me, either. My father would actually love to have a good excuse to stretch my neck. So we make it look like it Indians did it. You have some access to them, right? You can get some of their weapons, some trinket or other we can lay at his feet and make it look like a brave dropped it during an attack?"

"You still haven't answered why I would want to get involved."

"Because Ransom is worse than my father. I know you're probably waiting for Mothershed to die, trust me I am too. But when Ransom takes over he will be worse. He has all of the cruelty of my father with none of the religious morality, tattered as that may be. His aim is war and murder for war and murder's sake. He'll not hesitate to take the fight to you."

Deliverance wasn't sure about this, but she knew Erasmus wasn't telling her something. "And why are you petitioning me for this now? Why the urgency? And why do you care if Ransom takes over? I'm sure you and your white skin will be just fine."

"My white skin, maybe. But not the white skin of my sister. She's to be given to Ransom as a gift."

Of course Mothershed would use his daughter to strengthen his bond with the Paluxy Boys, it was a scheme she should have seen coming, but that preacher has a way of making her underestimate the depths at which he'd buried his humanity.

"And not the brown skin of my lover. When Ransom takes over the Paluxy Boys he'll flay Guadalupe alive and make a coat from his skin."

"Look, I'm sorry about the situation you're in, I really am. But I have a very fragile relationship with the Indians and I ain't going to risk that. The trade is good and is helping my people survive. Last thing I want to do is get them involved in a war with the Paluxy Boys."

"You're against the Paluxy Boys, you could fight them with the Indians. Tell them they're your enemies, too."

"No good. They don't see things that way. Best case scenario is they stop all dealings with people on this side of the river. Worst is they attack us, too. Either way, it's a bad outcome for me and my people."

"Talk to them. Make them understand. They're reasonable people."

Deliverance could sense the desperation in his voice. He was losing the petition and he could probably feel it slipping through his fingers. She felt bad for him.

"They got to where they was at before the Calamity by being reasonable. They ain't gonna make that same mistake again. I'm sorry, but this just ain't my problem."

Erasmus stood up. Deliverance expected an angry outburst but all she saw etched in his beautiful, delicate face was fear.

"Well Deliverance, thank you for your time. I hope I can count on your discretion regarding this conversation?"

"I won't tell no one, you have my word."

"And if you change your mind, if situations change your mind, maybe we can work out a deal then."

"Look, how about you have your boy come here? I'm sure we have some room. Serpent's Bluff ain't big by any means, but there's some empty homes still around town. He can find himself one, the Freemen will leave him in peace, I promise that."

He seemed to brighten up a bit at that. "Again, thank you. I'll encourage him to take you up on that."

He left, but the echo of his conversation remained. Deliverance was troubled by it. She had dismissed him, yes, but she couldn't shake his warnings. A showdown with the Paluxy Boys seemed imminent. Maybe she could set it off on her own terms. Maybe the killing of Ransom was a necessity. With him gone, who would take over his gang? A power vacuum there would work well in her favor. She scanned the room for Erasmus and cursed herself for not asking him. Amateur mistake.

Her mind raced and she needed to settle it down with some kind of diversion before she could separate the tangle of thoughts in her mind and make sense of them.

She needed Sovereign. She spied him across the saloon, with a sallow-skinned harlot on his lap. The woman was unfamiliar to her and Deliverance suspected she had come from Sorrow Draw. This conversation with Erasmus had reminded her of how precarious their position was, how fleeting their lives could be, so she would take both Sovereign and this white woman to her bed tonight. She would enjoy every pleasure in life before the inevitable end.

Chapter 10

Old Tennessee (August, 1881)

Cornelius White

Progress was slow moving upriver. The horses were unsteady at first, but Farhad, with help from Conny, managed to get them down on their haunches and that seemed to calm them a bit. The four men rowed in silence. Conny wasn't sure when the dogs stopped barking, but at some point, he realized that he wasn't hearing them anymore. He scanned the riverbank through the haze. Nothing. No movement. No sounds. No dogs. No Crowkiller.

"I think maybe we should call for him," Conny said. "Elsewise we might row right past him."

"You two call," Becker said. "I'm still a bit winded."

Conny put his hands to his mouth and called out. Farhad whistled. There was no response. They rowed on, slowly, calling and whistling toward the shore.

Farhad shook his head. "Maybe we should go ashore and have a look around."

"I agree," Conny said. It was a better idea than whistling from the scow. "This is about a half mile from where he took off. He would've been able to get his animal under control by this point. Then he would've followed the river back south to regroup with us. Might even be able to find some tracks and hunt him down."

"Sounds like a fine plan," Becker said. "I'll stay here with the animals and gear. Someone needs to keep an eye on our Mexican friend and make sure he doesn't take off with everything we own."

The ferryman sat on the railing, rubbing down his new Henry repeating rifle with an oiled cloth.

"Now Becker, don't be so inhospitable. I doubt the mistrust is entirely warranted," Farhad said.

"All the same I think I'll stay here and guard our gear." He crossed his arms and leaned back against his horse, a gesture that left no question about his intent to stay.

Conny gestured towards the Mexican. "Tell our ferryman to get as close to shore as he can. We'll jump off and have a quick look around."

Becker stood back up and came in close to Conny. "Don't be out there long. That bloody Indian knows his way around I think better than he lets on. If you find him—great. If not, we can't waste any more time looking. That clear?"

Conny nodded. Becker's plan to get as far from Memphis as possible in as short a time as possible wasn't panning out for them and Conny shared his concern. But a friend is a friend. Even one as questionable as Crowkiller. In Conny's world, friends were hard to come by.

When Farhad returned, they rowed the scow to shore and the two men jumped out. The river was cold, and the water was like a kick to the groin, but the bank was steep, and they were on dry land soon enough.

Tracking was never Conny's specialty, nor Farhad's he assumed. He told Farhad to walk the bank south and see if he could find anything, while he went north. He searched fast. horses aren't graceful animals—they leave large, heavy prints and the wind was light enough that they should still be easily visible. They heard no hounds, but Conny still kept his revolver in his hand. Three shots left. Enough, perhaps, to buy him some time to get to the scow if he should come up on any trouble.

The sand on the bank was smooth, undisturbed. No signs of man or beast of any kind. The top of the bank turned to dry grass, but with enough sand and dust to leave prints. His own showed easily on the ground behind him. The trees rose barren and lifeless, like the old skeletons that linger in the

Wastelands long after everything that had made them a living thing had been devoured by time.

Conny found his mind wandering. He hadn't had the time to think about the money—he intentionally tried not to think about it. Disappointment came hard and quick in the desert of the dead, but life hadn't handed him much to hope for in the last eighteen years.

California was a dream—a legend. It had achieved almost mythical status in the East, like the stories of the djinn and sultans and ancient demons of Arabia that Farhad would tell. People whispered that it was a paradise. Foolish people, of course. People who couldn't face the reality that the world was dead and there was no coming back from the Calamity that struck it down.

A flutter caught his eye. Something that didn't belong to the barren world. Hooked on a dead branch was a scarf. It was Crowkiller's *keffiyeh*. At the base of the tree, leading away north, were the horse tracks they were searching for.

Conny whistled. He waited a few moments and whistled again, giving Farhad enough time to find him through the haze.

"Found his tracks," Conny said when Farhad emerged from the dust. "And this." He tossed the *keffiyeh* to the Bedouin who looked at it as if he'd never seen it before.

"Now how do you reckon he lost this?" Farhad asked.

Conny shrugged. "Snagged on the tree? That's where I found it."

Farhad bent down to examine the tracks. "His horse wasn't running here."

Conny stopped. The tracks were spaced too close together for the animal to have been running. Farhad was right. "So, he had control of the beast here, no hounds in pursuit, yet he drops his scarf and keeps going north? It don't make a lick of sense."

"Unless," Farhad started. He spun around, looking in all directions. "Unless he was going north so he could cut back around to the east. Maybe he was trying to give the pack a wide berth, meet us farther down the river."

"You don't think he'd try to give us the slip, do you?"

"Not me and you. I'll allow that he might if it was just Becker. But not with us here."

"You're right, I 'spose." Conny had his doubts about that, though. Crowkiller was always a difficult man for him to pin down. The Indian had his own agenda, and he's perfectly helpful if that agenda aligned with Conny's. But if it didn't, the man would disappear. Sometimes for months on end. But how would it benefit him to separate from the group, unless he intends to go after the money and take it all for himself?

Conny tried to push the thought away. It ain't a proper thought to entertain for a man he did consider a friend.

"Well, I reckon we can follow the tracks, see where they lead." Farhad gestured north. "Or we can head back and let Becker in on our confidence."

"I 'spose we ought to do just that."

Farhad sighed. "Why did I know you'd take the reasonable option?"

"And why wouldn't anyone choose anything other than the reasonable option?"

They turned as one to head back to the ferry. "My friend... my dearest friend, the reasonable option is invariably the dullest option."

Conny laughed. "And you think that it's more entertaining to get lost in the Wastelands looking for a Goliath of an Indian who may or may not want to be found?"

"Infinitely." Farhad took out a cigarette and match from his coat pocket. "You see? Now you are once again Conny White. Now my friend has returned."

"I've been thinking too much lately, I reckon."

"A terrible pastime. I don't much recommend it at all." Farhad took a long drag, and they walked back to the boat together passing the cigarette back and forth between them. Not for the first, or last time, Conny admired the younger man. He felt a sense of pride for the person Farhad had become, a capable gunfighter, a dependable companion, a damn fine gambler, and, above all, a good friend. If there was anyone left in the world that Conny truly loved, it was him.

They stepped up to the edge of the river and looked out across the water. The ferry had drifted farther away since they came to shore and it was barely discernible across the water, like a ship drifting through the early fog. Conny whistled and waved. A figure waved back, Becker, judging by the height of the man.

Conny called for the ferry to come pick them up, and Farhad repeated the call in Spanish. Another figure, smaller than the first, emerged from the dusty haze and stood behind the taller man. The ferryman, no doubt. The small, stout silhouette leveled a rifle—a Henry Repeater—at the other man's head and fired.

Conny yelled. Shock and anger gave speed to his arms and his revolvers were in his hands in an instant, but the ferryman ducked behind the beasts that were still on the scow and there was no shot he was able to make.

The two men stood in stunned silence, revolvers drawn and leveled at the scow, helpless to watch as it drifted out of sight. Moments later, a splash. The unmistakable sound of something dumped overboard.

"Hasta Luego, pinche gringo." The voice sang out in the still air. "Gracias por los regalos."

Conny ran out into the river, but Farhad held him back.

"Con. Con! It's done. He's gone. Even if you could swim fast enough, he'd just pick you off as easy as we picked off them dogs."

"Goddamn...Goddamn bloody..." Conny sputtered. "I'll put a bullet between your eyes, you hear me, you son of a bitch? I'm going to kill that fucking greaser."

"You got some lead with his name on it, make no mistake. But right now, we have got to get ourselves right before nightfall because she's coming on quick."

Anger was something Conny couldn't easily set aside, but Farhad was right. Nights in the Uncontested Lands were bitterly cold and black as pitch. Moonless for eighteen years. Fortunately, the dead trees in abundance provided plenty of fuel for a fire, and Conny had a tin of dry blasting caps in his pocket. Before long they had a large campfire roaring and snapping. The dry wood caught quick and burned even quicker. They would have to take turns on fire watch throughout the night.

All of these tasks Conny performed in silence, lost in his melancholy, his thoughts fixed on Sam Becker. How far the man had come from Calamity survivor to governor of Memphis. Conny couldn't deny that the man had deserved to die, but he deserved to die with some dignity at the end of a rope for his crimes, not from a bullet in the back of the head by a stranger for the price of a few horses and some gear.

They sat for a long while beside the fire, neither man saying anything to the other. Conny was the first to break the silence.

"So now what? This rescue mission's turned into something, hasn't it? We're in the shit, that's for sure."

"Well, now, I'm not so sure it's as bad as all that. Becker getting hisself killed is a shame, of course, but, and hear me out here, I ain't saying it's a good thing, mind you. And I ain't saying we aren't in a damn fine mess but," Farhad licked his lips. "we're down two men if Crowkiller don't come back, of course. But we find Eudora and the preacher, and we find that money, we can split it fifty-fifty."

"Becker was our friend, Farhad."

"True. But truth be told, Becker was more your friend than mine. He didn't have much of a taste for foreigners, even when they're boys who wanted nothing more than to go back home."

"So, he was a rotten friend. But friends are hard to come by these days."

"Be a lot easier to come by with thirty thousand dollars."

"I thought I raised you better than this."

"Isn't it wonderful that I didn't turn out nearly as honorable as you?" Farhad winked.

As much as he didn't want to admit it, Farhad had a point. Becker was gone, and there was nothing Conny could do to change that. They couldn't go back to Memphis; Longstreet was likely already there and demanding a noose for all their necks. Or worse. Nothing to do but move forward or let the Wasteland take them.

"Alright. I'll try to look at the bright side of this. At least we're above snakes."

Farhad laughed, a sound that punched through the still blackness.

"That's the spirit. We ain't got our horses, we ain't got our supplies, both of us nearly out of lead, and no food. But we ain't dead yet."

In the starless night, they made plans and toasted the memory of their friends. Conny took first watch and in the quiet solitude, he despaired.

SORROW DRAW

Conny woke in the morning to Farhad pulling the body of Becker out of the water. The younger man had spent his watch digging a shallow grave—it must not have been an easy task with nothing but his knife to loosen the dirt. Conny fought off a piercing shame. That burden should have been his but instead, he spent his time on watch with his head in his hands feeling sorry for himself. Conny jumped off of his bedroll and took Becker by the legs, as Farhad had him already by the arms.

It wasn't the first time Conny had to carry a dead body, but it was always a strange thing. The heavy body, still here in our world, but the mind, the soul, gone to whatever spectral sphere the consciousness goes to when it's driven from the mortal form. Once, Conny would have called himself a good Christian man. But two kinds of people emerge from the annihilation of the world: those who see the presence of God in the endless fields of the dead, and those who see His absence. Conny was the latter. It was impossible to reconcile the God he had once believed in with the reality of the new world. The Wasteland they buried their friend in was enough proof that God had abandoned the realm of men.

They carried Becker to his resting place under a large white oak. The tree was leafless and dry, the bark worn nearly smooth on its east side from the perpetual sandstorms. One day the sands would completely erase the last of the trees, the way a river wears down a rock. They piled stones atop the grave to keep the dogs from digging up the corpse, but a marker was useless; the shifting sands would obscure any sign of Becker's crude grave.

The red sun rose behind a curtain of dust that hung high in the air like a lump of glowing coal under a bed of ash. Conny cinched up Becker's holsters and tested the fit, sliding his revolvers in and drawing them fast.

"My pa once told me that so long as someone somewhere remembered you, you wouldn't really die," Conny said. The two men stood unmoving looking out over the grave. "He said a little piece of you would live on in them. Course, that was right before he was hanged for cheating at poker."

Farhad stifled a laugh. "Jesus."

"Hey, I ain't no good at this shit. What about you? Your people got any last rites or anything?"

Farhad was silent for a long moment. "We did," he said at last. "But I don't remember them."

Conny nodded.

"That's why you took the man's holsters?" Farhad asked. "So, you can remember him?"

"I suppose so. When they cut my pa down off the tree and left him for me to drag home, he had a card in his pocket—the Two of Hearts—and I still have that to remember him by."

"So, he did cheat at poker?"

"Oh, without question. Ironic thing was he never was much of a poker player, my pa always preferred Faro. Easier to cheat at Faro. Hell, you're expected to cheat at Faro. But the Faro tables were full that day."

"That's some bad luck, my friend."

"Well, I reckon we ought to say our last words to him and head out."

"You were a bit of a bastard, but you gave a young foreigner a place to stay when most wouldn't. And you gave me a purpose, so I didn't despair. For that, I'm grateful to you. Allah maak, my friend"

Conny put Becker's hat on top of the stones, the only marker the man would get. "There you go, bud. We had our differences. But you were a loyal man, and I was proud to call you 'friend.'"

Farhad clapped Conny on the back. "Let's go. We have a ferryman to catch. And flay alive."

"I think I already found him for you."

The two men spun on their heels, revolvers flashing in the dim sunlight. Conny's reflexes denied what his ears clearly heard. It was Crowkiller.

"Is this the one you're looking for?" The big man stood tall and imposing, his hand held out a scalp of curly black hair.

"Crowkiller, you Cheyenne son of a bitch." Farhad grinned and took the scalp.

"I told you, I'm Blackfoot."

"Did you? I could have sworn you said Cheyenne."

"I'm glad to see the two of you. When I found the Mexican with our animals and gear, I feared the worst." Crowkiller leaned into the grave. "This Becker?"

"What's left of him," Conny said.

Farhad twisted the scalp in his hands. "Now don't misunderstand me, my friend. I am glad to see you, but I was really hoping I could get my hands on the owner of this scalp and show him my gratitude for his hospitality."

"I can dredge him up from the bottom of the river if you'd like."

"Not necessary my good man. I'm afraid that would be a bit superfluous now."

"What happened to you? We found some tracks, but they went off to the east," Conny asked.

"Had to circle around after my horse spooked. Took a while for the dogs to run off after other prey. When they were gone, I found your tracks and followed them up to a dock. Figured you had found a boat, so I went downriver but didn't see anything for a while."

"We didn't go south, we came back upriver." Farhad laid the scalp on Becker's grave.

"Didn't think Becker would let you come back for me."

"He almost didn't. But I have a way of being mighty convincing when I need to be," Farhad said.

"How'd you come across the ferryman?" Conny pressed. Crowkiller was a good friend, but he often had his own reasons for doing things that he kept to himself.

"I ran hard south for a while. When I didn't catch up with you there, I wondered if maybe you'd gone to look for me so I turned back. Not long after I spotted a boat with three horses and a Mexican with a Henry rifle. I sneaked up on him and asked him where he got the stuff."

"I can't imagine he was forthcoming with you." Farhad smiled.

"He told me many things. None of them the truth, though."

It was Conny's turn to smile. "Well, I reckon we can head out now, yes? You still have the scow?"

"I Pulled it up on shore about a quarter mile back to let the horses graze. I followed the smell of your campfire from there."

The three men walked south towards the horses, towards the scow, towards Becker's daughter, the preacher, the money, and away from Memphis, and Longstreet's gallows.

After brushing their horses down and beating out their dust masks, they boarded the scow and pushed off. The dead oaks slowly gave way to low shrubs and knee-high prairie grass that stall managed to survive despite the dust and ash in the air. Crowkiller spoke more about his adventure in the Wastelands, and Conny, dipping his oar into the muddy waters of the Mississippi, listened attentively. The big man had almost made it as far as Commerce before realizing the group didn't go south. He saw no sign of the dog pack after their first encounter, save a few lone howls in the long night he spent alone.

The recapture of the scow was of particular interest to Conny. Crowkiller saw the boat long before the pilot was in a position to see him. Having identified the horses and Farhad's rifle, the Indian laid low in ambush and waited for the scow to pass by. He took his clothes off and slid into the river. To hear him tell it, he moved like a water moccasin, gliding through the water soundlessly, easily overtaking the scow. He boarded the boat like a phantom and drew himself up behind the ferryman, who only noticed the marauder when the water dripping off his body pooled at the Mexican's feet. When he spun around—what a sight it must have been. Crowkiller's powerful, naked frame, the river falling off him in great drops, his hair clinging to his face and shoulders like wet, black grass. And the look of fury in his eyes.

He told of the interrogation, of the torture, and of the scalping. Conny didn't much care for killing in general, but he did listen to that part with a certain amount of satisfaction. Becker's soul, if such a thing existed, could rest a little easier. And once they found his daughter, he could rest easier still.

They pulled the oars in and rode on in silence. Conny manned the tiller, while Crowkiller slept and Farhad tended to his newly recovered rifle. The muddy waters of the Mississippi carried them at a steady pace. Conny watched the shoreline pass, more out of boredom than necessity. This area was patrolled frequently in the early days of the Memphis occupation and anything useful had long been scavenged. Conny had heard some of the young folk, born after the Calamity, or just before and survived, refer to things that humanity left behind as "relics" or "artifacts." The term rubbed him the wrong way, but he couldn't argue the accuracy of the word.

"Jesus Christ." Farhad stood and looked out at the shoreline.

Conny followed his gaze. The bank rose steadily up above the edge of the water. The prairie grass was tall and abundant, and the brush grew thick as far as he could see. A row of corpses lined the bank, impaled on crude stakes or crucified on improvised crosses, splayed at odd angles like ghoulish windmills. Conny choked back a sob. Most of the dead were children.

They passed in silence, watching from the ferry. Crowkiller joined them and took off his hat. The first few bodies were fresh. So fresh that Conny was tempted to see if any were alive, but he didn't have the nerve. The corpses turned blacker the farther they drifted downriver until the naked bodies were parched and hollow, jawless heads looking up to the sky, with not enough left on their bones for even the crows.

"Do you smell that?" Crowkiller lifted his nose to the sky and closed his eyes.

Behind the stench of rotting bodies, behind the smell of earth in the water and the air, a faint trace of smoke. "Commerce?"

"Likely whoever did this," Farhad gestured to the executions, "is the same whoever that has those fires burning."

"And they've taken up residence in Commerce." Conny sat back down at the tiller, driving the scow towards the shore.

"Now wait a minute, Con." Farhad took a seat next to Conny. "Let's not be too hasty with anything. We're gonna go and investigate first, right?"

"What for?" Crowkiller unhitched his horse. "Makes sense why we haven't heard from Commerce in nearly six months. The people who moved in aren't friendly. We go around."

"Well, why can't we just drift past them on the river? We'll take it slow and move real quiet."

"No good. Commerce is built on the river. Whoever is crucifying these people will have eyes on the water."

"And we can't sail any closer to the western bank," Conny said. "Indians will shoot us full of arrows if we do."

"They have rifles, you know," Crowkiller said.

"Fine. They'll shoot us full of lead if we do."

"Well, what if Eudora and the preacher are in Commerce?" Farhad asked. "And we just go around, then what? Then how long do we wander south looking for them when they were right here? Con?" Farhad looked to Conny for support.

Conny took his hat off and wiped his forehead. "Well since you're asking me, I say those two may be a couple of fools, but they ain't that stupid. They stayed far away from Commerce. But maybe we should go look for some signs. See if we can pick up their trail." Conny didn't want to go anywhere near the people who executed these children. The Calamity had drawn out a monstrous side of humanity he hadn't seen before. Scavengers returned sometimes with tales of depravity. Human sacrifices became a common occurrence in the untamed desert, as people desperately tried to appease God, or even lure a new god here, from wherever it was they thought gods came from. Any god gratified by the sacrifices that lined the river to Commerce was a god that Conny hoped would stay right where he was. The Wasteland needed no god. All it needed was a cleansing.

"Pick up their trail?" Farhad repeated incredulously. "There ain't no trail to pick up. This desert long covered any trace of them."

"True enough," Crowkiller said. "We don't really need their trail anyway, we know where they're going. We sail down the Mississippi to the Southern Corridor and head west. We may overtake them before we even get there if we can hurry."

"I ain't going anywhere near Commerce," Conny said. This was something that was not up for debate.

"Farhad, my friend," Crowkiller gave a wry smile. "You know Conny as well as anyone. If he sets one foot in Commerce and finds those responsible for all of this, he'll gun everyone down like he's on some religious crusade. We need to go around."

Farhad sighed. "It's a shame to lose the scow, is all. I suppose it was too much to ask for an easy trip."

Crowkiller clapped him on the back. "You wanted easy, you should have stayed in Memphis, bedding whores and chasing dragons."

"The worst part of that is I never really knew those would be the good old days."

They pulled the scow onto the bank and covered it with brush. It was a waste of time, but Farhad insisted, in case they ever came back this way and needed a river-worthy boat, and Conny didn't want to argue with him any more than he already had. Fortunately, the bank was overgrown with cotton bush and that made the covering a quick process.

By the time they finished, the sun hung low and it peered through the dust in streaks of rose and orange. The brush made riding difficult, so they struck out on foot to the east. Conny hoped to ride far enough out to avoid any contact with people of Commerce, and he reckoned that a good twenty miles should be plenty of berth.

They passed under the shadow of a crucified body, too mummified for even the flies. The urge to look overcame Conny's desire to keep his eyes averted, even out of respect for the pitiful soul whose body hung there in the sky for all the world to see. It seemed, judging by the slight frame, to have been a woman, but any other means of knowing had long since vanished. Her head hung down and she looked at Conny with her empty eye sockets, like gun barrels pointed right at him. The need for vengeance, for righteous judgment, burned in his chest, and Conny looked away again.

He was startled out of his fury by a scream. All three men snapped their heads up and looked to the south. It was a woman's scream, shattering the stillness of the wild lands like the crash of thunder.

"We should leave it." Crowkiller was always cautious and never quick to help. He often preferred discussion and debate to action. It was wisdom and prudence, of course, but Conny, already enraged at the inhumanity and degradation on display, mounted his horse and galloped to the south, one revolver drawn. He didn't expend any energy to see if his companions followed. If they were true, they'd be right behind him. Conny didn't think them anything other than true.

The gunfighter crested a small hill and spotted on the road below a group of armed men, six strong, escorting an oxen-drawn wain. The wagon was uncovered and stripped of everything but the flatbed. The entire wagon had been painted black and two enormous black oxen pulled it down the road. In the center of the bed, like the mast of a demonic ship, rose a cross lashed tight with rope. On the crucifix hung a woman, nailed by her wrists to the crossbeam, her light brown skin stood out bright against the painted black cross.

Conny spurred his horse. He raced down the hill and closed the gap quickly. Gunfighters often talk to each other about their experience in the heat of battle. Many men have told Conny that the world slowed down for them and that's why they were faster than their enemy. But the world didn't slow down for Conny. Men moved at normal speed. There was nothing magical about gunplay. He simply pointed his gun and pulled the trigger as fast as he could.

This is how it was when he rode up behind the gruesome caravan. He fired two shots and brought down two men before the others could gather their wits and their nerve. He circled his horse around and cocked his revolver, leveling it at a third man as he came round the back side of the oxen. The man drew his pistol, but not fast enough. Smoke shot out of Conny's Colt and the man's teeth came out the back of his head. He dropped to the ground, his legs twitching.

To his right, a red-haired man in a tattered green waistcoat had his rifle aimed right at Conny. The man's expression turned from grave to shocked when a new hole opened up in his chest. Blood and meat sprayed the wagon beside him. Crowkiller stood at the top of the ridge, his smoking rifle in his hands.

Farhad galloped past Conny. The last of the armed men stared about in disbelief, shocked at this sudden and unexpected turn of events. Farhad's boot connected with the man's jaw. It made a sickening snap and the man fell backward. He landed hard in a cloud of dust and didn't move.

Farhad dismounted quickly and knelt beside the unconscious man. "Kicked him a little harder than I had intended, Con. My apologies."

Conny paid no mind to Farhad. His attention had turned immediately to the crucified woman in the wagon. The men had driven nails through her wrists, but her feet were bound only with rope. The cross was made from scavenged wood. It was thin but strong enough to hold a woman small in frame.

"We're gonna cut you free, ma'am."

She turned her head and met his gaze. She had dark tattoos around her eyes, like twin suns, the lines radiated outwards, black as midnight. Conny shuddered. He tore his eyes away from her haunting face and instead examined the nails holding the woman fast to the crossbeam. They were bent behind the wood so he couldn't pull them out.

Crowkiller rummaged through the boot at the front of the wagon and found a coping saw. The two men lifted the cross on its side and Conny held it in place as the big Indian cut the woman free.

When the nails were uncoupled from the wood, Conny warned the woman to brace herself. He took a firm grip on the nails, one at a time, and pulled them steadily from her wrists. Blood drained from the holes, but Conny was prepared and he wrapped her wrists with scraps from Becker's old shirt. They had buried Becker naked. In the Wastelands, everyone was a scavenger and everything was scavenged.

Conny laid the woman down on the bed of the wagon and wrapped her naked body in his wool blanket. She stared straight ahead and spoke to no one, the shock of her ordeal had taken its toll on her, and Conny worried that her mind may be completely gone.

"Con, he's coming to." Farhad had busied himself tending to the remaining gunfighter. "I gave him a bit of morphine for the pain."

"Why?" Crowkiller knelt beside the man. "Let him suffer."

"I want him to talk. A man in pain don't say much. Least he don't say much of anything useful."

"What do you want him to say?"

"I'd love to know what the Devil is going on down in Commerce." Farhad looked into the injured man's eyes. "Call it curiosity."

"I 'spose it couldn't hurt to ask him some questions." Conny left the woman's side and joined the other two.

"Then we kill him?" Crowkiller asked.

"By all means," Farhad said. "Take his scalp. Give it to the woman as a gift."

Farhad turned his attention back to the man with the broken jaw. The side of his face had begun to turn a deep purple, and that jaw hung at an awkward angle. He looked something like a marionette, as if his mouth didn't belong properly to his head. His face was deeply pockmarked and his eyes rolled around in their sockets when Farhad whistled and snapped his fingers at him. He gazed at the men around him and groaned.

"What's your name?" Conny asked him in a pleasant, almost friendly voice.

The man groaned again. Saliva streamed from the corner of his mouth.

Conny and Farhad exchanged a glance.

"Can you talk?" Conny asked.

The man groaned louder this time. His eyes turned sharp as they darted from man to man.

"You kicked him too hard." Crowkiller gestured at the man's jaw.

"Well, I was a little preoccupied trying not to get shot."

"A man's face is a delicate thing. You can't just smash it with your boot if you want him to be able to hold a conversation later."

"I don't suppose we have enough time to wait around for him to recover, do we?" Farhad looked at Conny with a small smile flashing behind his mustache.

"Certainly not."

"So now," Crowkiller said, "we just have to decide how to kill him."

The man moaned, frantic now, and pointed to the wagon, then he pointed south.

"Now what do you suppose he's trying to get at?" Farhad looked behind them to the south.

"I don't know. Well, let's hurry up and get it over with. I'd like to put a lot more distance between us and Commerce before sundown." Conny looked at Crowkiller. "Make it quick."

Conny didn't notice the woman behind him. "He don't deserve no 'makin' it quick.' Not this one." Her voice broke, hoarse, yet forceful. "No, not this one."

The wind picked up and she pulled the blanket tighter around her shoulders. Her brown skin was the color of the sky and she looked as if she and the horizon were one, as if her fury caused the wind to blow and her anger kept the sun behind its veil of dust. She threw open the blanket to reveal a Bowie knife she had clutched to her breast. In a moment she was on him, the knife flashed at his throat, and bright red iridescent bubbles boiled out of the gash. He clutched at his throat and his body stiffened. The woman grabbed his hair and the knife slid across his forehead. She stood on his back and tugged at his scalp like she was pulling up a tuft of grass. There was a popping sound when the scalp pulled free and the woman stood over him, the ruin of his head in her hand. The man kicked in the dust for a long time and the woman watched, unblinking.

"Just die, you goddamned bastard," she whispered. "Just die already."

Conny picked the blanket up and wrapped her in it again, just as the man stopped kicking.

"That's it," the woman said. "That's it. I'm free."

"What's your name?" Farhad stood up and dusted his hands off.

"I'm free," she repeated.

"Your name's 'free'?"

"Nikki. My name's Nikki."

"Well then, Nikki Free, that sure was something else, make no mistake." Conny spoke tenderly, though truth be told, there was no need.

She frowned for a moment and nodded her head.

"Nikki Free," she whispered into the wind.

Chapter 11

Sorrow Draw, North Texas (August, 1881)

Hattie Mothershed

If there was one thing that Hattie could count on when it rained, it was always guaranteed to put her in a foul mood. Rain was loud and cold, and kept her trapped inside. It turned the dust and sand to mud for days and that would make walking around town much more difficult than it had to be.

She stared out the window of her mother's bedroom and watched the rain fall, watched it hit the glass and slide down and leave muddy streaks until it was too cold to stand near the draft.

She took a seat next to her mother by the fire. She remembered the rain when she was young. How welcome it would be when it arrived. You could see it across the green plain, falling from the clouds like a black curtain. Sometimes she would wait in the barn for it to come, wearing only her old nightshirt but sweating from the day's heat. When it came, it fell in cool, clean drops that smelled of earth and iron. It broke the silence of the prairie with a thundering roar that never stopped to catch its breath but screamed unbroken. She remembered standing in the midst of it, her nightshirt stuck to her body and her hair clinging to her face. Before long a close bolt of lightning would frighten her, and she would run back to the safety of the house. Sometimes her mother would scold her, have the maid, Clementine, dry her off, and make her lie in bed so she didn't catch cold. Clementine was a kind Negro. Hattie always liked her. Clementine's hands were warm and soft when she would dry the rain from her hair and she spoke to her soft and low.

"Where's my tonic?" Eula Mothershed asked, without turning to face her daughter. Each word came out choked and strained. "I need my tonic. My legs hurt." Her voice was hard, like a key turning a rusty iron lock.

Hattie opened a medicine chest at the foot of her mother's bed. Most of the tonics and oils in the chest had been offerings from the church. There were soothing syrups with cocaine, Indian elixirs, opium remedies, arsenic, and swamp roots. She took a bottle of Brigg's Remedy and pulled up the stopper. The tonic had formed a crust around the lip of the bottle, but she smelled it and the liquid inside wasn't foul, so she handed it to her mother. Eula took it with a thin hand. She was impossibly light and frail for her age, disease whithered her body and decayed her mind. The Calamity killed many people quickly when it struck, but some it killed intolerably slow.

Eula drank the tonic and spit it out, coughing up the dark green liquid that ran down her chin and pooled in her lap. "I can't drink this, are you trying to kill me?" Her thin voice was a needle. It took on a sharp point and Hattie did not doubt that if her mother had more strength in her, she would have shouted and hurled the bottle into the fire. "You gave me anise, you know I hate anise, it makes me shit for days. Give me something else."

"You can't really be too picky, mother. There's not much left."

"Well send James to the general store to get some rock oil and laudanum. There's no reason we should have run out. Tell him he'll get a lashing if he forgets and lets my stock run dry again."

James had been their stableboy and general laborer when Hattie was a girl. She remembered him as a big man with a powerful chest and gentle eyes.

"Ma, James is dead."

"Dead? What are you talking about?"

"He died in the Calamity. I saw it myself, remember? A twister threw a fence post right into his head."

"What are you on about? I don't like that kind of talk one bit." Eula suffered from episodes of forgetfulness. She would sometimes completely forget the last eighteen years and in her mind she was back in her farmhouse with her two young children and an old man for a husband. Hattie discovered that she could tell her mother anything she wanted to when Eula was in that condition, and she wouldn't remember it the next day. So, Hattie would sometimes confess her secrets, or tell her mother things she'd always wanted to tell her but was too afraid to. Sometimes she just used the opportunity to be cruel. She resented her mother's slow death. Most people, like James, had the decency to die quickly from the Calamity. Her mother insisted on holding on and dying slow.

"I don't really care if you like it or not, it's the truth. He died eighteen years ago, along with most of the world."

"You aren't talking sense. Go fetch James, please. I need him to get my medicine."

"You know I used to hide in the stables when I was a girl? I'd crawl under the fresh hay in the afternoon. It was hot as all Hell, but sometimes I'd get lucky, and James and Clementine would sneak into the barn. Clementine would hike her dress up around her waist and bend over and James would drop his trousers and take her from behind, right there in the barn."

Eula's expression remained unchanged. Hattie was sure that would get a rise out of her, but her mother just stared into the fire.

"Well, you're no fun tonight, are you?" Hattie asked, not expecting a response.

"Did you get a good look at his cock while you were down there?"

Hattie jumped. Erasmus stood in the doorway, leaning against the frame, an expression of delight written on his face. Hattie's heart pounded in her throat.

"How was that black shaft of his? Long as your forearm? Thick as your wrist?" He took off his top hat and made a show of dusting it off. "I imagine it was the finest in all of Christendom."

"I didn't mean any of that." It was a stupid thing to say, she knew. But she couldn't bear the thought of her brother having some of her forbidden secrets to hold over her head. "I was only funning is all."

"Or maybe it wasn't James' cunt-plugger you wanted to spy. Maybe it was the cunt he was plugging?"

"How dare you—"

"Now you certainly won't get any judgment from me, considering the company I prefer to keep. Don't worry, dear sister, your secret is safe with me."

"I said, I didn't mean any of that. I was just trying to get a rise out her is all. She's having a spell. She sent me to fetch James to the general store."

"Oh did she now?" Erasmus knelt in front of Eula and snapped his fingers in front of her face. "She's quite gone right now, isn't she?"

"She is, just now."

He leaned in, uncomfortably close, and touched the front of her dress. "Dousing her with wormwood, are we?" he said, smelling his fingertips.

"A bit of a tonic is all. She didn't like it, the hag did it to herself."

"You know she hates anise."

"We're running low. When she's lucid, when she knows what's going on, she understands that, and she'll take her tonic just fine. Maybe with a bit of grumbling, but she takes it. I didn't know her mind was stuck in the past today."

"Hmm." Erasmus opened the medicine chest and removed a small bottle. "Here. Just give her rock oil, nothing else. It's all she needs, and she won't give you any trouble no matter where her mind is. I think the old woman actually likes the stuff."

"We only have so much. The church gives what it can, but it won't last forever."

"The church gives what it must, or Father takes the Paluxy Boys off their leash."

"Even the Paluxy Boys can't find what ain't there."

"I get the rock oil, Hattie. It doesn't come from the church."

Hattie was surprised. He had always been flippant, at least on the surface, but sometimes he genuinely seemed to care about things.

"Really? Why mother? Why would you go out of your way to help her, of all people?"

"I'm a complicated fellow, Hattie, what can I say? It's the old love-hate relationship I have with our dear old ma."

Eula Mothershed had never been a caring woman. Her preference had always been to pass off the raising of her children to her maids. Eula had been an extraordinarily beautiful woman. Even after delivering four children—one died of cholera and the other in the Calamity—she looked no worse for wear. The cause of her misery and anger was her husband, Hattie's father, the Reverend Mothershed. He was thirty years her senior and she had been given very little choice in the matter of her marriage.

Reverend Mothershed had set his eyes on her when she was only fourteen. She had come to the Republic of Texas with her uncle in 1836 when her parents were killed by Apaches in Mexico and her uncle was eager to be rid of her. His wife was violently jealous of Eula's blossoming figure and the way her husband looked at the girl. When they arrived in Sorrow Draw, the Reverend took an immediate interest in her. The only tenderness her father showed to anything in all of God's creation was to Eula. His affection was a fountain that only she could drink from, a banquet where she was the only guest, yet she looked on it with disdain. When Hattie had been a child, she would have done anything to eat from that banquet, to taste just a bit of her father's love.

"Where do you get the rock oil from?" Hattie asked.

"That's not important. I like to have my secrets, too. Though my secrets aren't as scandalous as yours."

Hattie was convinced that he would never let her forget this. "Oh please, you think I don't know your secrets? You think I don't know about what you and Guadalupe do? Tell me, brother, when you and Lupe have your little dalliances in the barn, which one of you pokes, and which one of you gets poked? Or perhaps you take turns?"

"Are you sure you don't know? Maybe you've been hiding under the hay, watching us, too? Besides, we long since moved on from the barn. There's far more scandalous and dangerous places to consort and the danger is half the fun."

Hattie had many skills, but Erasmus could always best her in wit. It was infuriating, but she knew if she continued trading insults, she would lose, and it would ruin the rest of her day. The rain was bad enough, she wasn't about to let her brother add more misery.

"What do you want, Rasmus?"

"Want?" He held his arms out. "You know me, I want something new every day. I can never settle on one thing." He moved in front of her and put his hands on her shoulders. "Right now, I want you to find some happiness. You're positively miserable."

"In case you hadn't noticed, the world is dying around us."

"Yes, but why let something like that bring you down? You could use a little diversion from—" Erasmus waved his hand around the room. "All of this."

"You're right. I guess my chances of finding any happiness in life are about to dwindle to nothing. I can't imagine a life with Ransom is going to be anything but melancholy."

"Let's hope it never comes down to that."

"If it does, you'll be fine. You'll just run off with Lupe and leave me alone in my wretchedness."

"Possibly. Or maybe I'll find the time to abduct you and carry you off to Hill Lodge for a night of gambling and debauchery every now and again."

"You are singularly obsessed with that place, aren't you?"

"Mhm. I was there last night."

"I thought you went to Lupe's?"

"I went with Lupe. It's a long walk, but worth the trip." Erasmus yawned. "Coincidentally, I saw Clementine there."

"Our Clementine? Are you sure?"

Erasmus nodded. "Her face is harder, and her hair is gray and she somehow managed to become even more thin than when we were children, but it was her, make no mistake. She looked...happy. She was smiling, laughing. She had her arms wrapped around another woman," he said with a wicked grin. "She looked happy."

A flush of shame warmed Hattie's cheeks. But what had she to feel ashamed of? She had been a child. She had never owned, nor ever claimed to own, Clementine. In fact, she could scarcely recall even knowing that Clementine was a slave, yet her guilt was a palpable, burning thing that was made all the worse in hearing of Clementine enjoying life. Amid the end of the world, when the Earth itself had become a dying thing, Clementine found happiness in freedom.

"She was smiling? I don't think I ever saw her smile."

"She never smiled when old James was giving her the skewer?"

"I'm serious."

"Well, so am I. Of course she never smiled. What did she have to be happy about? What had any of them to be happy about? For all of Father's talk about treating them well, and how much they love serving, and how it's their lot in life, they were fucking miserable. They were slaves, Hattie."

"But they were treated well—"

"No Hattie. No, they weren't. That's something you'd say about a dog when you bury it, 'he had a good life, we treated him well, didn't we?' That's not what you say about a person. Father bought—and sometimes sold—people." He spoke firmly, but gently. If he had been talking to their father at this moment, Hattie did not doubt that his passion would have erupted. He would have flown into a rage, yet he seemed to hold back with her. She was grateful. She didn't know how she could tolerate such a confrontation with her brother.

"You should visit Hill Lodge," he said. "But I know you. You can't go and just look. I'll take you there and you can play cards or dance or sing…or fuck. But also listen to people. Let some of the Freemen talk to you. Listen to them. You'll understand why they give their children the names they do. Why they live life with such enthusiasm. You'll see why the Calamity was a blessing to them."

That was too much. Too unbelievable. "A blessing? This misery? This death?"

"Yes, a blessing. Come with me next Sunday. I'll show you. What do you say?"

Hill Lodge sounded like an invigorating place, but something held her back. There was a constant fear in the back of her mind. But a fear of what? Of enjoying herself too much? Of her father finding out? What if there were men there that showed interest in her? She didn't know them well enough to know which ones could offer her more than just a night in bed. She needed someone willing to take her away from Sorrow Draw. Deep down inside what she really wanted was to try for California, to see if it was a paradise, as some had said. But she would settle for anywhere else. Even the town where the Lodge sat,

Serpent's Bluff, or whatever the Freemen were calling it, would be preferable to living in this house, taking care of this woman who had the misfortune of being her mother and cowering under the shadow of her father.

As soon as the thought entered her mind, she knew it wouldn't—couldn't—ever happen. Hill Lodge was not far enough away from her father and the Paluxy Boys. He would send the gang in after her and there would be blood. She wondered if the Negroes had many guns, they might put up a fight if they did, but she knew the Paluxy Boys were well-armed and ace shots, even on horseback. If her father even contemplated a harassment campaign against the Indians, he must have enough men and guns to take the Lodge and everyone in it.

No, her father would never let her go. He would drag her back to Sorrow Draw, back to this dust-cursed town in irons. She had a vision—she saw herself being dragged up the steps of their church in chains, bound like a calf, and then pulled slowly down the aisle, the congregation looked down on her from the pews, faces with expressions of pity, disgust, and amusement. She struggled against the shackles, but it did no good. On the other end of the chain, standing at the altar, wearing a bloody waistcoat and a belt of black-haired scalps around his hips, was Ransom Eisenhardt.

Hattie shuddered. "Alright, I'll come with you. But you better not make yourself scarce as soon as we get there and leave me stranded and alone."

"I won't abandon you. It'll be your night and I'll make sure you enjoy every moment."

Fear tightened her chest, but she would do anything to rid herself of her impending marriage. Maybe she could find a man at the Lodge and let him ruin her for Ransom. Would her groom consent to wed a woman who had been ravaged by another man? What if she found a man like James, tall and broad-shouldered, with black skin and dark eyes and hands soft as velvet? Could she lift her dress and let him take her? And would Ransom know, or care, if she had done it?

Chapter 12

Uncontested Lands, Old Mississippi (August, 1881)

NIKKI FREE

DARKNESS CAME FAST ON the Wasteland and, like a secret lover, stayed long after it was due to leave. With the darkness, came also the cold. They were partners, arriving hand-in-hand, as was their way. Nikki Free sat close to the fire and shivered against both the cold and the unknown things that prowled in the shadow of the Earth. She was dressed in the clothes of the dead. The dead men who had crucified her and taken her out to the Wastes to die. She hated the clothes. She hated the look that reminded her of them, she hated the stink that took her mind back to the things they did to her. The blood on her shirt—his shirt—thickened and with every breath she could taste the iron tang of that blood in the air. It was her only satisfaction.

She watched her new companions around the campfire. They had saved her from execution and so far, none of them had expected anything from her. They gave her food and water and a blanket to keep her warm. What should she make of such men? Such basic kindness had been long absent in Commerce, though truth be told, it had only been a little over a year since things fell apart. But she had lived a thousand lifetimes in that one year and she was not the same woman coming out the other side as had gone in.

The older man, the one they call Conny, was the unofficial leader of the group. He was a bit too eager to be helpful and at first, Nikki thought he was sweet on her, trying to bed her down, but she paid particular mind to how he treated the smaller, darker-skinned man and he was tender on him, too. She decided that was simply this man's nature. She'd met a few men like this before, but they've been made less so since the Calamity. The end of the world had a way of hardening men like that.

The darker-skinned man looked the part of a foreigner, except his clothes. He had a taste for finery and wore himself a clean waistcoat and frequently dusted off his trousers. He had a quick smile and a quick wit, but men like that weren't to be trusted. Just as often they were also quick to anger. He was smooth with words and sometimes she couldn't tell if he was being charming or insulting. She got the drift that maybe that's what he intended. Still, she would try to play her part for as long as they were willing to keep her around, or a better opportunity came her way.

She had a harder time figuring out the big Indian. They called him Crowkiller. He carried himself like a bit of an outsider. A part of the group, but also separate. He sat apart from the other two. He ate apart from them. He busied himself with tending the animals as a way to avoid them sometimes. She hadn't seen an Indian in a long time, only when they made the occasional raids into Commerce from across the Mississippi. Most of them were a part of the Indian Territories and they kept mostly to themselves since the Calamity hit. But here sat a living, breathing Indian, traveling with a white man and a foreigner. And now a Negro, she thought.

"So how far do you think they could have gotten by now?" The man called Farhad asked the white man. "We should start figuring out how to ration our food and water now that we have unexpected company."

"Well, I don't know about that preacher, but Eudora sure liked her whiskey and pills. If I didn't know any better, I'd say they're likely moving slow as he'll have to drag her from every abandoned saloon from here to San Fransisco."

"You know he isn't a preacher, don't you?" The big Indian broke in. The other two stared at him.

"Course he is." Conny's expression was dumbfounded. "He's led services before, I've been to one or two. He does the funerals, too. Buried Miles Parker a few months back after he got caught sparkin' on ol' Cockran's daughter."

"No. He did those things because the people paid him. Whiskey slips and food. Second scavenger picks." Crowkiller lit a pipe with a stick from the fire. "But he's not a preacher. His name is Preacher."

"You can't be serious." Farhad looked at Conny and the two men laughed. "The bastard's name is Preacher! Do we absolutely have to kill him, Conny? Sounds to me like that man's an absolute treasure."

"Jeremiah Preacher?" Conny asked.

"Yes. When he arrived in Memphis two years ago, he told people he was called Jeremiah Preacher and the whole town believed he was a priest. He just never corrected everyone."

"If you knew about it, why didn't you set us all straight?"

Crowkiller's eyes narrowed, and his face hardened like steel. "What do I care about the white man's religion? You came with your Bibles and your Christ and you moved us off of our lands and tried to crush our spirits and even now the stink of your religion poisons the mind of Sanguin Corvus. He calls himself "The Prophet" and the Son of the Great Spirit. It made my heart glad to see Preacher fool your people."

They told stories of Sanguin Corvus to the children of Commerce. Stories of how he and his bands of raiders would snatch babes right from the tits of their mothers and dash their brains out on the rocks or roast the children alive to eat for supper if they strayed too far from the watchful eyes of their parents. That was before the people of Commerce became the real monsters. Once their parents started impaling them as sacrifices, made-up stories about Indians didn't seem so bad.

"Crowkiller, you Blackfoot son-of-a-bitch," Farhad said, his eyes wide. "You continue to impress me. You are one disturbed individual. I knew I liked you for a reason."

"I told you already, *sayed*. I'm Comanche. Do not insult me by calling me Blackfoot."

"Well now Crowkiller, I suspect you ain't bein' very true with me."

"The blood of the Comanche runs through my veins, Farhad."

Farhad laughed until he coughed. There wasn't anything unusual about that until he didn't stop, and the fit took him. Conny rushed to his side and gave him something that he accepted readily. Soon the coughing fit passed, and the foreigner sat pale and weak, sweat fell from his forehead despite the cold. The White Plague. Consumption. This man's days are numbered. Nikki felt a sudden pity for the man she hardly knew.

They went back to themselves, each man again returned to their solitude. The foreigner to his book, and the Indian to the horses. The white man mixed something in a tin cup and sat down next to Nikki.

"How are your wrists?" He held the cup in both hands as if it might leap out and scurry away into the darkness.

"They hurt." She held them up to the firelight. The strips of cloth—torn from her executioner's shirt—were dark from her blood, but none of it fresh. "I think the bleeding stopped."

"Drink this if you want. Helps to deaden the pain." He held the cup out for her.

"What's in it?"

"Whiskey...and a little laudanum."

"I'll pass on that, gunfighter." In Commerce, she wasn't allowed opium, on account of her being a Negro, and she had seen plenty of white people lose their will and their wits from it. The offer was enticing, and her body yearned for the pleasure of the drug, but she didn't know these men, and right now she needed a clear mind. "Looks like your foreign friend be needing it more than I do."

She studied his face, saw him look over at Farhad, and clench his jaw.

"He your lover?"

"What? No—"

"I see how you look at him."

Conny's face reddened. "You misunderstand, ma'am. It ain't like that. I found Farhad when he was twelve years old. He was wandering the streets of New York City alone. The Calamity had caused the ocean to rise up and flooded the whole city. Was something awful to witness. Least from what Farhad tells. He was damned lucky to live through that. If you can even say it's luck to be living in these times. Have you heard the stories?"

Nikki Free shook her head. No one in Commerce cared what happened in New York City. The unwritten rule in the City of the Damned was to never talk about your old life before the Cataclysm. That life was over, and you belonged to the Faith.

"Almost everyone in New York City died. Farhad himself doesn't even know how he survived. Waves of ocean water crashed so far inland that the entire island of Manhattan was covered. Fish of all kind, enormous whales, and some creatures of the deep that ain't got no names because no living man ever laid eyes on them 'fore, they was all left to rot in the streets when the ocean receded. It took everyone he came here with. His whole family. They was here to sell camels to the Army. Camels of all damn things. Twenty men from his family came here. Father, brothers, uncles, and cousins crossed the Atlantic all the way from the Holy Land itself. Now they're all gone 'cept him." Conny hung his head a moment and Nikki suspected he was gathering some inner nerve to go on with his story so she said nothing. "I had...just lost my wife and my own children to the goddamned Calamity, so when I found him, I took him in. I taught him our language and how to read and write. Truth is, he was a natural at all that stuff and I didn't actually have to do much in the way of the teaching."

"When did he come down with Consumption?"

Conny sucked in his lips. "About four years ago. Some drifters came through Memphis and Farhad got himself friendly with one of their light-skirts. He wasn't the only one who got it, but he is the last one of that group still alive."

"You take good care of him."

"Yeah, well, I ain't been attending my duties as well as I should lately. Making up for lost time, now. White Plague took my ma...and my darling little Bess. She was only two when she got sick. Poor little thing was always so small, didn't take long for her to go. Good thing too, she didn't have to suffer much. Though I'd have just as soon liked a little more time with her."

"I'm sorry, Mr. White."

"Con, you can just call me Con. What about you? You have any family in town? Who have you lost?"

"No family of my own. Lost them long before the dying happened, when I just master's slave. I looked out for the children in Commerce as best I could but you seen how that turned out. In the end, there was nothing I could do.

Hell, I didn't even know what they was doing until it was too late. It ain't uncommon for them poor orphan kids to just wander off and die somewhere. Happens all the time. But then it happened too many times and I found out the truth."

"I guess we both have some amends to make."

"I supposed now is as good a time as any to ask what you intend to do with me. I can't go back to Commerce, they'd put me right back up on the cross, and I don't know anywhere else I can go."

Conny nodded. "Well, if you're good in a fight you're welcome to come along with us. If fightin' ain't your thing, you're free to leave. At your earliest convenience, of course."

"I ain't never fired no gun before, but if it's all the same to you I'd like to stay, least for now. I'm a quick learner and I reckon I can learn as we go. You've already seen I got the nerve to kill a man when he needs killing. You got an empty horse and my executioners left more than a pistol or two behind."

Conny looked at her for a moment without speaking and she held her breath. Staying with this group, regardless of where they're going, is a far cry better than striking out through the Wastes on her own.

"I think that'd be fair." He stood up and stretched. "Get some rest, Nikki Free. We leave early."

She spent an uneasy night. When the men had retired, she stole a bottle of whiskey from the foreigner. She reckoned he had plenty. She drank enough to numb the ache in her wrists and to quiet the demons of Commerce and to forget the faces of the children she didn't save. She wanted to erase them from her mind, to forget they ever existed, to bury them forever and, with them, the pain they had added to her already painful life. In the end, the whiskey dulled the physical pain but didn't banish any memories so she settled instead for a few hours of restless sleep.

True to his word, Conny woke them all before dawn and they set off as the sky to the east began to brighten. Nikki Free passed a hard night at camp. Her wrists throbbed in pain and the woolen blanket, grateful as she was for it, didn't do much to keep the cold at bay. Every sound past the edge of the firelight was her tormentors, come from Commerce to wrest her back and nail her to the crucifix. When it had been his turn on watch, Conny had fetched their dead friend's tent and showed her how to set it up. It was small and had an odd sour smell, but it blocked the wind and provided a bit of warmth. She resolved to give it a good wash at the first opportunity.

They rode at a steady pace and put more distance between them and Commerce. The longer they rode, the more Nikki's spirits rose. She still wasn't sure about this group of men who somehow rescued her from death itself, but at that moment she tempered her fear and unease. The men, for their part, were kind and spoke easy with her. Crowkiller said little, but Conny and Farhad asked many questions which she gladly answered. Farhad seemed mostly interested in Commerce—the people, the Faith, why there were so many executions. Unfortunately, her answers were rarely satisfactory. The people, she told him, simply lost their minds. They followed an Irishman who went by the name of Abhartach. He promised blessings from new gods. The first victims were those who refused to renounce Christ, but that wasn't nearly as many as he had hoped for. Turns out that allegiances to gods are as shifting as the sands in the Wastelands. After the first few were impaled and put on display, Jesus of Nazareth became something of a pariah.

Abhartach then moved on to his political enemies and their supporters. He became mad with bloodlust and paranoia. Naturally, his new gods mimicked his savagery. He declared the sacrifice of children to be the most pure and holy in their eyes, and the people of Commerce did the unthinkable—they continued to follow him.

"How'd you end up on that cross?" Farhad asked.

"The town ran out of children. Wasn't many to start with on account of the end of the fucking world. When he ran out of children, he decided his gods wanted Commerce to be purged of what he called the 'lesser folk.'. Being a Negro, my time was up."

Conny snorted and shook his head. "They still care about all that shit in Commerce?"

"Well, they didn't for a time. It was just enough that we were alive, and the rest of the world wasn't. Not much of my kind was left, though. People acted like they didn't buy and sell us like animals, or at least tolerate the buyin' and sellin' of us." She shrugged. "Then came Abhartach. The men followed him and his new religion with a fervor that I ain't seen in a long time."

"Is that what them tattoos are for?" Farhad pressed her for more answers.

Nikki smiled. "Tattoos were quite popular in Commerce for a time. Right after the Calamity struck, we was all getting them. These," she said pointing to her eyes, "symbolize the return of the sun. I wanted people to look at me and be reminded that this will all pass in time. Someday the dust will clear and the sun will shine as it did before."

"You really believe that?" Conny pulled his horse up beside hers.

"I used to."

Conny nodded and they rode on again in silence.

When the sun rose behind the dust high overhead they stopped to water and feed their horses. Nikki took her tent to the edge of the water and took to scrubbing out the stink. Crowkiller silently knelt beside her. Of the three men her life was now entangled with, he was still the one she was most unsure of. He spoke very little, and seldom to her, so his presence now put her a bit on edge.

"Give me your guns." He gestured to the revolvers she had liberated from one of her would-be executioners.

"Why?" She had spent so much of her life being told what to do, that being ordered about now got her blood heated fierce.

"It's a good idea for me to show you how to load those. We don't have any cartridges. Loading a revolver is a tricky thing, but you're going to need to learn fast if you're going to be watching our backs. And you may have to reload in the middle of a fight, so you need to be able to do it with your eyes closed."

The big Indian made a lot of sense, so she did as he asked. She took both revolvers out and handed them over. Their polished wood handles looked small in his hands and the brass accents flashed in the muted sun.

"No." Crowkiller spun the revolvers around and pointed the handles at Nikki's face. "Never give anyone your guns."

"You said you were gonna learn me how to load them." Being played for a fool was almost as bad as being browbeaten. So far, this lesson wasn't going her way. "How can you show me when I got the guns?"

"I show you with mine, and you follow with yours."

"Well you should have said that instead of saying 'give me your guns.'" She grabbed her guns from his mammoth hands.

"No. There's no lesson in doing it that way. This way you won't forget. Now, pull the hammer back with your thumb halfway. Just until it clicks."

She did as he instructed. The cold metal stung her hands but moved smooth and precise. The hammer cocked back with the click of steel on steel. The cylinder had an engraving etched into it—a battle scene between warships. It was a marvel of art and utility, fluidity and precision.

"Good. Now spin the cylinder. Count how many chambers are loaded in each one." He pushed her hand away. "Don't point it at me when you do that."

Nikki spun the cylinder. It didn't spin as easily as she thought it would. Her hands were small and she fumbled the guns a few times, but she vowed to make it a practiced move.

"There's five in this one." She tilted the revolver in her right hand. "And two in this one."

"Alright. So first, we empty it."

"How do we do that?"

"By shooting it. Follow me."

They stood up and Crowkiller led her to a clearing a short distance away. Conny and Farhad were both there, and Conny gestured to a boulder a short distance away. The top of the rock was fairly flat, and on it, they had set up a line of various objects: smaller rocks, some tins, a chunk of bark that stood up on its own, and several glass bottles.

"Those your whiskey bottles from this morning, Farhad?"

Farhad looked aghast. "Why, I object to that positively scandalous accusation. If I was back in Memphis right now this would be a fraction of what I would imbibe, my dear."

"I have no doubt about that."

"I'm beginning to like her, Conny. I do hope we get to keep her."

"We'll see." Crowkiller folded his arms on his chest. "Now draw your gun."

Nikki pulled both guns out and leveled them at the glass.

"Fast enough," Crowkiller said. "But not both guns. Only one. We don't shoot both at the same time."

"Well now, some of us do," Farhad said.

"Yes, but only when you've had enough opium to kill a horse. The rest of us shoot one at a time."

"Then why do we carry two?" Nikki put the guns back in her holster.

Conny nodded. "They take too long to reload, so we keep two loaded at all times. When one runs out of lead, we draw the other." He appeared to be a simple man if you didn't look too deep, but Nikki never was one for not looking too deep at people. The other two men had scores of peculiarities that she'd made mental notes of, but this happened to be the first little oddity of his she'd cataloged; he nods when he thinks someone's asked a good question.

"Now," Crowkiller continued, "you favor your right hand, so draw the right gun."

Nikki drew the revolver and took aim.

"Pull the hammer back with your thumb." Conny continued the instruction. "It's got a notch on the top. Line that up with that little brass ball on the end of the barrel to aim. Then just pull the trigger."

Nikki squeezed the trigger. Everything felt right. The cloud of white smoke, the slight kick, the loud crack, the smell of gunpowder. Her heart raced and her hands trembled but she fought off the excitement. What would they think of her if she appeared so excitable?

"Well, you missed...damn near everything, but it was only—"

Nikki fired again, more sure this time. The trepidation vanished. She now knew what it felt like to fire, the jump of the gun in her hand, the flash from the barrel, the acrid cloud of smoke it left behind. So she could concentrate on aiming and breathing. Cock the hammer, aim at the target, squeeze the trigger. Hammer, aim, squeeze. She emptied the gun, slid it back in the holster, and drew the other, firing its two rounds. She wasn't as sure with her left hand.

Farhad cheered. "Goddamn, girl. You're five for seven."

"Not bad." Crowkiller nodded. "You missed the first shot on each gun. You'll have to watch out for that."

Conny smiled. "Now, shootin' at bottles and rocks is one thing. But shootin' at men is a bit different. When the time comes, we may be countin' on you. Don't lose your nerve."

"Don't worry, Con. I ain't afeared of killin' no man. I promise you that."

"Yeah. I remember."

The instruction she was given on loading the guns was decidedly less diverting than shooting them. Each chamber had to be loaded individually and one at a time, first the twenty grains of black powder, then the ball was pressed in with the charging handle, grease added, and a cap placed on the nipple. Once that's done, do it five more times. Conny said that some gunfighters leave one chamber unloaded to rest the hammer on so it doesn't go off when you least expect it to, but he carries the same guns she does, the Colt Navy he called them, and you can put the hammer between chambers so it don't go off and you can have your six-shooter shooting six rounds.

Twelve shots. She would have to remember that. Count them during a fight. The last thing she wanted was to have to reload in the middle of a fight, to leave herself—and her new companions—uncovered. Twelve shots. She would have to make them count.

They rode on. Crowkiller wanted to test her more, but Conny disagreed. He worried that they didn't have enough supplies to afford her proper training. He made a count of their stash of black powder, lead, and caps, and determined that it was prudent to wait. He reasoned that she'd be halfway competent in a fight as it is and eight guns firing was better than six.

"There's a lot more to gunfighting than the ability to point and shoot, Con." Farhad wheeled his horse around to face him.

"No telling what kind of nerve she has until men draw on her," Conny said.

"Then I'll either show you the quality of my nerve, or the Wastes will take me." Nikki broke into their conversation.

"Or you'll get one of us killed," Crowkiller said.

"Gentlemen." Conny put his hands up. "There's only one way to find that out and no amount of shootin' bottle or pieces of bark is gonna prepare her for it. So let's save what supplies we got and hope we can scavenge up some more soon."

They made camp for the night in a bend in the river. Nikki set her tent up and congratulated herself on the smell. It had an earthy scent, the same that blew in from the river, like sleeping in a hollowed-out log by a fresh stream.

"Found these." Conny held out a bundle of clothes. He had shaved his beard and now had just a mustache that turned down at the corners of his mouth. He still had the shadow of a beard left on his face and Nikki studied its contours.

"What's this?" She asked, still gazing intently. She decided he was a handsome man.

"Found them in Becker's old gear. I think he brought them for Eudora, in case she needed some traveling clothes. They look like they might fit you and I reckoned you'd like to get out of them dead men's clothes."

She snatched the bundle from him, eager to put something else on—anything else— instead of the blood-stained, oversized clothes of the men from Commerce. She undressed and put them on. She didn't bother to hide her nakedness from him, he had already seen her at her most vulnerable and for his part, he didn't shy away from her. That was unexpected, she had imagined he would turn a bright red and run back to his tent, but he watched without any outward expression.

The clothes fit better than she could have hoped. The shirt was a loose-fitting linen that tied at the top and the trousers were a brown duck cloth, a bit long in the leg but nothing that her knife couldn't fix.

"Thank you, Con. I'm obliged."

"It's nothing. I saw you frettin' in those dead men's clothes and thought you'd rather not be carrying them around with you anymore." Conny coughed uncomfortably. Another tell, she made a mental note of. "How's your wrists?"

She held her arms up. "Healing just fine. No sign of infection, I think Farhad's whiskey is a bit more potent than he lets on."

"Yeah, that stuff'll take the shine off ya, for sure."

"They hurt a bit from the shooting. Nothing I can't handle." She picked up the old, blood-stained garments and took Conny by the hand. "Come along."

They walked the short distance to the fire. Farhad was reading his book as best he could by the light of the campfire and Crowkiller was laid out on his back, his hat over his eyes and his hands behind his head. He lifted his hat back when the two approached.

Nikki tossed the clothes into the fire. No need for ceremony. No need to give those men any last words or any more consideration. She watched as the first tendril of fire caught, consumed the threads, pulled the fibers from each other, and dissolved them away, like time itself was already doing to the memory of those murderers. Somewhere, miles behind her, rested the bodies of six men. Six men who tried to end her life but failed. Six men whose bodies were, even now, being slowly buried under sand and dust, laid claim to by the desolation of the dead desert. No markers, no graves, nothing, and no one to bear witness to their final resting place, the knowledge of their existence already beginning to fade completely from all time and all reckoning.

In the flickering light of the campfire, Nikki Free smiled at the thought.

Chapter 13

Uncontested Lands, Old Mississippi (August, 1881)

Cornelius White

On their third day out from Commerce, Conny found the remains of a campsite. Whoever it belonged to had likely built it on the westward side of a slope on the banks of the Mississippi hoping to keep it out of the wind. The plan was a success, but it also left it intact enough for the men to determine that it might have belonged to their bounty. Two sets of tracks were visible in the shelter of the wind. One left by a man about Conny's height. The other was the slender bare-footed print of a woman.

The discovery energized and reinvigorated the men. Spirits were high, and even Conny celebrated when the whiskey bottle came around. Nikki Free put up her tent and retired early. Whatever the reason for her reticence, Conny couldn't deduce, and he chose to leave her be. When the conversation turned to one of reminiscence, as it often did with survivors of the Calamity, she abandoned her tent and returned to the campfire, her mood having greatly improved, and she behaved as if she had done nothing out of the ordinary.

Conny chose to let it alone, and the men, for their part, made no mention of it either. She listened attentively to their stories, asked them questions, and shared her own. She laughed easily, even playfully. He envied that. He let himself try—try to forget about where they were at, where they were going, that they were all laughing here at the end of the world.

And for a moment, he did forget. Laughter was sometimes like a plague. It was infectious, and Nikki's laughter had a unique potency. He thought how strange it would seem if a weary and half-starved traveler roaming the Wastelands had happened upon their group. What would someone make of them, an Indian, a Bedouin from Arabia, a white man, and a mulatto woman with tattooed eyes laughing around a campfire, surrounded by the ghosts of the numberless dead?

They arrived at the outskirts of Bolivar on the fifth day, the same day that the rains first hit. It didn't rain much in the Uncontested Lands, and when it did it was more destructive than anything else. Half of the ground was too arid to soak any of it up, and the other half would become a thick mud that could stick a horse fast. Last Conny and others had heard, there was a small group that had taken up in Bolivar, but when they arrived, they found it deserted. Everyone vanished—moved on or dead.

Conny had spent the last several days tending to the wounds on Nikki's wrists and they were now closed up well, but he worried the rain would set her healing back. He wrapped her wrists in his wool poncho, despite her protests.

They found a stable to board the horses next to a hotel and saloon that Conny suspected would be an ideal place to stop for the night. Farhad left to find provisions to restock his personal supplies so Conny, Nikki, and Crowkiller set out to investigate the hotel. Like most places, it had been stripped clean of valuables, or what passed for valuables in the Wastelands. There were plenty of fineries and ornamentation of all kinds—paintings still hung on the walls, trays of once-polished silver sat on the bar, coins, and bills—both Confederate and Union—scattered all over. Conny found a small tin of tobacco, sealed in wax, hidden behind the bar.

Conny took out his pocket Bible and tore out a page. He tore that page in half and handed it to Nikkie. "You care for it?" There wasn't much tobacco, but he didn't mind sharing, especially not with Nikki. Conny felt sorry for the woman who, as far as he could reckon, had as difficult a life as anyone could now and still be alive to tell.

Nikki took the paper and thanked him. When she saw it was from a Bible, she laughed. It was a flash of lightning in the dark. It was as if, for a moment, the clouds gave to and the sun shone again.

He read a verse quietly to himself, not wanting to share his ritual with Nikki for fear of how she might take it. She'd been through a lot already in the name of religion and he didn't want her to get the wrong idea of him.

In those days there was no king in Israel, but every man did that which was right in his own eyes.

They smoked together in the dimly lit saloon. The smoke hovered around them in the still air as if time itself had stopped. The scent of tobacco pushed out the stench of the dust. Conny inhaled deep through his nose and took in the sweet and woody smell.

"So tell me, Conny." Nikki broke the silence. "I know we aren't supposed to ask, but I feel like you wouldn't mind if I did, and I hope I don't come across as too forward, but what was your life before?"

It was common law in this new world that one did not ask about someone's life before. The before was gone and it wasn't ever coming back. It was perfectly tolerable to offer the information but considered unseemly to ask someone of it unless the pair in question had become close. Conny thought for a moment. He didn't feel riled by the question, as it came from Nikki.

"Well, I suppose it ain't much different than most others. I was born in Vermont. Met my wife there when I was young. Married young."

"What was her name?"

"Elizabeth. We had three children together. My littlest, my Bess, got consumption and passed away when she was two. The twins, George and Emma, didn't survive the Calamity. Neither did Elizabeth. I traveled home, alone, from Virginia right after it happened, right during the worst of it, when no one knew what the hell was happening or how long it would all last."

"Goddamn, Con. I remember it when it happened. I was still a child, but I remember it very well. How did you..." She shook her head in disbelief.

"Hope's a powerful thing. I believed if I made it back, they'd be alive. I thought God was giving me the strength to make it through because they were alive, and they needed me. Why would God give me that strength otherwise?" Conny took a long pull from his cigarette. "I never questioned it. Never. I believed it with every fiber of my being. But when I got home, I found the whole house buried in the sand. I dug and dug for hours, calling their names. When I finally got into the house I saw them, their bodies were dry and mummified, holding onto each other even in death."

Nikki took his hand in hers. "What were you doing in Virginia?"

Conny was grateful she changed the subject. Fifteen years and he could talk about it now without too much emotion, but there was something about Nikki that brought out a sense of regret in Conny, a feeling of what might have been. He gave her a half-smile. "I was a soldier in the First Vermont Brigade. I saw battle in Williamsburg, Antietam, and then Fredericksburg. It was in Fredericksburg I got laid up."

"Wounded?"

"Fell sick. It was December, and we was all sick all the time. I remember it just rained and rained and I was sick and alone. The Vermont Army marched on and left me behind to recover. Just when I was cleared to return to my unit, it hit. That's about all there is to tell."

"Oh no, there's much more there to tell, soldier. But I'll leave you to it. I've dug up more than I needed to today." She turned around and rested her back against the bar.

In the time they'd traveled together, a closeness had developed between them. It had been a very long time since Conny had met another living soul that he cared enough to get to know. He admired her resiliency. Nikki learned fast, laughed freely, and it always amazed Conny that this woman could find joy in the midst of so much personal suffering.

"What about you?" Conny pulled the ash out of his cigarette and put the rest back in the tin.

"What about me?"

"What's your story from before?"

"Same as most other slaves, I imagine. I worked in my master's house. He happened to be my daddy too, though he'd never admit to that. My momma told me and I ain't got no reason to think otherwise. Makes sense on account of my light skin. But even so, I always had a mouth on me, so I still got master's whip sometimes."

Conny had seen the faint traces of scars across her back when they cut her down from the cross.

"They ain't so bad," she said. She must read his thoughts. "My daddy had them go easy on me. That's what everyone always said. 'Master's gone easy on you' but I didn't want to believe it for the longest time." She shrugged. "I guess he did."

The door on the other end of the saloon swung wide and Farhad walked in. Nikki's hand had gone quickly to the gun on her hip. Good. The Bedouin was carrying a small canvas bag that clinked as he moved.

"Druggist on the corner. Got some fine medication. I honestly can't believe it was still there." Farhad frowned. "Am I...interrupting your confidence? I can come back later if you still need a moment."

"That'll be all, Farhad," Conny said pointedly.

"Are you sure? There's always more places to scavenge if you two want some privacy, although I must say that the obligation is really on you to find a secluded spot where your clandestine assembly won't be uncovered, but I will inconvenience myself for your greater good."

"That won't be necessary," Nikki smiled and shook her head.

"Now really, I won't be put out, I swear."

"What do you got in the bag?" Nikki asked.

"Now this..." He pulled out the items one by one and placed them on the bar. "I got laudanum, morphine, opium, and a few bottles of red eye."

"So nothing really useful, then?" Nikki fingered the small bottles.

"Give me that." Farhad put them back in the bag feigning indignation. "Some people are cultureless heathens," he said under his breath. "I assure you I can put all these to very good use."

"Where's Crowkiller?" Conny asked.

"With the horses."

The sound of rain on the rooftop grew louder. Conny looked out the door. "Well, he'd better hurry afore the floods come. I've been caught in downpours like this and they can carry a man away and he ain't never seen again."

"You think that's likely to happen?" Farhad asked.

Conny wasn't sure, but if it rained hard enough and long enough it would.

"I think your friend'll be just fine lookin' out for hisself." Nikki pulled the stopper from one of Farhad's whiskey flasks. "But yes, Conny's right. This one's gonna be a hell of a flood. I suggest we bring the horses in. Their chances are better in here. Then we take to the upstairs. Nothin' to do but wait it out." She took a short pull and made a wry face.

"How long?" Conny didn't like the idea of waiting. Their fugitives were out there in this weather, and a flood could wash Eudora, Preacher, and the money away and no one would ever again find any trace of them.

"I'd wager it'll be done by tomorrow morning."

Conny nodded. "That's my thought, too."

"Alright." Farhad sighed. "You want me to go out there and bring Crowkiller and the horses in?"

"Maybe we should." They stood at the door, the deck above offering some protection from the rain that fell. The sound of it was deafening and seemed to come from every direction with an unnerving constance.

A whinnying of horses broke through the downpour and four large beasts emerged from the gray tapestry of water that enveloped the town. The three jumped out and joined Crowkiller who drove the animals before him. Conny found a rein and pulled his horse into the back of the saloon, the others right behind him.

Even though he had only been out in the rain for a few seconds at most, Conny was as wet as if he'd jumped straight in the Mississippi, clothes and all. His companions fared no better and the floor was soon slick with water.

Crowkiller snapped his fingers. "Let's move the tables to the corners and give the horses some room. And less things to injure themselves on."

The four companions jumped to it and soon had the floor cleared. Conny and Nikki stacked a few tables in front of the door to keep the beasts inside. They were frightened and skittish and Crowkiller rubbed them down and threw blankets on them to keep them warm while he hummed a soft melody.

When they were finished, Nikki grabbed one of Farhad's whiskey bottles and walked to the foot of the stairs that led up to the hotel's rooms. "Alright, gentlemen. I'm going to find a room up here that has a soft bed and warm blankets and I'm going to get out of these wet clothes and sleep this storm off."

"Did you purloin a bottle of my whiskey?"

"I think you have more than enough to share, you rogue."

"Rogue? From where I'm standing it looks like you're the one who's stealing from me, and you have the nerve to call me a rogue?"

Conny laughed. "Looks like she's wise to you."

"He is like glass," the Indian said. "Fragile. And one can see right through him."

"Fragile?" Farhad scoffed. He turned to Nikki. "Do you see the type of abuse I'm forced to suffer? This kind of torment can destroy a man's very soul. But perhaps you have just the elixir I need to heal my wounds?"

Nikki looked at Conny and sucked in her lips. Conny met her eyes. She stirred some passion in him over the last few days, but nothing like the heat that look brought to him. He swallowed hard and broke her gaze.

She turned back to Farhad. "Not this time, lunger." She hustled quickly up the stairs. Conny thought about following her up. He thought about how her warm naked body would feel in his hands, the taste of her lips. He pushed those thoughts aside as fast as they came. He liked Nikki. He enjoyed her company; hell he might even say he was a little fond of her. But he had to steel himself. Like the great Pharaoh of legend, he had to harden his heart. The world after the Calamity was no place for any kind or virtuous person. He had saved her from the Angel of Death once, but he was still coming for her, just as he was coming for Farhad. And yet, here he was, untouched, endlessly passed over, doomed to wander the world of the living.

Farhad sighed. "Con, you gonna do something about her? The girl needs bedded, and I think she wants you to do the bedding."

Conny had a ready response to fire off at Farhad, but it stuck in his throat. The Bedouin's face was like a death mask, pale and wet. He looked frail and Conny was reminded again of his mortality. "You need to get out of those clothes and warm yourself up."

"I'm flattered, Con but you know you aren't my type." Farhad took a step towards the stairs and his eyes rolled back and he collapsed, the floor rushing up to meet him. Conny and Crowkiller were by his side in an instant, each took an arm and lifted him up.

"I got him," Conny said. "Get a fire going, quick. I'll get him out of these clothes."

Crowkiller broke a table apart and lit a fire in the hearth. Conny stripped Farhad and set him in a large chair Crowkiller had set near enough to the heat. They wrapped him in a dry woolen blanket. Farhad had regained some consciousness, but he drifted in and out of delirium, sometimes speaking the language of his father, sometimes in English.

Conny remembered the fainting spells his mother had to endure when he was a boy. Her strength faded, faster than Farhad's, until she was bedridden and Conny had to bring her food and change her bedpan and wash her down while his father drank and gambled at the Faro tables. She hung on, sick and weak, for months. Sometimes he had wished he would wake up to find her finally dead, for her own sake as well as his. Still, he would creep into her room in the morning with fear gripping his heart. She apologized to him once, for still being alive. Conny was never good at hiding his emotions, especially as a boy, so even so close to death she could see the dread carved into his face. His shame was instant. Even now his guilt was palpable if he gave himself leave to remember it.

"I'll stay with him." Conny pulled up a chair next to Farhad. "You go get into some dry clothes before you catch ill."

Crowkiller rummaged through his saddlebag and found a dry shirt and trousers. He threw the Saltillo serape he took from the Mexican ferryman over his shoulder. It was large and had a chevron pattern of deep reds, oranges, and white peppered with black. Farhad tried to win it from him in a game of hazard, but couldn't best the Indian, even with loaded dice.

"I'll watch him. Go clean up." Crowkiller pulled another chair beside Farhad and Conny thanked him. The Indian's loyalties could indeed appear questionable at times, but Crowkiller didn't seem concerned with appearances. He had his own methods and didn't take many into his confidences, but to Conny, he was as fiercely loyal a companion as anyone could hope for. He tended to Farhad with something bordering on tenderness. He draped the serape over Farhad's shoulders and sat quietly beside him.

"You should get the woman," he said to Conny. "She might know some medicine."

"Doubtful," Conny said. "She likely only knows remedies that we already know."

"Don't be so sure. She may have old medicine. Things like medicine can be passed down, and hidden from white men. She might have something like that."

Conny nodded. It was best not to disagree with Crowkiller on matters like this. Indian medicine was different, but no less effective in Conny's experience. Their medicine was of earth and sky, of water and old spirits, of tobacco and moss. White medicine was morphine and laudanum, amputations and blood-letting. They both had their place.

Conny took some dry clothes and went upstairs. He told Nikki about Farhad. She grabbed the bottle of whiskey and ran down to check on him. By the time Conny had changed, she had a pot of water boiling on the fire. She moved with astonishing quickness, gliding around the men with a liquid grace and when he moved out of her way, he inevitably found himself right back in her way again. She was everywhere at once and somehow knew her way around the tavern as if she had lived there her whole life. She stirred the pot, rummaged through a saddlebag, and scoured a cupboard, all while floating effortlessly between them.

"You think you can help him?" Conny's voice betrayed his fear for his friend.

"Some." Nikki stopped and rubbed her hands together. "It ain't the consumption. Well, not completely. He's cold. That makes his lungs worse. So we need to warm him up from the inside."

Conny nodded. "Alright."

"Conny." Nikki pulled him aside and lowered her voice. "I know you're trying to get to California, but I don't know if he'll make it. He needs someplace warmer than this Wasteland. And truthfully, no one knows if California really is a paradise or not, so we might get him all the way there only to find that it's just like here. Yes, he's going to die, but we can help him live longer and in less pain if we take him south."

"South? What's south? How far south are you talking?"

"Mexico. I knew a woman from Veracruz. She said it was warm and dry there, and the dust ain't as thick. It's the dust that's gonna kill him quick."

"I know it. But how do you know it's any better in Mexico than California? If it's so great there, what in the Devil was this woman you know doing in Commerce?"

"Well, I'm sure I never got around to askin' her that. Knowing Chaparrita, she was probably run out of Veracruz at gunpoint. But it's a better bet than California. How many you know can say they've been there and seen it for themselves?"

Conny sighed. "None."

"It's just a thought. I know if you ask him he'll follow you to the ends of the Earth, so maybe we shouldn't ask him what he wants."

"You want me to send him away? Farhad is a man, he ain't my boy. Least, he ain't no more. He makes up his own mind, I can't tell him what to do."

"Then you need to convince him it's the right move. You know it."

Farhad mumbled quietly by the fire. He coughed softly, too weak to muster any force in his lungs. The problem was, Farhad gave no indication that he felt ill or delicate, and told no one of his suffering. Would he tell them next time, or would he collapse again, like a freshly hewn tree? Would he be there to pick him up? Would she be there to nurse him back to health? They had time. The road to the Southern Corridor was still a few weeks hard riding through the Uncontested Lands. He could still have time to convince Farhad to leave them. To persuade him to go to Mexico alone. But Conny knew in his heart that he would not let Farhad go it alone. California, money, riches, all these things were empty without his friend, the man he considered to be his only remaining family.

Chapter 14

Vicksburg, Old Mississippi (August, 1881)

Eudora Becker

Eudora squinted at the orange smudge that rose from the ruins of Vicksburg. It was brighter than usual. The fact that she had to squint, she told herself, was proof that the dust and haze of the day obscured the sun less than it typically did, though the extra light didn't seem to translate into any extra heat. The cold, which at first sneaked through every seam, hole, and tear in her clothes, now ignored those completely and passed through every layer she wore like a phantom. It did the same to her skin and the flesh underneath and froze her very bones. Nothing stopped it, and she was quite positive that she would remain cold forever.

Jeremiah didn't understand. He didn't get cold like she did. He rode ahead of her wearing a wool cloak, indifferent to the chill that invaded her body. He drank and smoked as if the frigid air didn't bite at every piece of his exposed flesh. He could at least pretend to suffer, if only for her sake. But Jeremiah wasn't one for considering her feelings. That was now fully evident. Her resolve to abandon him at the first opportunity was strengthened with every miserable step.

The only thing that worried her about striking out on her own, was the fact that they were being followed. She didn't know by whom, but she was fairly sure it wasn't her father. The man following them had a larger build, from what she could see of him through the dust. He had been following them for several days, but he always remained a tolerable distance behind.

When she first noticed him, only a few days out from Bolivar, she had told Jeremiah. The shadowed man on horseback had crested a small hill and she could see him watching. The rain had finally let up and the steam rose from the hills and the dark figure looked more like a phantom than a man, a spirit rising from the mists to haunt trespassers.

She screamed when she saw him. "Someone's there," she grabbed Jeremiah and shook his arm. "Someone's there."

Jeremiah looked where she had pointed, but as usual, he didn't listen. "There's nothing there, Dora," he had told her. "The dust playing tricks on your eyes is all."

"It weren't no dust. There was a man on horseback up on that ridge."

"It was probably just some dead tree or other. There ain't no one daft enough to be out here, 'cept us."

"I ain't no green-to-the-Wastes fool, Jeremiah. I knowed what I saw. Besides, shit-for-brains, if it was a dead tree, it'd still be there."

He put his finger in her face. "Now goddamnit, Dora, I've done told you to stop talking to me like that."

"Or what? You gonna do what? Hit me?"

"Mayhaps I just might. Ain't no one here aside from the two of us, so no one to tell me I can't."

She punched him in the arm. "You won't lay a hand on me Jeremiah Preacher, so help me God." She punched him again.

"Ow, quit it."

"If it weren't so damned cold, I'd really give you a walloping. Now mind me, I saw a man on horseback up there."

Jeremiah grumbled, but he had gone and searched the area she saw the man in and reported back that he had found nothing. Since then, she had seen the shadowed figure a dozen times, always just far enough out in the distance that she couldn't make out a face, always where only she could see, and always watching them. The man didn't seem intent on doing them harm, so now Eudora kept quiet whenever she saw him.

She started to enjoy the thrill of her secret. After all, it was Jeremiah's fault that he didn't know about the man stalking them. She tried telling him, but he was a fool and refused to believe her. So she kept this new man to herself, and if anything happened to them because of it, if this man were to ambush them and kill Jeremiah, then it would only be no less than he deserved for dismissing her like he did.

She glanced backward and saw that he was still following. She smiled and waved. She wanted him to know that she knew he was there. If he was any smarter than Jeremiah, he'd already know. But this was a man, and one could never be too sure with men. The shadowy figure waved back. It was awkward, stiff, as if he was unaccustomed to the gesture. It was exhilarating.

If this man meant them no harm, she might be able to use him to get rid of Jeremiah. The man on horseback clearly had experience out in the Uncontested Lands. He could do a much better job of taking care of her than the man who currently held the position. There was no doubt that she couldn't get him, whoever he was, to take her to California. If there was one thing in the world that Eudora knew, it was men. They were simple. They were easy. She knew what they wanted, and she knew how to get what she wanted from them.

The man shadowing them soon disappeared again into the curtain of dust, but he'd return. Her plan began to take shape in her mind. Her next step would be to get close to him, to see what kind of man he was. That was important. Not all men could be seduced in the same way, or by the same things. Sure, there were things she could do that would work on most men. Certain looks she could give them to make their knees weak, but those worked best on older men. The batted eyelashes and the sultry smiles only went so far with men her own age. But the old men? She could get the old men to kill with just the hint and hope of more. Such promises didn't work on the young men. They needed guarantees. Married men were the easiest. Even the ones who were devout. Especially the ones who were devout. If a man was married, she could make him do anything.

They made camp without further sight of the stalker. Jeremiah told her they would arrive at Vicksburg the next day. The promise of warm lodgings and the chance to do some scavenging in a proper town lifted her spirits. After

Jeremiah had a fire going and she had warmed herself up, she told him she was going to do her necessaries, and she went, instead, to see if she could meet the man who was following her. The idea both terrified and thrilled her, but the time seemed right to make her introductions.

She reasoned she could get herself alone, away from Jeremiah's eyes, and that might lure the stranger out. Perhaps the presence of Jeremiah had him more cautious than he might otherwise be. Despite her confidence, she tucked a revolver into her trousers just in case. A girl still had to protect herself. She had met a few men who had no interest at all in women, and for men such as those, her only advantage against them was to act innocent. Sometimes those men could be moved by her childlike appearance and a wide-eyed stare. She hoped this man was fond of the gentler sex. In many ways, it made things easier.

She took off her headwrap and let her golden curls fall around her shoulders. She wore men's clothing out of need and utility—they were easier to ride in and kept her warmer than a dress, but she needed to make sure the stranger knew she was a beautiful woman, if he couldn't already tell. Even wearing men's clothes, there was no hiding her figure. Even so, some men could be brought to their knees by those gilded curls alone.

She ambled down a rough path to the river, her oil lamp scattered shadows in every direction. The cold hadn't let up, and she did her best to ignore it and put the right movement into her walk. Once, when she was a little girl, she had gone fishing with her father. He taught her how to bait the hook, how to cast it into the water, and how to use the rod to lure the fish to the bait. Small movements, slow and deliberate. The motion was a promise to the fish, a promise of a sweet, easy meal. She put that same idea into her walk. It was a promise to those around her, a promise of something sweet and easy—but like the worm on the hook, it could be just as deceptive.

She scooped up some water with her tin cup and tasted it. She knew not to drink too much, the water was near frozen, but it tasted like earth, and she savored it. She'd bring it back to camp and warm it on the fire, but despite her chill, she loved the taste—the sensation—of cold water.

She waited, probably too long, if Jeremiah had any sense, he'd be calling for her soon. She started to shiver, and her breath came in jerks. Not tonight.

Poise was essential. Some men love the innocent routine, but others liked confidence. Her instincts told her the stranger was a man who liked a confident woman. Shivering, sniffling, and chattering didn't signal strength. She had just resolved to head back to camp when a dark figure walked in from the veiling shadows and stepped onto the path in front of her.

She drew herself up, straightened her back, and lifted her chin, the cold forgotten. She held up her lamp to see if she could see his face, but the shadows cast were hard and crisp, and she couldn't make out any of his features. He stood in the path with his hands folded on his chest. He was one of the tallest men she had ever seen.

"Why, hello there," she said. Her voice sounded too loud in the darkness. "You nearly gave me a fright. I suppose you're the man who's been following me for the last few days?"

"I suppose I am." His voice was deep, and his accent was peculiar but oddly familiar. Eudora couldn't remember where she had heard it.

The man walked towards her and into the light. Nothing was threatening in his manner, and Eudora reminded herself that he could have killed her at any time if he had been inclined to. When she could see him clearly, she had to temper her shock. The man was an Indian. Eudora was sure he was the most beautiful man she had ever seen. But what kind of woman did she need to be for him? She didn't know. She was suddenly lost. Age? She couldn't quite tell. He could be twenty-five, or he could be fifty. Did Indians marry? She didn't know. She had only ever met a handful of them. But, she reminded herself, men were men. She would have to draw this information out, then she would know how to win his heart.

"So, what's your meaning then, following me across this Wasteland? Who are you?"

"The name's Joseph. Joseph Horsethief. If names mean anything anymore. I've been following you mostly out of boredom I suppose. It's not often that I see two so ill-equipped to travel in the Wastes make it as far as you have. You running from something?"

"For your information, Mr. Horsethief, I am perfectly capable and equipped to survive out here in these barren lands, though my partner is not."

It was imperative that this man knew she did not need him. He's a Wasteland survivor, possibly a raider or a bandit, and he would value self-sufficiency.

"A fact that did not go unnoticed," he replied. His eyes roamed over her. Eudora could see the hunger behind them, and she could see how he tried to hide that. Yes, men were men, no matter what color their skin.

"Where are you from?" she asked. "What kind of man are you who would stalk an innocent woman out of boredom? Does that pass for sport among your people?"

He smiled. "The Wastes are my home, and it's you that don't belong here. What are you running from? Do you know you have men pursuing you?"

Eudora knew her father would send people after her, but the news struck her in the gut and panic rose in her heart, but she forced it back down. There was nothing to be gained from losing her wits right now. "I figured as much. Have you seen them?"

"I have. Two men and a woman not more than two days behind you."

"What do they look like?"

Horsethief shrugged. "One's a white man. Older. The other's a young foreigner. From where, I can't say. He's dying from the White Plague, that I know. The woman is a Negro."

The people he mentioned could have been anyone. Eudora had her suspicions, especially about the foreigner, and she sure didn't know who the woman was. There were a few black women in Memphis, but none of them would have made a trip out into the Uncontested Lands willingly. She almost wished the old man was her father, but she reckoned he probably got that crusty bounty hunter, White, to do his dirty work for him.

"Maybe they ain't looking for me. Maybe they're lost, or headed across the desert to the other side, like me. They say it's a paradise on the other side, you know."

"I know. They say many things. Some of those things they say might even be true."

The cold bit her hands and her feet had turned numb. It was time for her to get back to her tent and her fire, to crawl under the blankets next to a man whose value is bound almost exclusively to his ability to generate heat to keep her warm at night. "Well Mr. Horsethief, I thank you for your warning, and for looking out for me, even if it was out of nothing more earnest than boredom."

"What's your name, girl?"

"Eudora. Miss Eudora Becker, if it pleases you."

"One more thing then, Miss Eudora Becker." He came in close, close enough that Eudora could smell burned tobacco and desert sage. She turned her head up to meet his gaze. "You will soon arrive in what was once the city of Vicksburg. Avoid it, if you can. There's a man there who calls himself The Magistrate and he is not a man you want to meet. There's a wickedness in Vicksburg. Go around it and don't linger."

Fear tightened her throat. But as quickly as it came, she snuffed it out like a candle. She had been looking forward to Vicksburg for days. She needed to scavenge a proper town. Her clothes were too loose, her blankets too thin. Vicksburg was sure to have remnants left. Maybe not in the stores, but the houses doubtless would.

"It seems I must thank you again for your concern. I'll do my best to convince my partner to skip Vicksburg. Maybe Natchez would be a better place for scavenging."

"I'm sure. But don't stay anywhere too long. Your friends are getting closer." He tipped his hat and swung his large frame back on his horse. As imposing as he was standing in front of her, nothing matched his figure riding on horseback. If the prairie had a god, it was him.

"Here." He threw a large bundle at her. Eudora caught it, but only barely, having been taken by surprise it nearly made her fall over. "It's buffalo. From back when you could still find them. Good luck, Miss Eudora Becker."

He was gone. She listened to the sound of the horse for a moment and then that, also, was gone. She wrapped herself up in the buffalo hide the Indian had given her. There were fragrances in it she had no name for, smells that had no memories. She imagined this was what he smelled like. She walked back to camp and found Jeremiah already asleep in the tent. She didn't get under his blanket and brace herself against his body. She didn't have to smell the stink of liquor and sweat. She pulled the hide tight around her and fell into a warm sleep.

Chapter 15

Sorrow Draw, North Texas (August, 1881)

Erasmus Mothershed

Three days after the rain stopped, the ground was finally dry enough to walk on without muddying up his boots. Erasmus Mothershed whistled as he strolled down Center Street towards the old general store. He was in a splendid mood. The dust was light this morning and he could see farther than usual. He wore his gray waistcoat with matching trousers and a pair of fine riding boots that Lupe's mother, Maria, found on a scavenging run. She traded it to him for a bottle of whiskey, some laudanum, and a beaver fur hat. Erasmus certainly got the better deal, but he took care of Lupe's family, and Maria never questioned her son's relationship with him.

He stopped in front of James and Son's tailor shop to look at his reflection in the large bay window. It was cracked and dirty, but it was one of the last windows still left unbroken in town. He adjusted his cravat, though it really didn't need adjusting. He had to touch it, though. It was a compulsion, a need. The cravat was beautiful—a paisley pattern of deep crimson color, like swirls and eddies in a stream of blood. If Erasmus Mothershed was sure about one thing in life, it was that if the end of the world finally came for him, he would look extraordinary when it did.

Satisfied that he looked like a proper dandy, he spun on his heel and continued on. He passed the post office and the jail. He usually never gave either of those buildings much thought when he walked by, but he was in a contemplative mood today. He had a cousin, William Perkins, who lived in Philadelphia that he used to write to on occasion. When he first learned to write, his teacher, Miss Mayberry, would give him paper and an envelope. She never let him draw pictures in his letters like he wanted to. She would tell him to draw pictures with his words. She would only give him one sheet of paper, so he had to practice writing as small as he could so he could say everything he needed to say. He would write out his whole letter first on his slate so he could copy it down onto the paper without making any mistakes or leaving anything out. He was a garrulous child. Not much has changed, really.

At lunchtime, Miss Mayberry would give him two cents and let him run to the post office, this post office, and mail his letter. In August of 1861, after it was clear that the war wouldn't end anytime soon, the post office no longer delivered to the North. Two years later, William was dead. So was Miss Mayberry and most of the other kids in his school.

He shook himself out of his musings. Why the devil am I thinking about William, and Miss Mayberry? His conversation with Hattie days before had affected him a bit more than he cared to admit. He was glad that Clementine was alive, glad that she had found happiness, at least for a time. Growing up he had loved Clementine, but unlike his sister, he was always fully aware of her situation. Father had made sure he was instructed in the proper social hierarchy. He needed to know exactly where the Negro slave stood, not just on Earth, but in Heaven as well. God had created the Negro race to be servants and they were happy to serve, both in life and in the afterlife.

Even as a child, Erasmus didn't believe that. He only needed to look at James and Clementine to see the misery wrought on their faces. He was eight years old when Clementine's son was sold. His mother told him that Negro women didn't feel the same kind of love for their children that white folk did and when Clementine screamed and wailed and begged it was mostly just an act of rebellion, a mimicry of how a white mother would feel, done just to sow discord. Erasmus was there when the child was taken. He looked to James, hoping he would do something to stop it. James was strong, powerful, and deeply kind. If anyone would stop them from taking Clementine's child, it would be him. But James had stood aside, head down, his own tears in his eyes. So, Erasmus ran. He ran to his room and covered his ears and sobbed. Father had Clementine whipped until she stopped screaming.

So much injustice left unanswered. He was doing what he could, in his way, to punish people who had done awful things before the Calamity, but it was a slow vengeance.

His good mood had turned sour. He needed Lupe to restore his spirits.

When he arrived at the general store, he smoothed his waistcoat and trousers one last time before he opened the door and strolled through. The sound of the bell over the threshold doused his melancholy like a candle snuffer puts out a flame.

"Guadalupe?" Erasmus called into the dark.

A cold object pressed against the back of his neck. He turned his head slowly—the tip of a cane. Lupe. He couldn't help but smile.

"I'm afraid you have me at a disadvantage, my friend. I am unarmed."

"This lie is unbecoming of you," he said in his thick accent. He tapped Erasmus' trousers with his cane. "I know you carry a big sword everywhere you go."

"For lovemaking, not fighting."

"Is all the same, I think."

"True," Erasmus said. He put his arms around Lupe's neck. "You make the same face in both activities."

Erasmus pulled his face to his and kissed him. Lupe's breath smelled of mint leaves. "You've been practicing your English."

"No, I just listen to you talk too much."

Erasmus laughed and kissed him again.

Lupe pulled away. "Not now, my mother's coming."

"I don't think we're in any danger of exposing her to something she isn't aware of already."

"No, I know. I just think she's still...hopeful."

"That sometimes appetites change?"

"She likes you."

"Of course." Erasmus let it drop. He considered himself fortunate that Maria del Sol was an understanding woman. Life after the Calamity was different, and sometimes the older survivors didn't change with the world. She understood that the world had changed and would never go back to the way it had been. She may not like it, but Erasmus figured he was fortunate that she at least tolerated it.

Lupe reached a hand out and touched his cheek. "Someday. I'm hopeful."

"It isn't even your mother we need to worry about." Erasmus knew that every time he met with Lupe, he put him in danger. There were rumors, of course, but if any of the Paluxy Boys got it into their heads to follow him, his father the Reverend would put a bounty on Lupe's head.

"You got what I came for?" Erasmus changed the subject.

"I have one of the things you came for. The other is going to have to wait."

"You are absolutely unscrupulous, do you know that?"

Lupe pulled a small bottle from his coat pocket. "Here."

Erasmus pulled his leather gloves on and took the bottle. He always hated handling mercury salts. He had visions of sitting in a chair by the fire, his arms and legs trembling and an endless stream of drool pouring down his chin.

Maria walked in from the back, a rooster following at her heels. "What you need all those bottles for, Erasmus?" She had a large piece of hardtack in her hands and she pulled small worms out and tossed them to the rooster.

"Maria, delightful to see you, as always."

"Sí, sí. But what you need those for? Those no good."

"I know, Ma'am. I need them to fix a little problem I have. Don't worry. I'm taking every precaution."

"Él tampoco me lo dirá." Lupe spoke in his native tongue. In one of his native tongues. He also spoke some Apache but didn't get as much use out of it. Erasmus encouraged him to keep using it. He feared that someday his father might come after Lupe, and after last Sunday's sermon, the fear had grown substantially. He hoped that Lupe's Apache blood could buy him acceptance into the Indian Territories. As much as it would pain him to lose his lover, he didn't want to see him swing from the end of a Paluxy Boys' noose.

Maria sent him away with a bundle of worm-infested hardtack, three fresh eggs, and a bottle of morphine, in case he needed some relief from handling the mercury salts. She knew his preference was for white medicine, which she had no use for. She always warned him that white medicine would likely kill him before any sickness did. Erasmus had no doubt she wasn't right, but whiskey and opium would at least make him happy before he died.

He turned to leave and heard a horse snort. They all froze. Horses were rare in the Wastes. They were hard to keep alive and died nearly as often as their own children did. In Sorrow Draw, only the Paluxy Boys rode horses.

"Get out the back," he whispered.

"They might just be passing through," Lupe said. "Besides, we have done nothing."

"You heard about my father last Sunday. I don't trust a single one of them now. They won't touch me, at least not yet. But get your ma out of here."

He watched them go, hoping that they were just passing through, that they didn't have the store surrounded, that they weren't waiting for Lupe and his mother to sneak out the back door.

He adjusted his cravat and slung his bag of goods over his shoulder. He walked outside into the dust and through the haze he saw a single figure on horseback. The figure kicked his horse into a walk and rode up to him. When he got close enough, Ransom Eisenhardt reigned in his horse.

"Erasmus. I thought I might find you here," he said.

Erasmus bristled. He sounded overly conversational. "Well, that's odd. I didn't expect to find you here."

"No, that's true. I don't do much scavenging myself." He took his hat off and wiped his brow. His short black hair glistened with sweat. "But I know you do. In fact, I hear you come down this way all the time. I'm surprised there's anything left in this store to scavenge. I'd have figured it would have run dry years ago."

"Well, that's what happens when you don't know shit about something. You tend to get it all wrong."

Ransom laughed. "I suppose you're right. You're a funny man, Erasmus. A bit of a flannel-mouthed dandy, but since I'm fixin' to be your brother-in-law soon, I figured I should get to know you better."

"Well, that does remain to be seen now, doesn't it? Though truth be told, I do desire for us to become better strangers."

Ransom sat up straighter in his saddle. "It's only a matter of time before we're family. If I were you, I'd make hay while the sun shines. Your father ain't gonna be around forever, and someday I'll run the Paluxy Boys. Just a friendly warning."

Erasmus knew this was a possibility. If there was one thing that he was good at, it was planning for the future, thinking of all possible outcomes and contingencies, following every thread in his mind to see where they might end up. Ransom assuming control of the Paluxy Boys would throw Sorrow Draw into chaos. While he wasn't as calculating as Reverend Mothershed, he had a far greater capacity for cruelty. Erasmus knew that the logical choice would be to get on Ransom's good side. But there were some things that he just couldn't do.

"If you're done, I'd just as soon walk home now. Alone."

"I'm done with you when I say I'm done with you." Ransom kicked his horse to block his path. "I know what you are and what you do. Don't think for a moment that I can't tell your father why you come here, you sodomite. Frankly, I don't give much of a damn that you bugger that Indian boy, but I'll bet a good pick that your pa does."

"My father's blind if he don't already know, I think."

"Then maybe I take my boys up to Serpent's Bluff and pay a visit to that little saloon you fancy. Seems to me that it could use a bit of righteous purification. You understand?"

"I take your meaning, sir," Erasmus said.

"Good. I will marry Hattie, make no mistake. But don't worry, maybe after I take Hattie, I'll make you my left-hand wife." He spun his horse around and kicked it into a walk. "Go on home, dandy."

Erasmus watched him disappear into the haze. He walked on, slower and joyless. He wondered if the town, absent the Calamity, would have accepted him better or worse than it did now. Would he have had an easier time hiding himself? Would he have been expected to court a woman, make one his wife, and then kill her slowly through his disinterest until his lack of love and affection for her pushed her into the arms of another man? Would he have been able to suffer the social humiliation, the whispers and stares and the behind-the-back comments? Or would he have been strung up a tree for his godless perversions?

That life, he decided, would have been a fate worse than Calamity.

Chapter 16

Uncontested Lands, Old Mississippi (August, 1881)

Cornelius White

THE RAIN LET UP by morning, but Nikki didn't think it a good idea to leave the hotel until Farhad's fever broke. Farhad, for his part, insisted that he lived most of his life feverish, and he needed only his laudanum. Conny knew that might be true, but he didn't care to travel so soon after a storm. Rain in the barren desert made riding difficult. Whole villages have been swept away by sudden mudslides, and men could scarcely tell the difference between dry ground and mud deep enough to swallow a horse. There are people from older deserts who knew how to navigate them, but the Uncontested Lands were only a desert for the past eighteen years, and the land, and its people, were still new to it.

When he wasn't watching over Farhad, Conny spent his time scavenging the houses and shops of Bolivar. Scavenging was easy in the beginning, right after the Calamity. Everything anyone needed could be found in the next house over, or the general store down the road. Clothes, blankets, and food could be had in abundance. But that abundance soon turned to famine. Few people took accurate stock of the situation, and they used up resources as if they were limitless, believing the Calamity a temporary thing, believing their lives would soon go back to the way they used to be. When the years passed and things got worse, not better, the survivors slowly started to panic.

They had to go farther and farther away from the safety of their homes to get supplies. Food was no longer able to be scavenged. Clothes rotted in dressers. Herds of cattle and pigs starved and died, left to rot in fields and pens. By the time people accepted their fate, supplies had been squandered, and no preparations had been made to secure their future. Rumors of help from Europe were never realized—no ships sailed to or from any port and soon new rumors emerged. Tales of devastation across the Atlantic on a scale far worse than any seen in America. Help, they realized too late, was never coming.

Conny scavenged for diversion, not out of necessity, and not out of hope. It kept his mind off of Farhad, off of California, off of Nikki Free, the woman whose sudden appearance had added an excitement to his life, some certain quality that he couldn't quite define and when he found himself looking after her more than he did Farhad, watching her more than he did anything else, he decided that scavenging was a needed distraction. He had to clear his mind and center himself.

In the first several houses he found nothing except Black Widows and scorpions, dust and useless fineries that had no practical purpose in the Wastelands. The only real luxury most people allowed themselves was books. They were more than a simple diversion, they served as a history lesson for the youth, and as a reminder of better times for survivors of the Calamity.

In a large chest at the foot of a once ornate bed with decayed green velvet drapes, Conny found a book, *A Tale of Two Cities*, by Charles Dickens. He held his breath and said a silent prayer to no god in particular that the book wouldn't crumble to dust when he picked it up. It didn't. The marbled cover was stiff, and the pages bound tightly with no hint of mold or rot. The book was in fine condition. Most found books were unreadable and would crumble like dry leaves. A good and readable book had high trade value, except for Bibles which were everywhere and easy to find. In his old life, he had been fond of Dickens' books. He hadn't heard of this book before, but he recalled reading *Little Dorrit* in *Harper's New Monthly Magazine* aloud to his wife, though she was a fine reader herself and had no need of him to read it to her. It had become something of a ritual for them before the start of the War. He paid twenty-five cents for each new edition at Norman's General

Store and he would always spend a little extra for some peppermint sticks or lemon drops.

He wrapped the book in a linen shirt from the same chest and stowed it carefully in his pack. If he found nothing else of use in Bolivar, he'd be content.

He slung the pack over his shoulder and walked back to the hotel. Back to the woman he rescued from the cross. Back to his dying friend who was drowning in his own lungs. Conny slowed his pace. His chest ached and the sorrow threatened to overwhelm him. What would his life look like the day he wakes up and Farhad is dead in his bedroll? He fought against the inevitability of that day, but nothing he did would keep it from coming.

He read the names on the dusty windows of the shops he passed.

Meyer & Khan Dry Goods Store.

R. Moffatt, Watchmaker and Jeweller.

Gauss & Shaw, Wholesale Grocers.

Mrs. G. Howard, Millinery.

Men and women who had lives before the Calamity. Families. Hopes and dreams and desires. Sometimes it was easy to forget these names were real people. But then, when he did remember, it was like a bullet to his chest. It took the very breath out of him, knocked him down, and left him stunned, wanting for answers, but knowing he wouldn't find any. For most people, the anger was long gone and, in its wake, it left only ugly bitterness, a rotting of the soul. It was something he could almost smell, if he tried hard enough, if the dust and decay would withdraw for a moment, he could smell the disease of the spirit or the stench of his blighted soul.

Conny could just make out the shadow of the hotel through the haze of dust. The people of Memphis called it the Fog of Calamity. Farther north the folks called it the Devil's Mist. What they called it elsewhere in the world, Conny didn't know. All he knew was it suffocated life. It was as if the world lived in perpetual darkness, and you had only a single candle to light your way. Everything beyond the reach of that flame was cast behind the veil.

Crowkiller leaned against a hitching post outside the hotel's saloon entrance. Conny hadn't seen him for a day and a half, but the man often disappeared for days at a time and returned without explanation. He smoked a long straight pipe, the rich earthy scent of tobacco lingered about the big man. He held the pipe out. Conny took it and drew a long pull and blew the smoke out slow.

"Thanks." Conny gave the pipe back to Crowkiller.

"What are we going to do about Farhad?"

Conny sucked in his lips. "We're going to wait until he's well enough to travel and then we're gonna move on."

"You like the man. I understand. I like him, too. There's some wisdom in waiting, but you see things through your heart, and not your mind. There's some wisdom in waiting, yes, but there's more foolishness in it. You know this in your head. We're going to lose the trail for good, if we haven't already. That money is still out there, and Longstreet is still after us. We have to move, whether the Bedouin is ready or not."

"I'm not gonna leave my friend here to die, if that's what you're suggesting." If Conny were being truthful, the money was no longer a concern for him. Finding Becker's daughter, maybe, but Conny tended to a growing suspicion that she didn't want to be found. His first priority was to Farhad.

"But he's going to die. Whether you leave him here or not. Whether we take him or not. Whether you dump him in Mexico or not. Maybe it's best he die here in the company of his friends."

"That ain't for us to decide." Conny's face burned. If Crowkiller thought he could convince Conny to put a bullet in his friend's head, even for pity's sake, he was dead wrong. Conny pulled his duster to the side, baring his revolver.

"Remember that." Crowkiller knocked the ash from his pipe with the heel of his hand. He ignored Conny's threat. "Remember that when the time comes and he makes his own decision, then. Let him go out on his own terms. It's the only way Farhad deserves to meet his end. On his own terms."

"He's got plenty of fight and plenty of good days still ahead of him."

"His good days will get worse and worse and sooner or later, a 'good day' will be what you would have called a 'bad day' before. You know better than anyone what he has in store for him, don't you?"

"I know it. But what you're suggesting is wrong."

"No. It isn't. You just can't let go. Sooner or later, he's going to need you to let go."

The Indian walked away without looking at Conny who stood tense, his muscles tight, bracing himself against the urge to lash out at his friend as if he were holding back a beast in a cage. He would not leave Farhad, the rest of them be damned. And it was far too soon to let the man kill himself.

Conny walked back into the saloon. The air inside was warm but reeked of horse shit and dust. They had moved the horses out to the stable when the floodwaters receded, and although Nikki Free cleaned out the bulk of the filth, the stench still lingered heavy. Indifference kept them from washing the floors and airing the saloon out. The same indifference that kept people from rebuilding, from reclaiming what they once had. It was as if people were waiting for the real end. The Calamity took most, and the rest are simply waiting to join them in the void.

Nikki Free sat with Farhad by the fire. She smiled at Conny when he came in. Since Farhad no longer required her constant care, she had allowed herself time to scavenge the area. She managed to exchange Eudora's clothes for a fringed buckskin shirt and trousers dyed a deep mahogany. She wore her hair in dozens of small braids underneath her dust scarf. She was beautiful.

Conny coughed. "How's your arms?"

She had been rubbing her wrists when Conny walked up. "Just tolerable. I had a few drops of laudanum last night for the pain and so's I could sleep."

"I thought you didn't touch the stuff?"

"I didn't touch the stuff when I didn't know if I could trust you or not. I think I got a handle on how you are now, though." She winked at him.

"Good. Good. You hadn't slept in a while. I was starting to worry."

"I knowed it. Come, sit." She tilted her head to the empty chair next to her. Conny sat and took off his gloves.

"Relax." Nikki pushed him back in his chair and took his hand.

Farhad opened one eye. "Now Nikki Free, I understand you are new to the company, but surely you've known Conny here long enough to know he ain't never going to relax." Sweat stood in fine beads on his forehead, but his voice had regained much of its previous vigor.

"Oh, I think he just needs some proper motivation."

"Maybe when we find Eudora and the money and we're free of Longstreet." Conny sunk back into his chair. It felt good to sit by the fire, to hold the hand of a woman, this woman, and to hear Farhad's wit.

Farhad put his finger to his lips. "Shhh. No talk about about Longstreet tonight. It's our last night here. Tonight, we celebrate."

"Celebrate what?" Crowkiller's warning sounded like a bell in his head. What had they to celebrate?

"Life, Con. Tonight we celebrate life." Farhad took a long pull from a bottle of whiskey and handed it to Conny. "I am still among the living, I think? Yes? Hard to tell sometimes with you, Con. Fortunately, we have Nikki Free here to show us that we are, indeed, still alive."

Conny drank the whiskey. It burned in his chest as it went down, and he savored the rich flavor of oak. The quality was surprising. This was no Red Eye. He took another pull and passed it to Nikki.

"Farhad," she said, turning the bottle over in her hands. "Tell me about your family."

Farhad shifted in his chair. "You already know Conny, he's my father. Crowkiller, well, I might call him a brother."

"Yes, but what about your real family?"

"They are my real family. But I suppose, little sister, I can tell you about my first family."

"I'm sure I'm older than you." Nikki took another long drink.

"Give me that, you're hogging it all. And I'm positive I have a few years on you." Farhad took the bottle. He emptied a tincture of opium into it and drank deep. He sat for a while with his eyes closed, and Conny wondered if he might have fallen asleep. The bottle continued to go around.

"What is it you want to know?" he asked finally.

"What's the Holy Land like?"

"The Holy Land," Farhad mocked the name. "Like these Wastelands, only not as cold and not quite as dead. Least, that's how I left it. Now I imagine it's gone from all knowledge. Scattered to the winds, the dust we breathe here is all that's left of it."

"What do you mean?"

"We had a German naturalist in Memphis," explained Conny. "He suggested that the Calamity was some kind of comet that came down and collided with the Earth, he said, like a shooting star somewhere in Africa most likely. He said it explains the earthquakes, the floods, and all the dust."

"Weltkiller-Komet. Der Todesengel. And if he's right," continued Farhad, "my homeland is nothing but a crater the size of Virginia."

"I ain't never heard a reason like that," Nikki said. "Mostly people blame God or the Devil. I heard some blame the Indians, but never comets."

"Yeah, he was a strange fellow," Conny said, "but to hear him talk about it, you almost had to believe it."

"Tell me about your mother." Nikki took Conny's hand again. It was warm and strange.

"Her name was Amal. She was the youngest wife of my father. She was small and beautiful. And my father doted on her in the most scandalous ways." Farhad winked. "I was her only child and so I consumed as much of her attention as I could get."

"Ahhh," Nikki said in a tone that suggested she had just realized something. "So that's why you are the way you are. Your mother spoiled you."

"What a dreadful thing to say. True, of course, but dreadful nonetheless." Farhad wiped the sweat from his forehead. "Yes, I was my mother's pride and joy. And, it seems, the source of most of her sorrow. When I was betrothed, she cried for weeks."

"Betrothed?" Nikki asked. "Didn't you come over here when you were young?"

"Yes, twelve years, by my reckoning, give or take. It wasn't an official engagement or anything that serious like you would have had over here, but I was promised to a girl. The daughter of my father's brother."

"What was her name?" Nikki rolled tobacco and put it in her mouth.

"Maryam."

"That's pretty."

"So was she."

"What happened to them? Con says you came here to sell camels or something? You never got word from them back home?"

Conny lit a page from his Bible in the fire and held it out to Nikki. She lit her cigarette and passed it to Conny.

"None for you, Farhad. I want you ready to ride tomorrow."

"My dear little sister, I will be more than ready by morning, and I'm quite sure that a little bit of tobacco is just what I need to clear my lungs."

"You and I both know that ain't true."

Farhad flashed his dimpled smile underneath his mustache. "You've been awful quiet over there, Con. How 'bout you tell us what you found on your little expedition today?"

"You were gone a terribly long time." Nikki sat up straighter.

"Nothing much out there. Spent most of my time just walking and thinking."

Nikki tossed the remainder of the cigarette into the fire. "Well, I like to walk and think, too. So next time maybe I can go with you."

"Of course." He didn't tell her that she was the reason he stayed gone so long, that he had trouble making sense of his thoughts and needed some time away from her to clear his head and think reasonably. He also didn't mention that it had done no good. As soon as he saw her again, he lost his senses.

Conny reached into his bag. "I found a book, though. Charles Dickens. You ever heard of him?" He asked Nikki, he knew that Farhad had read some of Dicken's stories.

Nikki shook her head. "They was never fixin' to let Negroes read, Con."

"Right. I forgot. I'm sorry."

"I know. That's why I like you, Conny White. You're a good man. After the Calamity, I did teach myself to read, but I don't know the man who wrote that. I had some religious shit to read mostly. The Talmud, Paradise Lost…The Bible, of course—those fuckin' things is everywhere—I did read this one story 'bout a man named Bartleby. That one had me laughing. I did enjoy that one."

"Who wrote that?" Conny asked.

"Don't remember. It was in a magazine. Putnam's, I think." Nikki rubbed her wrists. "Maybe you can read that one to me sometime. A little bit before we go to bed some nights if you care to."

It hit like a kick in the chest. It was almost as if the world, long out of balance, slowly fading away, was trying to right itself like a listing ship. To read a few pages each night to this woman would be some reclamation of what he once had, of what had long ago been seized from him. It would be a taste of sweetness he missed. He had been a king turned beggar, and here was a benefactor, dropping coins into his cup.

"I'd like that." His throat tightened. He made every effort to mask it from Nikki.

They sat in silence, as was the custom in the Wastelands. The fire cracked in the hearth and a gentle wind moaned outside.

Nikki stood up and draped a blanket over Farhad, who had fallen asleep. Conny didn't know when. She had a tender, delicate touch. A mother's touch, though she had never had children of her own.

"Put another log on the fire, would you?"

Conny went to do as he was asked, but he had drunk more than he thought and the room didn't want to cooperate. The floor shifted under his feet and the world insisted on trying to go in the opposite direction of the fire. With a great deal of effort, Conny managed to find his way to the hearth and throw in a couple of logs.

Nikki punched his arm. "Damn it. That hurt my wrist."

"Well, maybe you shouldn't hit people like that for no good reason."

"You're drunk."

"Just a little bit."

"Yeah, well it's my experience that the drunker a man is, the less drunk he claims to be."

"You have lots of experience with drunk men?"

"Unfortunately. Come along, vaquero." Nikki took his hand in hers. It was soft and warm and promised of things to come.

She led him upstairs to her bedroom. She had found clean blankets for the bed and a candle that she lit. It was strange, to be in a woman's room. He had only ever shared a room for any significant amount of time with his wife, Elizabeth. But this was a room in the Wastelands, a room *of* the Wastelands, as barren and empty as the land itself. *No. Not barren and empty. Not now.* Not with Nikki Free standing in front of him. *Is there anyone else in this dead* world so full of life as her? Had there ever been? In this new world or the old? He had ignored the women in Memphis for years, they were false, counterfeit. Farhad enjoyed that about them, he said they were real and Conny was caged by his old emotions, like a dog that refuses to leave his dead master's side. He would bed them when he had to, when the urge was overwhelming, or when the Law in Memphis demanded it, but it was always a dirty, ugly thing. But there wasn't a single thing false about the woman before him now. She was genuine and unvarnished, raw and unblemished.

Nikki put a hand on Conny's chest. Shadows from the candlelight darted across her face and over the sunburst tattoos around her eyes that seemed to spin and dance like black flames down her soft brown cheeks. "Conny—"

He cupped her face in his hands. He bent down and kissed her, soft and unsure. She pressed in and he found her tongue and the taste of whiskey and cigarettes, warm and wet.

Nikki pushed him back, letting his lip slide out from between her teeth. She pulled her leather tunic over her head and let it drop. He picked her up by the waist and sat her down on the room's empty dresser and kissed her again, savage and forceful. Slender fingers ran through his hair and she pushed his head down. Conny took a dark nipple in his mouth and Nikki exhaled slow and deep. She smelled of fire and musk. Of rain in a tin cup. Of sweat and marigolds. Conny's heart raced.

She leaned back and he untied her belt and let her breechcloth fall. He pulled her buckskin leggings off and ran his hands down her legs. Thin white scars crisscrossed her thighs. He often forgot that his kind had made slaves of others. No matter how far distant the institution of slavery had receded in their past, it would always be something that Nikki would never have the luxury of forgetting. She had once told him that her slavemaster took pity on her. What did he do to his other slaves if this was showing mercy?

Nikki must have sensed his thought. She grabbed him by the wrists and pulled him up to her face. "Don't." She pressed her lips to his, wet and hungry. "Not now. Please. Don't."

He picked up her small naked body and laid her down on the bed. They fumbled with his trousers, their fingers tangled, danced in between each other. She pulled him out, her hands soft and cold, and Conny hard and ready. The need to feel himself inside her became urgent, and he wasn't sure if his desire had yielded to pain, or if they were ever different sensations at all, but his body ached for her.

As if sensing his needs, or acting on her own passions, she lifted her legs and guided him in. Then he was on top of her and her hands gripped his back, fingernails raked his skin.

"Harder," Nikki whispered.

Conny took her in, her warm, tawny skin, taut breasts, the mass of coiled locks that spilled all around her, black as raven feathers, and her face fixed in an expression of agony that masked her pleasure. *This is the woman I've been waiting for.*

Conny pushed savagely, pressed her legs to her chest, and wrapped his arms around her. They were a tangle of skin and muscle, sinew and sweat.

"Harder," Nikki whispered, her voice deep, husky.

Conny drove again and again. He kissed her neck, buried his face in her hair. He inhaled deeply, a scent redolent of honey and milkweed. There was no one and nothing on Earth except this woman in his arms. There were no Wastelands, no Calamity, no End of the World. Not when Nikki Free still lived. For years he had been living in the past, terrified of the future. For the first time since disaster struck the world, Conny lived in the moment, took pleasure in the now, and thought of nothing but the immediate.

Nikki shut her eyes and groaned through clenched teeth. She pulled him closer, as if she could pull herself into him. Her pleasure was potent, an intoxicating drug, both sinful and divine. Conny held her while she shuddered. She tightened around him, quivering, and he gave in to the surge of release. He emptied himself in her and collapsed, breathless and alive.

Chapter 17

Serpent's Bluff, North Texas (August, 1881)

Deliverance Hill

It had been a few days since the rainstorm, and the trail from Sorrow Draw to Hill Lodge had dried enough to allow people to make the journey on foot, and they wasted no time in the coming. Deliverance had been on edge since her meeting with the Mothershed boy. The Reverend was always a threat, but things in Sorrow Draw must be coming to a head for his own children to brave the dangers of the Wasteland to warn her.

She rolled a cigar and smoked it in a dark, out-of-the-way corner. She wanted to be alone tonight and most people knew to leave her alone when she was brooding.

The Faro tables were busy, as usual. She sat opposite them on the far side of the grand saloon floor, the laughter from the gamblers was always loudest at the Faro tables, and she couldn't abide the noise tonight. Most of the painted ladies and gentlemen stayed on that side too, with the Faro players. They were most likely to win, most likely to drink, and most likely to end the night wanting to bed someone.

The Irishmen and the Germans stood at the bar. Lefty busied himself pouring drinks and running the exchange. He was a tough old man, and that's exactly who she needed at the exchange counter. The trade system at Hill Lodge was a work in progress, but Lefty was both fair and firm. She gave him the freedom to decide the value of the scrap and salvaged goods that the people brought in to swap for gambling chips, and those chips could then be traded for anything behind the counter—whiskey, gin, and *fuego del yermo*, a strong drink made from a kind of cactus that started growing in abundance after the Calamity. The Freemen traded what they could for it when the Mexican caravans came up the Brazos River with their boat twice a year.

People played at High-Low, Three-Card Monte, and even one table boasted a large chess board with pieces carved from local limestone. But it was her poker tables that drew her eye the most. Jacob ran one table, and the other was run by a tiny little light-skinned girl who called herself Independence. They were fine dealers, though Jacob's hands were too heavy, and she caught Independence cheating four times since she sat down to watch. She would have to remind her that the Poker was not Faro and she liked her face without a bullet hole through it, she would do well to remember that.

She watched everyone. She made it her business to know who was intimate with whom, which relationships were in trouble, who had a problem with rotgut, who was looking for opium, and who needed some private company. Friendships could be made by providing things people wanted, or by mending broken things. Loyalty can be found in disclosing the secrets of infidelity. It always amazed her what some people would do to keep their unfaithfulness confidential. She had very little interest in reserving herself and her pleasures for a single person. Most people who lived in Serpent's Bluff and frequented Hill Lodge felt the same way. It was those queer folk from Sorrow Draw who mostly kept that dead custom. They were also the first to run to the rooms upstairs to visit the scarlet men and women, always with their heads downcast, and incessant glances over their shoulders to make sure no one had discovered them.

A young Chinese woman made her way from across the grand hall towards her dark corner of the saloon. She moved on the tiniest feet Deliverance had ever seen. She had once told Deliverance that her feet had been broken and bound when she was very young, wrapped and folded under.

"They did that on purpose? Why?" Deliverance had asked.

"The men love the tiny feet," she replied.

"That must have been painful." It had been a foolish thing to say.

"They bind my feet so they bend under themselves. Then my mother and sister make me walk. Around and around in a circle. I walk for hours on the top of my feet until they crack and brake. Then they bind them tighter." She pointed to the drink in Deliverance's hand. "And no opium. No laudanum. Just pain and wishing for death."

"How old were you?"

"I was ten year old."

"Jesus Christ. All because men loved little feet?"

"It was desirable. A girl's value to her family increase the smaller her feet were bound."

"Well, maybe you girls should have decided that men with half a cock were valuable. Lash the boys down at age ten and tie stones to it until it snaps in two."

She walked slow and with a limp, but erect, with her shoulders back and her head high. She had an uncommon strength that had become so common in the Wastes. When the winds and dust had first hit like a canon, when the apocalypse came down on the world like the wrath of God, there seemed to be no pattern or logic to who lived and who died. But afterward—afterward it was the strong who endured.

Wu. She was strong. Like most of the people in Deliverance's gang, she had taken a new name for herself. Her given name was Lin, but she took Wu, a name, she said, of a powerful Chinese woman, an Empress who ruled long ago. For her, the Calamity had meant almost as much as it did for the former slaves. In a single day, in one grand catastrophe brought down by the hand of Fate, she had escaped a life of servitude to a husband chosen for her by her family. She had been emancipated from a desolate future as a creature whose destiny and purpose was to be stripped of everything but the expectation to produce children.

At Hill Lodge, Wu had found a purpose and a family. Deliverance loved her. Loved her as a sister, and just as often ached for her as a lover. Wu, for her part, rejected all her advances.

She pulled up a chair and sat next to Deliverance. She smoothed the front of her dress with her delicate hands. The dress was made from silk, and it was elaborately embroidered with flowers of reds and oranges and deep purples.

Wu." Deliverance handed her a tin of tobacco and paper. "You're looking passing fair tonight, as always."

"Thank you." She took the tobacco and rolled a quirley. "I saw you over here in the dark sulking."

"I'm not sulking. I'm thinking."

"You might be thinking, but you're also sulking. You're doing both, maybe." Wu often sounded upset, as if she were cross with you, even when she tried to show concern. Deliverance had made that observation to her once, and Wu had replied that this was the way she was, and Deliverance would have to learn to deal with it.

"Is that why you came over here, then? To bother me while I'm thinking?"

"Yes. To interrupt your sulking. Also to find out what's wrong, I suppose."

"Sorrow Draw. Something tells me they ain't right. Something's gonna happen, Wu. I know they've left us alone for a while now, but I don't trust them." She didn't mention the Mothershed boy, but the problem of Sorrow Draw had been plaguing her for some time. They were out-gunned and out-manned if it ever came down to a straight fight. And the Paluxy Boys were brutes. Cruel and wicked, born of the savage elements of the Wastes and nurtured by its inhumanity. Hill Lodge pacified some of them, but if the Reverend's grip on the community was as unyielding as his son suggested, then even this place wouldn't protect them.

"You worry too much about them. How many of them are here right now? You know what I think? I think it's a pity we don't use money. You would be wealthy woman right now."

"Maybe. But what would I do with money? Buy myself some nice clothes?" She pulled down on the top of her white dress, revealing more of her dark bust. "Or whiskey? Opium?"

"Power. You buy yourself power."

"I have that now."

"Sure, maybe. But it would give me something to count. I would love to sit in the back room counting money instead of bullets and tobacco and morphine pills and pieces of scrap not fit for ironmongery."

"I'm glad we don't use money. It's out of place, out of time. I don't even like rolling my tobacco in the stuff. Useless. From a time that's dead and buried and best left forgotten."

"What about the rest of it? All the scrap, the trinkets? They from the past too, yet you love those things. That dress? The jewelry? All from that Age you hate so much."

"Sure, but nothing symbolizes the very nature of that past like paper money. It's completely devoid of any real value, it's just an empty promise, a white man's promise that this paper means something. Backed by the United States government." Deliverance laughed, a laugh as devoid of real humor as the paper money was of value. "And people killed each other over so worthless a thing."

"You know, someday all this will be gone, too. All the opium, the morphine, the tobacco. Even the iron will rust away, and then what?"

"People don't really come here to bet, Wu. They come here to feel. To feel passion, to feel excitement, to feel—normal. They come to laugh and dance and listen to Dietrich on the piano. The bettin's just something familiar, something they remember as a part of the game. When they realize that it ain't an important part, then it won't matter no more."

"And when will they realize that?"

"I don't think in my life they will. But we'll always want pleasure, and that I can continue to provide. People will always want to fuck. There's no taking that from them."

"And so you should not worry about Sorrow Draw. They want to come here for that, too. That preacher can strut all he wants, but his people are no different."

Deliverance took her hand and kissed it. "You're right. You're right. I probably worry too much."

"Of course. But you keep worrying, won't you?"

"It's just...I know what religious passion can do to people. It can make them lose their heads and their senses. If that old man wants to, he can send the Paluxy Boys here and they'd butcher us all in his name and think they're right for doing it."

"Does this have anything to do with the conversation you had with Erasmus Mothershed the other night?"

Wu's accent stirred a hunger inside Deliverance. It was stranger than any she had ever heard, but her appetite for it was never sated. Wu was nearly twice as old as Deliverance, but that did nothing to temper her desire for the little woman. "I should have known you would have saw that."

"I did, of course. I wait for you to tell me about it, but you never did."

"No, I wanted to get my head wrapped around it all first."

"That's why I'm here. It's my job to wrap your head around things."

It was a subtle movement, so small that Deliverance wasn't quite sure why or how she picked up on it. She hadn't been watching Sovereign in particular but had been looking over the room, as she frequently did, when she saw the man at the bar pull out a knife. She called out to Sovereign from across the floor, who barely had a moment to react before the knife came at him, but that moment was enough. In an instant, there were half a dozen men on top of the would-be assassin and the saloon was in an uproar.

There had been stabbings at the Lodge before, even two shootings, but they were either because someone was caught cheating at cards, or the result of a spurned and jealous lover. Either way, they both were preceded by a great deal of shouting so when the knife struck, or the revolver fired, it wasn't an unexpected development.

But this had caught the crowd off guard. Some of her patrons had run for the door, others stood up at the tables, ready to fight or to flee if more knives came out.

Deliverance made her way through the throng of gamblers and dancers to Sovereign's side. The two worked to untangle the mass of men piled on the knife-wielder.

"Take him upstairs." Sovereign ordered his men to tie the assassin's hands and feet and they carried his body away, bound up like a rolled carpet. Sovereign gripped Deliverance by the waist, his massive hands could nearly wrap around her completely. "I'm in your debt, woman," he said.

"Yeah, don't forget it when I come to collect."

"Are there any more?" Wu asked. Her head snapped around the room. "There were a lot of men who ran out the doors in all the commotion."

"I don't know," Deliverance said. "You think there was more than one?"

"Like I said, there were a lot of men who left when it happened."

"Well we can't say for sure, can we? Maybe they just didn't want to get caught up in anything."

"Sure, sure. But it was a lot of white men I never see before."

"Only one way to find out now." Sovereign smiled. "We just have to ask our new prisoner."

"So do we ask him now, or do we make him wait?" Deliverance rubbed her hands together.

"First you tell him what you're going to do to him," Wu said. "Then you make him wait. Give him some time to think about what he has coming. Fear is quick thing. Terror take time to settle in. So, give it time to settle in."

"Why Wu, you are positively ruthless."

"I do know some things about terror." The little woman smiled. Deliverance saw a strange kind of sadness in Wu's face. It was the same look she saw in the faces of the old men who spoke fondly and sweetly of lovers long gone.

"Wu, one day you're going to have to tell me all about your past. Maybe over a bottle of rye. I think that would be very interesting."

Chapter 18

Uncontested Lands, Old Mississippi (August, 1881)

Eudora Becker

THE RUINS OF VICKSBURG came slowly into view. A low dust-shrouded wall ran along Eudora's right like a vein under taut, emaciated skin. The signs of a once populous city became more frequent as they drew nearer the hill that had been the epicenter of the town. Walls, fences, ruined shacks toppled like children's stacking-stones, wagons and carriages, ditches and trenches, structures hewn from wood and stone she'd never seen the likes of before, but to her, they were all the same—relics of an age and a people who were so far removed from anything she'd ever known that they might as well have lived on the other side of the world.

The people who lived before the Calamity, the life they had lived, the strange things they built, and the bizarre beliefs they held about God and women and the darkness of people's skin, were alien things, peoples and ideas that were out of place, and out of time. As derelict as the ruins around her. As threadbare as the wispy garments that still clung to the skeletons buried in the dust.

Jeremiah, in the lead, tried his best to keep them on the road. An easy task most of the time, one that Eudora could have handled on her own. This close to the city, the dust buried artifacts and stones that littered the countryside and filled in holes, all of which made the journey treacherous for their horses.

One misstep and she could find herself riding on the back of Jeremiah's horse the rest of the way, with her nostrils full of his stink.

She didn't want to be here. She had tried to argue against coming to Vicksburg. She wanted to heed the Indian's advice and stay far away. The place now had an evil aura to it that she couldn't escape. Jeremiah wouldn't listen. She had considered telling him about Horsethief, about his warning. She knew he would be angry, but what would he do about it? A competent man would bait the Indian, set a trap for him and kill him, she reckoned. But Jeremiah was not a competent man. He would take his frustrations out on her, but the cowardice in his heart would keep him from hunting down the Indian.

If she had any thought that he would take on Horsethief, she would have told him. The big Indian would put an end to him quick. Jeremiah would fall apart like the corpses her father had hung all around the walls of Memphis. But Jeremiah couldn't even go and get himself killed properly, and because of him, they rode straight into the heart of Vicksburg, and with each step her fear grew, and the Indian's warning played over and over again in her mind.

The buildings grew more frequent. They passed merchant stores that would, at any other time, have seemed promising. Jeremiah stopped at a general store with an intact window. There were straight razors, combs, canes, and hats still on display.

"Jesus, this looks like it ain't never been touched." He dismounted and looked through the dirty glass. "Let's go in and have a look."

At any other time in her life, Eudora would have been elated. Most of the artifacts left over from before the Calamity were of no interest to her, but some things she lived for. Clothes and jewelry, hats and hair tonics, laudanum and whiskey, these were necessities and luxuries, both the same to her. And yet, at this moment, she wanted none of it. She wanted only for Jeremiah to scavenge what he wanted so they could leave. There was an oppressive doom about the place and the Indian's warning continued to sound off in her mind.

"You want anything?" Jeremiah asked.

"Ink and quills. All the pencils they have, too. And paper if you find any."

"What for? You can't read or write. What do you need any of that for?"

"Never you mind what I need it for." She spit. "What kind of a man asks a woman what she wants and then tells her she don't need what she says she wants? Now are you going to look for any or not?"

"They ain't got any. Fresh out." He stood in the doorway with his arms crossed. Eudora was quite sure that if she had been in possession of a firearm at that moment, she would have put a lead ball right through his smug face.

"Get me nothing then. Show me how worthless you really are."

"Tell me what you need ink and pencils for, and I just might see if they got any."

"I like making drawings of things to pass the time."

"Since when?"

"You don't know a whole lot of nothin' about me, Jeremiah. A whole lot of nothin'. Get me my things or don't, but hurry it up, will you?"

"What has got you so riled up?"

"Just don't like this place is all."

"Just don't like this place is all." His mocking tone burned under her skin and moldered in her chest. He laughed and stepped through the broken door frame, glass crunching under his heavy boots.

Eudora stayed outside and waited. The wind screamed and moaned like a feverish mob, yet she scarcely noticed anymore. A thousand thoughts filtered through her head in the intolerable monotony of the windswept desert. How will she rid herself of Jeremiah? Will the Indian take her the rest of the way to California? He certainly seemed interested in her well-being so far. What is the danger here in Vicksburg? What if she were to find herself a gun and take care of Jeremiah herself? It wouldn't be the first time she killed a man. Yet, she didn't really want to kill Jeremiah. She wanted to rid herself of him, to be sure, but he probably didn't deserve to die, at least not by her own hand. Claimed by the Wastes, sure. Dead from his own foolishness, that's sure to be his fate. If she has some small part to play in that, so be it, but she won't murder the man, satisfying as that would be.

Her horse shivered nervously. A rush of air at her back pulled her out of her thoughts. Her vision filled with a blinding white light, and she tumbled from her horse and spun in the black void, and she knew no more.

First came the pain. Before the scent of the dust, before the cold stone on her cheek, before she could remember her name, she was aware of the pain. She felt it, but it was far away, detached, unmoored, and floating in a dark abyss. Gradually, it became clearer, focused. My head. My head hurts. She fought against waking. In sleep she felt no pain, it was only in waking that it came with renewed vigor, a twist of a knife in an old wound.

The earthen tang of dust overpowered her senses. A part of her marveled at the oddity of it. Her nose had long ago become deadened to the smell of dust, so omnipresent a thing as it was. She became aware of her body. One cheek cold and wet, she moved her toes, her legs took more prodding, but she eventually goaded them into a curl and tucked her knees under her chest. Her stomach hurt. Her hands were unbound.

She moaned and then cried. And then she remembered everything.

Vicksburg.

They should have stayed away. Jeremiah was a fool, and he didn't listen to her.

Something happened.

She hit her head.

No, someone hit her.

She fell. She remembered falling.

Off her horse. Now she's—where?

She didn't want to open her eyes. Opening her eyes meant she had to face her situation. She didn't want to face it. This is why she took Jeremiah. It was his job to deal with situations like this.

"Eudora?"

She spoke of the Devil, and he came.

"Jeremiah?" Her voice was hoarse. Her throat burned when she formed the sounds.

"Hey, it's me, Dove," he whispered.

"Where am I?"

"Still in Vicksburg. In a jail cell."

"A jail—" the words stuck in her throat. She opened her eyes. She was in a small room made of stone and brick with a wall of iron bars. It looked nearly identical to the jails in Memphis. Her father used to take her there to see the condemned. Men, women, and children—all awaiting the rope, new ornaments to decorate the walls of Memphis. Some screamed and cried. They pleaded with wide eyes and pressed themselves into the cold bars as if they could melt through and run away. Some were angry, they spit and cursed. Their eyes were narrow slits, accusatory, faces red they reached through the bars to claw at her father. Still others would lay in a pile on the floor, huddled up like discarded skins, they were more alive in death than they were in those moments of despair and quiet acceptance. Her father would bring her to teach her a lesson about the importance of obeying the law, of the consequences of disorder and rebellion. But she didn't listen. What was the use of those teachings when it was her own father who decided who lived and who died? She would never find herself behind those bars.

"They sneaked up on us. Caught me with my back to the door."

"So, I suppose I was right about this place? Wouldn't you say?"

"What?"

"I was right about this place. I told you to go around and you didn't listen."

"Alright, sure. You were right. Hell of a lot of good that's doing us right now. We need to find a way out of here, not point our fingers at each other."

"I'll point my fingers at whoever I like. Especially when I was right. If you had just listened to me for once, we wouldn't be here. You know something, Mr. Preacher? That's your biggest problem. You're too stupid to take care of yourself but even worse is you're too stupid to listen to someone who's got more brains than you."

"And your problem is you run your mouth too damn much. You're gonna end up in a bad way because of it someday. If these bastards here don't cut that tongue of yours out, I might do it my damn self."

"Oh, you ain't gonna do nothing of the sort. You spout off an awful lot, but you ain't ever man enough to back those words up with action."

Eudora put her hands on her temples and felt the blood pulse. Her head ached rhythmically. It hurt to argue, but some things could not be left unsaid. Now that she had said her peace, she sat in silence on the frigid stone floor. The only sounds were the winds howling outside and Jeremiah's heavy breathing. She sat so long she could no longer hazard a guess as to how much time had passed. More than minutes, less than hours.

In the cold dark of the cell, she had nothing to do but think. Mostly the same questions over and over again. Who is doing this to her and why? Where is her horse? Does the Indian know what's happened to her? Her mind reeled with all the possible answers, all the possible outcomes. Play her hand one way, and a thousand avenues diverge, probabilities multiply endlessly. She could act demure and clueless, a victim of this vagabond in the other cell, ignorant of his purpose and motives. This was the easiest course to take. Men don't pay any mind to a rattled woman. Sometimes men would chatter on together about things they wouldn't if anyone else was in the room, but she could be invisible, like a small child, they'd conspire openly, divulge their secrets while she listened. Secrets like the location of a hidden cache of money from the Republic of California.

Have they found the money, yet? Yes. That's almost a certainty. If there's one thing that is unchanging throughout this world it's the nature of mankind to be scavengers. She heard it wasn't always so. Another one of those realities of the Old World that seemed so unreal. There was a time, they say, when people looked down on scavenging and only the undesirables would scour the refuse piles, and only criminals would rummage through people's homes or take things from stores without leaving them money in exchange.

"Hey Dora," Jeremiah said.

His intrusion into her thoughts startled her and she felt her cheeks burn with embarrassment. She hated feeling like a fool, and that made her angry.

"What?" she asked, harsher than it warranted, she knew, but she couldn't help it. It was his fault she was angry, after all.

"I'm sorry." He spoke in a loud whisper, almost as if he were ashamed to admit it out loud. "You was right. I should have listened. We wouldn't be in this mess if I had. It's my fault. And I'll make it up to you. I'll get you out of here and we'll get to California."

Eudora laid her head on her arm. The throbbing in her head has lessened, but it had only made room for more despair. "Oh, Jeremiah. I don't think we'll ever get to California. I don't think we really ever had a chance to tell you the truth."

He sat up, a determined look on his rough face. "Nonsense. I'll get you there. Just as soon as we figure this out. I'll get you there. You got my word on it, Dove. Just have a little hope is all."

"Alright then."

But hope was something that she had abandoned outside in the ruins of Vicksburg with the other dying artifacts of civilization.

Chapter 19

Uncontested Lands, Old Mississippi (August, 1881)

Farhad

They rode out the next morning. Farhad drank his whiskey and laudanum to rid himself of the disjointed thoughts that often came to him in the morning. The drink and the opium cleared his head. He felt normal, focused. Not like a man dying, but like a man who had things to live for.

Crowkiller had disappeared. They searched around for him, but his horse and gear were gone. Conny told Nikki that this happened often with the Indian, but Farhad wondered if there was something Conny wasn't telling them. Nikki insisted on leaving a note for Crowkiller, in case the man came back, so Conny carved "Gone South" on the door with his Bowie knife.

The road out of Bolivar was easy and they made good progress. The flood had left debris scattered all over, but nothing that proved difficult to pass. Branches and brush littered the trail, black and wet but frozen in the early frost. Every year since the Calamity the frost came earlier than the year before and now even in the South, even in the summer months, the frost would cover the ground in the mornings when the sunlight first flared through the dust and clouds.

This particular morning was exceptionally cold, and Farhad wrapped himself in buffalo hide to keep warm. His horse snorted; its breath came out of its nostrils like gunpowder. Farhad took a pull from his whiskey bottle and shifted in his saddle. Soon the air would warm to tolerable levels and this whole damned trip might become enjoyable again. His temper soured and he had nothing to pass his time. Normally he would banter with Crowkiller about philosophy, about the mysteries of life. They would trade beliefs and stories like other men traded in liquor and blankets. Farhad shared secret tales and hidden knowledge meant for his people, but his people were gone and who would remember these things when he joined them? So he passed on what he knew, those things he could recall.

He thought briefly of talking with Nikki Free, of sharing an old story of two lovers, one a free man and one a slave, and a schoolmaster who learned of their secret love and the qadi who married them. But Nikki and Conny rode side-by-side, spoke quietly with each other, and smiled at each other often. Farhad began to feel a bit like the schoolmaster of his story, a discoverer of a secret love. It was a good thing. Conny was more of a father to him than his own father had been, and likely would have been even if the Calamity had never struck. His father was hard and reserved most of his affection for Farhad's mother and everything else he had to spare for his eldest son, Farhad's brother, the man who would inherit his wealth and position. He was nothing now but an heir of death. An inheritor of oblivion. A scion of the forgotten.

Conny deserved happiness. He had been miserable for so long. Farhad often worried about how Conny would get along once consumption finally caught up with him. If Nikki Free could stick around for a while, maybe he could finally die without being on the tenterhooks about it. Yes, this was good for Conny and Farhad was nothing loath to be pleased about it.

They traveled steadily for miles along the banks of the Mississippi. The river ran brown and cold, and the water was flavored of earth. It tasted ancient, antediluvian, as if the gods had transported them to a time before man. They met no one else on the road and the towns they stayed in were all very similar to Bolivar. Empty relics of a past that would someday be beyond recall.

They saw no sign of Crowkiller, or their quarry. On the far bank of the river were the *wechuge*, the effigies of evil spirits put up by Indians to ward off trespassers. They rose out of the mist and dust, black phantoms of branches and bones, tied together in the shape of men. Some of the bones were buffalo and deer, dog and bear. Some were unmistakably human. All were a warning to stay out.

Farhad shuddered, as much from the cold as from the chilling message. They instinctively drifted away from the riverbank, still following the water south, but they kept it firmly in the distance, just visible through the haze.

The road wound on, and the Mississippi coiled like a serpent. Their way would have been quicker as the crow flies, but none of them wished to risk losing sight of the water. It was their guide, their anchor in the world. They rode blind without it. Conny carried a compass, a vital tool in the Wastes where the sun was often impossible to find in the dark hazy sky, but the river was a comfort. It meant water, a guardian against thirst. It meant security from getting lost, from wandering the Wastes until exhaustion and terror killed you. It was a tether to the land, an umbilical cord to Mother Earth.

It also perpetually skirted death. The eastern bank was a trial, a grueling ordeal that many didn't survive. West of the river, death was certain, a fact that was uncontested. Eventually, they would have to cross, but it would have to wait until they were in the narrow corridor that the Indian Territories didn't claim, somewhere in old Louisiana.

"How will we know when it's safe to cross once we get there?" Nikki said she had never been this far from Commerce before and had always lived close to the threat from the Indian Territories.

"We won't see those things anymore, for one." Conny waved his hand at the black effigies lining the west bank. "The Indians would rather not have anyone even attempt to cross into their territory. The Prophet won't hesitate to kill, but they prefer to live in solitude, so they give us plenty of warning."

"Can't say as I blame them for that, I guess," Nikki said. "I remember what soldiers on both sides did to Indians before the world went to Hell."

"I 'spose you're right."

Farhad admired many things about Conny White, but it was his ability to see things from different points of view that the Bedouin valued the most. Conny didn't condemn the Indians like most as selfish, savage, or even cowardly for isolating themselves as they did, nor for their uncompromising dedication towards protecting their borders.

There were whispers about what it was they protected within their land. Most refused to believe they protected only themselves. Rumors of a paradise hidden within the Indian Territories spread almost as far as the stories of California. Occasionally someone would get it in their heads to mount an expedition into Indian lands. They believed with enough people, enough guns, or enough stealth, they could penetrate the heart of The Prophet's nation and discover what he had hidden behind the veil of dust and fear. No one ever came back out, and often it would be their bodies that would appear next along the river, more black wraiths to line the banks, a macabre partition of the dying continent.

"Why isn't Crowkiller in there? Do you think that's where he went? To rejoin his people?" Nikki asked.

Farhad shook his head. "Not likely. He's been exiled from the Territories. He's good as dead, same as us if he tries to go in there."

"Right. No one's told me why, yet. What'd he do?"

"Don't know. Ask him three times and you'll get three different answers and maybe none of them's true and maybe all of them's got some truth to 'em," Conny said.

"I ain't trying to offend, you understand, I know he's your friend and all, but do you trust him? He disappears whenever he feels like it, no one knows why his own people don't want him, I know you have a history but maybe your affection for him is clouding your judgment."

"It's not as simple as all that, little sister." Farhad rolled tobacco. His cold hands fumbled with the paper. "He's been there with us since the beginning. He has his ways of doing things, but he shows up when he's needed. Somehow, he always knows when that'll be. We don't really question it. He took a bullet once for Conny, and we'd likely do the same for him. But can he be trusted? Not entirely, no."

"Well that about clears it all up, now don't it?" Nikki laughed, the fog of her breath came out in great puffs like the chimney of a steam engine. She had an easy laugh, and it was difficult to not answer it with a ready smile. Farhad admired that in her. He had given brief thought in the beginning to trying to bed her, charming and beautiful as she was, but when he saw she was sweet on Conny he let it drop. He would find a new soiled dove the next time they found civilization. The women at the End of the World were nothing if not wholly devoted to bearing children by any means necessary, all of them brides of the multitude. Farhad shuddered to think of what life would have been like for him if the Calamity never happened—the idea of marrying only a handful of women, or worse—a single woman—seemed a fate worse than hell, Jahannam, itself. Perhaps a fitting torture in oblivion would be to suffer all the lusts he had in life, but with no physical body to satisfy them.

"Now what's your secret, then, Nikki Free?" he asked.

"Little brother," she teased. "I have no secrets from you. You two are my family now."

"What's your secret to such a happy life? Or is it all an illusion? A bit of prestidigitation? An elaborate ruse, perhaps?"

"I could ask you the same thing," Nikki said.

"I never claimed I was happy."

"Neither did I."

"You have me there." Farhad scratched his mustache. "My secret isn't exactly confidential. Whiskey, Laudanum, and women. Those are my vices and not necessarily in that order, though often they are."

"I can swear to that." Conny pinched a bit of chewing tobacco he found in Bolivar and gave another to Nikki.

"I suppose my secret to a happy life is to have a good sense of humor and a short memory," Nikki said. "I got the sense of humor. But I also got the good sense to forget nothing."

"A good sense of humor? Well, that don't explain how Conny lived so long, then." Farhad smiled despite the cold. Conversation lifted his spirits.

"Having a good sense of humor can be your downfall sometimes, too. They killed the Howington girl on account of she laughed too much." Conny spat.

"Tamsey? The redheaded one that caught her finger in the auger?"

"That's the one."

"They killed her?"

"Yep."

"On account of her laugh?"

"That's what they said."

"Sons of bitches." Tamsey was a good girl and it pained Farhad to hear they had taken another good thing from the world. "Someday I'm going back to Memphis and they'll all get what's comin' to them."

"Don't forget nothing," Nikki said. "Remember every last one of them bastards and everything they ever did. I gots some scores to settle, too. Maybe sooner rather than later."

"Let's not get caught up in talk of revenge right now. When the time comes, I'll ride in with both of you, my guns blazing if that's what you want."

"You better," Nikki said.

"Now that there is the true secret of a happy life," Farhad said. "A happy woman at your side. For me, many happy women at my side."

They made camp to water the horses and eat. The wind picked up, bringing a warmer air from the south, and by noon they shed their buffalo skins and went down to the wool blankets for warmth. Farhad was glad for the change in weather and his breathing eased. He made an inventory of his medicine. He had seven bottles of Laudanum and still over two hundred opium pills. He had six bottles of whiskey in a small cask in his saddlebag and a bottle of Jamaican rum.

He needed the whiskey to get him through until they reached Vicksburg. He reckoned there should be plenty of whiskey bottles to be found there. It's deeper inside the Wastes than most scavenger groups go. There were likely to be people there, but Conny figured on them being mostly friendly. Farhad prepared for the worst. Sometimes you had to ride into a new town and show the people you won't be trifled with. Sometimes that meant bloodshed, but it was best to ride in hard and show them who you are right away. Most folks who start trouble with you are the kind that deserve the killing anyway.

They ate a small meal of scorpions that Nikki collected in Bolivar during the long days when Farhad slept his fever sleep. Conny built a small fire and Nikki pulled off their stingers and grilled them with a bit of meadow garlic. Farhad checked and rechecked his revolvers. He wiped down his repeater. Sometimes you just know when bloodshed's coming, and the closer they got to Vicksburg, the keener he felt it, like an itch underneath his skin that he couldn't sate, growing more and more incessant and maddening with each passing mile.

Chapter 20

Sorrow Draw, North Texas (September, 1881)

Erasmus Mothershed

The town of Sorrow Draw had built a parsonage for their preacher. Long before the Calamity, before Mothershed arrived, when the preacher was a young fellow by the name of Budd Halifax, the townsfolk had erected a small house near the church. Halifax had likely intended to raise a family, grow old, and die in that house. He did only the latter. A bout of dysentery laid him up for six months. The doctor tried everything to relieve his symptoms, calomel pills, bloodletting, and eventually only laudanum for the pain, but the bloody flux finally took him.

"In this very room," Erasmus said.

Lupe lay still on his stomach, his naked backside glimmered with sweat in the low light. They both breathed heavily, exhausted. Their sex was merciless and inflexible, as severe as the Wastes, but unlike the Wastes, it was also passionate and vigorous.

"Probably on this very bed." Lupe pushed himself up on his elbows.

"Oh, I'm sure they changed it out." Erasmus mounted him from behind, and Lupe's sweat chilled his flesh, but the body he laid on was hot. He gripped the boy's shoulders and felt the muscles under the skin, solid, like steel rope.

"Who changed it out?" Lupe asked.

"You know—they did. Someone. I'm sure of it." Erasmus slid himself between Lupe's thighs.

"Don't go mousing around back there with that. You've had enough. I need to get dressed and get a move on. Your father's sermon will be over soon." Lupe pushed him off and sat up. He was tall and lean, and Erasmus never could stop drinking him in, like cold rainwater.

"Don't. He's been running long. Lots of damnations and hell-fires. He's gotta get them Paluxy Boys worked up before he sets them out."

"I know. Would you rather I stay here and let them find us? I wonder which of us would hang for it? The minister's son, or the Indian bastard?"

Erasmus knew it wasn't a question. The Paluxy Boys never really needed a reason to string someone up, but it sure made it easier to have one, and finding them both together, doing what they were doing in the plain sight of God Himself, were plenty of reasons to hang an Indian, even a half-breed one. And while his father never much cared for him, he certainly wouldn't have his son killed. He'd tell his congregation that Erasmus had been tricked and corrupted by the Indian, and when Lupe's body swung in the breeze, he'd declare the taint was cleansed.

It was unfair of him to ask Lupe to take such a risk. "You're right, you're right," he said.

"It's not that I don't want to."

"I know."

"You're angry?"

"No."

"No?"

"No. Just...sad. It's not your fault."

They dressed in silence. He loved Lupe, he was sure of it. His sister would disagree. Hattie would laugh if he confessed it to her. She would tell him that he doesn't really know what love is. The love a man feels for another man isn't real love, she'd say. She didn't mind that he fucked Lupe, but she would draw the line at love.

But he didn't need Hattie's approval to know his own mind and his own heart. At first, Lupe had been a diversion. A bit of fun. He had never really been interested in the pleasures of the flesh. He thought it odd, and a bit gross, that other men were. The first time he had been with Lupe, he understood what all those other men had felt. But he had found that desire in the arms of another man.

A slow realization was beginning to dawn on him. If wanted to be happy, he would have to leave Sorrow Draw. They would be discovered eventually, no matter how careful they were, if they stayed in town they would be found out. It was only a matter of time. They would be caught in the act, and he wouldn't be able to deny anything. He wouldn't be able to dismiss it as rumors and slander. And now that Ransom was on to him, their time was nearly up. They had to leave Sorrow Draw together.

He tried to bring it up as they dressed, but the words caught in his throat. What if Lupe refused? Would he leave his mother? What if he was just making light with him, and didn't want to run off and risk his own life for Erasmus' love? What if he told him about what Ransom said, and he turns cold and breaks off their courtship?

It was too much to think about. But for Lupe's sake, he did have one suggestion that might help, if only temporarily.

"Lupe, I worry about you and your mother here. Things are getting dangerous. I don't know how long it'll be safe for you."

"We have nowhere to go, gringo. You know that. Mi madre, she—she's worried about marauders in the Wastes. The devil you know is better than the devil you don't."

"What about Serpent's Bluff? There's places there you can stay. Hell, join the Black Bitch's gang, they'll take care of you. And no one will even care if I bed you down."

"I had been thinking about it. I was…worried about how you'd feel. But if I go there, what about you? You come too?"

"I can't." His chest tightened at the thought. "I wish I could, but my father would find out, and he'd find out right quick. Then he'd send in the Paluxy Boys to bring me back. Could you imagine what those Freemen would do if Ransom Eisenhardt and his gang rode into Hill Lodge?"

Lupe grinned. "That would be one hell of a gunfight."

"One for the Ages. But the Freemen would lose. The Paluxy Boys have more men than even I know. A part of me is beginning to think my father is amassing an army. It would be a slaughter."

When Erasmus had finished dressing, he held out his arms and spun around. "How do I look?"

"Like a positive dandy. How about me?"

"Like a Nancy."

"Is that good?" Lupe asked.

Erasmus laughed. "Yes, for you, that's good." He straightened Lupe's dust scarf. "Do you think your ma will agree to go to Serpent's Bluff?"

"I can convince her. She knows people are turning against her. I think she's tired of hiding."

"Good. Now let's get you back home and me back to church."

The wind outside whipped at Erasmus' clothes and the sand it carried pricked at his skin. Before the door behind them had even closed, he saw 3 figures approach from out of the dusty fog, all three of them wore dust scarves and were armed with pistols on their hips.

"Good afternoon, gentlemen." The man in the middle spoke first. "A word with you, please."

Erasmus knew the voice and his heart sank. "Another word, Eisenhardt? I had my fill of your words yesterday. I thought I was clear on that point."

"Quite. But you see, that was 'fore you went missing during your pa's sermon. He looked a bit upset, you understand. He was looking for you while he was preaching and, well, you was nowhere to be found." Ransom was the kind of man who loved to hear himself talk. Erasmus believed a man needed two important qualities to become a good preacher—he needed brains and a love of his own voice. Ransom had the second part, it was a God-given trait he's had as long as Erasmus had known him, but he didn't have the brains for it. Ransom would someday run the Paluxy Boys, and he'll likely make himself preacher, but he'll be piss-poor at both. That's not to say that Erasmus thought Ransom to be stupid. He had his own kind of intelligence, but a good preacher needed book smarts and he had to understand how to manipulate people's emotions. A good preacher could fire their passions and stoke their hatreds. Ransom wasn't subtle enough for all that.

"And what business is it of yours where I go?"

"Your father was worried, and he's my concern. He's my business. He's our guide through these trials and we'd be lost without him. We didn't want him frettin' none over you, so me and Hoyt and Bad Eye here, we came looking for you. We heard some laughter in the old parsonage here and came to check it out."

Erasmus cursed himself silently. His laughter brought them here. "My father shouldn't concern himself with my comings and goings. And neither should his goons. I'm no child to be fretted over."

Ransom pulled down the dust scarf that covered his face. "What was you two doing in the parsonage?"

"I was showing my friend here the spot where the old minister died. You know, the one that shit himself to death in this very house. A tragic tale. The mood was so somber afterward I attempted to bring in a little levity with some jokes and laughter." Erasmus feigned annoyance, but his heart threatened to beat out of his chest. *This is just what the Paluxy Boys would use to justify hanging Lupe. Why wasn't I more cautious?*

Ransom smacked his lips. "You know what they say about you, don't you? I mean, you have to know. And yet you still put yourself in this position. Doesn't the Bible tell us to abstain from the appearance of evil? Yet here you are, decidedly not abstaining from a god damned thing."

Erasmus put his hands into the pockets of his long coat and fingered his gun. The cold metal stung his fingers, but its touch gave him some comfort. He wasn't much for gunplay, but he always kept his Colt Pocket Pistol on him, and this was the first occasion he had to be glad for it.

"Well, if two men spending some time together is evil, I wonder what's to be said about three men? You three seem to always be riding around Sorrow Draw together. What kind of clandestine gatherings do you fellows have?"

"You keep that tongue back in your mouth, you filthy little shit 'fore I cut it out," the one called Bad Eye said.

Ransom held his hand up. "You're a lost soul, Erasmus. Lost. But we still have time to bring you back into the fold. That's what your pa says, anyways. Me? I'm not too sure. Might be it's too late. But for your pa's sake, and for Hattie's, maybe we just string up your friend here and be done with it?"

Erasmus pulled the revolver from his pocket and leveled it at Ransom. "Run," he said to Lupe. "Do what we said. Don't wait for me. Now run."

Lupe hesitated, then disappeared into the haze. Bad Eye made a move to run after him, but Erasmus pointed his gun at him, and he stopped dead in his tracks. "No one moves or they get a lead ball in the chest. All of you, put your hands in the air."

Bad Eye and Hoyt raised their hands, but Ransom kept his down "I'm a pretty quick draw, you know. And you ain't no killer."

A slow smile spread across Erasmus' face. "You have no idea what I am."

Ransom's breath came harder. He spoke through tight lips. "Boy, you'd best put that piece down because I ain't fixin' to turn tail and run. Not to you. Not to a fuckin' Mary like you, no sir, you dandified fuck. I ain't against your pa, but so help me God if you don't put that down, I'll put you down, make no mistake."

Erasmus faltered, his smile evaporated, and fear tore at his heart. He was never much of a fighting man, and confrontation made his knees turn soft. He tried to speak, but couldn't find the nerve.

"Ransom." A small voice cut through the wind, delicate and familiar. Hattie. "Ransom, what are you going on about?"

"Nothing, ma'am," he said, his voice losing a bit of its edge. "Was just having a pow-wow with your brother here is all."

Erasmus lowered his gun.

"Now Ransom, I know you aren't teasing him, are you?" She put herself between the two men. "You know he's always been a might sensitive. I saw you heading this way and thought I'd come talk with you and imagine my surprise to find you giving my brother a tongue lashing."

"Beggin' your pardon, miss. I may have gotten a little carried away. Seems your brother and I don't see eye to eye on the natural order of things. We was just having a little philosophical debate, is all."

"Philosophy get your dander up all the time?"

"Yes it do, miss. Again, my apologies."

"Walk me home?" Hattie held her arm out to Ransom.

He turned to Erasmus and tipped his hat. "Another time. C'mon, boys."

Bad Eye moved to pick up his gun.

"Leave it," Erasmus said.

Bad Eye and Hoyt followed after Ransom and Hattie. Erasmus sat on the porch, all the energy and courage drained from his body all at once and he shivered with latent fear as much as the chill in the air. Hattie saved him. Saved him and Lupe. He knew exactly how much it had cost her, too. This had doubtless stoked the fire Ransom had for Hattie and would reinvigorate his efforts to pursue her. Unless Erasmus could figure out a way to get Hattie out of Sorrow Draw, or kill Ransom Eisenhardt without drawing suspicion, she was as good as married to him.

Erasmus sat by the fire in his mother's room and watched Eula Mothershed's affliction torture her. She writhed and groaned, her muscles convulsed and spasmed, her arms lurched out in front of her so she had all the appearance of an infant suffering from colic. She wailed, loud then soft, cursed then cried. She begged for help as best she could, but her face had lost all feeling and she struggled to form words.

Through it all, Reverend John Mothershed sat next to her, at times he held her hand, whispered to her, or prayed over her. At times she thanked him, other times she cursed him, often she forgot who she was, forgot how to speak, and was like an animal, a primordial creature who knew only pain, only agony.

Erasmus controlled his breathing and kept his thoughts and emotions in check. His father didn't tolerate anyone else's emotions but his own—his and Eula's. Any display of feelings other than anger would be met with contempt. When he was small, it had also been met with a fist. Erasmus learned how to hide feelings when people were near, and how to let them all out when he was alone. Hattie hated to be alone, so for him, solitude was an elusive thing. Even as children they didn't play much with other kids, and Hattie anchored herself to him.

He was a devoted brother. He had protected her as much as he could from their parents, though it was their mother they had to worry about most in those days. Their father was easy to avoid. Stay out from underfoot and be silent when he came around. Eula was harder to give a wide berth to, and the woman seemed always to have gone out of her way to find them and punish them for having been born, for having ruined her body, caused her pain in delivery, pain in her breasts to feed them before she gave them to her Negro slave to nurse. Their father had been cold and uncaring, but their mother had always gone out of her way to make them suffer.

And so he sat in his mother's room and watched her body and mind go to ruin, to wither and perish, and he had to hide his smile.

"Bring some laudanum." His father spoke to him without any address, without taking his eyes off of his wife.

"I gave her some an hour ago—"

"Do you take me for a fool? I was sitting right here when you gave it to her."

"Yes sir." Erasmus forgot himself. He should never have attempted an argument, but he didn't want his mother to have any relief. He brought a small, brown bottle to his father.

"You forget yourself, boy," his father said when he took the laudanum. "I will not have my authority countermanded, are we clear on that? As far as I know, this is still my house."

"Yes sir."

"Yes sir," his father repeated, thick with contempt. "Did I ever tell you how much of a disappointment you are to me, Erasmus? I named you after my father, your grandfather. He was a great man. A strong, proud man. I named you after him and you soiled his good name. He was strong and proud but look at you. You turned into everything but. A womanly sodomite, that's what you are."

"Yes sir." Erasmus felt the flush of shame in his cheeks and neck. He tried to focus on his mother so he wouldn't have to see his father's sneer, the disdain etched into his face.

"I know what you are. I know your deviant behavior. Everyone in town knows."

Erasmus swallowed hard. "Yes sir," he whispered.

Eula choked, saliva drenched her chin and neck, and dampened the front of her nightgown.

"But perhaps worst of all is you're useless. I have to marry your sister off to a man just to have someone to take over the church for me and carry on my legacy, someone with the nerve to continue to fight the good fight. If the Lord don't return before then."

Listening to his father berate him was like grieving a long-lost love. It's a dull ache that's always there, but sometimes the pain returns swift and fresh, born again, it emerges anew. He wanted to run, to hide, to find comfort again in Lupe's arms.

The Reverend took his wife's head in the crook of his arm and poured the laudanum down her throat. He cradled her gently and rocked her in his arms until her shakes subsided and she fell asleep.

Erasmus watched this tender exchange and the rancorous irony was very nearly palpable. Despite his sorrow, it almost made him want to smile. The only person that John Mothershed loved in all of creation was a woman who was incapable of feeling it herself.

His father seemed to sense his son's thoughts and his bitter animosity lost its bite.

"Get out of here," he said. "You'll take no more pleasure in your mother's suffering today."

"Yes sir," Erasmus whispered again. He spun on his heel and grabbed his coat.

He went to his room and lay in his bed and he watched the shadows of the dead trees outside his window flit back and forth across the walls like crooked spinner's legs. He poured a glass of absinthe and a few drops of laudanum. Things would be happening soon, and he could see the cascading effects of events, each one altering the course of his life, one after the other, but it was these intolerably long waits that he hated. Like watching a storm roll in slowly, the lightning flashed in the distance, moving inexorably closer, he could do nothing but wait for it to creep in and brace himself against the coming rain.

Chapter 21

Vicksburg, Old Mississippi (September, 1881)

Eudora Becker

She woke to the sound of distant screaming. It had come to her in her dreams, she was sure, though when she awoke the dream vanished, along with its memory. But the scream...the scream remained. It was a raw scream, primal and full of fear. She blinked her eyes and forced herself to remember. She thought, for a fleeting moment, that she didn't want to remember. Something warned her to stay mindless and unaware. Ignorance is bliss, after all.

She opened her eyes to darkness and the scent of stale water and moldy hay. Rot. The cold stone floor bit and scratched her cheek and she remembered. The jail. Vicksburg. Her body ached from a long night asleep on the floor and she tried to sit up but could do nothing more than roll onto her back and shake from the cold. She thought of her buffalo hide and the Indian who gave it to her and of her wool blanket and the man she shared it with.

"Jeremiah?" she whispered in the dark.

There was no answering sound.

"Jeremiah?" she called out again, louder this time.

Still no answer.

She rolled onto her stomach and crawled to the bars that separated the two cells. She peered through, her eyes searched the blackness for a body, but the cell was empty.

Her heart jumped and panic threatened to take over her senses. Where did they take him? Why did they take him? Why didn't they take her? Eudora fought against the onslaught of questions. Right now it would do no good to speculate. Too many possibilities. And yet, time to think about all those possibilities was all she had. Why not sift through them in her mind and scratch out the one that was the most reasonable?

Well, you wanted to rid yourself of him, now you've got your wish.

But she never reckoned it would happen this way. Her teeth chattered. The frigid air had become too unbearable. Maybe that's what happened. Maybe Jeremiah froze to death, and they took his body out and now he's buried somewhere in Vicksburg. Then a sudden and terrifying thought occurred to her. Did those screams belong to Jeremiah? She recalled them in her mind. They sounded like a man's screams, so it certainly was possible. And Jeremiah is no longer in his cell.

She laid down on her side and hugged her legs to her chest. Eudora wept. Everything had fallen apart. She knew when they started that it was a dangerous thing. She knew her father would send someone after them. She knew it was especially dangerous for Jeremiah. Governor Becker would never punish his little girl and she had planned to let Jeremiah take the fall if they ever did get caught. She'd tell her father that he stole not just the money, but her as well. Her father wouldn't hesitate to believe her. But this was something that her smile and innocent rouse couldn't fix.

That remains to be seen. She reminded herself.

She lay curled up on the floor for an intolerably long time, her body wracked with spasms and her feet and hands painfully numb. She started to drift off to sleep, and a part of her knew that if she did fall asleep, she would never again wake up. Once she accepted that, it became easier for her to stop fighting. She was tired of being cold. Each convulsion sent waves of pain through her body.

The mechanical clank of a key turning a lock wrested her from her thoughts. She sucked in her breath. They're coming for me now. The screech of iron on iron echoed through the jail, and the door at the end of the corridor opened.

The man was tall and had to lower his head to walk through the door but, unlike Horsethief, he appeared thin and wiry. The matted clumps of hair seemed to sit atop his head, rather than being a thing that grew out of it. He carried a small bag and something else that Eudora couldn't quite make out.

"Jesus, it's colder than the Dickens." He stood in front of the cell door and appraised her. He had a thin beard that grew sparse. In the darkness, Eudora couldn't tell if that was from youth or from living a lean and severe life, as most of them did.

She struggled to decide on the right course of action—which Eudora should she be to this new man? But the sight of him made her bile rise and she decided she didn't want to be any Eudora to him.

"Here." He slid something large between the bars of the cell. "This was yours, I believe."

Her buffalo hide.

Eudora found an instant reserve of strength. She lunged for it, pulled it through the bars, and wrapped the thick fur hide around her whole body. She collapsed back on the stone floor and breathed deeply the scent of the Indian again.

"You look hungry." He tossed the bag he carried at her feet and crossed his arms. Eudora picked it up. As soon as she did, she smelled the sweet aroma of cooked meat. The bag was a cheesecloth wrap that her trembling and numb fingers struggled to open. She didn't know who this man was, or what he wanted from her, but so long as he gave her meat, she would stomach the sight of him. How much farther she could let it go remained to be seen.

She had eaten meat like this on occasion. There were still small animals that scurried around the Wastes that could sometimes be caught, and she could often convince men to part with the best pieces. Horses tended to get old, sick, or lame and have to be put down. Those times there would be an abundance of meat and her father would make sure that she got the best cuts.

When she had finally got the steak unwrapped, she devoured it. The bites she took were too big and she had trouble breathing while she chewed, but she couldn't help it. The meat was so hot it still steamed in the frigid air, and the heat warmed her fingers and they started to tingle and burn like they were being pricked by a thousand thorns. She ate through the pain, the weep from the meat dripped down her chin and her arms. The man looked at her with a smile.

"Delicious, yes?" he said.

Eudora nodded, still eating. The food had caught her off-guard but, even as she continued to eat, she thought again about how to best play her part. The man seemed to have some interest in keeping her alive. Warm and fed. Yet why didn't he come sooner? Why leave her here so long, almost to the edge of death itself, before he came to revive her? And what of Jeremiah? She considered for a moment, then thought against asking after his well-being. Perhaps it was best to distance herself from him now. Eventually, she'd find out. No sense in setting up Jeremiah as a rival to these men here by demanding to know where they took him. No, he would have to take care of himself, wherever he was.

And I am on my own, too.

She swallowed the last piece of steak and licked her fingers. Perhaps it was because she had been traveling through the Uncontested Lands for weeks eating nothing but hardtack and scorpions and she was on the verge of death and starvation, but she couldn't remember the last time she had meat that tasted so sweet.

Eudora awoke to the soft pat of water dripping somewhere beyond the walls of her cell. She couldn't tell how long it had been since she had spoken with the ugly fellow who brought her buffalo hide and gave her food. Days and nights were meaningless. They barely had meaning outside the confines of a prison and inside the difference between the two were impossible to discern. She knew only darkness and pain. A few times, someone had left her meat that she would quickly devour. She relieved herself in the corner and after a time, she could no longer smell that either.

At times she cried and longed to be back in her room in her father's mansion in Memphis, sitting by the fire and eating boiled eggs and buttered bread, still warm and steaming. No more thoughts or possibilities came to her. No more plans or schemes. She waited for whatever fate would bring, and when nothing came, she waited more.

There was a turn of a key and the shriek of iron hinges. Footsteps echoed down the short corridor to her cell and Eudora struggled to turn over and see what new thing had come down to visit her.

"Good, you're awake." It was a woman's voice. "I was afraid I'd have to wake you up before I started." She carried an oil lamp in one hand and a bucket in the other. Water splashed from the bucket when she set it down in front of Eudora.

"Drink," the woman said. "Drink as much as you can first. Then we'll wash you."

Eudora crawled to the bucket; her forgotten thirst came back with a sudden force that threatened to drive her mad if she didn't drink. She took great mouthfuls of cold water and her body shed its weariness with each swallow.

"That's enough for now," the strange woman said. She slid the bucket away with her foot. "Time to get you cleaned up a bit."

"I don't want a bath, I'm cold." There was still a chill in the air, though it wasn't quite as bad as when Eudora was first brought to the cell. But the prospect of cold water splashing over her bare skin didn't sit well with her.

"You'll have to get used to that," the woman said. "We're all cold here. The Magistrate keeps it that way. He likes the cold, so as I said, you better just get used to it."

"I want to go," Eudora said. Sometimes she could convince women to do what she wants, same as men. Some women liked to be mothers, and this woman looked like she played the part of a mother. Eudora could play the role of child as easily as she could play the harlot. "Please. I don't want to be here. I'm not supposed to be here."

"I know, child, I know. But that's out of my hands. I can look out for you while you're here though." She soaked a rag in the bucket and scrubbed Eudora's face.

The cold water stung, and the pain gave her new vitality. Like a broken dam, her mind flooded with possibilities. She could overpower this woman and make a run for the desert. She could survive on her own, she just needed some supplies. Those could be scavenged from the nearly untouched shops on the main road. She'd be without her horse, but her tracks would disappear quicker without one. The only thing that stood in her way now was the woman in front of her.

I could take her out like I did that bounty hunter. She looked around for a rock or something she could use to club the woman over the head with.

"If you're thinking about running, you won't make it," the woman said. "There's guards outside the door. Besides, in your condition, a little thing like you couldn't get passed me."

All the fight drained from Eudora.

"My name is Delilah, but my friends call me Lily. What's your name?"

"Eudora."

"What do your friends call you?"

"I ain't got friends."

"I'm sure you do."

"I don't. Just Jeremiah. He called me Dora. Where is he?"

"That the man you come here with?"

"Yes. He's my man. Where is he?"

The woman hesitated. There was something behind them, either fear or pity, Eudora couldn't tell which. "I think maybe the Magistrate should tell you about your man. That one's on him. It's only my job to wash you."

"Who is the Magistrate? What does he want with me and Jeremiah?"

"He's my son. His father was a city judge here before the Calamity and Edward—that's my son's Christian name—he just sort of took it upon himself to take his father's place. That was about a year or so ago. Things were awfully uncivilized back then and the men here needed some law and order, something fierce."

"Yeah, I've seen men's ideas of law and order in the Wastelands and I want none of it. I ain't done nothing wrong, so I ain't broke no laws. Just give me my man back and let us go."

"I'm sorry, sweetheart, it ain't my decision to make. I'll do my best to make you comfortable, but first I need to wash you up. And if you keep refusing me, I'll just bring the Magistrate in here and I can hold you down while he does the scrubbing."

Eudora let the woman called Delilah wash her body. The frigid water burned her skin, and she took to shaking so badly by the time it was over, that Delilah had some warm coffee brought in for her, with a bit of hardtack. The coffee was old and tasted terrible, but it warmed her gut. Eudora let the hardtack soak for a few minutes before she ate it.

Once Delilah left, Eudora tried to take stock of her situation. She wrapped herself in her buffalo hide and planned what she might say to the Magistrate. Delilah had told her that she would have to stand trial soon but warned her that the trials were something of a farce and the Magistrate already knew what he was going to do with her. She became tight-lipped from there and wouldn't answer any more of Eudora's questions.

***

It was sometime later that Horsethief came. He crept in silently, the creak of the iron hinges made only a small sound, but it was loud enough for Eudora to hear it, even above the howling wind outside the jail. As soon as his silhouette came into view, Eudora knew it was him. Her heart raced and her legs found renewed strength. She stood up and ran to the cell door. The Indian meant rescue, escape, and freedom.

"Horsethief," she called out to him.

He smiled and put his hand through the bars, touching her cheek.

"How did you get past the guards?" she asked.

"There's no guards."

"Delilah told me there were guards at the door."

"Delilah must have lied to you then."

"That bitch." Eudora seethed. She could have escaped earlier but she made the mistake of believing a strange lady who came to her jail cell with a bucket of water.

"Your captors will always lie to you, remember that."

"Well, I don't plan to get myself captured again any time soon, so hopefully I won't have to worry about it. Especially now that I have you."

"That's a good plan."

"Speaking of plans, how do you plan to get me out of this cell?"

Horsethief pulled a key from his pocket and put it in the lock. It turned with a metallic clank and he swung the door wide. "It was hanging on the wall," he said.

He lifted her and she allowed him to carry her out of the jail to his waiting horse. The air outside was colder, but he held her tight against his chest and kept her warm. Darkness was on the Wastelands, but Eudora scarcely noticed. Her fear of the dark and of desert nights had been tempered by her time in Vicksburg, and this man who carried her away from it.

Horsethief pulled a bag off the saddle and handed it to her. "Your things," he said. "They left your saddle bags lying around. They didn't even care to go through them."

She grabbed the bag and rifled through it—everything was still there. Her clothes, revolver, and all the money they stole from her father. All here and all untouched. Did Horsethief look through the bag, she wondered. How much did the Indian know about her situation now? She figured she'd have to tell him everything soon enough anyway if she expected him to take her to California.

She dressed quickly and wrapped herself back up in her buffalo hide as soon as she had her clothes back on. Horsethief waited for her in the saddle and put out a hand to help her up.

"Wait," she said when he had mounted his horse and settled her in front of him. "I know he's a bit of an idiot, but can we find Jeremiah? I don't think it would be right for me to just leave him here."

"I checked on him. Your man is already dead."

She was afraid to hear those words, but her heart had told her it was the truth before she even asked. "How did he die? What did they do to him?" Her voice sounded so small.

"You don't want to know, girl."

"Yes, I do."

"I won't lie to you."

"I know."

"These people are cannibals," he said.

He kicked the horse into a canter and Eudora bounced rhythmically with it. She thought about Jeremiah, about his promise to her to take her to California, about the money they took, and how far they had come together. Tears fell and she didn't know why. There was no great love between the two, least not from her, but she cried, and that made her angry. She thought of the meat they fed her, how the weep dripped from her hands, how sweet it tasted. She leaned over the saddle and vomited. Horsethief pulled the horse to a stop. He dropped the reins and put one arm around her waist, the other held her hair back as he hummed a soft and sad melody into the winds.

Chapter 22

Vicksburg, Old Mississippi (September, 1881)

Nikki Free

It was in Vicksburg that Nikki found out what happened to Preacher. They arrived at the outskirts of the city the morning of the fifth day, the cold made the travel slow as the horses got ornery in freezing weather. The bulk of the town sat atop a terrace that, under better conditions, would have overlooked the river. Nikki couldn't see the town from where she sat on her horse, but the signs of battle were all around her. Something big had happened here, a long time ago. Channels and ditches were cut out of the ground in long lines, running parallel to each other, half buried in sand and dust. Cannons, great wooden engines, scaffolds, and gantries knifed out of the ground like heinous skeletons, titanic horrors of war. Evidence of an arduous conflict, long buried under dust and sand.

"What happened here?" Nikki asked.

"A battle," Conny answered. "Union army laid siege to Vicksburg for months trying to gain control of the Mississippi. Both sides dug trenches up and down this area. They fought like hell for every inch of ground. When that got them nowhere, they tried damming up and rerouting the whole river. Eventually, they just surrounded the city and starved a surrender out of the Rebs. It was quite a victory. Made for great headlines in the Northern papers. A few weeks later, the Calamity hit, so it was all for naught."

"Imagine all that death and for nothing." Nikki imagined the bodies lying under the dust, frozen and mummified. Men ordered from their homes to fight far away. Rebels torn apart by cannon shot, taken to the sawbones to have their legs and arms cut off, screaming in agony. It made her heart glad. They got what they deserved. She felt a little sympathy for the northern soldiers, most of them died a few weeks before they would have died anyway, but also most of them likely didn't give a damn about her or slavery, they fought for the same reason the Rebels fought: because they were told to. She wondered how long their bodies would lie there under all that dust, mouths open in silent, fleshless screams.

They took a road that went straight up to the city center. Nikki was tense and uneasy. They expected people, Conny thought perhaps a hundred or so, but Vicksburg showed them no signs of life yet. Nikki wasn't sure if that was an ill omen or not. Good or bad, she kept her free hand on a holstered pistol at her side.

"Alright." Farhad spoke up first. "What's the plan, Con?"

Conny reigned in his horse. He looked unsure. "I suppose we look for signs of Eudora and Preacher. See if anyone lives here. If they came through, they'd be able to tell us how long ago they'd been here. If we're lucky, it wasn't that long ago. If we're really lucky, they're still here."

"Shit. Don't seem like anyone's here at all." Farhad's eyes darted this way and that. *He's as nervous as I am.*

"We'll start in the middle," Conny said. "First, we check out the courthouse. And we stay together so no one gets lost. And in case there's any trouble."

Conny led the way up the road. At the top of the hill, Nikki could just make out the rust-colored silhouette of a large building. It had all the markings of a white man's courthouse. It loomed over the town from its highest point. Its garish columns, like a row of fangs, echoed the influence of the Romans, another dead empire, the model of the white man's justice in America. But it was false. Black and rotten from the inside. Justice for the few, justice for those with money to spare, with the right color skin, with a cock between their legs. She had none of those things and would not have found any justice in that place.

"Keep your eyes skinned." Conny kicked his horse forward.

Nikki figured they must be on the main thoroughfare through town. The wide street had plenty of old shops lining its gutters. Nikki counted two grocers already, a farrier, and a Merchant's Bank. After a row of homes and saloons, she made note of a small haberdashery with a second-story millinery once run by a Mrs. Emma Buchner, as the sign in the window advertised. Haberdashers and milliner's shops were excellent places to scavenge luxury items and so long as she had some extra room in her saddlebags, she didn't see the harm in picking up a few incidental items. Least of all Conny wouldn't trouble her over it. No, that poor boy was too taken with her to trifle over some hats and gloves.

The wind started to pick up and they had to stop and put dust masks on the horses and wrap *keffiyehs* around their faces. Conny handed her a pair of goggles. They were made of green-tinted glass set in a thick leather frame.

"Where'd you get these?" They were a curious artifact. She had never seen anything quite like them before.

"Feller back in Memphis goes by the name of Lefty Richardson. Said they had something to do with steam engines. They used them for shoveling coal into the boilers so they didn't get ash in their eyes."

"Well, I'll be."

"Lefty always was full of horseshit, Con." Farhad tied his goggles behind his head, then settled his *keffiyeh* back in place. "Boy had that wobblin' jaw. Even he never knowed what he was sayin' half the time."

"No matter I 'spose. They work out here all the same." Conny helped Nikki with her goggles. The world closed in on her. It was surprising how much she relied on the edges of her vision, and when they were gone, a silent panic settled in. It was like looking at the world through a dulled and dirty window with the curtains half-drawn.

They rode up to the courthouse at the top of the hill. By the time they reached the steps of the lofty building, the savage wind threatened to cut through her scarf. Nikki marveled at how well it held up. Farhad taught her how to wrap it so it wouldn't come undone, but she knew the Wasteland desert had a way of getting what it wanted and a relentless hunger to tear things down, to uncover and erase the memory of mankind.

They hitched their horses on the windless side of the courthouse and rushed in. Nikki pulled the goggles off her face, thankful for the relief, but something wasn't right. She looked around and took stock of the situation. Conny and Farhad were behind her, taking their glasses and scarves off. She smelled the air. Just dust. The long hallway in front of her was lined with portraits, local politicians and judges, most likely, lit sporadically by oil lamps—shit. She dropped the goggles, and her revolver was in her hand before they hit the floor.

"Conny, lamps are lit," she whispered. She heard the two men behind her draw. "Someone's here."

"Yeah, looks like it." Conny's voice didn't travel far over the sound of the wind outside. "Alright," he whispered, "we move slow, check the courtroom, that's where they'd likely be."

"Why?" Nikki asked.

"I don't know, just feels right. Biggest room and all."

"What if there's only a few of them and they don't need a big room?" Farhad moved in front. He walked slowly down the hallway.

"Well, my guess is if there isn't many of them, then they wouldn't need to be holed up in the courthouse. One of them smaller places would do."

"Maybe they just wanted to feel—" A woman's laugh pierced the low rumble of the maelstrom outside.

The gun in Nikki's hand trembled, but it wasn't fear. Fear was a familiar sensation. No, Nikki wasn't afraid of what they might find—she was excited. The possibility of a shootout in the courthouse filled her with a warmth that confused her at first. But why not? She had spent so much of her life as someone's chattel, as a commodity for another man, then for The Faith in Commerce. Here, though, she had power. She held life and death in her hand, and it was beautiful. The smooth grip, the trigger on her finger, and the weight of the iron in her grasp, all felt right. She could put a bullet in a man's head before he could lay a finger on her. Her heart raced at the thought.

They inched slowly down the corridor, guns level. Muffled sounds beat against the door at the end of the hall. Laughter. Breaking glass. Someone played a piano. More laughter. Flickering light escaped from the bottom and through the cracks, catching the dust that drifted through the air. Nikki took a deep breath.

They reached the end of the hall and Farhad stopped them. "Sounds like this is some honest festivities, Con. Maybe we shouldn't kick in the door with our irons skinned. Might give them the wrong idea and start some bloodshed for nothing."

"What do you suggest?" Nikki asked. She had been itching for a fight and the thought of losing it now that they were so close didn't sit right. Vicksburg was an old rebel holdout. Some of the men here likely were Confederates long ago. Some may even have owned slaves. Least of all, they tolerated it. Maybe some were Union soldiers, like Conny, but killing a few Confederate men seemed a bit like justice deferred, rather than cold-blooded killing. But no innocents needed to die, either.

A scream tore through the air from behind the door. The unmistakable sound of pain. Nikki knew it all too well. Any doubt about how to handle the situation vanished. Conny leaned back and kicked in the door, the wood around the frame exploded in a cloud of splinters.

Nikki was the first to rush in. The revolver in her hand searched for a target, for someone to level on, someone responsible for the woman in agony. Every sound stopped. In the tense silence, Nikki managed to get a quick sense of her surroundings. The room was large but mostly empty. The piano sat in the corner, with a naked woman at the keys. In the center of the room, there were bodies, naked bodies, in a mass behind the sweet smoky haze of opium. Arms and legs tangled, every limb frozen and eyes stared, wide-eyed at the new intruders and the guns leveled on them.

They were all, save one, women.

The lone man sat in a high seat at the judge's bench in the back, an unclothed woman lying on the bench in front of him. She looked like a meal set out for some demonic villain. The man stood and Nikki watched him from down the barrel of her revolver. He got up on the bench and held out his arms, as naked as the rest.

"Firearms are not permitted in the Vicksburg courthouse, friends. I'm afraid I'm going to have to ask you to leave them at the door."

His thin frame was impossibly lean, and his sallow skin seemed pulled tight across his skeleton.

"Who are you?" Farhad asked.

"I'm the Magistrate. This is my courthouse." Long hair clung together in thick cords that snaked down the skin of his pallid back. He stepped down and walked towards them.

Nikki felt the bile rise in her throat. "We heard a scream." She let her hand relax but still kept the gun pointed at the Magistrate.

"Ah, that was poor Constance." He pointed to a woman in the center of the writhing mass of flesh. "She gets a bit—vocal in her pleasures."

"We're mighty sorry to have disturbed your—" Conny searched for the word.

"Proceedings?" the Magistrate offered.

"—Proceedings. We're looking for some people who took something that doesn't belong to them. If you could give us any information, we'd be obliged and on our way." Conny also still had his gun leveled at the Magistrate.

"You bandits come into my courtroom—a place of law and order—brandishing firearms, and you have the nerve to make demands?" He waved a dirty finger at them. "No no no no no."

"We're bounty hunters from Memphis," Conny said. "We're looking for a woman, goes by the name Eudora, and a man who calls himself Preacher. If you seen 'em, just point us in the right direction. If not, then I'm sorry to have troubled the lot of you."

Conny had patience, and Nikki loved that about him, but she didn't see any sense in indulging a troupe of naked opium smokers. This Magistrate suffered from delirium and in her experience, the best way to deal with a man whose mind was addled with drugs and whiskey, was to be as direct as possible. "Have you seen them?" she asked. "Yes or no. It's as simple as that. Yes or no."

The Magistrate walked right up to Nikki, his chest inches away from her revolver. Her finger twitched. She didn't quite know why, but she just knew the world would be a better place without this wretch drawing any more breath.

The Magistrate licked his lips. "Since when does a woman—and a Negro besides—come into my courtroom and sling directives at me?" He spoke to her with a contempt that startled Nikki. She had almost managed to convince herself that her days of being talked to like she was a dog, full of contempt and loathing, were over. Conny and Farhad had treated her so well, and talked to her so kindly, as an equal, it made her forget that there were still people in what was left of the world who looked at her as if she were an animal.

But Nikki had something now that she didn't before. A revolver in her hand. She smiled. "Listen to me, you filthy shit. Tell us if you've seen the two we're after or not before this Negro puts a bullet through one of your knees." She lowered her revolver. "Or maybe I'll shoot off that that sorry little thing between your legs."

A woman laughed.

Nikki felt as if the Magistrate was appraising her, judging her value. It wouldn't do to shoot him now, but it couldn't hurt once they had gotten what they needed from him. In fact, it might just help tip the balance of the world a little back to the good side.

The Magistrate laughed, an exaggerated caricature of a laugh. His open mouth flashed a row of jagged, broken teeth like a line of shattered whiskey bottles. The stench of rot nearly made Nikki gag. He walked back to his bench along the back wall and sat down. "You're bounty hunters. I assume you operate with the full consent of the law?"

"Jesus Christ, man," Conny said. "What law? Open your damn eyes. Come to your damn senses. We both know there ain't no law out here in the Wastes."

"No law? No, my bounty hunter friend, there has always been law. Maybe you've been eager to rid yourself of it, but the law has been written and it is unchangeable." He held up a thick book. It could have been a book of law, it could have been a Bible, Nikki couldn't tell. "The law doesn't care about the weather outside. It was written by the hand of man and codified by the blood of our brothers."

The Magistrate's voice echoed through the empty room.

Farhad holstered his revolver. He motioned to Conny and said a single word in his tongue. "*Sakoud*." He drew himself up, stiffening his back, and bowed to the Magistrate. It was a pompous, theatrical bow with a hint of concealed mockery.

"Your Honor." He addressed the naked man sitting at the judge's bench. "Forgive my friends, here if you please. We've traveled long in the Wastes, and it does tend to addle the mind."

The Magistrate offered a conciliatory nod.

"We do indeed operate under the full consent of the law in seeking to apprehend two known fugitives and bring them to justice. Being a man of law yourself, we hoped to presume that you might counsel us on our next course of action."

Nikki saw little point in appeasing the man. They held all the power here and yet now they seemed reluctant to use it. They had him dead to rights, three gunfighters against one man whose mind was lost to Calamity. He held these women against their will, or at the very least, failed to provide for them and she saw no scenario in which these women would not be better off if she didn't just shoot this Magistrate where he stood.

"I like your tone," the ghoulish man said. "Where are you from, foreigner?"

"Memphis."

"That's not what I meant. Where is your ancestral home?"

"Syria."

"The Holy Land? I see. Well, I'm afraid for you, that I've already accomplished one step in your task, the other, however, eluded me."

"What step?"

"We brought one of your outlaws to justice already, but the other has escaped us."

Conny looked first at Farhad and then at Nikki, his brows furrowed in confusion, a look that Farhad returned.

"Who have you brought to justice, and how?" the Bedouin asked.

"Preacher. He's stood trial here in this very courtroom no longer than a week ago, I'd reckon it was. They both did, him and his girl."

"What crime did they commit here?"

"Heresy. Preacher was a charlatan. Claimed to be a man of God, but I saw right through him. The man didn't know his scriptures to save his life. So, we put him on trial in front of a jury of his peers and they were found guilty. The man was sentenced to death, but the woman, well, she was guilty only of fornicating with a criminal, so she was spared the severest punishment. She was sentenced to live out her days here, never to see the promised land they sought."

"So you executed him?"

"Yes."

Nikki suspected the cock between Preacher's legs is what earned him an execution. And if Crowkiller's description of Eudora had been remotely accurate, it was her lithesome figure and full tits that spared her. Every single person in the room was a woman or a girl, except for the Magistrate himself. Most were women of child-bearing years, some with scars to prove it. Some were of age, yet had never carried a child, and some were only children. Yet all of them were naked, dirty, and thin, even by the standards of these remote and desolate places in the Wastes. A picture began to emerge, a vision of what happened in this place years ago that brought it to its current state, and it centered on the Magistrate lording over what was left of this town from his high bench.

"Can we see his body? So we can identify him as our man? No sense in chasing after ghosts, but we'd like to make sure it's our guy."

"There is no body." The Magistrate flashed his wicked brown teeth. "A few bones you can look at, if you want. Not enough to tell who it was when he was living, though."

"Did you burn him?"

"In a manner of speaking, yes." He trailed a finger down the side of the girl in front of him. She hadn't taken her eyes off of Nikki since the gunslinger came in. Nikki shivered at the thought of that skeletal finger on her own skin, like one of the bone necklaces Abhartach made from the hands of his enemies.

"We ate him." A young girl, withered in frame, sat up and spoke. How old is she, Nikki wondered. Twelve? Thirteen? Hard to tell when starvation can delay the body from maturing. "We were hungry."

Cannibalism was a far more common practice in the deep places of the Wastes than anyone would like to admit, but it was still reviled among civilized people. And Nikki considered herself, if nothing else, civilized. The Wastes hadn't taken her humanity, and she'd sooner die than let it. Whatever obligation she had to decorum that stayed her hand, whatever kept her instinct to end the life of this man in check, had withered and decayed like an atrophied limb, like the flesh from the bones of the women surrounding her.

"God, and the law, provided in our need," said the Magistrate.

"Amen to that." Farhad voice strained just a bit. He swallowed hard.

Conny didn't meet the Magistrate's gaze, but stood with his head down now, shifting his weight from one foot to the other.

"So any idea then where the woman went off to? You said she escaped?" Farhad pressed on.

Nikki no longer cared about the girl, the money, or California. Right now she wanted to set this situation right, and that meant this man on high, who stank of piss and rotted meat, this living corpse, would have to be removed from the world. Conny had told her once that when he rode into Memphis with Becker, Farhad, and Crowkiller, he felt like they were the Four Horsemen of the Apocalypse spoken of in *Revelation*. Now the three of them were the Furies. The Erinyes of myth, and she would exact retribution on those who violated the natural order of the world, starting here.

"I don't know," the Magistrate said. "She ran off into the Wastes by herself, so I assume she's as good as dead. She headed west. The three of you should have no trouble catching up to her. Especially if you came with horses? Yes?"

Farhad didn't fall for the bait, of course, he was too clever for such an obvious ruse. "Sadly they were stolen back near Commerce a few weeks ago. Indians got to them. We've been trudging through the Uncontested Lands on foot ever since, always one step behind our quarry." He shook his head dramatically. "You wouldn't happen to have any horses we could trade for, would you?"

"Vicksburg hasn't seen a horse in over a decade, I'm afraid. No, it seems you'll have to just walk faster than that wench if you want to catch up with her. She's a quick little thing, that one. If I were you, I'd leave right away."

She had to get herself into a better shooting position. The Magistrate was positioned just above the woman on the bench, and Nikki didn't trust herself enough with a revolver to risk accidentally shooting her.

"Conny? Nikki? What do you think?"

Conny spoke first. "I 'spose it would be right if we left these good people to their revelry. I think it might be best, like he says, to head out now before we lose Eudora's trail. We are obliged to your hospitality, though Your Honor."

Nikki understood the need for diplomacy, but it sickened her all the same that these two men were so easily persuaded to leave these women to their fates. They had rescued her, after all, why not these women? Were they not also in desperate need of liberation as she had been? She inched her way to the side, feigning interest in the young girl who had spoken to them.

"There is the small matter of payment for the court's hospitality, and for doing your job in apprehending a known outlaw. What was your bounty worth? The court will levy a fee of half the bounty's value."

Nikki could already see where this was going. She had been treated as a commodity her whole life, and this man valued only one thing. She could feel Conny's eyes on her, boring into her. She knew if she met those eyes, she might lose the nerve that she had built up.

"Well, like I told you, Your Honor," Farhad said. "We have no horses, no real gear that we can part with and still survive. Only food we got's a little bit of hardtack. You'll have to make do with our thanks and promise to pay once we can collect on the bounty."

"You have the Negro. Mississippi is a slave-holding state, by God and by law. That would be sufficient payment, I reckon."

Nikki seethed.

Conny drew his revolver and took aim at the Magistrate. "You best hold that diseased tongue of yours inside that mouth. It seems you forgot who has the weapons here and who don't and I've had enough of this little game you're playing. Now this woman right here is Miss Nikki Free and you'd do best to remember that name. You understand me? Say it now before I put a bullet between those eyes."

That was unexpected, and Nikki felt a brief moment of guilt for doubting Conny.

"Get out of my courtroom." The Magistrate growled.

Conny pulled the hammer on his revolver back. "I said 'say her name.'"

Farhad fingered the pearl-inlaid handles of his revolver. "You know, you'd be a daisy if you did. I'd go ahead and say her name, if you want to stay above snakes, friend."

Nikki held back tears. These men, who had rescued her from torture and death, who had accepted her as she was, as another human being traveling through the world, of no less value because of the color of her skin or former life as a slave, these men had stepped up to defend her honor.

She belonged. They were family.

Conny walked up to the bench, through the crowd of women and girls on the floor who now almost all were sitting up, some with expressions of fear, others curiosity, still some more with a hope bordering on hunger. "I'm going to give you one more chance. Say her name. Or I paint the back wall with what's left of your brains."

"Nikki." He spat the name out.

"Nikki what?"

The Magistrate swallowed hard. "Nikki Free," he said.

Nikki went to Conny's side, her revolver still aimed at the Magistrate's head. "You're goddamn right."

She almost pulled the trigger right then and there, but Conny put a gentle hand on her shoulder.

"Let's go, Miss Nikki Free. There ain't nothing else for us here. We got a trail to pick up."

Nikki allowed Conny to lead her away. A sea of faces looked up at her. Most of them had that thin sort of hopeless expression—a common look in the Wastelands. She saw a young child, reckoned her age around eight or nine, with skin darker than her own and wide brown eyes like saucers blinking in the torchlight. The girl's small, naked body shivered in the cold. Her bloated belly and tiny swollen breasts bore witness to the sins of the man behind the bench. Nikki stopped. Her guns were heavy on her hips and the reek of urine burned her nostrils. Every breath the Magistrate took was one more than he deserved.

Conny put his hand back on her shoulder. "Come on," he whispered. "He has no power over you."

Nikki put her left hand to his face. His unshaven chin scratched at her palm. His face was hard and rough, like a pumice stone. "You really are a good man, Cornelius White. But this ain't for me."

She skinned her revolver clean from its holster and fired. The Magistrate's neck blew open. A fountain of blood sprayed out as if it had been desperate to escape. He grabbed his neck with his hands, an expression of shock and confusion on his face, and fell straight to the ground as if a hole had opened from Hell itself to swallow him up.

The woman on the bench screamed.

Nikki closed her eyes and inhaled the sulfurous cloud of gunsmoke and the flesh rose on her arms.

Somewhere behind her, a girl laughed.

Chapter 23

The Wastes, Somewhere Between Sorrow Draw and Serpent's Bluff (September, 1881)

Hattie Mothershed

The sun had gone down on the Wastes by the time Hattie left Sorrow Draw for Hill Lodge. The wind had died down, but the dust still thickened the frigid air, so she pulled her scarf tight around her face. Visibility on the flats between the two towns was so poor that Erasmus had been forced to tie a rope between them to ensure they didn't get separated.

He had brought his lover, and his lover's mother, with them. They walked behind, and Hattie couldn't help her irritation at the intolerably slow pace they set. The mother, Maria, limped along, weighted down by the accumulation of years. Lupe walked attentively beside her, himself burdened with what little he could carry across flats.

Erasmus carried a full carpetbag that Hattie suspected belonged to their companions. It irritated her that he put himself out like he did. He had never given much thought or attention to anyone other than himself, yet the dandy had that carpetbag over his shoulder and walked across the Wastes with not so much as a single complaint.

She scolded herself silently. To be fair, Erasmus had dedicated a good deal of his life and attention to her. Growing up he had been her protector, her strength, and her shield from their mother. If he could now find the room in his heart for someone else, perhaps he had earned that happiness. Jealousy is an insidious beast, Hattie.

But her legs ached with the need to move faster and no one else shared in her frustrations, so loneliness and a sense of isolation set in. She pulled on her rope, drawing Erasmus closer.

"How far have we come?" she asked him.

"My guess is we're about halfway. Five miles by my reckoning," he answered.

"How do you know which way to go? I don't see any trail." She had been wondering about this for a while. The constant wind made trail-making a difficult task. Those who tried found that a trail would begin to vanish in the dust before it had even been finished. The people of Sorrow Draw learned long ago that roads were not sustainable in the Wastes.

"There's markers. They're tough to find, especially in the cover of darkness, but they're there."

"What markers? I haven't seen anything." She glanced about and saw nothing but the unbearable ocean of dust and blackness.

"Cairns," he said, in a manner that suggested he thought the matter to be closed.

"What? What's that?" She hadn't been this far from Sorrow Draw since the Calamity, and if something happened to her—if she got lost—she needed to know how to find her way back.

"Cairns," he repeated, as if that cleared up her confusion. "They're stacks of rocks. They line the road, ten or so every mile."

"There's lots of rocks out here. How do you know they aren't just any old rocks?"

"Well, they're stacked, like I said. I'll show you the next one. They're not stacked in any natural way. Each one points in the direction of the next and there's almost a hundred between Sorrow Draw and Hill Lodge."

"If we passed so many, why haven't I seen them?"

Erasmus shifted the carpetbag onto his other shoulder. "They've mostly been out in the distance, at the edge of the torchlight. Didn't really have a reason to walk right up on them. And if you don't know to look for them, you'll likely miss them altogether."

True to his word, after a few minutes, he tapped her shoulder and pointed out to her left. She saw it in the shadows before they were on it. It was as he said, a column of rock about as tall as she was. It looked precarious and delicate, and Hattie wondered how it could stand up to the gales of the Wastes. A dead tree limb marked the direction they needed to take for the next cairn. It pointed west like a skeletal finger.

"Who built all of these?"

"There used to be only a few. No one would make the trip unless the conditions were perfect. Even then it was dangerous. People just started adding to them to make the journey safer. Less chances of getting lost."

"Did you make any?"

"A few."

At the base of the cairn, half submerged in the sand, Hattie spied a large wooden box. She could just make out the rope handles on the sides jutting up out of the ground like fat worms. "What's this?" she asked. She bent down to get a closer look.

"It's an old cartridge box. For storing things. Travelers to and from the Lodge leave supplies in them. Food mostly, sometimes medicine."

"Aren't they afraid people will steal it?" It seemed ill-considered to her. There wasn't much distinction between theft and scavenging in the Wastes, and this seemed like an opportune target.

"No. You can't steal a gift. They're left to help out other travelers. The people who put supplies in them know that someone else will take them. That's the measure of it, really. They're gifts to help the weary. If you need it, you take it and no one questions you. If you don't, you leave it for someone who does."

The whole idea was foreign to Hattie. At first, it bothered her enough that she wanted to take everything in the box, just to prove her brother wrong. There's no benefit in helping people who will never know that it was you who helped them. But the more she thought about it, the more she felt like this was something singularly special, and in a small way, she was a part of it.

She bent down and opened the box. Inside she found some hardtack wrapped in cheesecloth, a pair of buckskin gloves, and a small, unmarked bottle. She opened the stopper and smelled the lip—camphene. She felt an urge to add something. She knew it was silly, she only brought with her what she needed, but the sense of belonging grew overpowering. She felt like a saint making a holy pilgrimage, though Erasmus would no doubt have likened her more to the Wife of Bath than any holy person, had she confessed her thoughts to him.

She took out her scarf and delicately placed it in the box.

"Someone might need it more than I," she said. "The Gales might be blowing fierce next time." She had to explain, though no explanation was necessary.

"Do they all have these boxes?" Lupe asked. He had watched the exchange in silence.

"No," Erasmus said. "Many of them do. Some have boxes like this, some have small tins, and some have nothing at all. At least, nothing yet. Maybe someday someone'll come by and put a box or tin under one of the empty ones. Eventually, maybe they'll all have one."

"Maybe I can bring one next time," Hattie offered.

They moved on at the same slow pace as before, but Hattie scarcely took notice this time. She dreamed instead of Hill Lodge. Of travelers from far-off lands, a caravan of camels from Arabia. Of a small girl, brown of skin, who shivered in the cold, and warmed herself with a black scarf she found in an old wooden box under a cairn.

By the time they arrived at the Lodge, it was well into the early morning hours. The sun was not yet up, but the dregs and drunks of the saloon had mostly retired for the night, gone home or to a room on the upper floor to enjoy the company of one of the lodge ladies. Others were sprawled out on the floors and benches to sleep off their drunkenness until the doormen came round to throw them out.

Hattie took it all in with no small measure of disappointment. Her imagination had taken a life of its own on her walk over the flats, and the reality of the lodge couldn't equal what she had built up in her mind.

"It's not much right now," Erasmus said, as if he read the disenchantment carved in her face. "But when this place is busy, it's truly a sight to behold."

Hattie had her doubts. Tobacco spit covered the floor, its sickly-sweet stench threatened to overpower her and she put a delicate hand to her nose. She tried to picture in her mind how it must be when it's full and the whiskey is flowing and the crowd is loud, when the people are playing games of chance, telling stories, and forgetting the outside world. She would withhold any more judgment. She would sleep and wait for the crowd to come back.

Erasmus knocked on the counter. A few moments later, a tall man with dark skin burst through a door on the far side of the wall. "Rasmus," the man called. He held his arms out wide, and the two men embraced. "Back so soon? I didn't expect to see you again for a few weeks, at least."

"What can I say? I can't stay away from this place."

"It's not an easy journey, even for a man as... capable... as you."

"Grueling is an apt word for it, Ezekiel," Erasmus replied.

"Terrifying is more like it. I've been out there once, and it had just barely gotten dark. I swear, every sound out there on the flats was something just outside the lamplight waiting to devour me. I wouldn't make that trek, not for some gambling, not for some whiskey. I'm sure you got whiskey there in Sorrow Draw, can't tell me the red eye is better over here."

"The red eye is better over here, to be honest." Erasmus quipped.

"Still, I'd rather drink some real tangle-leg shit than make that walk," he said with a shudder.

"What about for a toss in the hay with a little bum roll?"

Ezekiel thought about it for a moment. "I reckon that'll do it. If I had to walk ten miles across the flats to have a pair of fat tits in my hands, I'd do it."

"There's more men in Sorrow Draw than women, Zeke. And the ones who have the women don't like to share. Some of them do what I do and bugger other men, but most who do still prefer the ladies."

Hattie's face burned at the way her brother talked to this man. He laughed and talked openly about the shame he kept hidden in Sorrow Draw. He made introductions and the man named Ezekiel stared at her, brazen and lustfully.

"This is her first time here, Zeke. Go easy on the girl, would you? Besides, she's already taken."

"The Devil take your tongue, Erasmus Mothershed," Hattie said. She turned to Ezekiel who looked at her quizzically. "That business is a bit of a misunderstanding mixed with some unfortunate circumstances. Circumstances I'm hoping to remedy soon."

"Indeed?" Ezekiel asked.

"Indeed?" repeated Erasmus.

"Never you mind." She turned back to Ezekiel. "Can we get a room? I am exhausted and my feet are positively aching."

"Of course. There should be a few open rooms upstairs. But it looks like you folks are here for more than a room for the night." He gestured to the bags they carried.

"Not Hattie and I," said Erasmus. "My friends here, yes. You know of any places in town that are empty? They're staying indefinitely. Where should we look?"

Ezekiel tightened his lips. "If you're looking to hide out for a few days, I can help you out, but anything more than that I don't recommend. The Freemen don't take kindly to folks setting up in Serpent's Bluff."

"It's alright, Zeke. They got the rights from Deliverance."

Ezekiel raised his eyebrows. "If you say so, my friend. You may have to go out a ways, or board up with other folks, maybe. This place...this place is becoming something special, now." He spoke with a look that was a mixture of pride and wonder. "People used to come through sometimes, just stay a night and pass on through on their way to God knows where. Now they come here to pass through, and the Freemen have to force them out. Deliverance has created something amazing in this place."

"You two still sweet on each other?" Erasmus asked.

"Oh no. No, she plays this game too well for me. I'm a simple man, Rasmus, a simple man. She ain't fit for just one fellow, you know? And I ain't the kind of man to share if I'm being serious. And with Deliverance, I wanted to be serious." He spoke with a hint of regret that passed so quickly, that Hattie wasn't sure if it had been there or if she had imagined it.

"Well, you know what they say, Zeke, these aren't our father's times."

"They certainly aren't. But some things are hard to shake."

They gave no remittance for the room, Hattie had suspected they would have to, but Ezekiel told her that Hill Lodge was free for travelers. Anyone wishing to drink and join in the games or other diversions would have to pay for them, but a room for a night or two never cost a thing.

"There's no reason to come here unless it's to gamble and drink, so they always profit in one way or another," Erasmus told her. They found two empty rooms. Erasmus and Hattie took one, and Lupe and his mother stayed in the other. There was some brief debate as to who would get the bed and who would get the floor if they had to share a single room with one bed. Hattie breathed a sigh of relief when Lupe found the adjacent room empty. "The point of Hill Lodge isn't profit, though. Profit helps, of course. The extra food and supplies go to the Highwaymen and that keeps the road safe. But this place...this place ain't about that. This place is a beacon for humanity. It's like the fucking lighthouse of Alexandria, it sits in the middle of an ocean of darkness and guides people to something safe, someplace they can forget about who they are and forget about the end of the world. It gives people hope. When you're here, it feels like you can finally dream again. Dream of a better life, of a future."

"And then you have to go back to Sorrow Draw," Hattie said. She regretted it instantly, her brother's talk of this place made it sound preternatural, or otherworldly, a divine place like Olympus or the Garden of El in Canaan. She despaired that she brought it down so.

"If I could stay here, I would. You know Father would have the Paluxy Boys come after me if I went missing. We're risking an awful lot coming here today as it is. The both of us, I mean. He's going to be sore at us that we aren't taking care of Mother."

"With any luck, she'll be dead when we get back."

"Hattie, is that any way to talk about your dear old mother?"

"Certainly. I think dead relatives are better relatives. They can't burden you with constant disappointment. Present company excepted, of course."

"Of course, dearest sister."

Hattie took off her traveling clothes and sat on the edge of the bed and sank into the mattress. She felt heavy. The weight of her flesh pulled on her bones, and they ached under the strain. Her weariness, she knew, was more than physical. She felt melancholic, a disease of the mind that her mother suffered from all her life. She feared her constant misery would mirror her mother's in the worst ways, like a sinister echo, and she would find herself someday bedridden, drooling on her nightclothes and shitting herself. Only who would she have to take care of her? She had no children to indenture, and no husband to fret and dote on her through it all. She pushed the thought of Ransom Eisenhardt out of her mind. No doubt he would put a bullet in her head before he wiped her ass and changed her sheets.

"I'm going to scavenge out a place for Lupe." Erasmus had taken his coat off when they arrived at Hill Lodge, but he put it back on and headed for the door.

A wave of loneliness and fear hit her. It came on suddenly, with all the force of her father's boot to her gut. "Don't be gone long," she pleaded. She sounded weak, but she didn't care.

Her brother bent down and kissed her forehead tenderly. "I won't," he said.

He opened the door to leave, but turned around on the threshold, a wicked grin on his face. "If you get cold or lonely, I think Ezekiel wouldn't mind warming your bed."

Hattie's face burned. She couldn't believe he had just suggested such a thing. "Erasmus! He's a Negro," she whispered.

His smile faded. "No one cares anymore, Hattie," he said. "He's a man. You're a woman. That's all that matters. Get some sleep, dear. Your eyes will be opened wide tonight, make no mistake. I'll be back soon."

The door closed softly. Things were different in Hill Lodge, that she knew full well, but exactly how different were they? Her father's mission was to keep the old traditions and values alive in Sorrow Draw and he preached often lately of the excesses of the outside world, never mentioning Hill Lodge by name, but all in attendance knew what place he called "Sodom."

A gust of wind rattled the window. Somewhere outside a man sang a funeral dirge.

She laid back on the bed and closed her eyes and reminded herself that she did not believe in omens.

Chapter 24

Vicksburg, Old Mississippi (September, 1881)

Cornelius White

They stayed in Vicksburg for two more days while Eudora's trail grew colder. Nikki refused to leave until the women of Vicksburg were properly cared for. That sat well with Conny, though his appreciation for her thoughtfulness was tempered by his impatience to get back on the road. Still, Nikki had killed a man who had kept himself a harem of women. Kept them cold, drugged, and starving. He had poisoned their minds, bodies, and spirits. He had bedded them, even the young ones, and murdered and cannibalized the men. Her ability to shift from fierce killer to tender mother was impressive, and Conny discovered that he couldn't help how fond of her he had become.

Nikki had set to work immediately after killing the Magistrate, to taking care of the women. She saw to their illnesses and injuries, both to their bodies and spirits. Conny and Farhad deferred to her expertise and she sent the two of them out regularly to scavenge supplies from the shops and homes of the city. The Magistrate had whittled the population of the whole of Vicksburg down to only those few who had been holed up in the courthouse, and those he kept cold and malnourished, so there were more provisions in the city than Conny could have believed. The Magistrate must have begun his reign early into the Calamity. They found a good stash of wool blankets, some hardtack that was free of worms, and plenty of clothes of all sizes to go around.

The women moved themselves out of the courtroom and into one of the larger houses down the road that still was mostly above the sand and dust. After some discussion, they chose to leave the corpse of the Magistrate where it was and let Conny and Farhad burn it. Some of the women felt it would be some kind of justice to eat it, as many of them vividly recalled eating their husbands, fathers, and sons. The majority simply wanted to be rid of his filth. Conny was glad to oblige—anything to end the discussion of cannibalism for good.

He erected a large bonfire outside the courthouse steps made from broken furniture—chairs, tables, hat racks—and pieces of wainscoting they ripped off the courtroom walls. Farhad helped him carry the body to the pyre, though there was no need. The man was so thin Conny could have carried him slung over one shoulder like a sack of grain.

Conny went back to the house that the women now gathered in to see if anyone wanted to be present before they lit up the body. He found Nikki, sitting with her legs crossed in front of an older woman. From her tone, he knew that she was giving instructions. His thoughts went immediately to his wife. She had been a teacher when they met and when Conny asked her to marry him, she had to give it up. Married women were not allowed to teach. Though she agreed, she still wept when she left the schoolhouse for the last time.

He had visited her once in her classroom while they still courted. He stood in the doorway, so he didn't stir up any gossip and watched her instruct her class.

Teachers have a way of talking, a cadence, or rhythm, to their words. From the right mouth, it can mean not just just knowledge, but compassion and understanding. It can mean safety and love. He had been taken aback by her command and authority, as well as her gentleness. He saw her then as the children saw her—a tender guide and a kindly mentor. How could he uncouple her from something that must have been so unconditionally interwoven into the very fabric that made up her soul? He knew if he did that, he would destroy a part of what made her *her*.

This was what he also saw now, in Nikki Free. Her's was a hardened teacher, made more severe by a life of bondage and survival in the Wastes, but it was every bit as intrinsic in her as it had been in his Elizabeth.

And yet he had still pursued her, and still selfishly made her his wife and took her from her classroom and her students.

He sat down in an ornate chair, padded in burgundy velvet, dusty, yet somehow still beautiful. He listened and waited.

"Let the moss dry out real well first. Collect it when it's wet but put it in some heat to dry it out," Nikki said. The woman who called herself Delilah turned a piece of lichen in her hands. "Then you can put it to the mill. If you can't do that, roll it up real fine in your hands."

"Which one is best to use?" Delilah picked up a sprig of amaranth, what Nikki called pigweed.

"Both. You have to mix them up in equal parts. You can make the hardtack with the pigweed alone, but not the moss. You gots to mix it up with the pigweed. Use less moss if you don't like the flavor, but make sure you use some of it to keep the worms out."

Delilah shook her head. "It don't make no sense. Where did these things come from? They weren't never here before. I even lived up in Massachusetts as a girl, came down here when my daddy deserted the Northern army, he said they had no right to coerce the Southern states into giving up their sovereignty." She laid a pale hand on Nikki. "I know what that meant."

Nikki took a deep breath. "Well, it brought you here. That very well might have saved your life. Not a lot of people made it out of them Northern states, you know."

"You saved my life."

Nikki gave a small, tight-lipped smile. Conny noticed she had trouble accepting compliments.

"So I think that the plants started changing after the Calamity hit," Nikki said, to answer the woman's earlier question. "Changing in small ways, but those small changes can be very important. I think this moss comes from way up north. Farther than them Northern states got up to. It's cold enough down here for them now, so I think they moved down here, kinda like people move. Like you did. Even the pigweed is different than it used to be. Tastes better and stays longer as hardtack. The worms like it, but the moss flour keeps them out."

"How'd you figure all this out?"

"There was a woman that lived in Commerce with me. Her name was Augusta. She used to go on foraging runs with the scavengers. She didn't care nothing at all about scavenging, though. She collected all kind of plants and seeds and cooked them into all kinds of things. Some worked. Most didn't. A few made her sick. She got real sick one time and I wasn't sure she was gonna make it. After that, I had her test her cooking on me instead. I wasn't as important as she was. We would have been lost if not for her."

"Is she still there, making her batches without you, now?"

"No, she died. And then we were lost."

"I'm sorry. Was it her cooking?"

"In a way. She was accused of witchcraft, and they killed her. Sodomized her with a wooden stake and pushed it all the way up into her chest. Raised her up on the banks of the Mississippi."

"Oh, dear God," Delilah said.

Conny hadn't heard this story before, nor had he even heard of this woman, Augusta. He listened intently, eager to know everything he could about Nikki's life in Commerce, but always afraid to ask.

"Hours later she was still alive. I sneaked out and brought her some whiskey laced with enough opium to drug a bull. I soaked a rag in it a lifted it to her on a stick, like the Romans did with Jesus. I don't think I've ever seen anyone suffer that much. Going to her that night was the hardest thing I've ever done. I was terrified. I didn't want to see her. I didn't want to see her agony with my own eyes. I was a coward."

"But you went," Delilah said. "Being afraid don't make you a coward, letting the fear keep you from doing the right thing—that's what'll make you a coward."

Delilah meant well with her comment, but Conny felt the sting of it like a sharp blade. Nikki once told him that she didn't do enough to help the people of Commerce, especially the children, escape the wickedness of the man who called himself Abhartach.

Conny walked over to them and cleared his throat. "Pardon me, misses. I hope I'm not interrupting anything."

"We were just talking about baking hardtack." Delilah dusted off the front of her apron. "Nikki here is an absolute treasure and I think we might just make it out here thanks to her."

"Yes, ma'am. She is something special, make no mistake." He knelt by the women. "We're ready to light the fire. I wanted to give y'all a chance to be there if you want. You know, to see him go up in flames. I thought I should give you the choice. There's a lot of strong feelings about it, and I didn't want to deprive anyone of the satisfaction of seeing it."

Delilah was silent for a moment. "Give me a half hour. I'll meet you there with anyone else who wants to go."

"All right. A half hour then."

Conny moved to rise, but Delilah stayed him with a hand.

"Let's make one thing clear," she said. "This isn't a funeral. No words, no Bibles. We're going there to watch the monster burn. Nothing more."

Conny could feel her anger, a rage so palpable that he swore it took up physical space, and for Delilah, it was all around her. Then her eyes softened, and she made her face sullen. Conny sucked in his lips. "I promise. No Bibles, no prayers for the wicked. We burn him and let the dust and sand claim what's left."

A half-hour later, they were gathered in front of the pyre. Conny was surprised that most of the women in town came to bear witness to the end of the Magistrate. Each woman carried a small, lighted torch and at Delilah's signal, they all threw their torches in as one. With a little help from some kerosene Conny found in an oil lamp in the millinery, the old, dry wood caught fast and burned hot.

The wind blew soft and low. The dust was light, but Conny wore his *keffiyeh* to keep the ash out of his mouth. He watched in a gruesome fascination, a kind of macabre compulsion as the flame devoured the Magistrate's hair. His body turned deep red then black. Pieces of wood popped and cracked and at times would shift and settle as the fire began turning them to ash. When the man's body hissed and sizzled, and oozed fluid that caught in the flames below to flash like muzzle fire, Conny decided he had seen enough, and he started back to the warmth of the house in the center of town. A cold, small hand slipped into his and Nikki walked wordlessly with him along the street.

When they shook off their ponchos and scarves and stood by the heat of the fireplace, Conny took her face in his hands and kissed her. They hadn't been together since their night in Bolivar and Conny feared that she might not want any more from him than that one episode. But Nikki accepted his mouth eagerly and pressed back on him. Her tongue tasted of anise and tobacco.

"I know we have to leave soon." Nikki pulled herself away from him. "But I want to thank you for letting us stay. It...it meant a lot to me. This was important."

"You did something good here." Conny took her hand and kissed it. "I would have done the selfish thing. I would have just left so I could catch Eudora's trail. You put these people first, and that was a damn good thing. You're a better person than I am, Nikki."

"Now I don't believe that at all, Con." She slapped his chest. "You didn't leave me to die on that cross."

"No. No I guess I didn't. But I didn't stop to think about that, either. I just acted out of anger. But what if I had stopped, even for a moment, to weigh my options, like I did here. Would I have rode on and left you there?"

"So, in the absence of time and logic, your first instinct is to do the right thing? That's because you're a good man, Conny White. I think I'm quite fond of you."

"How do you think they'll do here now?" Conny changed the subject. Compliments came difficult for him, and more often than not, when Nikki told him he was a good man, he felt like a fraud, as if he was hiding his real self from her.

"I think they'll all die sooner rather than later."

This was not the answer he had expected. "Are you being true right now? You don't think they'll make it?"

"No Conny, I don't. I think they're going to die. The opium has its hooks in them. They need it and they'll fall apart without it. Things are fine now, but when we leave the cravings will hit and things here will be in a bad way."

She was right, he realized. Their chances were slim.

"It's alright, caballero. We still did a good thing here. And they might make it. Might be I'm all wrong about them."

He kissed her forehead. "I hope you are wrong."

"Me too."

A figure walked in, wearing the thick blue wool coat that marked an officer of the Union army and a long scarf, expertly wrapped about the face and head in a style he recognized immediately as Farhad's. The bundled man pushed the two aside to stand in front of the fire.

"You shouldn't spend so much time out there in the cold, Farhad." Nikki scolded him.

"Well little sister, we're going to be spending a great deal of time out there very soon, so that's an inevitability."

"Then you should spend as much time until then in as much warmth as you can."

"Oh, I'm plenty warm. Some tenderfoot Major or other with the Union army thought to bring his overcoat to gods-forsaken, dust-choked Mississippi. It's lined with beaver fur and warm as the fires of Perdition. I can't imagine it did him a lick of good before the Calamity."

"You look cold," Conny said. Farhad had the maddening tendency to trivialize his discomfort, which is an admirable quality in a healthy person, but Farhad was far from healthy and Conny had to stay vigilant for warning signs. Not if he wanted to avoid a repeat of Bolivar. The Bedouin might not survive another episode like that.

Farhad coughed. "I feel fine, Con. Fit as a fiddle. By the by, I saw the fruits of our handiwork from the farriers across the bridge. That was a disturbing smell, and that's the truth."

Conny had left the bonfire early, right as the odor of the burning body hit. He had never tasted human flesh, and the practice had been outlawed in

Memphis, but the Uncontested Lands were an immoral place—a Wasteland that favored sin, a domain that rewarded wickedness and malice and punished charity. Cannibalism, the most wretched of human indecencies, was too often tolerated. When he rode into Memphis with Becker's gang, it was the first crime they put on the books. A simple rule, but the folks in Memphis had developed a bad habit of it and some examples had to be made.

He still remembered the first time he found people eating human meat. It was also the first time he realized that the world he once knew was never coming back. They had been huddled in the back of a distillery. They ate the flesh with their hands dripping with fat. Their mouths tore into it with great bites, ripping the tender meat from the bone. Conny found them because of the smell. The aroma had cut through the walls of the building and through the dust to where he walked on patrol. After a year of eating wormy hardtack and moldy bread, the smell of cooked meat had made his mouth water. And he has never forgiven himself for that.

Nikki broke the silence. "When do you want to head out?"

"Early. We should leave while it's still dark," Conny said.

"At the absolute coldest time of the day?" Farhad asked. "You have a strange way of trying to keep me warm, Conny White."

They rode out of Vicksburg before the sun's first light crept through the dust and haze of the sky. A thin layer of frost crunched under the horse's hooves and the Wasteland gales cut sand and ice across Conny's face. He pulled his *keffiyeh* as tight as he could, leaving only a slim space to see out of. His long coat kept out all but the bitterest of winds, but the cold wormed its way through every hole and seam to bite at his skin. Before long, his muscles spasmed and his body shook.

This section of the Mississippi had shifted since the Calamity hit, so Conny decided to follow the old, dried riverbed. The new course took the river beyond the effigies that still lined the old bank. Conny didn't know if the Indians claimed the old bank still, or moved their border farther west to keep it in line with the new river, but he didn't intend to find out. The devil could keep the river. He just needed to follow his old map and hope that the diversion was only temporary, and the waters would eventually flow back into the old bed.

They rode like this for days, the cold chilling them to their core until it became as much a part of their existence as the air they breathed. They stopped at long-dead towns to dig into the houses for the night. Houses whose roofs barely emerged from the dust and dunes of the Wastes. Sometimes there would be bodies inside, dry and brittle, the air robbed them of moisture and whithered their skin, pulled their lips back in hideous grins, and left only wisps of hair, light and delicate like smoke. When there were corpses inside, Conny and Nikki would take the bodies out and commit them to the Wastes and Farhad would tend the fire.

Eventually, the effigies stopped. Or, it appeared to Conny that they stopped, but Farhad pointed out that they continued west. They had seen small signs of what they believed to be Eudora's passing. Discarded pieces of hardtack, the occasional torn fabric, and hastily covered fires with still-warm coals. Conny could feel them getting closer, but why was Eudora still running? Now that Preacher was no longer with her, she seemed to be running even faster. She may have been worried about the Magistrate trying to pursue her, or, if Crowkiller was right, she was the mastermind behind the heist of the money, and Preacher was only caught up in her schemes.

Either way, the Indian Territory fled west from here, and this would have been Eudora's earliest opportunity to strike out toward California. She certainly wasn't heading back to Memphis. Nikki brought up the possibility that they were chasing a phantom, some other marauder of the Wastes who has no connection to them whatsoever. An outcast, doomed to exile. It was possible. People did on occasion traverse the Wastes, cold and deadly as it was. But this was Eudora, Conny was certain of it. He had no hard proof, but his gut told him it was, and he had no reason to suspect his gut would lead him wrong now. Eudora came this way, and he was going to track her down and make sure she got to California. He had already resolved in his mind to let her keep the money. With Preacher gone, it no longer felt right to rob Becker's little girl. He would let Farhad have his share, but Eudora would keep his own. He was certain that Nikki would agree.

He stopped and examined his map, turned it over this way and that, and tried to make sense of what the map said, and what his eyes told him.

"What is it?" Nikki asked.

"I'm not sure. My map says the Indian territory should cut west at Natchez, but…" He gestured at the barren land around them. "No Natchez."

The ground around them rose and fell in uneven mounds, grasses, and sparse Yucca dotted the undulating landscape, and limestone rocks jutted out of the ground like shipwrecks.

But no Natchez.

"The Wastes have claimed it." Nikki Free smiled despite the cold. "The Devil himself dragged this whole place down to Hell."

"You sure you're reading that right?" Farhad asked. "River's shifted course and the land's always changing."

"I'm sure. We've following the old river. And the land can change all it wants, but the old river was here, and so was Natchez. But now it's gone."

"This place was evil." Nikki spat. "It's here, but the dust has taken it. I say, let the dust have it. Let it bury it for the rest of time. We'll start heading west and Natchez will be nothing but a lost memory."

"You have some history with this place?" Conny asked, though it was a question that didn't need asking. Nikki's vehemence was proof enough.

"You could say that. But it's a memory that can now die for all I care."

"I have a few of those myself, little sister." Farhad spurred his horse forward and the rest followed. "It's time we start heading west. Somewhere this way," he nodded towards the setting sun, "is the end of our journey. So let's go. And let's be glad in the offing."

Conny tried to be happy for Nikki, who seemed to him to be far too elated that the city was gone, but he didn't like secrets, especially not from her. He reminded himself of his own secrets and felt a brief stab of shame. There was plenty he hadn't told her about who he was, about the things he had done. Especially in those early days in Memphis, when he worked for Becker on the outskirts of the Uncontested Lands, attempting to bring civilization back into the world. Back when that seemed like a possibility, before he realized that humanity was a dying thing, before he accepted that the world wasn't for them anymore.

The wind blew and the bitter cold pierced through his long coat. He scanned the area once more, hoping to find some small piece of Natchez, anything to give some indication that the town had even existed. He saw nothing around but the boundless expanse of shifting dunes.

Chapter 25

Serpent's Bluff, North Texas (September, 1881)

Hattie Mothershed

Hattie had no idea how long she had slept, but it felt like an intolerably long time. Her body still ached, but now it was with the dull pain of sleep, the kind of which the only remedy was to get up and move.

It was the sounds that had woken her up. From under the floor came the din of people. She had never heard so much laughter in one place before and it both thrilled her and terrified her. She had been to Hill Lodge once, not that long ago, but the noise of the crowd was nothing then compared to what it was now. The murmur of the crowd ebbed and flowed like an ocean in a tempest, punctuated by howls and calls and the crystalline tap of glasses coming together. A piano began to play, and a few drunken souls took up singing. Laughter was rare in Sorrow Draw, and usually not done in the presence of other people. It had become an affront, a blasphemy almost as sacrilegious as sex.

She threw off the blanket. Though fatigue wore her down, she pushed through it and dressed quickly. The room was empty and she suspected that Erasmus might already be downstairs several drinks in on a bender when the door opened and he walked through.

"I was just coming up here to collect you," he said. "The night's just getting started and I wouldn't want you to miss it."

"Thank you for waiting for me. I didn't want to go down there by myself."

"I know."

He wore a dark blue waistcoat and gray wool pants. Hattie often wondered where he scavenged his clothes from. Most folk had a change of clothes, but Erasmus seemed always to have on something different for every occasion.

"Are you ready?" he asked.

"I suppose so." She hesitated, unsure. If it was possible to live entirely in that instant right before she had to act, in that breath that preceded a moment of bravery, she would have gladly existed right there.

Erasmus looked her over. "So then, a fair bit of warning—you're going to be a popular item tonight. You're new, beautiful, and more than available. The men downstairs...the men—and women—are going to be very interested in getting to know you."

"Alright. How do I let them know that I'm not interested?"

"You could try telling them. See how that works for you. But I don't think they're going to let that stand in the way of a fair bit of strange cunny."

"They're not going to—"

"No, nothing like that. I wouldn't bring you here if they did things like that. But some of them might get a bit persistent. You may have to be firm. Or, if you meet one you like, take him up on his offer." He stopped abruptly and pursed his lips. "You aren't actually wearing that, are you?"

She smoothed the front of her traveling clothes. "What's wrong with this? I told you I don't want all the attention, not tonight."

"I know you're planning something. I practically raised you myself. I know when you're scheming. But what if it doesn't work? What if you find yourself at the alter saying 'I do' with Ransom Eisenhardt?"

"I would sooner hang myself." She spat out her oath like it was venom.

"I know it. Even so, this may be your last chance for some excitement, for some pleasure."

"Rasmus...I don't know...I—"

"What is the last thing that Ransom Eisenhardt would want you to do right now?" he reached into his bag and drew out a dress, if it could be called that. It had a very low-cut top and the skirting wouldn't barely cover her knees. She had nightclothes that left more to the imagination than this harlot's dress. Still, she snatched it out of his hands.

"You are the Devil himself, Erasmus Mothershed."

"Not the Devil, dear sister. Just his son."

She put the dress on. Erasmus had to help her fit her bust into the top, and still, she feared her breasts would boil out. She lost her nerve.

"I can't do this. I look silly."

"No, you look sexy."

"How would you know?"

"I know. And I'll be right there with you. What are you afraid of? Having a good time?"

"As a matter of fact, yes. I've heard it's positively dreadful."

"Well, it's certainly not worse than cleaning up mother's piss and shit, or I imagine, spreading your legs for Ransom." He took a step back and looked her up and down.

"If you could please leave his name out of your mouth for the rest of the night."

He took her hands. His youthful face turned serious. "Hattie. We'll figure this out. I'm going to get you out of this, I promise. Believe me, the idea of that man putting his hands on you gets my blood boiling as much as yours."

Tears threatened to fall but she choked them back. Erasmus would defend her. If it came down to it, he would face down Ransom and all of the Paluxy Boys to keep her safe. But he had never hurt another person in his entire life and would likely get himself killed. That's why she needed to make sure it never came down to it. This problem had to be fixed before he took matters into his own hands.

She put her arms around him and buried her face in his chest. He held her for a moment.

"Come on," he said at last. "Let's live like it really is the end of the fucking world."

They walked downstairs, arm in arm. The noise that had once been a muffled sound she heard through the floor was now sharp and sometimes piercing. There were more people by far this night than she had ever seen in one place. The constant barrage of sights and sounds made that difficult for her not to stare wide-eyed and slack-jawed at everything.

She stopped at the landing. Where would they sit? The bar was full. About a dozen men and women lined up, some alone, others were on openly friendly terms with each other. One man, she noticed right away, had his hand up a woman's skirt. The longer she stared at them, the more she became convinced that the woman in the skirt was actually a man. A boy, rather, with the down just starting to show on his chin.

The gambling tables had some space, but Hattie never cared much for cards, and no one had ever taken the time to teach her how to play any games other than faro. Those tables were the most raucous of them all. The bets on the table were a jumble of arbitrary scavenged items—lead balls made up the bulk of it, but there was also some powder, what looked like bits of jerky, tins of pomade, candles, tobacco, and metal scrap.

Small groups of dancers scattered about the main hall, both men and women with their arms raised and their bodies moving rhythmically together. The man at the piano played a fast song. Hattie could just make out enough words to know it was about a girl who loved a farmer, a preacher, and an outlaw. She gave her heart to one, her soul to the other, and her body to the third. The dancers spun and clapped with the music, laughed at the bawdy words, and the women lifted their skirts when the piano man sang "but the outlaw got her gold." She had never seen people so free from worry. Free from worry, or ignorant of it. No, not ignorant of it. The Calamity had marked their faces just as it had everyone else. They didn't live a carefree life; they were just carefree right now.

But although all of this promised fun and excitement, the dark edges and corners of the saloon promised other diversions. In the shadowy margins of the hall, Hattie saw bodies intertwined, naked arms and legs weaved together like braids. They were shrouded in those dimly lit edges, and the unclothed bodies looked to her like people drowning, flailing about trying to stay above the pitch-black waters.

She recognized many of the people here from Sorrow Draw. Jake Chambers was the man with his hands up the boy's skirt at the bar. Hattie wondered if he left his wife at home. Or maybe she's one of those bodies in the dark.

Matilde Hoagland just threw two lead balls into the faro pot. Two lead balls that the Highwaymen might one day use to shoot one of the Paluxy Boys.

She glanced about for Clementine. Hattie wanted to talk with her, to tell her she was sorry they had treated her ill all those years ago. To apologize on behalf of her father for taking her babe away from her. But Hattie also hoped she wouldn't find her here. A part of her hoped she never saw Clementine again because as much as she needed to ask for her forgiveness, the very thought of talking with her old nanny put a fear deep in her belly. A fear that threatened to make her turn and run, run back to Sorrow Draw, back to her old room, and to the safety of that old, cursed, and dreadful house. You can't run from your shame, Hattie Mothershed.

Erasmus pointed to a table at the far wall. "There's Lupe, at the table over there." He waved and took her arm again. "Shall we head over?"

He seemed to sense her losing her nerve and he gave her arm a small pat, as one might do to a hungry child who's just beginning to understand that food is scarce in the world and hunger is her natural state. Still, she was grateful.

They made their way across the floor to her brother's lover and sat down with him. Erasmus kissed him soundly on the lips and Hattie's face burned with shame, though she knew it wasn't necessary. Still, it took her back to how open they could be in this place. Not a soul cared. So why should I? But that didn't stop the scandalous fire that blazed under her skin.

"Where's your mother?" Erasmus asked him.

"She's going to stay home. Places like this aren't for her, gringo. My mother's a fucking saint, you know?"

"You're in a rare mood." Erasmus sucked in his lower lip.

"This is some real firewater they got here." Lupe grabbed a bottle and filled a few glasses with a clear liquid. "This stuff hits hard."

"Where do they get it?" Hattie lifted the glass to her nose and sniffed. "What's it made from?"

"Mexicans from down south make it. Some kind of cactus. They says it's something new. Born from the Calamity. *La Calamidad.*"

"I've heard stranger things," Erasmus said.

"Well, I believe them. And it's better than whiskey, I think. But if whiskey is your drink, Hattie, they have plenty of that, too." Lupe pointed to barrels stacked around the room.

"I can't believe there's still that much whiskey left in the world," Hattie said. "And surely they don't make it themselves. Can they still do that? Make whiskey?"

"No idea." Lupe drained his glass. "But the area up north, up in the mountains, the old wagon trails going west are still full of caches of whiskey. Casks and abandoned wagons. The folks out in the frontier drank more of this shit than you could well imagine."

Erasmus frowned. "Yeah, but the Freemen can't get that stuff up north. That's Indian Territory."

"That's what I thought, but I hear rumors that she has some kind of trade deal worked out with Sanguin Corvus. Mostly for whiskey. Keeps the lifeblood of Hill Lodge flowing."

"Impossible," Erasmus said. "No one trades with Sanguin Corvus. No one."

Lupe shrugged. "That's the rumor. Maybe you could ask Deliverance yourself." He pointed to a small table on a slightly raised platform in the corner of the saloon. Seated there was a young woman, dark of skin, in an elegant dress, more revealing even than the one Hattie wore. Next to her sat the most beautiful woman Hattie had ever seen. She had seen Chinamen before, but this was the first time she had ever laid eyes on a Chinese woman. She wore a silk dress embroidered with flowers of oranges, pinks, and light blues that covered much more of her than most others in Hill Lodge, yet despite that, somehow seemed to conform to her body as if it were made of wax, leaving little of the shape underneath in any doubt. At first glance, Hattie thought the woman to be a little girl, so small in frame she was, yet the curves of her hips and chest left little doubt that she was a woman. Hattie found her so impossibly delicate, that despite her tiny proportions, she suddenly felt like a great ogre, some beast in a comically oversized dress.

"Is that Deliverance?" asked Hattie.

"I think so." Lupe rolled a quirley and lit it with a candle.

"Don't look now, but I think she's spotted us," said Erasmus.

"You think she knows who you are?" his lover asked.

"We're...acquainted."

"How?"

"How do you think I managed to get you a place here? I ambushed her here, turned on my charm, and won her over."

"I don't understand," Hattie said. "How does a girl like that control all of this?" She waved her arms around.

"See that big guy?" Erasmus inclined his head at the table. "His name's Sovereign. She has him firmly in her, um, pocket, you could say."

Hattie had been so focused on the tiny woman seated next to Deliverance that she scarcely saw the enormous man sitting on her other side.

"He's the leader of the Highwaymen," Erasmus continued. "When Deliverance had the idea to start Hill Lodge, most people didn't think much of it. Just a silly dream. A foolish dream for a foolish girl. But she got Sovereign on her side. She showed him her vision and he bought into it. Some say he was just cunt-drunk, but it don't really matter. What matters is he got his Freemen involved. They were just a loose bunch of kids with nothing else to do at the time, but after this really got going it gave them a purpose. They're a real outfit now, no denying that. They owe it all to this place. To her. No one's dared try and take it away from her, not with that man by her side."

"What does she get out of this?" Hattie took another drink.

"Power? Purpose? I can't tell you that one. The Freemen get most of the spoils."

"Loyalty?" Lupe asked. "Maybe that's just it. These people are fiercely loyal to her. Sovereign might be in charge of the Freemen, but they all know they owe everything to her and to this vision she had."

"Loyalties are fickle, Lupe. Fear rules best. Sovereign and his posse are a thing to be feared. She had the vision, sure, but he ensures that the vision became a reality."

"Come on, *cabrón*. Even you aren't that jaded."

"No, it's true. Show me a man who swears loyalty and all you've shown me is a liar. Or a dreamer, whose sensibilities are as easily swayed as dust in the wind."

"There are some men who actually have convictions, Erasmus. Men who live by their beliefs."

"And die by them, too I suppose."

"If necessary."

"How tedious and predictable. I prefer my men more fickle."

Lupe pulled at his single long braid. "Fine then. I think I'll go find a card game to join. Something less tedious than listening to you talk."

"I'll have you know, my conversation is perfectly tolerable. But I think I'll come join you. My little sister needs to give the appearance of availability, or the poor thing is never going to find a man to go to bed with."

A sudden jolt of panic overwhelmed Hattie. "Don't go," she pleaded.

"Now, now. You need to have a good time, and you can't do that with me keeping the men at bay. I'll be back, and I'll be watching to make sure no one's too lewd with you. Unless you seem to be enjoying it."

He disappeared through the crowd. Hattie stared at the table. She had never been more confused in all her life. Everything Erasmus said sounded delightful and terrifying all at once. She wanted to enjoy this. She wasn't sure if she'd ever get the chance again, but the thought of enjoying anything frightened her. Pleasure was sin. Sin was eternal torment. Sin risked the wrath of her father. Put that man out of your mind Hattie. He has no place here. She took a drink straight from the bottle and lifted her head, determined to at least try to appear confident and see what became of it.

"I thought the only Mothershed I'd ever see in here was that dandified brother of yours." In the span of a few breaths, Deliverance had made her way across the hall and now stood before her, hands on her hips. She had the look of someone appraising an old, rusted gun, attempting to discern whether or not the tool was worth the time it might take to make it useful again. "May I?" She gestured to the chair.

"It's your saloon," Hattie replied. "I mean, it is, isn't it?"

"If you're asking if I'm Deliverance Hill, then yes. The saloon is mine, so to speak." She pulled up her ruffled dress and sat indelicately in front of Hattie. She wore a white petticoat, not unlike Hattie's, but the contrast of the bright fabric on her dark skin made her beautiful and alluring. Hattie felt plain in comparison, as if there was no difference between her dress and her skin. She imagined that from far enough away you couldn't rightly tell where one ended and the other began.

"I suppose that's what I was asking."

"And you are Hattie Mothershed. Daughter of Reverend John Mothershed and his wife Eula." The woman in front of her was young but spoke with an authority born of confidence. This was a woman who knew her place and didn't question or doubt it. Or, at least, she knew how to appear not to doubt it. Hattie wondered if there was much difference. "What I'm interested in knowing, is why are you here? I tolerate your brother jus' fine. He's a good man, now I don't hold it against him that he's a Mothershed. I think his loyalty is to his conscious. But I don't know you. I don't know whose side you're on. And make no mistake, there are sides."

"I don't suppose you'd be inclined to allow that I'm on my own side?"

"Depends." Deliverance leaned back. "Maybe for now you just tell me why you're here. Pleasure? I don't think so. You look about as wrong in that petticoat as a whelk on a white ass. You ain't here to visit no whoremongers. So why are you here?"

"I—I don't entirely know, and that's both the long and the short of it, truly."

"You understand my concern, don't you girlie?"

"Of course." Hattie twisted the ruffles of her petticoat in her fingers. This woman made her lose her nerve, and cornered her like a beast, yet she may only have this one chance to ask for help. But she wasn't yet ready. The words caught in her throat.

"My you are dreadfully pretty, ain't you? Nervous, though. Quit beatin' the Devil around the stump and get to it."

"I need your help." She said it. She couldn't take it back now if she wanted to. Not that she expected Deliverance to help, why would she? Still, she'd plead her case.

"There it is." She seemed satisfied with herself. "I don't know what I can do for you, or what I'd be willing to do, since we ain't kin, and I don't really know you from Adam, but out with it."

"I'm promised to wed—" she felt the panic rise in her chest. "I've been promised to wed someone, but I won't do it. I won't, I can't."

"Promised? Who can promise you to anyone? Your life is your own to give. Tell 'em to fuck off. What do you need my help for?"

"It's not as simple as all that in Sorrow Draw. My pa, he runs things. If I don't do what he wants, he'll pepper me for sure. But I can't marry this man. I want you to help me...to help me kill him."

A hint of a smile played around the corner of Deliverance's lips, but her eyebrows registered surprise. "You really did just come out and ask, didn't you? Who is it?"

Hattie feared to tell. What if this woman betrayed her, went straight to Ransom, or her father? Hattie could think of no reason why she would, but the mere existence of the possibility made her afraid to go on. Yet she had no choice. Better to burn than to wed.

"Ransom Eisenhardt."

Any hint of a smile dropped from Deliverance's face. The woman sighed. *She's not going to help me.* "That's a shame right there, girl. You have my sympathy. He's a sick man, plum wicked if you ask me. But I know you know that. I know it took a lot of nerve to come here and ask for my help. But did you know that your brother already asked me to do the same thing? Kill that Eisenhardt boy? Now what makes you think you can convince me when he couldn't?"

Erasmus hadn't told her that. Her heart sank.

"He's coming for you, you know. For this place. It's only a matter of time. My father's been sending them on raids north to the Indian Territories. They come back sometimes with fresh-blooded scalps. Now my pa's been preaching against you and this place. He runs things, you know. He's not officially one of the Paluxy Boys, but he runs them all the same. They do what he asks. They always do what he asks. He just has to preach on it, and they'll do it. They're coming for you and this place soon enough. You could surprise them. Take out Ransom, maybe the rest'll think twice before messing with you."

Deliverance sighed. "Your dandified brother already made the same argument and I'll tell you what I told him. Look around, honey. This place is teeming with folk from Sorrow Draw. They don't want to see this place go up in flames. They need this place as much as anyone else. Hell, I reckon there's folks here who ride with Ransom. I bet they don't tell him what they're up to. That they come here to gamble, play cards, drink, and whore. Do you think they want to give that up? I don't. That's the beauty of this place."

Deliverance didn't understand. She wasn't raised in Sorrow Draw, in that church, and reared by a man who commanded the kind of devotion paid to him by his hordes of fawning lickspittles. "They're here because they know this won't last. Because they know that sooner or later, my father's coming to burn this place to the ground and everyone in it. They want to experience it before it's gone. Make no mistake, Deliverance. He's coming for it. He wants this House of Sodomy extinguished. And he wants all you Negroes back as slaves, as he sees is right and Biblical."

Deliverance stood up, slow and measured. "If you think to use that to bring me into your scheming, it ain't gonna work. Look, I'm sorry for you, I wouldn't wish marriage to Ransom on anyone, especially one who seems as fine as you. But I'm not risking war with the Paluxy Boys to save you from him."

Hattie's face grew hot, and tears fell down her cheeks. She hated herself for crying. She wanted to be strong, to be fierce and angry. Instead, she broke down like a child. "What am I supposed to do?" she whispered.

Deliverance took her hand. "Forget about him today. Have some fun. Play cards. Dance. Find a man to bed. Or a woman, it's not my business to judge. If you want, Sovereign and I can make you forget about your troubles, least for tonight. But I don't think you could handle the two of us."

Hattie laughed a bit, despite her misery.

"Maybe Ezekiel would be more to your liking. He's tender. Man's got soft hands. I could put in a word for you, maybe send him over here to meet you if you'd like."

"We've already met." At first, Hattie was quite sure that taking a man to bed wasn't exactly the kind of relaxation she needed, but it quickly crossed her mind that perhaps it wasn't relaxation that she needed at all. Perhaps it was diversion, or impudence, or rebellion. Maybe she could ruin herself for Ransom. She wondered if he would be able to tell. Would he know if she had been with a man? How much would it matter to him? She thought of Ezekiel's hands on her. She didn't want Ransom's murderous hands to be the only hands she ever felt. She felt her muscles twitch, as if the very thought of that touch made them recoil in disgust.

Deliverance bid her goodbye and turned to leave but stopped and turned back around. "Maybe," she said, "there's a way we can both help each other."

The sudden possibility made Hattie's heart race. Had she been snatched out of the fire at the last moment? "How? I'll do whatever you want."

"I need you to talk to someone for me. See if you know him. Find out what he wants and why he came here. And, most importantly, find out why he wanted to kill my man. Then we can discuss your…options."

Chapter 26

Uncontested Lands, Mississippi (September, 1881)

Cornelius White

THEY CROSSED THE MISSISSIPPI on September the twenty-fourth, by Conny's reckoning. The boundary of the Indian Territories ran west after Natchez, but they continued on south to give the Indians a wide berth. Conny's spirits were high, despite the cold. Their quarry was still on the run, and they were still in pursuit.

The going was easy after the vanished city of Natchez. The Wastelands were merciless and unforgiving, cold and relentless. Things that Conny knew how to deal with. He was strangely comfortable in them. He understood the Wastelands. He recognized himself in them. Kindred spirits. Yet, when he glanced over at his riding companion, Nikki Free, he burned with a warmth that was completely foreign in this dead stretch of land. Like him, she had been molded by the Calamity, hewed and whittled down to her foundations. She had been shaped, scarred, and tormented by it. But unlike him, she built herself back up again. The sunburst tattoos around her eyes were a resistance to it, a tenacious opposition to the unrelenting degradation of the spirit that's almost inevitable at the end of the world. He envied her strength. He envied her for having it within herself. He had begun to build himself back up, but he drew strength from her to do it. Without her by his side, he feared he would crumble and in the shifting sands of the Wasteland, he would disintegrate like the city of Natchez, remembered by no one in all the measureless years to come.

They had some trouble crossing the Homochitto River. The water was low, and the mud frozen over enough for the horses to walk on it and not get themselves stuck, but the ruins of a bridge dashed any hope that they could make the crossing without getting the horses wet and Farhad suggested they head west across the Mississippi rather than ford the Homochitto, but Conny wanted to see if there were any provisions at the nearby Fort Adams. They all remained doubtful, but it seemed to him that the further south they went, the less scavenged the towns were.

They had passed through a small village after Natchez that had never seen the hand of a scavenger. Clothes, bolts of cloth, candles, ink, boots, tack, paper, tobacco, whiskey, all untouched for eighteen years. They had taken what they could. New clothes, new saddles, a couple of rifles. Whiskey and medicine. They looked for round balls and powder, but the black powder they found wouldn't catch a light. Conny hoped that they could find some barrels at Fort Adams that were wax-sealed so the powder inside would still be fresh.

When they arrived at Fort Adams, they found it had been abandoned long before the Calamity. The place had been deserted, and the outlying village must have been in pitiful condition even before the Wastes claimed it.

"What now, Con?" Farhad asked. "We can cross the Miss here. Start heading west."

"I 'spose so." There was no point in going further south, but Conny was still unsure. "We ain't seen no trace of Eudora in a while, and that's starting to worry me."

"She likely already crossed and is heading west. If she was smart enough to stay away from the Indian Territories, we can be reasonably sure we're still following her."

"True." Conny took out his map. "We're only about a week's ride from Port Hudson, though. We can make it that far south, maybe there's some munitions there we can scavenge."

"Yeah, or it's taken over by some cutthroat bandits or religious zealots and we walk in and get ourselves killed." Farhad pulled a bottle from his saddlebag and took a pull.

"There ain't no Port Hudson, Con." Nikki sucked in her lips. "There ain't nothing left about a day's ride from here. It's all ocean now."

"It's all ocean?" Conny repeated.

"That's right. The whole southern coast. The water came up and drowned it all. Or the land came down and drowned itself, I don't right know which. But there ain't no Port Hudson, regardless."

"Goddamn." Farhad pulled his *keffiyeh* down and smelled the air. "Well Con, I do smell salt water."

Conny tilted his head back and sniffed. "Yeah, I do too. Jesus Christ, what kind of thing can cause the ocean to swallow entire cities?"

"Well, that settles it." Farhad rubbed his hands together. "We head west now. No sense in going any further south, right?"

"I 'spose so."

"Why don't we stay here for the night and make the crossing in the morning?" Nikki asked.

"Sounds like a good idea, Con. We can scout out a decent spot to make the cross, see if we can find a ferry or a big enough raft."

"All right, boys," Nikki said, "what if we can't find one?"

"Then we build one," Conny said.

They set up camp in the old barracks of the abandoned fort. No windows faced the wind, so the inside was relatively free of dust and sand. Conny insisted that Farhad stay behind to build the fire and cook the food. He needed as much warmth as he could get. Farhad protested until a coughing fit convinced him that staying behind by the fire was in his best interest.

Conny and Nikki rode a length of the Mississippi and searched for docks with rafts, ferries, or boats. Conny didn't want to abandon the horses, but if he had to cross the river, he would. They had no choice.

The sun set rapidly, and the desert grew dark. The two didn't talk. Neither of them felt the need to fill the silence of the desolate land with conversation. There were things about Nikki that Conny wanted to know, but he had time to get to know them. He didn't want to learn everything right now.

He savored not knowing. He enjoyed her anonymity and feared her history. Would he discover something about her that he couldn't reconcile? Yet, try as he might, he could think of nothing that she could have done that he couldn't look past. Maybe what he truly feared was that she would discover the skeletons in his own closet. Could she look past them?

"Conny, there's a light up ahead." Nikki pointed south down the river.

Conny saw it. A soft flickering glow through the rust-colored haze. "Let's check it out. Be ready."

Nikki drew her revolver and tucked it under the wool blanket she had wrapped around her. Conny pulled his coat away from his holsters. They closed the distance between them and the light quickly. Stealth wasn't necessary as the wind masked the sound of the horses and the veil of night would conceal them from anyone's eyes.

Wordlessly, the two split apart, Nikki slowed and approached from the north, and Conny rode around wide and came up from the south. His heart raced and the familiar sense of excitement and anticipation rose. He took off his gloves and felt the handle of his revolver, smooth and cold. When he got close, he reined in.

He dismounted and saw Nikki do the same. Conny had suspected a campfire, some exiles, or scavengers from a nearby town, but instead what they found was a large, hollow cairn. It towered half again as tall Conny and was made from the rocks of a dry-stone wall nearby. Inside, a fire burned, visible through small windows at the four cardinal points.

"I've never seen anything like it," said Nikki, a hint of wonder tempered with caution in her voice.

"It's an Indian cairn." Conny kept his hand on his revolver. "Looks like it was built in a hurry. Whoever made it was skilled, I'll give them that. The fire's been going for maybe half a day."

"Whoever built it was trying to signal somebody. Maybe we should go back to camp. Maybe we don't want to be here when they come."

Nikki was probably right, but Conny couldn't shake the suspicion that the signal, if that's what it was, might be for them. It wasn't a foolish thought. They hadn't met a single living soul since they left Vicksburg. The Wastes were empty, so the number of people the message could be intended for was a short list.

"Let's look around first. See if the builder left anything behind."

Conny lit an oil lamp, and they walked around the cairn. On the far side, they found a line of rocks on the ground in the shape of an arrow, pointing west.

"Con, look at this." Nikki bent down and lifted a piece of paper from under the rock that formed the tip of the arrow. "Give me some light."

She unrolled the paper and read.

"Found the girl. Cross here. Leaving you a ferry. Will slow down as much as I can so you can catch up. She has the money."

She gave the note to Conny who read it again out loud, then again to himself.

"Your Indian friend? Has to be."

"Crowkiller. That son of a bitch, I thought he was gone for good this time. But we got her! We just have to cross the river and she's good as ours."

Nikki took his face in her hands and kissed him. "You're taking me to California, Cornelius White, you hear me? You're taking me all the way. You ain't leaving me behind now that you've got your girl and your money."

Conny had spent so much time lost in his worries and fears that he scarcely gave any consideration to this woman's troubles. The thought that he would abandon her seemed like an absurd one to him, but only he knew his mind.

"Nikki Free, the only thing that's made this all worth it is you. Maybe California's a paradise. Maybe it ain't. I don't right know. But when we get there, if you're by my side, it won't matter. Cause I think I'll have all I need."

She kissed him again. "Don't forget it."

Conny folded the note and put it in the pocket of his long coat. "You know, I didn't even know he could write."

"That doesn't surprise me. You have to talk to people to find out things about them." She slapped him on the chest. "Now what, gunfighter?"

"We head back to camp. Let's get a good night's sleep. We won't cross the river at night, we'll wait until morning. Hopefully, the boat Crowkiller left for us is big enough for the horses, too."

Conny looked out towards the west and tried to see beyond the ruddy haze. Somewhere beyond that cloud of dust was Crowkiller and Eudora, down the Southern Corridor was the ruins of Texas, and farther still sat California. Whatever awaited them there, whether wasteland or paradise, he took joy in the prospect that he would meet it with Nikki Free at his side.

"Let's go, bandito," Nikke said.

They made their way back to camp and Conny tried to temper his excitement. He reminded himself that this was still the end of the world, and Providence has a way of dangling something good in front of you long enough to make you believe you can have it before it snatches it away. He centered himself, came back to the immediate, to the present, to the only time worth considering. The past was over and done, ain't never coming back. The future was out of his hands. The here and now is something he could exert a small bit of control over. That's why he didn't hesitate to leave Memphis when it came down to it. It's why he didn't shy away from Nikki Free.

But if there is a paradise in California...

Conny had no desire to plan for a future that likely would never come. Hoping for a hopeless dream could drive a man insane.

And if I made it there with Nikki Free...

When they arrived back at the ruins of Fort Adams, Farhad had three bowls of wasteland gruel bubbling over the fire. The gruel was a meal he was fond of and when the opportunity presented itself, the Bedouin would, more often than not, forage the area for the seeds and stalks he needed to make it. What those were, Conny didn't quite know. But the gruel was soft, thick, and warm. It filled his belly better than hardtack or a bowl of scorpions and grasshoppers.

As they ate, Conny brought Farhad into their confidence. He told him of the Indian cairn, and of Crowkiller's note.

"That Comanche bastard, I knew he wouldn't let us down, Con." Farhad beamed and shoveled in more gruel, suddenly he appeared ravenous, as if hope had stirred a hunger in him.

"He ain't Comanche, *sadiq*," Nikki said. "He's Oglala Lakota."

"Are you sure?"

"I'm sure."

"How do you know?"

"I talked to him and he told me."

"Well, he told me, too. And each time he told me he was a different kind of Indian. How do you know he wasn't playing you false?"

"He wasn't. The name Crowkiller is a bit of a hint. The Lakota and the Crow used to be fierce enemies. Before Sanguin Corvus came along. I wonder if that has something to do with his exile. Maybe he couldn't let go of his enemy, you know? He would have had to have killed a lot of Crow for him to earn the name Crowkiller."

"With a name like Crowkiller," Conny said, "that's a good possibility."

"Now hold on, none of that is even remotely solid evidence," said Farhad. "All you've given me is speculation and that's hardly convincing."

"He wouldn't lie to me," said Nikki. "That's what he does with you, not me. That's your game, not mine."

"I think she's got you there," said Conny.

"Of course you would think that. Wouldn't do for you to go against your darling, now would it? Me, on the other hand, I require more than speculation and the musings of the fairer sex."

"He speaks Lakota," said Nikki.

"He also speaks English, but that don't make him a white man."

"He tells Lakota stories."

"He also told you *Das kalte Herz*, but that don't make him German."

"He sings Lakota songs."

Farhad pursed his lips. "He also sang *That Ole Wasteland Roan*, but that don't make him a scavenger, neither."

"Boy, you got an answer for everything, don't you?"

Farhad winked. "You know I do, little sister."

"Could have been a lawyer for all your quick retorts."

"Now how dare you slander me like that," Farhad said with mock pain in his eyes. "Better for you to call me a junkmonger. A man's likely to get more use out of what the junkmonger peddles than the lawyer."

"Well now that you've both had your fun, I can tell you the truth," Conny said. "He's a Comanche from Texas."

"And how do you know that?" asked Nikki.

"He told me."

Both Nikki and Farhad laughed. For a time, they all talked in the fluttering light of the campfire. Conny enjoyed these nights and these conversations. He was content to sit and listen, as words didn't come as quick to him as they did to his companions. There was something good and pure in their bandying, and Conny held on to these moments as long as he could.

When Farhad finally relented to Nikki, after he had stood up and bowed deeply to honor her unerring logic and powers of persuasion, Conny knew the time was right to try and convince Farhad to go south into Mexico, to leave him and Nikki, to find a dryer climate and ease the burden on his lungs.

Almost as if Fate handed him an opening, Farhad fell into a coughing fit.

"Farhad, I think we should discuss something," Conny said after the Bedouin's hacking subsided. He began awkwardly, uncomfortable and hesitant to broach the subject. He didn't want Farhad to think he was trying to get rid of him, and he didn't want the man to go, but it was for the best.

"I don't like that tone, Con," Farhad said. "Anytime you use that tone, it ain't never good." Although he joked, his smile was wide, and he looked as if he would take whatever news Conny could give him with that same detached grin. Sweat beaded on his pale forehead despite the cold.

"Yeah, and this is a hard one." It wasn't in Conny's nature to dance around a subject, so he would have to just come out and say it. "You're dying, Farhad."

"I've been dying for years, Conny. That ain't nothing new."

"I know it, but being out here is making it worse. It's too cold. There's too much goddamn dust."

Farhad turned his gaze to the fire, his smile gone. "There ain't nowhere else any better, except maybe California from what we heard. I just got to make it there, that's all. I can make it there."

"I don't know if you can. It'll be months before we get there, and who knows if it's a paradise or not? It likely ain't, I reckon. It's just a hope and only fool's hope."

"You just bring this up just to put me in a sour mood? Was I too jovial for you, so you had to remind me of my mortality? Of the inevitability of me drowning in my own lungs?" There was a sharp edge to his words that suggested he didn't like where this conversation was going. "If not, I think you ought to get to the real point right quick."

"Mexico," Conny said. "I think you should go to Mexico. I hear it's warmer there and the air ain't so dusty. I heard you can see the sun, and even the stars at night."

"Yeah, and I heard there's whole fields of wild tobacco and the whiskey grows on fucking trees."

"Farhad—" Conny started.

"I know what this is about, Con. This isn't about me, it's about you. You don't want me around because you don't want to have to watch me die. So you'll send me packing to Mexico so I can die alone, that it? A foreigner in a foreign land?"

"That's not fair, Farhad." Nikki had kept silent so far, but she spoke up now. "You want to be mad at someone, be mad at me and the Indian. We both put Conny up to this, but he don't want you to leave. I don't either, for my part. I haven't known you long, but I love you like a brother. You're a drunk, a rogue, and a scoundrel, but goddammit I want you to live." Nikki's voice broke and she tightened her lips.

Only the low howl of the wind on the Wasteland filled the silence that followed. After what seemed an intolerably long time to Conny, Farhad finally spoke. "I don't call you 'little sister' lightly, Nikki Free," he said, smiling at her. "I do believe that I sit in the company of two of the finest damn people left in this world. But I am the master of my own life. I ain't about to lose the only thing that's sparked any emotion in me, any enthusiasm, in years. I will see California, for good or for ill, before I die. Mark my words. I am not going to Mexico. Damn fine place it is, I'm sure, but I'm not going there. I'm taking my cut of the money and living out my final months or, if I'm lucky, my final years in the Republic of California."

Conny sighed. This was exactly how he thought this would play out. Farhad was never one for taking orders or doing what was best for himself. He was a man of vice and pleasure. A man who did what he wanted and damn the consequences. But surviving the Calamity in New York, then living for years with Consumption had molded him to be that way. There never was any other fate for the Bedouin after all that. He would do as he wished, and no one was going to tell him otherwise. In a dead world, Farhad was a dead man who had learned how to truly live.

"That settles it then," Conny said. "The matter is over. I won't bring it up again."

Farhad nodded and turned his pallid face to Nikki who nodded in agreement. "Alright, you both got that off your chests. Your consciences are clear. I relieve you of any obligation you think you have to my well-being, so you can all stop fretting over me. Now I think it's time for me to get some rest. Dawn comes early."

After Farhad left for his tent, Nikki laid her head on Conny's shoulder and buried her face under his arm. He held her tight against the cold, against the wind, and against the sorrow that had invaded their night. Under the blanket of dust that shut out the stars, he held her until she stopped crying and fell asleep.

Chapter 27

Serpent's Bluff, North Texas (September, 1881)

Deliverance Hill

The man who tried to murder Sovereign had been laid out on one of the upstairs beds, tied to the wrought iron frame by his hands and feet. He was older than Deliverance, but younger still than she had expected him to be. The single candle that lit up the room burned bright enough for her to see the face of the terrified man. His eyes looked like great round stones pulled from the river, polished by eons of moving water, gleaming in the weak light. His breath came in panicked rasps devoid of cadence or rhythm and he whimpered like a child when anyone approached.

Deliverance almost felt sorry for him.

Behind her stood Wu, small and silent, watching everything. She was Deliverance's eyes and ears when her own were inadequate. Also behind her was Hattie Mothershed, lithic and timid, her hands kneading themselves in front of her.

"This is him, Hattie." Deliverance gestured to the cowering thing on the bed. "Take a good look. Tell me everything you know."

At the name "Hattie," the man's eyes widened even more, though Deliverance wasn't sure how that was possible. There was recognition there. Recognition and a bit of wild hope.

Hattie put a hand to her face, either from shock at the sight of the man or from the overpowering stench. The smell of urine burned her eyes and triggered something primal in her gut, some need to purge herself of anything rotten and foul. Deliverance felt her bile rise but held it in.

Hattie bolted from the room and vomited in the hall.

"Wu, can you help her back in? I don't have the patience for weakness tonight." Normally, Deliverance could handle a girl like Hattie, one who seemed to still live a privileged existence, even here at the end of the world. But tonight, her prisoner upset her. She didn't like to keep a man bound and helpless like this. Much better to hang him from a tree without ceremony and be done with it, but Sovereign wanted answers. And who could blame him? If this man had tried to murder her in her saloon, she'd want answers, too.

When Wu returned with Hattie, the Mothershed girl's pallid face was somehow more pale than it was before.

"Let's try that again," Deliverance said. "Do you know him?"

Hattie nodded. "That's Fogg Bailey. He's one of Ransom's men. They all call him Sharp on account of he's a bit of a dullard. I don't know much about him, though. Other than that."

"You live in Sorrow Draw," Deliverance said. "How do you not know more about him?"

"I don't mind other people's business. I keep to myself."

"Does he have a family?"

The girl paused for a moment. "He does. A wife, I think."

"Kids?"

"I don't think so."

"How important is he to the Paluxy Boys?"

"He's one of their dogs. I ain't never seen him unless he was trailing behind Ransom."

"I see. Would he have tried to kill Sovereign on his own, do you think? Someone who's a bootlicker might hatch a scheme like this to gain favor. But some can't get their nose out of your ass long enough to think for themselves."

"Why don't you ask him?" Wu asked.

"I ain't got the stomach for torture." Deliverance couldn't even look at the man tied to the bed for more than a few moments before her courage failed her and she had to look away. She could admit that to Wu, maybe, but no one else.

"Then we find someone for you who can. There are men here who would love the opportunity."

"Yeah, I'm sure."

"Some of them would take great pleasure in carving up a white man." Wu spoke slowly and deliberately and the prisoner, this man named Bailey, squirmed and whimpered.

"He don't got the brains or the nerve to even breathe on his own unless someone told him to," Hattie said. "He wouldn't have done this unless it came directly from Ransom Eisenhardt's lips. That much I can guarantee."

"Then there's a plot," Deliverance said.

"More than likely. But this man, he was just doing what he was told I reckon. Don't you think? Don't you think that he could tell us what he knows in exchange for letting him go back home?"

"That's the problem with you, girl. You are, in your heart, still loyal to that town. Sorrow Draw got its hooks in you, and ain't let go of you yet. Might not ever."

"No, it's just that I don't like killing. I don't like none of it, that's all. I don't like it when they get killed, I don't like it when you people get killed either." The girl's body shook fierce. Deliverance didn't much care for the killing either, but this would have to be done. But she needn't let Hattie know, not yet. Not until this man gave her everything he knew.

"Alright Mr. Bailey." Deliverance spoke in a slow, almost sultry voice. She had learned long ago how to speak to men to get what she wanted from them. She had no desire to seduce her prisoner, by any means, but it didn't hurt to make her voice more pleasing. "Hattie here wants me to let you go if you tell me what I want to know. I'm not so inclined, but I can be persuaded if you tell me what I want to hear."

Bailey's eyes darted around the room as if he couldn't decide which of the three women deserved more of his attention, but his breathing began to slow.

"That's good, Fogg. Just listen to Deliverance and you'll be out of here and back home in no time." Hattie spoke to him as if she were comforting a child. "Wouldn't you like that? I'll take you home myself. My brother and I, I suppose. He's here, too. We'll both take you back home."

Bailey turned to Deliverance. "That true?" he asked. "I tell you what you want to know and you'll let me go home?"

Deliverance hated a liar. At the poker tables, lying was an art form. It was necessary and expected. Those who didn't expect it were either fools or liars themselves. But outside of the game, she hated a liar. So she chose her words carefully. "Yes, Mr. Bailey. If you tell me what I want to know, I'll send you home. You have my word."

"It was Ransom," he said. He spoke fast, as if he were afraid to stop once he started. "He's trying to get things moving, you know? The preacher's been talking a lot about the end of the world and Jesus coming back and all, and so Ransom, he thinks he can help it out. Maybe give God a little nudge is all. Reverend Mothershed says once all the heathens is dead Christ can come back and make the world a paradise for us again. So he sent us here to kill the big guy and start a war. There was supposed to be others, but I guess they turned tail and ran. None of them had the gumption to do what I did, but we was supposed to stab him all at the same time, like that Julius Caesar story. I guess I should have knowed better."

"Does Ransom really buy into that old man's preachings?" Deliverance asked once the man stopped talking and took a breath.

"No, I don't think he does. We do, though. Most of us, anyway. Ransom will believe someday. When it all happens, you know? But right now, he's just itching for the fight. Well, for the fight, and for Miss Hattie there. Once the fighting starts, he reckons the good Reverend will join the two in marriage. And that's what he really wants right now. Miss Hattie."

Hattie shrank back into the shadows.

"Tell me something, Mr. Bailey. Are you afraid to die? You're shaking something fierce."

"To die? No. I already know the end is coming. The Reverend says so. I ain't afraid of the dying so much as the pain. Once that's over with, I reckon I'm good. I suppose I'm also a bit afeared for my wife. If I were to die, she'd belong to the Boys. They'd pass Constance around like a harlot. They call our widows the brides of the multitude and they are wed to the gang. We all get equal rights to them. Only serves me right, I guess. I've enjoyed more than a few myself. When young Waller Overton got hisself killed by some Indians, we all took a turn on Mary Ann. Hell, we're still sharing her around and Waller's been dead for over a year. Clem said it was Indians, but you know I don't think it were, truth be told, we all wanted that Mary Ann."

"Jesus Christ, shut the fuck up," Deliverance said. He spoke almost casually about the men passing the widows around between them and whatever pity she cultivated for him whithered away. She opened the door and called for Sovereign.

"He's all yours now," she said.

Sovereign and threw the bound man over his shoulder. Bailey kicked and yelled, cried for Hattie and the Lord, for Ransom and Mothershed.

Soon they were gone and Deliverance stood in the room with Hattie. She wanted to leave. To go back to her saloon, to play poker as if nothing out of the ordinary were happening. Even more though, she wanted to be the kind of person who could watch what Sovereign and his men were going to do to Bailey. She wanted to be able to watch him suffer. She was sure he deserved it, and worse.

Instead, she stood there with her head down, unable to move, unable to look at the girl standing next to her.

"You said he could go home if he told you," Hattie said, her voice shaking like a baby fawn.

"I didn't lie. I said I would send him home. And so I will. Whatever is left of him after tonight, I will send home."

"That's monstrous, and it's beneath you."

"Don't you dare tell me what's monstrous. Do you think the Paluxy Boys'll give me the same courtesy when they come and shoot up my saloon? You think I won't end up skinned? Hung upside down and burned alive? How do you think defeat ends for us here?"

Hattie cried silently.

"Looks like the Eisenhardt boy wants to start a war. My people ain't gonna win, I can tell you that. We ain't all green, but a lot of us are. We're families, not cold-blooded killers." Deliverance wrung her hands and outside the cheers of the mad crowd ebbed and flowed.

They stood together in silence. The acrid air burned in her nostrils. Hattie's shoulders shook. The crowd yelled.

The Mothershed girl turned and put her arms around Deliverance and cried into her chest. Deliverance patted her head like she was a child.

"Shhhh. I know, girl. I know. It's alright. Everything will be alright."

Chapter 28

Sorrow Draw, North Texas (October, 1881)

Erasmus Mothershed

After the killing of Fogg Bailey, Erasmus and his sister made their way home as fast as they could. The Freemen planned to sneak into Sorrow Draw and leave Bailey's body on the church steps. Erasmus wanted to be back in town well before that happened to avoid suspicion. Deliverance had promised they would allow them plenty of time, but Hattie told him not to trust in that woman's promises.

Eula's voice echoed down the dark and dusty hallways of the Mothershed manor. It was a shrill, creaking sound like a door closing on great rusted hinges. She called for her son.

"Erasmus."

When he didn't answer, his mother would call again, and the house would carry her voice through the unlit corridors like blood through veins, so it felt to Erasmus like the manor itself was a living thing and Eula's voice—his mother's voice—was the black ichorous gore that pumped through its rotting heart.

He ignored her wailing and continued to measure out his liquid into a small cup. Mother's medicine. He poured a small dram of arsenic into the tin and stifled a smile. He felt evil. But the evil he felt also gave him an equal measure of satisfaction. He briefly contemplated giving her more. He could put an end to it all right here, right now. He could end her suffering and, in turn, end Hattie's suffering. Perhaps it wasn't fair that she had to endure the countless hours taking care of their mother. The feedings, cleaning the soiled bedding, and on those days when mother was lucid enough, tolerating her abuse. He could end it all tonight.

He returned the stopper to the bottle. No, not tonight. Not yet. He wasn't willing to let her go. She hadn't yet paid for her sins. He hadn't yet delivered restitution to those lives she had destroyed. God had delivered the Calamity to him, this opportunity for divine punishment, and he would not let it go to waste.

Eula Mothershed called again, and still, Erasmus felt evil. He took a pull from a bottle of whiskey. This wasn't the first time he had to give his mother her medicine, but it never got easier. He remembered the days in the beginning, when she was sick of her own accord, or that of Providence. He had genuinely tried to ease her suffering at first. Her cries had filled him with terror and dread, he would feed her and she would vomit it up on his waistcoat and he would cry for her and for his clothes. Back then her screams were louder, her face fuller, and her body, dying as it was, still more full of life than the gaunt, ghoulish husk that lay in the big velvet-draped bed on the third floor.

Sometimes he would cradle her head in his lap and stroke her hair until she was herself again and she would tell him that she didn't want any molly or sodomite putting his hands on her. In those days he still had that primitive love for his mother that all children have, no matter what she had done, to him or to others. But he also hated her. He hated the mask of beauty that she wore to cover up her cruelty and how that beauty would often be enough for people to forgive and forget the harm she so often caused. He hated how that beauty would make his heart hurt when he looked at her and he would want nothing more than to fall in her arms, to smell the sweet scent of bluebonnets, cradled in her embrace.

Lucifer, he had been told, was a beautiful angel, too.

Those were childish thoughts, and Erasmus remembered them now only as sad and foolish memories, ashamed to have felt them at all. No reconciliation could ever be found with such a woman, not one whose hateful words had pierced so deep, who herself found joy in the suffering of others, yet Erasmus feared he was becoming the very monster he intended to slay.

He took up the small tin cup and walked the long halls of the Mothershed manor to his mother's room. Her thin body contorted on her bed. She looked at him with dark, deep-set eyes, and in the low candlelight her face took on the form of a skull. She had pulled at the front of her chemise until it had torn and fell to her waist. Her breasts glistened in the firelight from drool, sweat, or vomit. Or perhaps any combination of the three. Her wet skin gave her the appearance of a polished marble statue, so smooth it still was, so pale. But what had once been a faultless, pearlescent body was now a wan and anemic corpse.

The room smelled of urine and Erasmus put a finger to his nose.

"Finally," she said, her voice scarcely above a whisper. "I've been calling for you."

"I know, mother. I've been mixing your medicine. This should help you sleep."

"Sleep? What for? So I can dream? Dream I'm a young, beautiful girl again, not this thing covered in piss and shit? So I can wake up?"

"Yes, Mother. Waking up is generally what happens after one sleeps."

"Well, I don't want to wake up, Rasmus. I want to sleep forever."

"Come now, mother. You don't mean that."

"Do I not? Don't tell me you don't wish the same thing. Why wouldn't you, boy?"

"You're my mother—"

"And what kind of a mother have I been? You have been the worst kind of son, but I know how you must see me."

"The worst kind of son? How have I wronged you, mother? How, as a child, did I possibly wrong you?"

"You live, that's how. I never wanted you. I never wanted you or that sister of yours. I never wanted to come to this filthy town and I never wanted that old man to put his hands on me. I was supposed to become a city girl. That's what he promised me."

"Father? Father promised you that?"

"No, not your father. I was never supposed to be with him. It was Albert. He promised to bring me up in society. Swore that I would live in San Francisco. Said it was going to be the new New York. Said I would even have me some Jewish servants so I wouldn't have to stomach having any Negroes around my house."

"What happened to the two of you?"

"He had left to get the house prepared and arrange for our wedding. Some Apaches shot him full of arrows somewhere in New Mexico or so I heard. After that, your pa paid a lot of money to my uncle for me and dragged me down here."

Eula's lucidity was astonishing. Erasmus hadn't seen her this aware in years and his throat tightened listening to her.

"Give me some morphine," she said. "And give me too much. So I fall asleep and never wake up. Take some pity on a woman who had never got a choice to live the life she wanted."

"None of us got that chance. The Calamity took that from all of us. Besides, what would Father do without you?"

"Oh, yes, your father." She coughed. "My only regret is that somehow that old bastard outlived me. My God, I wanted him to die a long time ago."

"I know."

"You know?"

"Yes, I know. I know a lot of things you think I don't know."

"Like what?"

"I know about Arthur Swink. I know the two of you were intimate. I've often wondered if Hattie was his child. I never told her, of course. Or father. When poor Swink met his unfortunate end, I saw no use in it. I always did find it interesting how he died. What was it, the paper called it? Bilious fever? I always thought that was interesting."

"He was going to tell your father." Eula's body seemed to sink further into the bed. "He knew Hattie was his. When she was old enough…when she grew into her face, he became certain of it. He wanted her. He wanted me and her, but he wasn't fit to be a husband or a father."

"Maybe that's because he was still a boy."

"A boy? He was eighteen, hardly a boy."

"Eighteen when you poisoned him. How old was he when you took him to bed?"

She waved her hand in a dismissive gesture. "Old enough to know what he was doing. I wanted to hold out for your father to die but I suppose I should have poisoned him instead."

"Yes, I suppose that would have been the easiest solution."

"I don't know why I couldn't. I had no problem poisoning Arthur, but your father? I couldn't bring myself to. The very idea terrified me. I always thought he would rise up from the gates of Hell and drag me down with him if I tried."

"It seems we have something in common after all."

"You know, I'm surprised you never told her the truth, Hattie I mean. You never told her who her father really is? I would have thought something like that would have given you a great deal of pleasure in tormenting her with. You two always hated each other."

"No mother, we never hated each other. If cruel words were ever spoken between us, it was from a place of love and affection. We learned how to be vicious to each other, alright. You and Father taught us that. Murdering family with words is the Mothershed way, after all. But the two of us have had to endure living in this home, our own private little Purgatory, for so many years. I wouldn't have survived without her. I love Hattie. Probably more than I love anything else on Earth. I love her more than I love even myself, and you know how much I love myself."

Eula snorted. "I wasn't so awful to you. Your father, maybe. But not me. I could have been a better mother, but being a mother wasn't something I wanted. It was something your father forced on me when I was just a child myself."

"Believe me, mother. That's something I had to remind myself of every day of my life." He put the tin cup to his mother's mouth. "I put extra laudanum in it tonight. It should help make you more comfortable."

"What is this? Where's my silver teacup? You take me for some nigger to drink out of a cup like that?"

Erasmus leaned in and whispered in her ear. "No, those of that noble race are far too good to drink from a cup like this. This is a cup for a murderer. Now drink it."

She let him pour the liquid in her mouth and she swallowed it silently. She turned her head away. "Close the door on your way out. I won't be needing you anymore tonight."

"Of course, mother." Erasmus turned to leave.

"One more thing," Eula said. Her voice took on an unnatural deep quality, one that Erasmus knew well. "Are you still a sodomite?" she asked.

He wasn't ashamed, and he refused to allow her to hear any trace of shame in his voice. "When I do bugger someone, it's another man. So yes, I suppose I am."

Eula nodded slowly. "Then I'll see you in Hell."

Erasmus closed the door behind him. Ahead, the long hallway felt darker than usual, and the walls loomed oppressively high. He left the manor in a hurry to walk the deserted streets of town. He walked past shops with their broken windows and bare shelves and he imagined how they were before the Calamity. He tried to remember the iron ring of the blacksmith's hammer, the sound of horses in the livery, the piercing smell of liquor, and the din of raucous laughter from the saloon. He stopped at the haberdasher's and saw a vision of himself finely dressed and freshly shaved, chatting with another gentleman about the newest selections.

Have you tried Captain McLure's Macassar Oil yet?

I have, and I've sworn that I'll never again buy anything else.

And to think, just two summers ago the only thing you could find here was a tin of bear's grease.

If one was lucky!

Ah, hello. A bottle of Alopecian balm. Perhaps you could purchase it for Mr. Schumacher?

Indeed, the old balmer gets balder by the day!

He roamed the town for hours and he watched the ghosts of Sorrow Draw walk with him. Carriages rolled past and filled the air with the clatter of hooves. Laughing children ran by on their way to school. He heard barking dogs and the gossip of men and women in their separate places. He wandered the streets until the darkness of evening threatened to conceal his path back home.

Hattie was waiting for him when he arrived back at the Mothershed house. She wore a plain gray dress that fit loose enough that she could wrap more of it around her to stave off the cold.

"I was getting worried. I didn't know if you were coming back tonight or even where you had gone."

He kissed her forehead. "Do you love me?"

"What kind of question is that?"

"A serious one."

"Of course I love you."

"No matter what I've done?"

"Rasmus, I know about the things you do."

"No matter what I've done?" he said again.

"Rasmus you're starting to scare me."

"You know everything I've done has been to protect you, right?"

"Well, I'm sure that now I don't really know what you've done. But I know you've always looked out for me." Her voice quavered, and a gust of wind blew her brown curls into her face.

"Goodnight, Hattie," he whispered.

"Rasmus."

"Yes, Hattie?"

"I do love you. No matter what you've done."

In his room, Erasmus poured himself a drink from a bottle of absinthe. He crushed a morphine pill into a fine powder and watched it swim and swirl in the green liquid.

He fell into a restless sleep and in his sleep, he was a child again, hiding behind the folds of his mother's dress, hiding from his father. His mother picked him up, but she wasn't beautiful. She was old and sick and she pulled a breast out from her dress and gave it to him to suck but it was covered in filth and vomit and he cried for his nanny Susan, the woman with the dark skin and the warm smile and this made his mother angry and she said terrible things to Susan and mother made him watch as some men came and put a rope around her neck and hung her up outside until her body swelled and her dark brown skin turned black and her eyes fell out from her head.

Chapter 29

Uncontested Lands, Old Louisiana (October, 1881)

Farhad

It had been a week since they crossed the Mississippi into what had once been Louisiana. They had found Crowkiller's ferry buried under a thicket of dried brush. It was small, but their horses were light and thin, born of the Wastelands, and they were able to fit everyone on and it made the crossing easy.

When they had landed on the opposite side, Farhad said a silent prayer that it would be the last time he needed to ride in a boat. His first experience on the water was when he sailed from Jaffa for the United States when he was a boy. He had never seen so much water. His father had told him before they arrived that it was like the desert—deadly if not given the proper respect. Like the desert, it could pull you under, bury you, cover you over, and keep you hidden for eternity. Or it could leave you adrift on its desolate waves, lost to sorrow and despair, only to die of thirst.

Farhad had marveled at what his father said. How could there be so much water—more water than he even knew existed in the whole world—yet a man could die of thirst? He had stood on the dock full of sublime wonder, his eyes wide trying to take it all in. The waves lapped up against the side of the ship, threw themselves at the pier again and again, and he wanted to drink it, to dive in and open his mouth and let the water fill his belly but his father refused to allow it. That very day he found his way up to the front of the ship after they had unmoored and set sail. The water sprayed up over the railing and he opened his mouth to it and discovered the awful truth. The ocean was as his father said. As deadly as the desert. Maybe even more so. Unlike the desert, which always took its time, the ocean could kill someone quickly if it desired. But if it wanted to savor it, it could make it a slow thing. He imagined himself drifting endlessly on the unbounded waters. The salt air leeched the moisture from his body and turned him into an arid husk. The waters themselves mirror the sun to blind him, all the while offering not a drop of relief to deliver him from his withering agony. Ash-Shaytan himself could scarcely conceive of a worse hell.

It was seventeen days from Jaffa to the United States and Farhad had spent most of those miserable days below deck, sick, unhappy, and terribly alone. He listened to the shrieks and groans of the ship as it fought to keep the infinite power of the ocean at bay, and he passed his time reading from the Quran. His uncle Osman had been teaching him to read, though his father saw little importance in it. But Farhad had the least responsibility among his brothers, and so Osman saw an opportunity to tutor him, and his father relented. He had been an eager student, and a quick learner, so his uncle had told him. In truth, those things had always come very easy for Farhad. Even now, if he were to spend a few minutes with a group of people who spoke an unfamiliar tongue, he could start to pick up some words and phrases. A few hours and he could have simple conversations. Give him a few weeks, and Farhad could speak their language as if he was born into it. It was a skill he didn't even know he possessed until the Calamity hit and he found himself stranded in a foreign country. There were so many languages spoken in America that he quickly found that with a little patience, he could begin to understand them. First the words, then how they are arranged, which words come first when you're speaking, and how to talk about things that happened in the past. It took a little longer to understand a culture's expressions and what Farhad called "unspoken words." Those, along with the forbidden "curse" words, were the most appetizing of all.

His brothers and cousins fared much better on the rolling waves than he did, and they amused themselves by playing games with the ship's sailors.

Farhad had suspected at least some of them of drinking alcohol, which was haram, and it angered him. If his father knew, he said nothing of it. In the years since, Farhad would often wonder if his father might not have indulged a little himself in those terrifying days and nights aboard the ship.

The thought once again made him smile. He would give up California, leave Conny and Nikki for the void, and face the rest of eternity in darkness for a night drinking with his father. He pulled the stopper from his whiskey bottle and took a long pull.

"Easy there, bandito." Nikki pulled up beside him. The road in front of them stretched out as far as he could see through the dust. The monotony of it all began to take a toll on them. Conny took the lead, a ruddy silhouette at the edge of all that was visible. It was a familiar sight, and Farhad could do nothing but continue to follow it.

"I am never easy on whiskey, Nikki Free. Whiskey requires a forceful hand and a stern demeanor. Without that, she's likely to take advantage. But why call me a bandito? What have I done to deserve that kind of oath so early in the morning from the likes of you?"

"Oh, aren't you right, of course," she said. "What's a word in your language that means bandit? I can call you that instead."

Farhad thought about it for a moment. "Qutaa al turuq." He didn't get the opportunity to speak his native tongue much and it tasted sweet.

"That's a lot for my mouth to say. I'll stick with bandito. The sentiment is the same, at least."

"You knave." Farhad took another drink.

"I have a question for you," she said.

"Ask your question, little sister, and we'll see if I have an answer to match."

"If you're from Arabia, and Conny, a Yankee, taught you English, why do you speak with a southern accent?"

"We had a few people in Memphis who came up from Texas. I fell in with them. Good people. One was a woman named Josephine. Her accent was as beautiful as she was. I spent so much time talking with them that I just picked it up and I've just never let it go. I find it soothing. This accent is like butter, smooth and sweet, and everything is better covered in it. It feels rich rolling off my tongue and makes me want to savor every word. Conny, now his accent's just fine and all, but it isn't... delicious."

Nikki wrapped her blanket tighter around her shoulders. "I think his accent is positively charming."

"You would."

"Were you and Josephine ever sweet on each other?"

"Why do you ask? Is that jealousy I detect?"

"Not a bit. Curiosity is all. You do seem to enjoy the company of women when the opportunity arises. I seem to recall a little white woman back in Bolivar who you got real friendly with."

"Ah yes, lovely Lulah. I must admit, it's my memory of her that's been keeping me warm at night."

"I'm surprised she didn't want to come with you."

"No one said she didn't, darling." He made an effort not to smile. "But I ain't Conny and it takes more than a pretty little face and a warm and willing body to convince me to take on another traveling companion. 'Sides, you got the last horse, and I don't think these beasts can manage two riders."

"You have to admit, I'm pretty handy to have around. I think Conny made the right choice."

"I have no doubt you think that. And I will say, it was one of his better ideas." The wind stabbed at Farhad through his coat, and he lowered his voice just a bit so it wouldn't carry too far. "Now, let me ask you a question if you could oblige."

"Certainly."

"Why Conny?"

Nikki stiffened in her seat and drew herself up almost imperceptibly. "What do you mean?"

"Now don't get me wrong, I love this particular coupling. You are two of my favorite people, after all. But you aren't like Conny. You're like me. We are products of the Calamity, you and I. We weren't born into it, but we are better off for it. For all its death and destruction, all its inhumanity, for all the suffering it caused, you wouldn't change it, and neither would I. Admit it. If you could go back and somehow stop it from happening, you wouldn't."

"Ain't no one could stop it from happening, so there's no point in speculating on it."

Farhad had no intention of letting her go that easily. There was a mystery about Nikki, not just her past, which she guarded like an overprotective mother, but also her intentions. Though he trusted her with his life, there was so much about her that he didn't know. "The way I've been seeing it is this. There are only two kinds of people in the world. Those whose lives were destroyed by the Calamity, and those whose lives were saved by it. Now, the former outnumber the latter by a country mile, that's for sure. But Conny, he's of the kind that if he could by some miracle reverse the course of time and stop whatever otherworldly thing it was that turned the world to ruin, well, he'd do just that."

"For Elizabeth?" she asked.

"Ah yes, for his fair-haired maiden long lost. And for his children and his god-damned sense of honor."

Nikki sniffed and rubbed at her wrists. The wounds from her crucifixion were still dark but healing well. "What was it that you said to Conny back in the courthouse?"

"Back in the courthouse?"

"With the Magistrate. You said something in your language. What was it?"

"I said *sakoud*. Conny and I, we sometimes use my language as a sort of secret code. We can say things to each other in situations like that and our enemy doesn't know what we're planning."

"So why your tongue? Why not French or German if you speak those, too."

"The likelihood of someone here understanding French or German is much higher than someone understanding my language. Those odds are about zero. As Crowkiller is fond of pointing out, I am probably the last native speaker left in the world."

"So what does it mean?"

"I told him to let me take the lead."

"Why haven't you taught me any of this? Shouldn't I know these secret words?"

"I'm sure you have your own secrets."

"I don't have secrets. Only things I haven't told him about yet. But since I do intend to tell him someday, they aren't really secrets."

Farhad laughed. "Now if that ain't the most womanish thing I ever heard. Alright Nikki Free, I'll teach you some of my native tongue. It'll give us something to do to pass the time, at least."

Up ahead, Conny slowed and let them catch up. "What's so funny?"

"Farhad here doesn't think that a woman is entitled to her secrets, is all."

"Not true, little sister. But I do think maybe the two of you ought to do a little more conversating and a little less..." he gestured in the air, "whatever else you've all been doing with your lips and tongues." He laughed again and rode forward to take the lead.

He sank into his coat to ward off the chill. He could hear the occasional fragment of conversation behind him, carried to him by the wind, followed by long moments of silence. Jealousy stabbed at his heart, but he pushed it away. Conny was a man of the past, his soul was stuck in the old world. He could easily give himself over to one woman and live happier than if he had his own harem of tender-fleshed girls. Farhad could not love only one. His trickster heart burned with passion for a new love, but like gunpowder, it consumed itself in a flash, in an instant the fiery lust would be gone, and he was made all the emptier for it until a new desire beckoned. And he would always answer.

Life would be easier if he could love as Conny loved. Conny loved as he lived, slow and measured. This affair with Nikki, at first, seemed out of his character. Too quick, too sudden. But in truth, Conny had been building up to it for eighteen years. Eighteen years since the Calamity, eighteen years since his Elizabeth had betrayed him. No, this love affair was not formed in haste but had been built up slow and gradual, like the great bonfires of the wandering scavengers, it was tended to layer upon layer, needing only Nikki to come along and set it ablaze. Theirs was a fire that would burn hot and long.

Lost in his thoughts, he almost missed the sign. A small cairn on the side of the road. A large, flat rock at its base had a stylized drawing of a crow.

Crowkiller. They were going the right way. They stopped for a moment to celebrate and to see if there was anything else that the Indian might have left for them. Farhad was disappointed that Crowkiller hadn't left a note or any other cryptic signs, but when they returned to the road he was filled with renewed vigor. They rode on through the dust like men stumbling in the dark with only a single candle to light their way.

Chapter 30

Uncontested Lands, Old Louisiana (October, 1881)

Eudora Becker

She had given herself over to Horsethief too soon. That much she knew, and Eudora had spent the last few days admonishing herself for it. It was a terrible mistake, and one she can't get back. Once she's given herself to a man, it's not possible to make him desire her the way he did before he had her. That's something she learned with Jeremiah. Now her influence on the Indian has lessened. Desire, it would seem, is as unsteady as the shifting dunes of the Wastelands. An unfair truth, but one she must fix as best she can.

Horsethief busied himself with his carving. He was always carving. The knife flashed in the firelight and his powerful hands darted back and forth like a woman with a sewing needle darning a pair of socks. Days ago, it had been a flute. Tonight, it was a figure of some kind, too small for her to make out from across the fire.

The wind blew and stabbed at her skin, but Horsethief seemed unperturbed. He didn't flinch in the cold, his skin didn't prickle, he didn't shut his eyes to the icy gale. He just continued to whittle at the figure taking shape in his hand.

She could deny him his appetites. If familiarity bred this disinterest, she might make herself unfamiliar again. There were no other men around to feign interest in. That often stirred the mad blood in men. Back in Memphis, she could juggle the interests of many men. When one became indifferent, she would show him some attention, and rouse his passions a bit. Then make sure he saw her with another man. She walked a fine line at times. There were some men whose jealousy angered them too easily. Other men would be more likely to give up entirely. Some, she had heard, would kill a woman for less. But she was Becker's daughter. No man would be fool enough to hurt her if she didn't take things too far.

But Horsethief didn't care if she were Becker's daughter. No one out here did. Her protections were stripped, and she was laid bare like the corpses that lined the grand entrance to Memphis. Corpses her father had put up to keep people on the outside away, and people on the inside in line.

She shuddered. The memory of her father stabbed at her with a ferocity not unlike the wind. She had abandoned him. It must have hurt him to find her gone. She didn't think about that when she left. Of course, he would have been angry, but she hadn't thought about the pain it might have caused him. Tears threatened and she pushed them aside.

If not for her new companion, she would turn around and head back to Memphis. It wouldn't be too difficult. With poor Jeremiah dead, she could blame him. When she returned the money, he would adore her. Then again, if it hadn't been for Horsethief, she would be dead like Jeremiah. She felt the bile rise. Sometimes when she slept, and hunger gnawed at her, she thought of the Magistrate and his offering of meat. On those nights her mouth watered, and shame devoured her.

Returning to Memphis was not an option for her, not as long as she had her silent companion. But what kind of man was he? She needed to know his heart. She needed to know how much of his heart she could have. She doubted that she could make him see things her way, the way she could with Jeremiah. Then again, he was still a man, after all.

"What are you making?" she asked. She needed to talk to him to find his mind and know his heart. A difficult task with this one. He doesn't care much for conversation.

The Indian stared at her for a minute, almost as if he was surprised she had spoken. Then he held up the tiny figure in his hand. "It's a crow."

Eudora held her hand out across the fire. Horsethief gave her the crow and she turned it around in the dim light and studied it. It was, of course, beautiful. The wings were spread out as if it had been frozen in mid-flight, the feathers splayed behind it like spread fingers. She touched the beak, impossibly small and open wide in a silent cry.

"It's beautiful." Eudora handed it back. "What's it for?"

"A flute."

"A flute?"

"Yes."

"I've never seen flutes with animals on them."

"Then you've never seen the flutes that my people play."

"Why a crow? With a name like yours, I'd have thought maybe a horse would suit it better."

"This isn't for a man named Horsethief. It's for a man named Crowkiller."

"Crowkiller? I'm not sure I like that name. Why is he called that? And why use a crow for his flute if he kills them?"

"Perhaps he doesn't kill crows. Perhaps he is a Crow that kills."

"I hadn't thought of that, I guess. Well, either way, he's sure to love the flute."

"Yes, I believe he will."

She needed to press him, to know more about who he is and, maybe more importantly, who he knows. Did he know her father? If he does, that's an advantage she can use.

"So where are you from, Horsethief? Are you from the Indian Territories? I've always wondered what they were like. But I suppose someone like me could never be fortunate enough to see for herself."

"I am from the Indian Territories, yes. And you could see for yourself what they are like. Only it would be the last thing you ever saw."

"Wouldn't you protect me? If you were with me, I mean?"

"I am only one man. In the Indian Territories there are many men."

"You could tell them I'm only one woman. I can't hurt them at all. It wouldn't do them any good to kill me."

"It's your blood they don't like. They fear your blood mixing with theirs."

"But you don't fear that."

"No."

"Why?"

"Because I know the truth."

"What's the truth?"

"That it doesn't matter. The world is dead. They fear your kind coming back, but I know you won't. I know that nothing is coming back."

"Then maybe you can tell them. So I can come to your home and live with you."

"I have told them. They don't believe me. Some of them are too cautious. Others are too angry. Your people are cunning and fight well. But your men can't be trusted."

"Why are you out in our land then, and not your own?"

"You don't have land here. Eventually, my people will reclaim all of this. When the dust finally settles, and the sun returns. When the trees come back and the rivers flow clear again, we will come back for it all. My people believe that a great battle will happen between us and the white men, but I don't think so."

"You think we'll all get along then?"

"No, I think you will all be gone by then. All we need to do is wait."

Eudora's heart sank. She didn't like this conversation. It wasn't answering any of her questions, and she didn't think her people would all die. They had survived this long. Someday, women will start having babies again the way they used to. Her father told her that, and she believed him. He was the smartest man she had ever known.

"Well, how far have you traveled?" She needed to know if this man knew her father.

"Far. I've crossed the harrowed mud fields of Lukango's kingdom in the south, to the dunes of Carolina, an ocean of sand so vast that if the sun could pierce the clouds, it would stretch farther than your eyes could see. You could go to sleep there at night and when you wake up, it would seem a different place entirely, because the dunes shifted in the winds. I've seen the Great Ice in the north and fought alongside white men who were fighting against other white men in the ruins of Boston. I've killed Mexicans and White men in Tejas and beyond. I've even journeyed into desolate Mexico until the wind blew the sand so hard it could scour the skin right off your bones and I was forced to turn back."

For a moment, Horsethief's words filled Eudora with wonder. Then wonder turned to despair. Could a man who had seen so much, endured so much, ever care for such a small, insignificant girl? Then she reminded herself that she was Eudora Becker, the daughter of Samuel Becker, the governor of Memphis. Someone as well-traveled as this Indian should surely know who she is and recognize her importance.

She drew herself up. A governor's daughter shouldn't be seen hunched over. "Have you ever been to Memphis?" she asked.

"A time or two, yes." He smiled. "I recognize the street and those shops you've put there on your paper." He pointed his knife at the drawing she held in her lap. Horsethief had pencils and paper that he used to write notes and make maps and he had given her some. She spent her nights by the fire making drawings of people she knew and places she had been.

"Oh, you do? I wanted to see what they would look like if I could see them all at once, you know? Without all the dust covering them up." She had drawn the road where Purdy's saloon sat across from the general store. She had drawn it from memory alone, as best as she could recall and she put them down on paper as they would have been before the Calamity, before the people boarded the windows against the dust and wind, before the passing of time had reduced them to ruins.

Crowkiller nodded. "I like your Memphis better than the real one. The last time I was there will likely be my last."

"Oh? And how recently were you last there?"

"Would it surprise you to learn that I have followed you since you and that white man left like the ghosts of the Wastelands were chasing you?"

"You didn't tell me that."

"No, I didn't."

"Well, if you've been to Memphis a few times, you should know my father, and so I should offer you a warning, though I hesitate to do so for fear you may try to ransom me." She took a calculated risk in revealing her identity. Should Horsethief prove false, he could take her prisoner and ransom her back to her father. Or he could take her to the Indian Territories where they could torture her, mutilate her, and send her back to her father to goad him to war. But Horsethief had protected her and cared for her so far. And she desperately needed someone to trust.

"You're Sam Becker's daughter."

He said it so plainly, as if he wasn't guessing, but he knew. "You knew already? I should have known. You're here to take me back to him, aren't you? That's just like him, to send someone else to come collect me. I told Jeremiah—"

"I am not here to return you to him. If I was, we would never have crossed the Mississippi."

He had a point. They were headed in the exact opposite direction of Memphis. "So, what are you going to do with me, then?"

"We will keep going. Follow the road to California. Take the money you have and make a life there."

"So you know about the money? You looked through my things?"

"Yes. I saved your life, and I saved your things. It was my right to look through them and see what I was saving."

"Well, you're still here, so I suppose you want the same thing I want."

"I do. We'll go to California. You and I."

"But what about the Indian Territories?"

"What about them?"

"You aren't going back?"

"No, girl. I am banished from them. And even if I were not, I would not return." He picked up his knife and went back to work on the crow carving.

"Banished? Why?"

"I tried to kill my brother."

"Why would you do that?"

"I believed he was leading our people down the wrong path."

This news was great for Eudora, though she knew Horsethief would appreciate it if she showed sympathy for his unfair banishment. "Why are you here alone? Did no one else stand by your side and fight with you?"

"A few did. They weren't so fortunate as I to be given exile as punishment. What's left of their bones now lie scattered on the border of the Indian Territories."

"That's awful."

"There are worse fates."

"Well, if you know who I am, and you know who my father is, and you know what I'm carrying, then you must not be a bounty hunter come to take me back to Memphis."

"No, I am not."

"So, my father might still send out more. We should be on the lookout."

"No," Horsethief said. "There may be more people who will come for you, but they won't be sent by your father."

"Why not? He's not going to let me go. He'll keep looking for me until he has me back or he thinks I'm dead. He'll find a way to drag me back to Memphis unless we can move quickly."

"Your father's not in Memphis anymore."

"What do you mean? He has plenty of trackers to come after me, he has no reason to leave Memphis, certainly not when I might have gotten bored of this whole thing and found my way back on my own. He'd need to stay there for me."

"This was a more serious thing you did than you realize, girl."

Fear gripped her heart. She didn't like Horsethief's new tone. It had gotten more somber, more serious. Which was quite a feat coming from a man who was already the most serious person she had ever met. "How so?" she said. Her voice stuck in her throat.

"Well, he had already sent a letter to Longstreet about the money you took. So, Longstreet was coming to collect it. When he realized you and your phony preacher took it, he knew he couldn't stay in Memphis, or it'd be his own body that decorated the front gates. So he went after you himself. Him and a few of his friends. I followed them, for a time. But things happened that kept them away, and so I found you first."

"What things happened? Is my father alright?"

"Come here woman and sit with me."

"No, tell me."

"Not until you sit with me."

Eudora's legs barely held her up. She was afraid of what he was going to tell her, but she went over and sat next to him. He put his arm around her and told her. Told her terrible things, things she didn't want to hear, but her mouth wouldn't form the words to tell him to stop. He told her about a ferry, about a Mexican man, about a rifle. She shook, and the man put a coat around her. It was heavy wool, gray, her father's. He gave her a hat, too. It had been his. It smelled like him. She shook some more, and the man put her head on his chest and held her. She clawed at his arms, and she sobbed and sobbed and when she thought she was done, when her chest burned and her belly ached and the tears wouldn't flow, she sobbed some more, and the wind took her sorrow and bore it away.

Chapter 31

Uncontested Lands, Old Louisiana (October, 1881)

Nikki Free

Nikki held the paper at an angle against the firelight. She had taken to reading during her time on watch, and this was a *Harper's Weekly* that Conny found in an old shack that had been half buried in the sand and dust. He fit himself in through a small open window on the roof, but the roof was now only just above the ground. He found it mostly untouched, as was the case with most of what they encountered in Louisiana. The area wasn't very populated before the Calamity, and it certainly wasn't after.

The biggest problem with recovering artifacts in Louisiana was the decay. Nothing lasts long in the barren land. Iron rusts, leather cracks and crumbles, paper turns to dust. The best places to look are the houses like the one Conny found this paper in. Houses that are buried in the earth, that protect what's inside as much as possible from the consuming Wastes.

Nikki loved reading the papers. Petty problems, useless and trivial. White man's problems.

Winchester Occupied
Evacuation of New Madrid
Capture of Newbern
Memphis in Anarchy
Our Wounded and Dead Scalped and Mangled

White people who killed other white people over slaves. She read the accounts of the war and the fighting, the hundred dead here, the thousand dead there. Names and places with little meaning to her now. She wondered how things would have played out if the Calamity had never come. Would the Yankees win? Most people thought the Yankees would win, but then again most people didn't expect the rebels to put up such a fight. A part of her was glad they put up a fight. The longer the war, the more their bodies piled up.

She wondered how things would have fared had the Yankees won. She knew right well how things would have turned out if they had given up the fight and let the rebels have their own country. But what if the Yankees won? What if they beat the rebels into submission and outlawed slavery? Some whispered that they would have freedom, that they would be equal. Nikki believed it when she was a girl. But she knew better now. The end of the world had done nothing if not show her the true nature of humanity. They would have been granted freedom, but they never would have been treated as equals.

She wondered about Conny. Would he have survived the war? Would he have gone home after all to his pretty little white wife? Would he have thought, at the end of it all, that it was a war worth fighting? It was an unfair thought, but it came unbidden and intruded on her mind. She pushed it away.

Whatever may have been will never be. These stories in this paper were white man's problems once, but the troubles of whites and blacks had merged, at least for now. But her people still knew other fears. The white man didn't secretly dread the end of the Calamity. They didn't fear the parting of the veil of dust and the warming of the world again and what that would bring, but they longed for it. Dreamed of it.

But isn't that what she also dreamed of? California. A place where the Calamity had already vanished like an overlong winter and the green and the life had returned to the world. Yes, she dreamed of that, too. But she dreamed of the return of Mother Earth on her own terms, one where she was not bound and captive. Where her children would not be taken from her and sold to another, where she would toil for herself and not a master, and where laughter and joy would supplant the bitter tears of slavery. If such a place could even exist.

Farhad awoke to relieve himself and when he was finished, she asked to do the same. She belted on her revolvers and walked uneasily to the edge of the light.

"Expecting trouble?" Farhad teased.

"I think Crowkiller would tell me to always expect trouble."

Farhad laughed. "You're an impeccable judge of a man's nature, Nikki Free. Why I'd say you know what we're going to do or say even before we do."

"Men ain't at all complicated, Farhad. And it don't matter the color of your skin, or where you're from, even if you come from a land all the way across an entire ocean."

"I'd be insulted if I weren't so inclined to agree with you. Hurry back, I'm likely to fall asleep waiting."

"Hadawa," she said.

"Nikki Free, I have not been teaching you my native tongue so you could turn it back on me like that. Now you skedaddle. Hurry up and piss and I might forgive you for this grievous insult."

They had made camp under a small outcropping of rock next to some shallow, slow-moving river. Conny told them he wasn't sure what its proper name was since most of the rivers had run off course after the Calamity. They were about a week out of crossing what Conny believed to be the Calcasieu River, though he couldn't be entirely sure. The Calcasieu, and all the other rivers they had to cross so far, were much easier fording than the Mississippi. Nikki could sense Farhad's relief every time they found they could cross a river without needing a boat. Many of the rivers were frozen over and passing them was slow, but not particularly difficult.

Nikki made her way down the bank and found the edge of the nameless river, keeping the soft glow of the firelight always in view. When she had finished relieving herself, she cleaned up with a neckerchief she took from one of her would-be executioners, and then washed it in the icy waters.

Raised voices cut through the wind, voices she didn't recognize, and Nikki froze, her heart in her throat. Sounds of shouting and the whinnying of horses. She pulled her pants back on and quickly buckled up her gun belt. She took a moment to test the fit, to make sure her revolvers felt right on her hip.

She drew one and made for camp. The sound of the wind muffled her feet some as she made her way slowly and deliberately back to camp. Nikki's skin prickled and her mind screamed for her to run. The Wastelands were teeming with hazards, but even in this place that wanted nothing more than to choke out all life, the most dangerous of them all was still a stranger. Conny and Farhad would speak to each other at length about the man they feared might be on their trail. Bounty hunters working for someone they called Longstreet, they said, may be gaining on them.

How they could track them in this dust and darkness, was a mystery. Had it not been for Crowkiller, she didn't know how they would have been able to follow this girl Eudora as far as they did. The men she traveled with seemed competent enough, but it was a task that bordered on the impossible. She had asked Conny once how these men might be following them if they left no tracks.

"A few ways," he had told her. "Most important is they know where we are going. Since they know our bearings, they just need the occasional sign to tell them they haven't lost us yet. We try to be careful about picking up our campfires, but there ain't a whole lot we can do about the horse dung. Collect and burn some of it, but no matter what we do we leave traces of our passing. These men—Longstreet's men—they're good at what they do."

"How? How'd they get so good? I can't imagine there's a need for bounties and bounty hunters in the world anymore," she asked.

"Oh. You'd be surprised. Especially up north. Longstreet's been doing his damnedest to turn back the clock, so to speak. Trying to run a proper empire. A man like that makes enemies real quick. Hell, even when he didn't have real enemies, he'd invent some just to make sure people knew he was important enough to have them."

"Seems an awful lot of work for very little reward."

"You are right about that."

Impossible task or not, she feared these men had found her friends. She crawled on her belly up the embankment. Two men on horses had guns drawn on Conny and Farhad. Their horses looked lean but strong and the men themselves were much less road-weary than her friends. They both sat atop their horses erect and fixed like man and horse were the same creature.

Powerfully built for the Wastelands, bodies that were used to being nourished.

"I told you they wouldn't be shit, Dobbs. Look at 'em. Scrawny, just like I'd expect from a bunch of junkmongers from Memphis." The man with the rifle said.

The other man, the one with the two black-handled revolvers snorted. "So this is the great Cornelius White. I'd heard you got soft, turned into an old mollycoddle, but I didn't want to believe it," said Two-guns. "I was hoping to bring in the legend. Now look at you."

"Now you," Rifle pointed his firearm at Farhad. "You somehow look better than I expected."

"I do get that a lot," said Farhad.

"You look like you might live for another ten more years. Not bad for an old lunger. I got your bounty right here, says one 'Farhad the Bedouin from Syria. That you?"

"My name is Hamad bin Abed Al-Hadid. Only my friends may call me Farhad."

"Where's the other one?" Rifle asked.

"It's just the two of us," said Conny.

"Bullshit." Two-guns spat. "You got three horses, and I got a bounty for Crowkiller."

"Crowkiller took off," Farhad said. "Left for the Indian Territories."

"Even Longstreet's arm ain't that long," Conny said. "That horse belongs to Becker."

"Terrible thing what happened to Becker," said Rifle. "Found his grave way back up the Mississippi. Didn't make it far, did he? We ain't getting a full bounty on him, no sir. Bring 'em back dead is only half bounty. Longstreet's gonna be awfully sore about it, too. Yes, he wanted Becker alive most of all. He'll have to make do with just the old man's head, I suppose." He patted the saddlebag at his side.

Conny's face flushed with rage. Nikki had to stop this now, or Conny might do something foolish in his anger. She took a slow, deliberate breath to steady her nerves and ran through her plan once in her mind. Satisfied, she stood, revolver in hand, and took careful aim. She shot Two-guns in the back and cocked her pistol before the smoke cleared. In an instant, there was a flurry of motion. Horses squealed, Two-guns tumbled from his saddle, Conny and Farhad dove for their weapons.

Through the smoke and haze, the bounty hunter spun his horse but before he could level his rifle at her, Nikki fired. He fell, twisted in the air, and landed hard in a billow of dust, his leg still in the stirrup.

The scent of gunpowder lingered a moment before the wind bore it away. Two-guns lay in a heap on the ground with a hole in his back and the earth drank up his blood, eager to devour, to knit another body into its macabre tapestry.

"Nikki Free, you are a beautiful woman," said Farhad. "Beautiful and deadly. I am certainly pleased that I decided to bring you along."

Conny attempted what passed for a smile. "I wish Crowkiller were here to eat his words."

Rifle groaned.

"Well, maybe you aren't nearly as deadly as I thought." Farhad checked on the man. "You got him in the shoulder, Nikki. You clearly need to work on your aim, little sister. You disarmed him well enough, so I'll still give you a point in your favor."

"Are we keeping score, now?" asked Nikki.

"My girl, we have always been keeping score."

Conny snaked his way past Farhad and the injured man and pulled Nikki to him. He smelled of cold water and wet leather, but it was not unpleasant, and Nikki's breathing slowed, and she no longer felt as if she were drowning and couldn't get enough air and for the moment, she was good again.

Metal flashed in the firelight, and Farhad caught the man's arm and wrested a wicked-looking knife from his grip. Conny punched the man in his wounded shoulder. Rifle cried out and rolled over.

"I admire your determination, friend." Farhad patted him on the back. "Still fighting against all odds. If you're going to go down, take as many as you can with you, I always say. The trick is to never go down, though. Might want to work on that one."

"Fuck you, lunger." Rifle groaned.

"What do we do with him, Conny?" Farhad asked. "I don't reckon we need to put the screws to him for information. I don't think there's anything pressing we need to know. Longstreet's after us and he almost got us. Not much else to tell."

Nikki cursed herself for her poor aim. Now a decision would need to be made about the fate of this man and if she had shot truer, there'd be no debate. Just some bodies to scavenge and two graves to dig.

"No, I suppose you're right," Conny said. "Put him on his horse then, and set him out is about the only thing we can do."

Farhad's head snapped up. "Put him out on his horse? Have you gone mad, Con?"

"What good will killing him do us? We got his guns and his knife. Could set him out. He likely won't even make it back to Memphis."

"Con, I appreciate this newfound pacifism, but you know as well as I do that we need to kill him."

"Then why'd you ask what we should do with him?"

"I only meant 'how'd you want to kill him,' not 'do you think we should set him free.'"

"Nikki?" Conny asked. "What do you think?"

Rifle had to die. Conny had to know Farhad was right. "Conny, if this man goes back to Longstreet, he could send more men after us."

"He's like to do that regardless," Conny said.

"Yes, but only after it becomes clear that these two ain't coming back. But we let him go, he'll run back to his boss, and he'll send more out after us."

"Not to mention he'll be privy to our last known location," Farhad said.

"We kill him though, and it might be months before Longstreet knows they failed."

Conny spat and nodded his head.

"Conny." Nikki took his head in her hands. "I hate this just as much as you do. But this man has made a living killing people and he's getting what's coming to him."

Conny bent down and kissed her forehead. "And when will I get what's coming to me? Farhad? How are we doing this? Let's make it quick. I know it's still dark out, but I'd prefer to break camp and head on out as soon as we're done."

"You don't have to kill me," Rifle said.

"Shut up," Farhad said.

"Please," he cried. "I won't go back to Longstreet. He'd likely kill me anyhow. He don't like people who can't get the job done."

"I said shut up." Farhad hit the man with the back of his hand.

The man's voice only got louder. "Please, I can fall in with some scavengers or some of the hill folk around here. I don't want to die like an animal on the Wastes."

"But you didn't have any misgivings about killing us like animals, did you?" His pleading didn't have the desired effect on Nikki, and a familiar anger swelled in her chest.

"Mr. White, please." He turned to Conny. "Don't do this, I'm begging you, now."

"Farhad," Conny said. "Let's make it quick." He had grabbed a rope from his saddle bag and fashioned a noose on one end.

The man Nikki called Rifle sobbed. Terror wrote itself on his face and he looked every bit like the cornered animal he feared he would become. "Don't! Please!" His breath came in quick puffs like the sound of a great steam engine, and it repeated over and over "Don't! Please! Don't! Please!"

"None of us take any pleasure in this." Farhad looped the rope around the man's neck and pulled it tight. "For what it's worth, I am sorry."

Conny measured out a length of the other end and tied it off on the bottom of a great dead tree. Its branches were too dry and brittle to serve as gallows, but the roots still held fast in the ground.

"Don't, Please."

The two men grabbed Rifle and pushed him off of the embankment, a drop three times again as tall as Nikki. She fought the urge to turn away. But if she's going to vote to put a man to death, she had to have the nerve to watch it happen, or she was nothing more than a coward herself.

The rope snaked quickly down after him and then snapped taut but then went slack. The corpse tree held firm. Nikki feared the man had slipped the noose and instead fell to the earth below. The three companions peered over the edge. Nikki retched. Rifle's headless body lay at the bottom of the cliff, his head nowhere to be seen.

"Head must have bounced away," Farhad said, peering into the dark void.

"We should have just put a bullet in him, I reckon," Conny said. "The rope always seems like it's going to be more civilized, but it just ain't."

"Ain't no civilized way of killing a man, Con." Farhad wiped the sweat from his brow. "You and I know that about as well as anyone."

"What happened?" Nikki asked.

"Rope was too long," Farhad said. "If the rope's too long, you cut a man's head off. Too short, and he swings in the wind choking to death."

"So should we bury him?"

"No sense in burying him," Farhad said. "The Wastelands will bury him soon enough. I'll fetch the rope. The wind and dust will do the burying. It's an irrelevant and, dare I say, a redundant custom now."

"You buried Becker," Conny said. "Was it not irrelevant and redundant then?"

"I buried Becker because I knew you'd insist on it, Con. You are painfully predictable sometimes."

They set about their tasks, each one working in silence. Nikki broke down camp while the men scavenged what they could from the other man. Connie found Two-Guns boots fit him better than his own and were less worn.

After some debate, they decided to butcher one of the new horses and take as much fresh meat as wouldn't spoil and bring the other along. Butchering both of the horses was a waste of meat and a senseless killing, but they couldn't take on two new animals. Food in the Uncontested Lands was too scarce. They considered letting the second one go, but Farhad noted that they could always slaughter it for food in a few weeks when the meat from the first had run out. Conny suggested they replace their worn-out horses with these new, sturdier ones, but none of them were willing to butcher the animals that had born them across the Wastelands and had done so without demand or complaint.

Conny built a small sled from deadwood. He stripped Two-Guns bare and used his clothes to lash the wood together. Farhad and Nikki cut backstrap and strips of meat from the rump, enough that would not spoil in the cold, and they wrapped it up in the canvas tarp they used to line the bottom of their tent. They all agreed that fresh horse meat was worth the loss.

They mounted up and rode on, eager to put the camp far behind them.

Chapter 32

Sorrow Draw, North Texas (October, 1881)

Hattie Mothershed

Hattie sat in the ruins of her old schoolhouse and planned how she would murder the man who would be her husband. She had never plotted a murder before, at least not in any serious fashion, and it was more complicated than she had hoped it would be.

The schoolhouse had long been a place of refuge for her. A place where she ran to when she needed to be alone, to think, or to read, or to pray. Often, to just get away from the Mothershed manor and the still-living mother that haunted it.

She wanted to be a schoolteacher when she was younger, before the Calamity. Her mother told her it was foolish, schoolteachers weren't permitted to court men, or to go to social halls, or indulge in alcohol—all the things her mother loved to do—but Hattie didn't care for any of those things. She adored her teacher, Miss Mayberry. She had been young and kind and gentle, all of the things her mother was not. She had been put up in the Mothershed house for a time when she first arrived from Cincinnati. Hattie had loved having her there. The house was plenty big enough, with rooms to spare, so she didn't understand when, after only a few months, Miss Mayberry left to take a room with Margaret Wells, a frightening old widow with crooked fingers. Whatever the reason, Miss Mayberry seemed to be happier, so Hattie didn't question.

Hattie had cleaned up the schoolhouse years ago and visited regularly to make sure it stayed in good condition. When Mother had gotten sick and Hattie found the courage to leave the house and make small journeys into town, the schoolhouse was the first place she headed for. There was nothing in it of any value, and so the first scavengers mostly left it alone. The slates would soon disappear, as well as the chalk and the ink, as people became increasingly desperate for resources, and scavenging close to home was always preferable to leaving the relative safety of Sorrow Draw. The desks hadn't yet been carried off, and Hattie could sit in her seat and remember Miss Mayberry and smile sometimes, and other times cry.

The old iron stove still sat in the center of the single room, and Hattie put in some wood she had collected from the Mothershed house. Broken picture frames, table legs, pieces of a wooden bucket, and a broom handle—all things that no one would notice she had taken, if she did it slow enough. How long would it take for her to cannibalize the entire house, to eat away at it bit by bit until she had burned the entire thing down in this schoolhouse stove?

A terrible thought crept into her mind, one that came often and uninvited. The terrible, terrible idea of burning down the Mothershed house, her childhood home, of locking the doors with her father and mother inside and setting it alight, and watching the flames eat away at the rot and filth. It would be a cleansing of sorts, a baptism by fire, and she could be born again a free woman. But the Mothershed house was one of the most untouched and unsullied places in Sorrow Draw, and as far as she knew, of the whole of the world. All the wood, the fabric—linens, velvets, and brocades—that still occupied it, clothing still untouched for the last eighteen years, all of it an obscene display of decadence her father used to manifest his prophetic claims and to show evidence of his divine favor. To destroy such a place and waste the wealth of resources, would be to commit a grievous sin against humanity itself. Greater perhaps than even her father's sin of squandering it.

Hattie put it out of her mind. There may be time enough for that one day. But today she needed her mind focused on one thing. Murder. Deliverance still wouldn't commit to sending someone to kill Ransom, even after Bailey's confession. The woman was afraid. And if a woman like that was afraid, Hattie knew she should be afraid, too.

Now, there were many ways to kill a man, that had become apparent as soon as she began making a list. She had to concentrate on the methods that existed within the realm of possibility. As satisfying as it would be to tie Ransom to a wagon wheel and roll him down Bowden Hill, she would have to settle for methods that were physically possible to pull off.

A revolver or a rifle of some kind might work. They were certainly deadly, she knew, but they were also loud and likely to attract unwanted attention. Shooting Ransom would have to be done in private, somewhere the sound of a gunshot could fade away before reaching any other ears. That would mean she would have to lure him away with promises of things that men loved and that she had no desire to promise him. Of course, there was also the fact that she had never fired a gun in all her life. She thought about shooting him—and missing—and what he would do to her, and she crossed guns off her list.

She immediately dispelled the very idea of using a knife. While she was unsure even if she had the strength to plunge a knife into a man's chest, she was certain her nerve would fail if she attempted it. And what if she somehow gathered the nerve, but found she didn't have the strength? What if the knife only stuck a bit into Ransom's chest and all her hopes would be dashed into the dust? She shuddered.

That left poison. She had once heard Erasmus quip that poison was the weapon of a woman and, sometimes, of a dandy. If her first foray into assassination was any indication, she might be inclined to agree with him. Poison was a weapon she could wield. It required no strength on her part to kill, and she needn't even be in the same room as Ransom when the weapon did its killing.

But what poison would she use, and how would she acquire it? And when she did acquire a suitable poison, when could she find a chance to administer it?

She knew her answer before she asked it, but she hoped to leave her brother out of her plans. Most of the townsfolk would like nothing more than to hang him from a tree for being an abomination so the very suggestion that he was involved in a murder and father's tenuous protection of him would be severed. *Father himself might use it as an excuse to get rid of Erasmus for good.*

No, there could be not the slightest hint that Erasmus was involved. She would sooner marry Ransom and live a life of misery and shame than watch the people lynch her brother.

Hattie despaired. Any use of poison would likely be associated with Erasmus, as most of the supply ran through his lover, and he had a sizable collection of tonics and tinctures that, if used more liberally than suggested, could cause a speedy death.

She was out of options. She could run away and live among the scavengers in the south. They might take her in, or they just as likely might gut her and fashion clothing from her skin if the tales the townsfolk tell could be believed. She could chance a journey to California where she would certainly die along the miles and miles of sandstorm desert Wastelands.

If only she could stay in Hill Lodge. Her visit there had stirred a passion in her, some kind of awakening that her mind tried to turn aside but it persisted. Each vivid memory was a sword thrust that her frightened, rational mind parried. These two sides of her spirit have waged constant war with each other. Her passionate side never had the advantage, it never gained ground. Fear and rationality kept it constantly at bay. Even at the end of the world, when many people had given themselves up completely to passion and emotion, she still held on to her fear. Fear of her father, fear of God, fear of her future, fear of no future, fear of death, fear of life.

If only she could stay at Hill Lodge. She would let her emotions overcome her fears. They could claim victory in this war she fought against herself. She could give in to her appetite and drink all her terror away. She could give in to her lust and ruin herself for Ransom.

If only she could stay at Hill Lodge. But she couldn't really fool herself. If she were to stay at the Lodge, she would still be Hattie. Her fear would come with her. There was no destroying it. There was no winning this war. She was her fear. It was as much a part of her as her own skin.

"Excuse me, ma'am?"

Hattie started. Ransom stood in the doorway and that familiar fear gripped her heart.

"Ransom. What do I owe this pleasure?" Anger wormed its way through her fear. He intruded on her private place. He left this stink in her house of worship.

"I smelled the fire. I know you enjoy coming here and I wanted to make sure you had everything you need." His cheeks flushed with cold, but his features were more than fine. He had trimmed his beard neat, but not so much as a dandy like her brother would.

"I do, thank you. I've been fortunate that the townsfolk haven't raided this place as much as they could have. I still have my stove, my desks, and a few Bibles left for me to read."

He nodded. "I've made sure they all know this place is off-limits. I know you need to get away. I can't imagine what you have to endure with your mother and, if it ain't too bold for me to say, your father too."

"I am much obliged to you, then." Her voice was calm and measured, but inside she reeled. Ransom was the reason her schoolhouse, her temple, had been left unspoiled. She wanted to disbelieve, but as soon as he said the words she knew the truth of them. This building should have been dismantled for its raw materials long ago. The stove should have been melted down; the wood should have been burned in fireplaces throughout town.

Ransom cleared his throat. "Hattie," he began. "I know I can come across as a bit rough. At times I can be somewhat of a dull blade, if you catch my meaning."

"I hadn't noticed." She tried to sound sincere.

"I appreciate you saying so, but I know that's true. I can be crass and crude. I can lose my temper with the boys. What you may not understand is, I do it for them. Sometimes I'm the only thing that keeps them alive. Your father, he wants to start some feud with the Freemen over at that lodge everyone's talking about. You know the one?"

Hattie shook her head. "No. I mean, yes, I've heard of it. Heard people talking about it."

"My own father has the idea to throw in with yours any time he so much as breathes in our direction. They're both so bloodthirsty they get all the Paluxy Boys riled up good. Then it's up to me to stamp out the fires, as it were."

Hattie didn't know what to say to him, so she nodded and turned her attention to the floor. She couldn't look him in the eyes. She didn't trust herself. Bailey's confession burned in her mind. She knew that he had sent men to murder Sovereign at the saloon. She knew that he directed them to start a war. And she knew he did it for her.

But she wished she didn't know any of it. How nice it would have been to believe him. He's good at talking, that's for sure. He's good at making sweet on her one moment, then threatening to kill her brother the next. He's a mighty handsome liar who speaks with a forked tongue. Still, it was best to be cordial.

"You must find it all terribly wearisome."

"It's only tolerable, miss. In truth, I can tolerate it just fine really, knowing that someday I'll lead the Paluxy Boys and you'll be my wife."

Hattie's skin prickled. "Well, a lot can happen between then and now, Ransom."

"Nothing short of Jesus himself coming back is going to keep me from becoming your husband."

"So much more than that can happen. In fact, I think that might be the least likely thing to keep us apart."

"I'm not so sure, to hear your father talk about it. Sounds like if we don't wed soon, the Kingdom of God might come first."

"My father's been saying that for as long as I can remember and it ain't come yet."

"You don't have faith in your father, Hattie?"

"It's not that," she said quickly. "It's just—" She struggled to find the words.

"It's alright. Sometimes I doubt it all, too. Hard to doubt it when the world is the way it is, but I admit, I still do. For me, it don't matter. Your father won't live forever. If he lives to see the kingdom of the Lord, so be it. If not, then I reckon, being your husband and all, I'll take the church. But none of that matters much to me. You know I've had my eye on you for a long time, Hattie. It's you I want. God can come back and rule over this dust, but I want you before this world finally dies."

She was keenly aware of her vulnerability. Ransom stood in the only door that led in or out of the single-room schoolhouse. She stole a look around the room for a weapon, something, anything she could use to defend herself, and found none. Ransom likely wouldn't try anything, but the resolution of men often fails in the presence of a woman, and reason can swiftly surrender to lust. For all the strength men possess, there is an abundance of frailty there, too.

When she didn't speak, he continued. "I know you hesitate. I think I know why. Being with a man for the first time can be a frightening thing. I know I look rough at times, but I will be gentle, I promise you that. You've got nothing to fear from me. But I have good news to bring. Very good news. I've just come back from talking with your father. He's with your mother right now, the poor thing. We were discussing our wedding plans. Monday after next is All Soul's Day and your father has agreed that this is the day he will marry us. Right there in the church for God and all the people to witness."

Hattie smiled at him. In a few moments, she knew, the panic would strike. Her heart will beat out from her chest, her breath will come in short, quick spasms, her palms will ache and her knees will buckle. But right now, she only smiled at him. A warm, gentle smile. "Well then I look forward to it and on All Soul's Day you will find yourself a bride eager to make you her husband."

He blew out a breath like a swimmer who had just come up for air. "That makes me very glad to hear, Hattie. Very glad indeed."

She needed him to leave soon before the panic set in. "In that case, you'll excuse me, won't you? I have prayers to make, and I should read my Bible to gather my courage from the Word of God."

"Oh, of course." He took her hand in his and kissed it. "If I don't see you again until our wedding day, take care and be well."

When he left, Hattie sat in the far corner of the schoolhouse and allowed herself to panic. Loneliness closed in on her and she missed her brother. She wrapped her arms around her chest and pretended she cried in Erasmus's arms.

She gave up her plans. She couldn't play the killer anymore. Why did she think she could have the nerve to kill Ransom? And what good would that do anyway? The Paluxy Boys—and her father—would find some way to blame her brother, and even if they didn't, they would punish the rest of the town. Her father might have been the brains of the Paluxy Boys, but Ransom was its heart. They were devoted and dedicated to him and their rage and fury at his murder would know no bounds.

The wood cracked and popped in the stove. Hattie slid across the floor to sit near it. She sat so close that she watched the heat redden her skin and when she finally had to back away, the air felt all the colder.

She would run away. She wouldn't allow the possibility that her brother could bear the wrath of the Paluxy Boys if anything were to happen to Ransom, and she couldn't marry him. She would flee Sorrow Draw and though the Wastelands might very well be the death of her, she did not care. The parched earth would be her wedding bed and she would make the dust her veil.

Chapter 33

Unknown Lands, North Texas (October, 1881)

Cornelius White

Conny pulled his keffiyeh tighter across his face. The wind blew steady across the immense Texas plains. It brought frigid air from the north along with dust and sand that ate at their exposed flesh. Conny wore his cinder goggles and wrapped his horse's head in a wool blanket. They were trained to walk blind through sandstorms and trusted their riders to guide them.

They had eaten well over the last week. They had dried much of the meat, but a good deal of it would spoil soon, so they ate like they did before the Calamity. They ate like kings. They devoured the tender backstraps at night after roasting them on a spit. They laughed around the campfires, licking the weep from their fingers. They kissed, the taste of sweet meat on their tongues. They fell asleep to the scent of still-burning fat.

Their trail had been marked with frequent signs from Crowkiller. The flat and bare landscape looked the same in every direction they turned. They kept their course with a compass, always heading due west. Conny reckoned Crowkiller either had a compass of his own, or some other ability to navigate through the haze and fog of Calamity.

They crossed the plains for days, with empty riverbeds and the occasional hilltop the only break in the monotony. Despite the sand and dust that whipped across the prairie, the orange glow of the sun behind the wall of dust burned a little brighter than usual. When it rose in the morning, they could even make out a separation between land and sky as the silhouette of the distant horizon cut across its face. It had been eighteen years since any of them had seen anything so far away. But once the sun broke free from the edge of the earth, the horizon disappeared again into dust and haze, and they were back at the end of the world.

This morning it began to snow. Longstreet's bounty hunter, the one Nikki called Two-guns, had a large tent that was big enough for the three of them, and they had taken to using that and a small fire inside to keep warm. Farhad didn't care for the idea, he said that sleeping so near them with consumption might pass it to them, but Nikki insisted, telling him not to worry, her own mother had told her that consumption was hereditary, so he had nothing to fear. Still, she told him to sleep with a keffiyeh on if it worried him so much, but they had to conserve as much fuel as they could, and a small fire inside would keep them much warmer.

"Won't matter a bit getting sick if we freeze to death," she had told him.

So Farhad slept with his head opposite them and kept his face wrapped. The nights passed a little warmer after that.

The horse they didn't butcher back in Louisiana had become a pack horse, useful for carrying their fuel for campfires. They kept it well strapped with wood they scavenged from the ruins of houses, barns, fences, wagons, and dead trees they passed on occasion. Conny reckoned they would keep it along for a good while since shrubs and the sparse desert grasses now dotted the trail west, so the horse had plenty to eat. Conny was glad for it. The killing of a horse still didn't sit right with him, even if it was for their survival. Horses were rare things, and they were loyal, too. Killing a creature that's loyal and trusting felt like the worst kind of betrayal.

They encountered no other living souls in the days since they crossed into Texas, though signs of them were all over. They passed through Marshall, Canton, and Kaufman, but all of them had been laid nearly bare. The scavengers in this part of the world were thorough and disciplined. Everything of use and value was gone, and the wood from the houses and shops had been taken in a precise and orderly way. Some structures had already been leveled, their wooden boards cut, bundled, and tied off with twine, ready to be hauled away.

"This ain't nothing like back home, Con," Farhad said when they saw the first stacks.

"It's almost like these people plan to live through the end of the world," Nikki said.

"The absolute audacity. It is the pinnacle of human arrogance to insist on surviving when God Himself is doing His damnedest to kill us all off. I myself plan to do my part and die like I'm supposed to."

"In that case," Nikki replied, "I don't think you're supposed to for quite some time, my friend."

"Well just for you, I'll make sure I don't slip into oblivion too soon."

"I'd appreciate that."

"Well, Conny. We'll be passing near Dallas in a couple of days, I reckon. What are your thoughts? Poke around a bit or steer clear?"

"I'm still all for steering clear of Dallas," Conny said. "There's a fairly well-run scavenging collective somewhere around here and I wouldn't be at all surprised to find them in Dallas. Last thing we need is to run into any sizable group of people who might be armed."

"I wouldn't mind a run-in with some other faces. No offense to you two, but I need some stranger company."

"From scavengers, Farhad?" Nikki asked.

"I love scavengers. They're almost always good people. Their lives are simple, but they can see the use and value in everything. Other people are wasteful. Even now when everything is scarce, people are wasteful. But not the scavengers."

"But isn't that what makes them more than likely to carve you up and take what's yours?"

"No, little sister, that's mostly a myth. The junkmongers might. People think they are the same, but they aren't. Junkmongers will rip the teeth out of your mouth if they can make a trade with them, but the scavengers are the true heart and soul of the human race. Once people like us are gone, they will remain."

"Have you spent a lot of time with them?"

"A bit, yes. In Memphis I'd often go on runs with them for the company."

"For the company," Conny asked, "or for the feminine companionship?"

"Both. They are tolerably good at both, Con. I suppose they remind me of home. They have the same kind of life, the same kind of society. They're always on the move and they treat everyone as family. Though, they are a bit more free with their love."

"I think I'm starting to see why you enjoyed their company," Nikki said.

"Why of course, the always lewd and salacious Farhad must have the company of women as his prime motivating factor in all his decisions, is that what you think of me?"

"Not in all decisions, but in most I suspect it's the case."

"Very true, you have me dead to rights."

"That reminds me, though. I do have a question for you."

"Ask away, my dear."

"When the bounty hunters asked you for your name, you gave them another."

"I did."

"So? Care to elaborate?"

"That was a statement, little sister, not a question."

"You are frustrating sometimes."

"Yes." Farhad took a long pull from a whiskey bottle. "Yes I am."

"Alright. What was the name you gave, and why did you give it?"

"I'll answer the second first. I gave that name because it is my name. My true name is Hamad bin Abed Al-Hadid. It is the name I was given as a babe. Farhad is the name my brother gave me."

"Why did he give you the name Farhad?"

"To tease me. He found it funny that I was in love with the girl who he was to marry. Farhad was a man in a Persian story who loved a woman he could not have."

Farhad told Conny the story once, but he again listened all the same, curious to see if Farhad would tell it in the same way. Nikki loved Farhad's tales of adventures and love, of magic and trickery.

"It begins with Shirin, a princess. She is bathing one day when she is greeted by a man dressed as a peasant. She doesn't know him, but he professes his love for her and for her undying beauty. She rebukes him for spying on her naked body and sends him away. Later, she sees him again, only this time she knows him for who he is. His name is Khosrow, and he is a king.

"Naturally, she agrees to marry him, but not until he regains his throne, which has been seized by one of his generals in his absence. When he returns home, the general agrees to give him his kingdom back, but only if the king agrees to marry his daughter, Mariam. The king wants Shirin, not Mariam, but he agrees and reclaims his throne.

"One day he hears of a man named Farhad, a sculptor, who is courting Shirin. This Farhad, he loves Shirin above all else, and Khosrow, who cannot have her, agrees to let Farhad marry her. Provided he can carve a road through a mountain. An impossible task, to be sure. Khosrow has no intention of actually allowing anyone else to have Shirin. But rather than be dismayed by this impossible job, Farhad gets to work. When Khosrow hears that he is almost finished with his road through the mountain, he sends him a letter telling Farhad that his beloved Shirin had passed away. It was a lie, of course. But Farhad was struck with such grief that he threw himself off the top of the mountain."

"That's it?" Nikki asked when Farhad didn't continue. "The story ends like that?"

"No, the story doesn't end like that, but it ends for Farhad like that. It's really the tale of Khosrow and Shirin, not Farhad. He played but a part in it. His part ends there."

"Well, I hope those two got what was coming to them."

"They do indeed, little sister. They do indeed."

"So you kept this name? The name Farhad?"

"I did. I love the name, as I love the character from the story. He was a lover. A man of passion, who let his love for a woman help him move mountains. His was only a tragic story because he loved the wrong woman."

"Farhad, but you love many women, not just one."

Farhad laughed. "I love many women, yes. There's so little love left in the world it would be a sin for me to give all I have to only one."

"I thought the same for a while. But I think that sharing my love with others only watered it down and lessened it, maybe."

"What do you think, Con?" Farhad asked.

Nikki had told him of her life after the Calamity, before the folks in her town went mad and started sacrificing children. For her, things were good. She enjoyed liberty without slavery, and people of her town made love freely. It was this way for many places in the Wastelands. Either they clung to religion with vigor, or they abandoned it to live a life of freedom and vice. Her town, it seems, had done both and did them both with equal zeal.

"Seems to me that everyone needs to make that particular choice for themselves," Conny said. "I bedded women in Memphis when I needed to, but I never loved them. Never was one of them I could see myself devoted to. I think when you find that person, then you won't care to spread your love around. You just can't imagine giving it to anyone else."

Farhad laughed again. "It's like I knew you'd say that before the words came out of your mouth, Con."

"I think it's the perfect answer," Nikki said.

"You would." Farhad took a long pull from his whiskey bottle. "So what about the two of you? Are you together for the convenience of it, or are you devoted?"

Conny coughed. Nikki looked at him, her eyes questioning just a little. "I think," Conny said, "I think that I'd be in favor of being committed myself, but I'm only one half of the situation."

"I have no designs on anyone else. And no desire to meet other men either here or in California."

"What about other women?" Farhad asked.

"Not my thing, gunfighter. But it ain't my place to judge."

"But you can't tell how sweet a wine is unless you take a drink, Nikki."

"Well, who says I haven't tried wine a time or two before and found it not quite to my taste? I prefer whiskey. It's harsh, it's fiery, and it makes me feel positively delightful real quick like."

Love in the Wastelands was a freer thing than it was before the Calamity. All the same, the direct questions, and Nikki's equally direct answers to them made Conny somewhat uncomfortable. But he smiled despite it all. Eighteen years ago, his good sensibilities would never have allowed him to listen to a conversation like this.

SORROW DRAW

They rode the rest of the day talking and sharing stories. Farhad told them about his life in the desert of Arabia, about his tribe, his family, and the tales his people told. Conny learned more about Farhad than he had ever known before. Nikki brought that out in him. For her part, she shared her own stories. Stories of loss and love, about her good years after the end of the world. Conny told them about his father and his father's hanging, about his children. He told Nikki about Elizabeth, and about how he had received a letter from her sister while he was laid up, about how the letter told him that Elizabeth was with child again, only there was no possibility that the child was his. He told her how he had deserted the Union Army to go home and confront her.

Nikki asked him what he had planned to do, and he told her it was a question that he had asked himself many times before. He told her all of this without grief, without sadness. She listened to him and showed him sympathy and kindness. His sorrow, he knew, was really nothing compared to what she had endured as a slave and he felt foolish sharing, and even more foolish when she gripped his hand tighter and put her hand on his leg to comfort him. He thanked her for it but told her it wasn't necessary, that he was over the pain.

Conny reckoned it was an hour before nightfall when Farhad spotted what would be the last of Crowkiller's cairns. It was sheltered by the side of a small cliff that protected it from the wind. Nikki spotted a note under a rock at the base and read it out loud to the men.

"Girl and money still safe. Town up ahead. Nice big saloon. Seems friendly. Won't stay long. Have to keep moving. Don't let the Bedouin drink too much there. Could get into trouble. Using the name Horsethief for now."

"Horsethief?" Nikki asked.

"One of the names he goes by," Farhad said. "Now, what do you suppose he meant when he said I 'could get into trouble'? Mighty odd thing to say if you ask me."

"Well," Conny replied, "if they got themselves a saloon, I'd be inclined to agree with Crowkiller. You might get yourself into trouble there. In any number of ways."

"Why Horsethief?" asked Nikki.

Farhad shrugged. "Might be his true name for all we know. He has a few more he goes by. I'm more interested in this saloon. I wonder if it's better than old Purdy's saloon in Memphis." Farhad smoothed the front of his coat. "Only one way to find out, really."

"Tomorrow," Conny said. "It'll be night soon, and Crowkiller didn't mention how far away this town is. Could be a mile, could be twenty mile. Let's make camp here and head for this town in the morning."

"Good idea," Farhad said. "I'd like to get a good night's sleep before a day of drinking and debauchery."

"How do you know there'll be any debauchery going on there?" Nikki laughed. "They might be a town of prudes for all you know."

"Nonsense. Crowkiller said I could get into all kinds of trouble there, and he knows I can handle my liquor. The only thing that will get me into trouble in a saloon is gambling and women. Either way, I'm sure to have a good time."

"Just be ready," Conny told Nikki. "We may need to leave in a moment's notice if he gets caught cheating at cards or bedding down a girl he shouldn't be bedding down."

"Conny I am once again shocked by your lack of faith in me. I know how to use discretion when I defile myself."

"We'll stay alert," Conny said again.

They set up camp on the side of the same small cliff where Crowkiller built his cairn. They ate from their supply of horse meat. The meat had begun to smell, and Conny thought it best to leave the rest of it behind in the morning. They sang songs by the campfire, anticipating what the next day would bring. A saloon meant people. It meant drinking and dancing and song. They might be able to trade, to play cards, to gamble their scraps and artifacts, get supplies, and hear new stories.

Conny didn't want to think about the possibility that these townsfolk could be an unfriendly lot. They had met up with enough of those on this journey. Sleep came hard for him. His thoughts were seized by the ferryman who killed Becker, by the men who crucified Nikki, and by the Magistrate who drugged his women and ate the flesh of men.

Chapter 34

Sorrow Draw, North Texas (November, 1881)

Erasmus Mothershed

The coal in the iron stove burned hot. Erasmus opened the door and stoked the glowing bricks, coaxing them into sharing more of their heat. The warmth soothed, but the scorching heat made him feel alive. It burned at his skin and the decadence and extravagance of hoarding heat aroused him in ways he couldn't describe. He loved Lupe, his smooth form, the hardness of his body, the way the ropes of muscle tightened under his skin, but heat—real heat—the kind that reddened flesh and brought pain, that was like a drug. It roused him, excited him, and like opium, it left him cold and wanting more in its absence.

He stepped away from the iron stove and the chill in the air returned. The coal bucket was still half full and they had a few hours before his father's morning service, but Erasmus didn't want to risk putting off too much smoke, so he left it alone. They weren't exactly in a remote location, the barber's shop sat near the saloon, a once prominent building in town before his father had it razed to the ground. Erasmus still enjoyed the danger of bedding Lupe right under the noses of the people in town. Yet another of his vices. The risk, he told himself, was its own reward.

"Come back to bed," Lupe called. "I get cold."

"Should I put some more coal on the fire?"

"No, we not go on another coal run until February. Save it. Just come to bed. I'm cold. warm me up, por favor."

"It's not much of a bed," said Erasmus. "It's hard and the floor is cold."

"Que está mal, Rasmus?" Lupe said. "I say 'I'm cold' and you no come."

"I'm sorry, love." Erasmus bit down on the inside of his cheek. "I haven't really been myself lately."

Lupe stood up. He wrapped the blanket around his shoulders. He pulled up a stool and sat by the stove next to Erasmus. "You and me, we feel the same. We cannot keep doing these things and not getting caught."

"No, we can. There's a few people standing in our way, but if we get rid of them, we can live how we want."

"What do you see for the future for you, Rasmus?"

"My future?" He thought for a minute, unsure of the question. Most people he knew never spoke of the future. Only people like his father, who thought the end of the world was only a temporary situation ever considered the future. The rest of them just lived. Survived from one day to the next, not expecting their lot in life to ever really change. They were only a part of the last gasp of humanity. Erasmus shrugged. "I'm going to just keep trying to survive as long as I can, I suppose."

"That's it? Only survive?"

"That's it. We get rid of those who stand in our way, and then we survive until the end."

"There must be more than that."

"What else is there? Take on an apprenticeship somewhere? Travel to California to seek my riches in the gold mines? Perhaps I could take a commission with the Confederate army?"

"I want more."

Erasmus thought about Lupe's profoundly simple statement. He downed the remains of a tincture of laudanum. Church wouldn't start for a few more hours, but he hoped it would be enough to get him through. "What more is there? We find a way to send our enemies to Hell and we live the rest of our lives getting drunk and fucking in peace."

Lupe smiled. "That would not be so much a bad life, I suppose."

"No it wouldn't."

"Who is first that you to send to Hell? Which one of tús enemigos?"

Erasmus fought a wave of nausea. "My mother," he said.

"She does refuse to die, no?"

"I've helped her along in that regard, but yes. She's always been a stubborn woman."

"What do you mean?"

"I've been…mixing her some special medicine." He had never told Lupe, or anyone else, about what he'd done. Would Lupe be angry? Would his lover see him differently? The thought terrified him, but he told him now anyway. The need to tell someone, anyone, overcame his fear.

Lupe didn't look at him. "I think as much," he said in his broken English.

"You knew?"

"I think," he replied. "I thought, I mean. You get a lot of bad medicine from me. Very bad medicine."

"Well, some of it is very good medicine. Just bad for her."

"No, is bad medicine. Solamente."

"I think it might be time to end it. To let her go. But if I do, I'd be a murderer. I've made her suffer enough, haven't I?"

"Who now isn't? Who can get this far into end of the world and not be a murderer?"

"Hattie," Erasmus said without hesitation.

"Yes, Hattie. Yes, yes. Things are going to happen here, Rasmus. Bad things. You can sit back. Watch it happen. Or, you can make it happen. I like 'make it happen.' This way you know who, where, and when. You are in control."

Lupe had a point. Erasmus dropped his voice to a whisper. "I need to get rid of Ransom," he said. "He's going to force Hattie to marry him and I can't let that happen."

Lupe laughed. "Ransom is only a man, like any other man. Not hard to kill."

"Yeah, but people will know. I'll get caught and people will know. They'll come after me, or they'll come after Hattie. It isn't that simple."

"It is that simple. The End of the World is a big place. Big and loud and full of places to hide. Hide yourself, hide your sin, hide a body. Lots of hiding. Kill a man and his friends will never know where he is. The Wastelands will claim his body. How can they find it? They can't. You don't kill Ransom because you afraid of him. Or you afraid your world changing. Which one is it, Ras?"

Erasmus's heart dropped in his chest. He wanted to argue, but it was true. "Both, I suppose."

"Is alright to fear. Is alright. But maybe now is time to do something about it."

Reverend Mothershed's sermon began as usual but ended in a frenzied fever of vengeance and righteous fury. The Paluxy Boys had rounded up all the townsfolk and brought them in, the reluctant ones were marched in last so the preacher could look them each in the eyes as they took their seats. He had lit only half the candles, and their faint light lit him from below as if he had ascended above all the heavenly hosts themselves. God incarnate on Earth. The Second Coming of Jesus Christ.

Erasmus twisted in his seat. His wool waistcoat itched, and the wooden bench offered no comfort other than a distraction from his thoughts.

Hattie sat next to him. She said nothing to him and kept her face and eyes downcast. He wanted to say something to her. Something crude and witty, something to make her smile, but his voice stuck in his throat.

The congregation rose and sang *"It Came Upon the Midnight Clear,"* and *"Fairest Lord Jesus."* Hattie, who usually sang loud and joyful, barely moved her lips. The church murmured when the crowd sat, then silence.

Mothershed smoothed the front of his worn coat. He didn't keep himself groomed. He preferred to spend his time in prayer, in the study of the Bible, and in devotion to his wife. The windblown mass of white hair on the top of his head gave him the appearance of a frenzied dog. "What a beautiful message, isn't it?" he asked.

No one answered. Mothershed's questions weren't meant to be answered. They were statements. They were demands that hung in the air like the stench of rotten meat and everyone closed their mouths to avoid tasting it.

"Fair are the meadows," he said, quoting the song. "Fairer still the woodlands. Too many of us look upon the sublime expanse of the meadows you call the Wastelands and the barren trees of the old forest and we see only ruin and destruction. We see only what it is, compared to what it used to be."

A bead of sweat rolled down Erasmus's back.

"In our earthly eyes, there can be no comparison. For those of us who remember, who were there before God's great Calamity, we yearn sometimes for the return of the beauty, do we not? We yearn for the green leaves, the rolling waves of grasslands, the clear water running through the streams and rivers of our land, but I am here to tell you that these are not things of true beauty. They are not things of Godly beauty. God told Samuel that 'the Lord sees not as man sees: man looks on the outward appearance, but the Lord looks on the heart.' Well, we are the heart of this land. This town, this congregation, we are the heart of this land, and the Lord looks on us and sees our beauty."

Ransom, standing on Mothershed's right-hand side, shifted his gun belt.

"And if we are the beauty of the land, then it is us who make it beautiful in the eyes of the Lord. But there is a stain on the land that we all know well. The stain of the savage. I know I've talked about this before, but I will not stop preaching against the heathen until the heathen is no more."

Hattie's thin arms trembled. Erasmus took his overcoat off and wrapped it around her.

"Now, our boys have been doing a mighty fine job of taking care of the savages that come into our land." Mothershed reached behind his pulpit and pulled out a mass of severed hands, each one tied to a string, with the other end bound to a large iron ring. Some in the congregation gasped. A few of those hands were small, Erasmus noted. The bile rose in his throat, and he put his hand to his mouth. Hattie's eyes were wide like polished river stones, and she stared unmoving. "This is a small collection. Each hand represents one Indian. One savage that we have scoured from our land. I show this to you so I can harden your nerve. To brace your heart against the coming storm. It must be a bulwark for your courage.

"Look at them. For all these hands we've gathered here, not one of our boys has been lost. Old O'Leary took a bullet to the leg on Friday, but he was far past his prime for Indian killing, so it was no great loss. But the Lord is protecting our boys, and no one can argue against that." He put the grotesque mass of hands on the altar in front of the pulpit. "The Kingdom of God, the new Kingdom, belongs to the courageous. There is no place in the Thousand Year Reign of Jesus Christ for timid men."

Erasmus straightened up in his seat. He said a silent prayer that his father was right, and he wouldn't have to suffer eternity with the Paluxy Boys. Wouldn't it be the final irony of them all if he managed to kill Ransom but found himself feasting at God's table right next to him?

"Now our brave lads might call themselves the Paluxy Boys, they've been called that since before the Calamity, but make no mistake, they are the Army of God and they carry his righteous banner, and they fight with the sword of truth, and they are protected by the seven pieces of the Armor of God. This is His sanction. It's a new covenant He has made with you as His new Chosen People, and with me as your shepherd. As Moses reincarnate, I will guide us through the desert to the Promised Land."

Joseph Cooper shouted "Amen!" and a few others in the crowd muttered an answering "Amen." Erasmus scanned the congregation. All heads were turned towards the pulpit, save for the few bowed in silent prayer. Even those that were brought in at gunpoint gazed on the man Erasmus called father with a look of adoration that he knew in his heart was not feigned. Reverend Mothershed could captivate an audience, but even more than that, these people wanted to believe. They had lived a life of quiet desperation and they wanted to believe it was going to get better, and his father made it easy for them.

"But the Israelites failed to remain loyal to God and wandered the wilderness for forty years. Forty years was the price of their disloyalty to Him who delivered them out of bondage in Egypt." Reverend Mothershed stretched out his hands and gripped the edge of the pulpit. "Anyone who knows me knows that I am loyal only to the One True God. I have earthly loves, as does everyone else, but my fealty is to God first and foremost and always will be."

Another "amen."

"Fealty, loyalty, service, duty, sacrifice. These are solemn and sacred words. Solemn and sacred words that require solemn and sacred actions. Now the Good Book says that all have sinned and fallen short of the glory of God. That includes me. I have been a sinner." Mothershed paused, but there was no "amen" from the crowd. "Oh yes. I have. But today I will atone for that. You see, I have been neglectful in my duties as a father. Both to my earthly children and as a father to my church."

Panic seized Erasmus. Before the Calamity, his father had never neglected punishment. Since then, he had abandoned the very idea of being a father in place of being a preacher and of maintaining some control and order in Sorrow Draw. Erasmus hated him, but he also knew that without his father's leadership and control, this town might have died long ago. It might have devoured itself like so many others.

"And so today I will rededicate myself to our Lord. In front of all of you as my witnesses, I will give myself wholly to this church, our People, and our God."

"Amen."

"Before I can do that, I must divest myself of certain bonds. My own children must be set on the right path first. I cannot make them follow the righteous path, but like you, I can only set them on it and trust in the Lord to keep them walking in the Light."

Erasmus gripped Hattie's hand, his mind emptied of all thought except the intense desire to run, but his legs wouldn't move. Ransom and Mason had come around to his side of the bench. They grabbed him by the arms and pulled him down the aisle to the altar.

Hattie screamed behind him. "Let him go," she said. "What are you doing to him? Leave him alone." The panic in her voice drove it to a shrieking pitch. He wanted to tell her it was alright, to comfort her and tell her he would be fine but his voice, like his legs, wouldn't work.

"My son," Mothershed began when Erasmus had reached the altar, "has a wandering eye."

He could hear thrashing around behind him and the muffled screams of his sister.

"The Lord demands a sacrifice. He demands a punishment that fits the sin. For the price of my sons wandering eye, that looks upon the ruin of Sodom and Gomorrah, and in his Pride he says, 'I do not care. I do not submit to His will. I will commit the same sin as them and He will not rebuke me.' For this sin, the Almighty will have his wandering eye plucked from his head."

Hands seized his head and more hands pressed down on his shoulders and dropped him to his knees. Ransom bent over him and pulled his hair back, turning his face to the ceiling. He had a knife in his hand, and it flashed in the light of the oil lamps. Ransom put the tip of the blade right below Erasmus's left eye.

"Brace yourself, boy," he whispered.

Arms wrapped around his head. Erasmus couldn't move. He struggled against them but their grip on him was iron-clad. He tried to scream, but no sound came out.

If his father hoped to put the fear of retribution in him, it worked. He would leave Sorrow Draw, take Lupe and his mother, and leave forever. Flee to the Wastelands and live as marauders and exiles. He prayed to an absent god that they would let him go and not slit his throat or cut off his tongue or castrate him at there at the altar.

"Don't struggle now." Ransom's breath burned hot in his ear. "It'll just make it worse."

His captor looked him in the eye and winked. The knife slid under his eye, the sharp blade burned through muscle and vein. In the searing pain and darkness, Erasmus found his voice. It came out of him like the bursting of a great dam. He thrashed about but they held him firm. His left eye burned hot and someone put a rag to it and told him to hold it there. He took the cloth with shaking hands that could barely hold on. He pressed the rag to his eye—to where his eye once was—and cried out in pain. He took the rag off. The cold air blew into the new hole in his face and it burned and the blood flowed onto his cheek like tears, and he cried out again.

Ransom pressed the eyeball into his hand.

"Here, do something with this. It's wicked and shouldn't defile your father's holy temple."

Erasmus clutched his eyeball in his palm. Despite the agony, it felt strange, wet and larger than he thought it should be.

"Gird yourselves," his father to the hushed crowd. "Penitence is not a pretty thing. It is as ugly as the sin it forgives. My son has been forgiven. He has been washed in the blood of the lamb. He will carry this mark of redemption with him for the rest of his days."

A woman came to him, and they carried him away, but Mothershed stopped them and told them that his son needed to be a witness to what would happen next. The woman cradled his head to her chest and Erasmus sobbed in silence. He still had one eye left, he told himself. His father hadn't completely blinded him. He made himself small, curled up in the woman's arms, and tried as hard as he could not to make a sound, only the quivering of his shoulders betrayed him.

A wave of nausea overtook him and the world spun. He heard his father's voice through the roar in his ears, high and rough, as if he had to strain to push each syllable out of his throat. He heard an invocation, a blessing, and wedding vows, and Hattie sobbed. He glanced back at the altar with his good eye, the only one he had left. Hattie sat on her knees with Ransom by her side. She wept and looked over at Erasmus and reached her hand out for him, but Ransom grabbed her hair and turned her head away.

He lunged for her, desperate to reach her and protect her as he promised but someone punched him in the gut and he choked and vomited and his world spun until he fell into darkness.

Chapter 35

Serpent's Bluff, North Texas (November, 1881)

Deliverance Hill

Deliverance had a lot to worry about.

First, it had been two days since Horsethief had come by to trade. That in itself wasn't unusual, but he had a woman with him this time. A white woman. And he traded for supplies. Normally he trades in other pleasantries—whiskey usually, sometimes a night with a woman. The women at Hill Lodge were no soiled doves, they gave their bodies to whoever they wanted. Sometimes for a price, but often for free. It was their business. She suspected that Horsethief knew this, but he traded her for it anyway, so she didn't bother correcting him. He had been coming through this way for years, and always it was the same. But this time it wasn't alcohol, drugs, or women. It was a handful of supplies. The kind of supplies that a man gets when he's going on a long journey through the Wastelands.

Second, the folks from Sorrow Draw had stopped coming. It wasn't all at once, but in the last few weeks, they had seen fewer and fewer of them, until tonight when there wasn't a single white soul from across the Wastes. That was a problem.

Third, Sovereign hadn't returned from patrol yet. Every night the Highwaymen sent out patrols to scout around the outskirts of town. People joked that the patrols kept them safe from wild dogs and scavengers, but their real aim was to watch for the Paluxy Boys. Deliverance didn't trust the people of Sorrow Draw, but she tolerated them. What she didn't tolerate were the Paluxy Boys. Known members were banned from the Lodge and the Highwaymen had occasional shootouts with them on the fringes of their territory, though nothing ever came of it.

The attempt on Sovereign's life troubled her more than she cared to admit. The Lodge was hers, everyone knew that, but she only controlled it because Sovereign allowed her to. She was too young, too unimposing to command respect and loyalty on her own. She needed his power and muscle. Without him, she would lose her grip on the Lodge.

"Wu," she called to her confidant.

"I'm here." The little woman shuffled over on her impossibly tiny feet and sat next to Deliverance.

"Have you heard from Sovereign yet?"

"No. I don't think the patrol has returned. Why?"

"Because it's not like him. He's usually here."

"And do you worry for your lover?" Wu sipped from a small teacup.

"Yes. He might be my lover, but he's also my anchor here. What do you think would happen to this place if Sovereign were to die? What would happen to me if the Paluxy Boys find him and kill him?"

Wu looked thoughtful. "Well, as it stands now, I think someone else would take over. Maybe Ezekial. Or that George Stout. He a big man. People like him."

"Right. So, it's in our best interest to make sure that Sovereign doesn't find himself in front of a Paluxy Boys revolver."

"That is not really something you can control though, yes?"

"I should convince him not to go on patrols anymore. That could help keep him safe."

"Sure, sure. But he almost gets stabbed to death here at the Lodge? I think patrols might be safer."

Deliverance poured a glass of whiskey. "Alright then, that's fair. What can I do?"

"Start by ridding yourself of the need for Sovereign. No need for him, no worry that he die. Simple."

"How do I go about doing that? People are loyal to me, sure, but I think they are only loyal while I'm sitting next to him."

"This maybe not so true."

"How so?"

"Maybe, maybe not. Up to you. You make yourself important. All things go through you. Maybe they try to take over, but before long they realize they need you. Only you know contacts. This you control. You control exchange and inventory."

"Well now, I really don't. Lefty does exchange, and Zeke looks after inventory."

"But they are not Freemen. They answer to you."

"They also answer to you, Wu."

"Yes, yes. This means they answer twice to you."

"So I replace all the gamblers with people who aren't technically Freemen?"

"Yes. And be quiet about it. Not all at once. No need for people to take notice."

"Waller and Douglas at the Faro tables. They'll go first. But we'll piss them off fierce. We have to give them something else to do. Something that'll satisfy them."

"We could. Or you could let me take care of it."

"You? How?"

"Horsethief owes me a few favors."

"Wu, I can't kill my own people."

"This isn't just about the Lodge, you know. This about everything. The dust, it settles. Yesterday I saw a star. For first time in eighteen years, I saw a star. No one believes me, but I know what I saw. As clear as anything I've ever seen, the dust parted for a moment and there it was, high in the sky shinning down on me. The world isn't dead. It is coming back. There will be a new land to rule when the dust is gone and it starts here, at this Lodge." She took Deliverance's hand, her eyes wide. "Listen to me. It must not be a land ruled by men, where people like you and me have to live a life of servitude. I cannot go back to that. I will not. I will do anything I have to do to keep that from happening."

"Do you really think it would go back to that?"

"Of course it will. Men will make sure it does. I will not go back."

Wu's passion terrified her. She had heard stories, when she was younger, about her parent's lives as slaves, she read books and monthlies with stories about white men and their adventures and in those stories the people of her race were childish clowns, characters meant to get a laugh out of the white men who read them. And she had read the newspapers where they advertised the sale of her people.

"Waller...he's a Negro like me. How does it save my race to be killing people like him?"

"It's not just about your race, Deliverance. It also what's between your legs. You a woman first. And the new kingdom will need a queen, not a king."

A part of her admired Wu's boldness. There was a certain truth to her words that Deliverance couldn't deny, but some of these men were her friends and lovers, and killing them had never once crossed her mind, though it was clear that Wu had thought about it often enough to approach her with a plan.

"As long as the Paluxy Boys are a threat, I need all the men I can get. The answer is no. And I don't want to hear any more about it."

"It is a plan that requires boldness and nerve," Wu said. "I should have known it wasn't for you."

"You go too far, Wu. You want to gamble with your place here, that's on you."

Wu stood. "Good men have always stood by and done nothing about the tyranny of the wicked men. Remember that. When this is over, and they have taken this saloon from you, and they have taken your hope from you, and they have taken even your very voice from you, you will remember what I said. I would sooner disappear into the Wastes than let that happen to me."

She left, and Deliverance sat alone the rest of the night. She sent away the men and women who came calling, who hoped to share a drink or a card game with her, or those who hoped for more. Wu had spoken the truth, she knew. It might not have been her truth, but it was Wu's truth, and she couldn't dismiss it entirely.

It felt like a problem for another day, another year, another lifetime. Something that may happen when the dust blows away. It was a war that may or may not come, but if it did, it wouldn't come until after the dust war, the war against Sorrow Draw, was long over. And she might not even be around long enough to worry about it.

Chapter 36

Sorrow Draw, North Texas (November, 1881)

Eudora Becker

Eudora didn't understand why Horsethief wouldn't stay another night at the lodge. It was the most magnificent place she had ever been to and she wanted to stay. Men and women danced to music, sang lewd songs, gambled, and drank. There were an awful lot of Negroes and Mexicans, and she was sure she had even seen a Chinese woman, if the stories of how they looked could be trusted. She saw very few people her father wouldn't have called foreigners in Memphis.

She cursed at herself for thinking about her father. Ever since Horsethief told her about his death, thinking about him made her sad, and being sad made her angry. She hated being sad. It accomplished nothing other than making her look foolish. She could feign sadness, which was often a necessity, but that tool should be wielded with intent and precision. Genuine sadness had no place, especially not right now when any false move could spell the end of her.

Besides, her father should never have come after her. It was his fault. She expected him to send men to come and get her back, but when they were unsuccessful, she expected him to give it up. Why would he deny her a life in California? Horsethief told her that Longstreet would have killed him for losing the money, but that wouldn't have been necessary. Why lose a good man just because he made one mistake? And her father wouldn't have allowed that. He had his men who were loyal and would have fought for him. Who is Longstreet anyway? Why did he inspire more fear than her father?

She felt tears threaten to fall, but she knew it would not affect Horsethief. The man was impervious to her sorrow, or her innocence. She could be warm right now. Warm under the blankets and lying on a mattress filled with sawdust. Instead, she was trudging through the falling snow that carpeted the dust-covered ground.

They made their way through a dead forest, the land here rippled and folded like a cloth. A thin layer of ice underneath the snow made the going slow and difficult, but Horsethief seemed intent on making his way inch by plodding inch. They followed a slow-moving but wide river. Eudora had asked how long they were going to follow it. The big man told her they would continue alongside it for many days before it finally disappeared into the Wastelands, all the way to the New Mexico Territory.

"What's on the other side? More of...this?" she asked, gesturing to the dead landscape around them.

"No," he had said. "It's the Indian Territories. I wish I could take you there. Our journey would be over."

"Well, yeah but they don't use California money, right? All that money would be just as worthless there as it was in Memphis."

"But if you were there," he said, "you wouldn't need the money. You wouldn't want the money. We look for a paradise in California only because we cannot have the one to the north." He told her of his banishment from his home and family, about his brother, and his brother's religion. Eudora didn't understand why he made such a fuss over the religion. If it made people happy and it brought them together, why care so much? If the Indian Territories were truly a paradise, why risk losing it over some foolish beliefs? Men were simple in their wants most of the time, but sometimes they were impossibly confusing.

The supplies they got at the lodge did little to stifle the cold. She still had the buffalo hide, which kept her mostly warm, but the icy air had a bad habit of worming its way through the folds to burn at her skin. Horsethief pulled on the reins and their horse came to a stop.

"Wait." He pointed to the ground. "There's horse tracks here."

She saw some markings half buried in the new snowfall. "So what?" she said. "Could be anything, how do you know it's horses?"

"I know what horse tracks look like."

"Doesn't look like anything special to me. Could be a pack of dogs."

"Those are hoofs."

"Maybe someone lost a cow out here. Some people still have those. I think a cow would live quite well out here. There's some brush that still grows around the river. They might not get very big, but they could survive."

"No one is going to lose a cow. And I know the difference between a cow and a horse. And I also know that you are angry because we left the Lodge, but I told you that you did not have to come with me."

"Oh, no. You're right. I didn't have to come. But you would have left with my money if I had stayed."

"Yes."

His honesty was maddening. "Yes? That money bel—"

"Shhh." He put his hand out to her. "No talking. Listen." He lifted his head up to the sky, but all Eudora could hear was the wind.

"I don't hear anything."

"We need to ride. Now."

He spurred the horse to a run. She pressed her back into his chest, a sudden fear taking over. But fear solved as many problems as sadness, and so she pushed the fear aside with more anger. Anger was a problem solver. Anger could help her see things clearly. At this moment, she saw this gallop through the forest as a distraction. Horsethief needed to stop running from her and understand why she was upset. Once he's apologized, things can go back to normal between them. She didn't want to end things with the Indian the way she ended them with Jeremiah.

She had just started thinking about Jeremiah when Horsethief fell from his saddle and hit the ground hard, nearly pulling her down with him. A loud crack echoed through the dead woods followed by the sound of men hollering in celebration. They were close, yipping and howling like mad dogs.

Eudora jumped from the horse to help the injured man. He rolled onto his back; his teeth clenched in pain. He pressed his hand to his side.

The sound of galloping horses drew closer. Eudora didn't know what to do. Horsethief needed help, but these men who shot him would be on them any second and she couldn't be seen helping him if she wanted to get out of this situation herself.

It didn't matter. Horsethief had been good to her, and she would help him as best she could. She took a bonnet from her saddlebag, one she had gotten in the lodge. A man there had taken a liking to her and gave it as a gift. She hadn't been aware of the local customs though, and he had demanded more than she wanted to give for it. He had been close to taking what he wanted whether she cared for it or not, when Horsethief found them and the man quickly decided he didn't need what he thought he needed after all. Now, she pressed that bonnet into the bleeding wound on Horsethief's side as the strangers rode up and circled them. They were not Indians. They were all white men.

"Well, well. What do have here, gentlemen?" said one of the men. He had a pleasant-looking face with a short beard and wide shoulders. Something about him made Eudora uncomfortable, though. He had the air of a man who spoke politely in company but turned wicked and cruel when no one else was around. Eudora had known plenty of men like that. The truth was in their eyes. They always looked at her with sharp eyes that never relaxed.

"Curly, what does this look like to you?" he asked the man next to him.

"Looks like we got ourselves an injun and a pretty little shickster," said another man with a thick tuft of curled black hair.

Eudora counted fifteen men. Fifteen men, all on horseback. How they had that many horses, she didn't know. She had never seen so many mounted men all at once. She needed more information before she played her hand, and so she waited.

"Not just any injun, mind you. This here is the one who calls hisself Horsethief," said the first man.

Eudora had known enough men like these to know that more than often the first man to speak in a group was the man in charge. This man carried himself as if he were used to being in charge.

"Ain't that right?" he continued. "You Horsethief? You call yourself Nanabozho and Edward Crowkiller too, don't you? Mothershed thinks you might even be Sanguin Corvus hisself. That true?"

Sanguin Corvus. Horsethief told her about him. His brother. Could he have lied to her about that? Could he actually be Sanguin Corvus? And is he really the same Crowkiller that had been a part of her father's posse so long ago? This revelation made sense to Eudora. This is why he knew where to find her. It wasn't a coincidence that he had tracked her and Jeremiah. He didn't just happen to be wandering the plains when he spotted them. He had been sent by her father to find them.

Her anger returned. She didn't care if her father had sent him. That wasn't what angered her. He lied. What else had he lied to her about? He had a lot more to apologize to her for when this was over.

Horsethief, or Crowkiller, spat. Blood from an ugly gash on his forehead spilled down his face and he appeared wild and fierce. "Sanguin Corvus can burn in your Hell," he said through blood-stained teeth.

"Now those ain't my words, injun. I don't care one way or another. But Reverend Mothershed does. I reckon he's gonna be pleased to see you."

A man with a flushed face and whiskey nose kicked his horse alongside the leader. "Ransom, if we're gonna take the injun we best do it now. Men are getting uneasy being so close to the Red River and all. They fear an ambush."

The man named Ransom nodded. He whistled through his teeth and pointed at Horsethief with his head. Men with ropes surrounded the wounded man. He fought them off, but they beat him with their rifles until he couldn't move any longer.

Eudora cried. She wanted to yell at them to stop, but the words didn't come. A voice deep inside reminded her that she had a role to play, and it wouldn't do for her to be seen crying. She must appear grateful. She didn't want to be grateful though, even if it was just the appearance of it. Every step of the way, men have done everything in their power to ruin all her plans.

"And what about you, little dove?" asked the man named Ransom. "Who are you, and why are you riding with this Indian?"

At the edge of her vision, the men loaded her companion and lover onto the back of a horse. "He took me," she said. "My name is Eudora. Eudora Becker. My father is Governor Becker from Memphis."

"Memphis?" asked a man behind her. "There's folks still up in Memphis?"

"Why yes," she replied. "Quite a few, actually. We have several hundred, I'd reckon. I don't really know all that much. I'm just the Governor's daughter is all."

"Of course," Ransom said. "But what's the governor of Memphis's daughter doing all the way out in Texas and riding with an Indian?"

"He took me," she said again. "Stole me in the middle of the night, can you believe it? He meant to ransom me, I think, if you'll pardon me for saying it. I mean no offense to your unusual name, of course."

"No offense taken, ma'am. My father is Prussian. He just liked the word. He thought it sounded very American." He shrugged. "Well Miss Eudora, I can't leave you wandering the Wastelands all alone. I'll take you back to my town and we'll see if your father or his men come calling after you. I'm sure the good Reverend has a room he can spare for you."

"That would be most agreeable, sir." Eudora flashed him her most childlike and innocent of wide-eyed smiles. This man looked at her with hunger in his eyes. It was a look she knew in men well, but she had always the protection of another—her father, Jeremiah, Horsethief—but she had no protection now. So, she played innocent and hoped this man would not reveal himself to be the kind whose desires only intensified when she played modest and chaste.

They rode south through the dead woods. They allowed her to ride on her own horse, but Ransom kept it tied to his so she couldn't ride off. Once again, she found herself in need of a plan. Once again, she was caught up in the tangled mess of lies and deceit that men make of their lives. Ransom's eyes grew more eager by the mile.

Chapter 37

Unknown Lands, North Texas (November, 1881)

Farhad

Farhad woke before dawn to bathe. A stream wound its way past their camp, and he took the opportunity to clean himself, despite the cold. He couldn't do much more in the shallow water than splash it onto his body and scrub away the worst of the dirt and grime. The stream was either a new, post-Calamity addition to the landscape, or it was too small to warrant inclusion in Conny's map, but Farhad suspected it was new. It flowed on top of the land, not through it. In the absence of eons, it hadn't yet had the time to cut its path into the earth.

The icy water burned, but the washing served a ritualistic purpose. They would encounter civilization today. Or, at least the remnants of a civilization that still clung to life. He had washed his clothes the night before and hung them over the fire to dry with twine he lashed to the top of the tent. This morning they smelled of smoke, but they were clean. He doused them in perfume he picked up in Bolivar.

Whether the day would end in a bed with a woman or two, or in a shoot-out, he determined he would meet it looking and smelling like a gentleman.

He closed his eyes and fought off the urge to cough until it became a demand that he couldn't defy. The Graveyard Cough, the doctor in Memphis had called it. The Great White Plague. Unable to stand, he fell to his hands and knees in the water and coughed his throat raw and it stung as if he inhaled broken glass. He didn't know how long he sat there, but the water had numbed his legs, and he couldn't stand so he rolled himself out of the stream. The wind tore at his wet flesh, but it masked his cough and so he was grateful for it. Conny and Nikki would have rushed out to him, carried him back to the tent, and refused to move on until they were sure he wouldn't start back up again. He could refuse Conny. Refusing Nikki proved a greater challenge.

He pushed his thoughts of Nikki aside. With any luck, he would bed a woman tonight. If not, he would gamble and cheat until he got into a gunfight. Either way, he would feel alive.

The tent hung at the edge of his vision. He forced himself to stand on unfeeling legs and walk, slowly and deliberately, back to it. He could not let his companions see him crawl back on his hands and knees and so he teetered back to camp.

He sat with his cold legs next to the fire until they returned to life and a thousand tiny knives stabbed at them. He grit his teeth against the pain and kept his face turned away from his friends who still slept quietly together.

He closed his eyes and concentrated on the pain in his legs and throat. Someday his eyes would close for the last time and he would never again feel any pain so he savored it for a time. He focused on it, the knives and the broken glass, until he thought of nothing else, knew nothing else, until pain and life merged into one.

A bitter taste blazed in his mouth and he swallowed. Warm hands cradled his head until the pain dissolved and a rush of heat replaced the agony. Nikki's hands were rough, not like the coddled girls in Memphis who were set up from a young age to breed like stock, but like someone who had worked outside with her hands, in an age before the coming of the dust, when crops grew in the fields and life was an endless cycle of work and sleep with little time or opportunity for love, especially in one with skin as dark as hers.

Farhad understood. They were the same, and so he loved her because he loved himself.

"We're two of a kind, you and I. You know that, Nikki Free?"

"How's that? I don't do near the amount of whoring around that you do."

"There, you see? Right there. You're the only person I've ever met who could put me in my place with a wit as sharp as mine."

"Nonsense. My wit is far sharper."

"That's true." He tried to look at her but his head swam and she was nothing more than a blur in his eyes. "In truth, the thing we most have in common is we were both prisoners before the Calamity. This fucking thing, this end of the world, this Great Dying…it set us free. We'd be nothing without it."

Nikki said nothing for a long time and Farhad wondered if perhaps she didn't feel the same about their fate. "I know it," she told him at last. "I know it, but knowing it don't make it any easier to live with."

"What's hard about it, Nikki? They didn't make it, we did. Ain't nothing to feel bad for. The world's ended and we get to watch it choke out its final breaths. We're fortunate, you and I. I see you reading your newspapers. You read about the old war and smile. You smile at the battles, don't you? Reading about the dead soldiers gives you joy, doesn't it?"

"It does," she whispered. "And I take no pleasure in that."

Farhad laughed. "It gives you joy yet you take no pleasure in it. Once again, Nikki, you speak like a true woman."

"Maybe that's because that is exactly what I am."

"Give me more laudanum," Farhad asked.

Nikki raked her fingers through his hair. "Not yet, gunfighter. Not yet. You've got a long day ahead, and you're going to want to be at your best. You're gonna gamble, you're gonna drink, and you're gonna whore until you can't gamble, drink, and whore no more."

"You really know what to say to a man, Nikki Free."

"I know it. Now get up, get yourself dressed, wax your mustache, and put some of that pomade in your hair. You are going to have your pick of the women. They will swoon when you walk through those doors."

Nikki helped him sit up, then she slipped back under the blankets she shared with Conny. Farhad drew in a deep breath and filled his chest with the warm air. His lungs still burned from his fit by the stream.

They heard the saloon long before they got their first glimpse of it. Sound cuts through the dust and haze with ease while light is conquered by it. The wind carried the music to them, the tinkling of a piano, a raucous song, the laughter of men and women, glasses slamming onto tables. At Purdy's saloon in Memphis, these sounds were subdued, shackled by the constant unease and fear, and the bitter loneliness of life. But this place sounded for all the world as if it had joy to spare.

They hitched the horses to a dead tree far past the outskirts of town. Conny insisted on staying behind with them. Their horses and gear were likely the most valuable things for hundreds of miles in every direction and it wasn't wise to leave them unattended. Even though the odds of someone stumbling upon them by chance out in the thick dust were low, it still didn't sit right with him. But when Nikki told him that if he stayed, so would she, he relented.

"I can't be the thing that keeps you from having a good time tonight," he had said. "I know you wouldn't miss this for the world."

"Maybe not for the world, mister, but I would for you. The world ain't much, for sure."

When they were close enough to see the light spill from the windows and cracks of the saloon, Farhad picked up his pace. He walked with a lightness and his mustache twitched. He fingered the handle of one of his revolvers.

"Farhad," Conny said. "Let's get the feel of this place before you go running off. We stay together until we know what we're up against in there."

"Cornelius White, you do know exactly how to bring wreck and ruin to any and all fun, don't you? You positively raze the very notion of enjoying yourself to the ground."

"We're here mostly for supplies, not fun. I want to make sure that the three of us are safely leaving this place tomorrow morning. Together. Just as we came in."

"We will, vaquero, we will." Nikki put a hand on Conny's chest. "But let him gamble and drink and bed a woman. You can show me a fine country dance and we can always keep one eye on him."

"I am positive that I can take care of myself, Nikki Free. Don't you children stay up late on my account, I guarantee I will have a long night and if I come to a bad end from it, there ain't nothing the two of you could do to stop it."

He had heard rumors of California since Conny first found him wandering the streets of New York. Golden beaches on the Pacific Ocean, the wild and untamed wilderness, the fields still producing grain, farms, and cattle, the ringing of the blacksmith's hammer, the ships sailing in and out of port up and down the coast, more sights and sounds than he could imagine and yet if he died right here tonight, he would be content with it.

Farhad opened the door and a wave of sensations struck him like a steam engine. Wall-mounted torches lit the main hall brighter than anything Farhad had seen in years and he had to squint a bit, though the sun used to shine brighter when he was a child in the desert, his eyes had become accustomed to the perpetual dark. But here the fires blazed hot and bright and bathed the dancers in a brilliant golden hue. The air blew out warm and smelled of fiery whiskey, sweet tobacco, and the peculiar aromas of human bodies—of sweat and piss and sex.

The lodge was big and alive and full of motion. Bodies everywhere moved and swirled like motes in a stream. Men and women danced and glided across the floor, gamblers twisted in chairs and stood up, then sat back down, lovers in corners squirmed and writhed. Then all motion and all noise stopped and the whole of the lodge turned to face the newcomers.

Two large men on the left and right with revolvers. The man on the left looks slower. First him, then the man on the right. Bartender across the hall likely has a rifle under the bar. Three shots, then turn and run. No, dealers are armed. Too many. Shoot guards left and right, then run. Should be able to escape under the cover of dust unless they have horses.

The piano man started playing again, and after a breath, the people resumed their activities. Gamblers turned back to their cards, lovers turned back to their partners, and dancers took to their feet once more.

The three crossed the hall to the bar at the far end. Eyes in the dark places watched them with either suspicion or eagerness, Farhad couldn't tell which. After some negotiating about costs, Conny traded some powder for three shots of whiskey.

"I don't like this," Conny said.

"Well, that's a real shame Con, because I am in my element right now." Farhad tipped his head back and whiskey went down fiery but smooth. It was quality stuff.

"Welcome to Hill Lodge." A Chinese woman with impossibly tiny feet limped up to the bar. "I am Wu. I have a table and drinks for you if you will follow me."

"Follow you where?" asked Conny, suspicion always at the front of his mind.

"Over there." She pointed to a round table in one of the dark recesses. A small black woman sat there looking over at them. Farhad couldn't read her expression. It could have been a look of distrust and anger every bit as much as a look of interest or desire.

"And to whom do we owe this pleasure?" Farhad asked.

"My mistress, Deliverance. She is the proprietor here."

Farhad pointed to the table. "That Deliverance?"

"It is she."

"A bit young to be the proprietor here, isn't she?" he asked.

"Some would say so, but not many. This new world is for the young, after all."

"New world?" Conny asked. "It's the end of the world."

"Yes, one world ends and another begins. Now, come. Young or no, you stay here at her desire."

They followed her to the back corner where the young woman waited and she sat them down. A man with a shaved head placed a bottle of whiskey on the table and Wu poured a glass for each of them while Deliverance appraised them.

"A white man, a mulatto, and a...I'm sorry," she said to Farhad. "I don't know your kind."

"Bedouin. From Syria."

"Right. A real-life Arab in my saloon, well I'll be."

"The pleasure is all mine, this here is a mighty fine establishment it would seem. If you pardon me, ma'am I've only just arrived but I've never seen the likes of it anywhere else."

"Thank you." She seemed unsure.

Farhad found her beautiful. She held her glass of whiskey in her dark hands with white palms and she looked at them with large, bright eyes that glistened in the torchlight.

"My name is Deliverance, and this is my saloon. You're welcome to stay, if you don't cause trouble. You're all well-armed and I'd ask you to not fire those guns in my lodge and don't pull them out to threaten no one either. You'll be exceedingly popular tonight, I have no doubt, and you'll likely attract a lot of attention. Some good, some bad. Keep your tempers in check. We simply don't get strangers around here and yet we've had four now in just as many days."

"Four?" Conny asked. "Who else has come by here?"

"Tell me who you are, stranger, and what you're doing here and I'll see if I'm going to tell you any more."

"Fair enough," said Nikki. "My name is Nikki Free. This here is Cornelius White, and that devilishly sly conman to his left goes by the name of Farhad."

"And what brings the three of you out this way?"

"Just passing through. We're traveling to California. We've heard it's a paradise and we're going to see for ourselves," Conny said.

Conny kept their details too well-guarded. They were an interesting group to these people, and they would want a more interesting story from them.

"We're following someone, to be honest," Farhad told her. "Someone who has something that belongs to us. Might have come by this way not too long ago. Might be those strangers you mentioned. But there would have been two of them, not just the one, so maybe it wasn't them."

"There were two of them," Deliverance answered.

"Ah, well perhaps my math ain't what it used to be, but when you said you had seen four strangers, and there are three of us here, I calculated that there was only one other stranger who came through here recently and we've been following a pair as it were."

"You do have a very roundabout way of getting to the point, don't you? Like you take the longest route to get there when the shortest would do just fine."

"That is one of his many failings," Conny said. "But he speaks the truth. We are looking for two people."

"Yes, two people came through here, but only one was a stranger to me." She looked at Farhad. "Which is how I managed to count to the four of you."

"I see." Farhad tipped his hat. "Would the pair happen to have been a young white girl and an Indian?"

"What do you want with the Indian?"

"How do you know him?" Conny asked.

"What business you got with him?"

"He's a friend," Nikki said. "These men rode with him a long time ago."

"A friend?"

"That's right," Conny said. "He's going by the name of Horsethief. We've followed him all the way from Mississippi. We've crossed the great river of the same name, across Louisiana, and across the plains of Texas and now we're here."

"Sounds like you're chasing him to me. Why should I believe you're friends of his?"

"Look," Conny took a paper from his breast pocket. "Here. He's been leaving us notes on how to find him. You read?"

"I read." She looked over the note for a moment and handed it back. "Says his name is Crowkiller. Is that Horsethief?"

"It is. How do you know him?"

Deliverance exchanged a look with Wu who only raised her eyebrows. "He's...my trading partner. The supplies to run this saloon don't come easy out here in the Wastelands, but inside the Indian Territory? They are apparently plentiful."

Surprise registered easily on Conny's face. The man never seemed able to hide his feelings. Farhad suppressed the urge to smile. This certainly got more interesting.

"Crowkiller...Horsethief, he...he gets you supplies from inside the Indian Territories?" Conny asked.

"He does. He can cross back and forth, but he's the only one I know that can do that, and so you understand how important it is for me to protect him, right?"

"This is very interesting news indeed, isn't it Con?" Farhad reached for the bottle of whiskey. "You mind?"

"Help yourself," Deliverance said.

"OK, look." Conny sat up straighter. "I need to find him. The girl he's with is the daughter of an old friend and I've sworn to keep her safe. We all have, well, except Miss Nikki Free, here. But anyways, we're sworn to keep her safe and we're supposed to meet up with our friend here and travel together to California."

"Well then, it would seem that your luck may have run out here. They've been taken."

"Taken?" Conny asked. "By who?"

"The Paluxy Boys. Look, you're all new here so let me tell you that you've walked into a big old hornet's nest. We're on the edge of an all out war with the people of Sorrow Draw, so I'd recommend to you that you forget about your oath to your friend and get the hell out of here and take your chances in California."

"Maybe you should start from the beginning," Nikki said.

Deliverance called for another bottle of whiskey and a tobacco pouch. They sat together and drank. They rolled the tobacco in papers from Conny's Bible and smoked while she told them about Reverend Mothershed, about the Paluxy Boys, about the history of the conflict between them. She told them about Sovereign and about the rising tensions, and finally about how a man from Sorrow Draw came to the lodge this morning and told her about the capture of Horsethief and the girl.

Farhad could scarcely believe that something as wondrous as this saloon still existed in the world. His life since the Calamity had been filled with mostly pain. Dusty saloons with watered down whiskey and ancient tobacco, knives in the dark, hangings and betrayals, and only the occasional night of bare women and strong opium to forget about the savagery of it all. But here were people who lived a life of pleasure day in and day out and he wondered if they ever gave any thought to the barbarity that exists among the rest of humanity.

He could live here, for a time. But endless pleasure is as dull and meaningless as endless pain. Farhad needed to feel. Too long doing one thing and a potent and persistent urge would take hold of him. An urge to feel something different. Perhaps knowing that he would die soon had awakened in him a crucial need to experience all he could, to see and feel everything before he could no longer see or feel anything.

Desire took many forms with him. Women, drugs, drink, even killing sometimes offered gratification, if the man deserved killing. In truth, anything was a vice. A new food, a new scent, a new stretch of land beyond the fog of dust, the feel of fine clothes, the banter between friends on the road, he reveled in it all.

Once he had drank his fill and smoked enough tobacco, he leaned back in his chair and listened to Deliverance talk. Conny and Nikki were caught up in her tales and he should have been as well, his friend had been taken and was either dead or would be soon. There would be time to mourn or to stage a rescue later.

Another yearning took hold of him now. The woman who called herself Wu had stolen more than a few sidelong glances his way when they first sat down, but now she looked at him openly and Farhad returned her gaze. The familiar hunger for the tender flesh of a woman burned in his gut and he stood and offered Wu his hand.

"Ma'am, might I have the honor of a dance?"

Wu's eyes opened wide and she put a hand to her mouth. "I'm sorry, sir," she said. "I don't dance."

"She's crippled," Deliverance said. "She walks with a limp. I ain't never seen her dance with no one."

"That's alright." Farhad kept his hand out. "We'll tell the piano man to play something real slow."

She took his hand and they walked together to the dance floor. The man played a song he called "*Oh to the River Went my Scavenger Bride*". A woman came up from the crowd and sang next to the piano. A white brothel gown hung loose on her dark-skinned frame, and she sang in a low tone of love and loss, of death in the time of dust, and of new brides and old sorrows.

Farhad and Wu danced and when the music stopped, they went on dancing. When her feet hurt too much to go on she took him upstairs and they locked themselves in a room and undressed each other. They lit candles and burned incense. At times they opened the window to the cold, other times they locked it tight. They pleasured each other and smoked opium and shared their most intimate memories of the time before and of the blessing of the Calamity that brought them both their freedom.

The two of them lay on the bed, naked and sweating. Farhad ran his hand over her body and her gooseflesh rose.

"Take me away from here," she said to him.

"Where do you want to go?"

"Anywhere."

"My friends and I are going to California. You can come with us."

"No us. Just me."

"Just you?"

"Just me."

"You want me to leave my friends?"

"Yes."

"And what do I get out of this deal?"

"You get me."

"I have to admit, that's tempting." He kissed her breast and ran his fingers through the soft hair between her legs.

"I can teach you my language. Do you know Cantonese?"

"Not yet."

"I want to see how fast you can learn."

"I can learn fast."

"So you say."

"Why do you want to leave?"

"I don't want to be here when the men take everything back. I don't want to live like that again. I saw my mother's sadness every day of my life before the Calamity. I will die first."

She had told him of Chinese culture and the role of women. She allowed him to take her shoes off, her impossibly small shoes, and see for himself what they had done to her.

"You aren't afraid of me? I don't know if you noticed or not, but I am also a man."

"You are Farhad. A man, yes. But you will love me."

"You're very confident of that, aren't you?"

"I am."

"Why?"

"Because we are same. Have you met a woman who can hold her own with you?"

Wu had matched him drink for drink with and without laudanum. She had smoked when he smoked and when he thrust inside of her, she had met him with equal vigor.

"No, I haven't. But how long can that last? This is my natural state."

"I live in a saloon. It is my natural state, too."

She kissed him. He tasted the salt of her skin and the cactus liquor she told him the Mexicans made. They kissed for a long time and Farhad wondered if he could leave Conny and Nikki for her and how his friends would be better off without a lunger dragging them down.

"I can heal you," Wu whispered to him.

"Maybe you can at that, woman. Maybe you can."

Chapter 38

Sorrow Draw, North Texas (November, 1881)

Hattie Mothershed

It was the morning after her marriage to Ransom that he brought in the girl to live with them.

Ransom had wasted no time after the sudden wedding to take her to his bed. Hattie hadn't fought, she hadn't struggled, and she had made no effort to make the act a difficult one for him. After she watched as they cut her brother's eye out of his head, she had no strength left to fight. She spent all her vigor on her tears. She wept for her brother and the memory of his bloody eye on the church altar. She wept for her lost virtue and for the shame she suffered under Ransom's heaving body.

The crying had put him in a sour mood, and he berated her for turning their consummation into something he should feel guilt over. When she only wept more, he struck her on the jaw with the back of his hand and told her how sorry he was that she made him do that to her on their wedding night.

Hattie pulled up her blanket to cover her nakedness. Her arms and legs trembled violently and shook the iron bed frame. The sting in her jaw quieted her grief for a time and her mind cleared. It was her fault. She had plenty of time to poison Ransom, and yet she delayed time and again. She could have left and taken her chances in the Wastelands by herself, or Erasmus could have gone with her and together they could have made a journey to California.

When she was young, she took a long trip with her father and mother to a port in Galveston and saw the waves from the Gulf of Mexico crash into the sand and recede, only to swell and crash and then recede again. She had watched it transfixed, and she felt the terrible presence of God when it struck her that those waves had crashed onto that shore long before she was born and would continue long after she was dead. There were things in this world that were impossibly big, and those things didn't care at all about her. The shame she felt now crashed like those waves, and when it receded, it exposed her anger like the sand that lay buried under the surface of the water.

Her new husband had brought her a bowl of water and a cotton rag and told her to clean herself up. She sat so long staring at her hands that her blood, and Ransom's seed, had congealed and her thighs stuck to the sheets. He watched her soak the rag and scrub between her legs.

When she had finished, he told her he would leave to patrol the Red River. Her father thought that they might draw some Indians out of hiding if they rode up and down the shores for a while, so he and a group of Paluxy Boys were to play the bait and try to trap them.

"I hope they put a bullet in you," she had whispered. She thought he would strike her again, maybe put his hands around her neck and choke out what life she had left in her, but he didn't.

For a moment his expression was unreadable. He simply looked down at her and breathed hard. "Don't wait up," he said at last, and he left.

Now, the girl called Eudora sat in front of the fire in Hattie's room at the Mothershed house humming to herself and combing her hair. Ransom had moved her back to what he referred to as "her childhood home" so she could keep an eye on this new girl he had found and keep her company. The Mothershed house, being larger and a good deal warmer and better maintained, would be a more ideal location for two ladies to make themselves social with each other.

Hattie agreed immediately. As far as she knew, her brother still lived in this house, and he needed her care and attention. But when they got to the house, she found his room empty. She checked on her mother, and he was not with her either. If he wasn't here, he would be with Lupe, licking his wounds and finding comfort with him. So she took to caring for the girl. God willing, Erasmus was somewhere safe, and that he would come back soon.

As it turned out, this girl proved to be more than she was prepared to handle. At first, she sat by the fire, aloof. She spoke no more than a word or two when Hattie questioned her. She had no idea where the girl came from, how Ransom came to find her, or how long she would need to stay in Sorrow Draw. The girl held herself in high regard, that much was certain, and Hattie got the distinct feeling that this Eudora would hand her over to the wild men of the Wastelands on no more than a whim.

When Hattie brought her a meal of dried meats and coffee from the cellar, her demeanor didn't soften gradually, as one would expect, but the girl went from cold and haughty to doe-eyed and fawning in an instant, and all traces of the former girl vanished in a flash of smiles and fluttering eyelashes.

These wild mood changes would be typical over the day, and Hattie wondered if it was the result of some ordeal she had suffered on her journey here, or if this was simply her way.

"So you still haven't told me where you're from." The urge to know the little blonde-haired girl's story grew. She provided a distraction from Hattie's constant worry about her brother.

"How long do we have to stay in this room?" Eudora asked.

"I don't know. Why do you want to leave, though? Believe me when I tell you that things out there are much worse than they are in here."

"How? There's a whole town out there. There's people. There's relics to look at. I even saw a millinery on my way here. Is it empty?" The girl's eyes widened.

Hattie had known few girls who still cared for things like that. Rings and baubles to wear on their hands, necklaces to wrap around their necks. "Well, I'm sure I don't really know. I haven't been."

"You live here and you haven't been? Where do you go? Please tell me you leave this room sometimes."

"I do. I...I spend a good deal of my time in my old schoolhouse."

Eudora rolled her eyes. The disgust evident on her face was replaced by one of disappointment. "Of course you would spend your time in the schoolhouse."

"What's that supposed to mean?" asked Hattie.

Eudora gave her a look that said you know exactly what that's supposed to mean, then she sighed and looked out the window at the falling snow. They sat in silence for a while. "I'm from Memphis," she said at last.

"Memphis?" Hattie said. "That's pretty far away, I think. You came all this way? How long did it take? Where are all the men you came with?" Conflict was a way of life in the Wastelands, and she prayed that Ransom and the Paluxy Boys didn't have a hand in the fates of her companions.

"I didn't really come with a bunch of men. Just me and Jeremiah." The girl spoke in barely a whisper, and she laid her head in her hands and reclined against the divan under the window. "He went and got hisself killed."

"I'm sorry."

"He was eaten by some folks in Bolivar, I think it was. They almost cooked and ate me, too but I got away."

"Good Lord." The thought of cannibals in the Wastes terrified Hattie. Hunger on the windswept plains was a real threat, and more than a few men have claimed to have been tempted by the flesh of another person. The people saw a victory over the temptation as the sign of a righteous man, someone who had walked the boundary of Hell and survived. Like Christ tempted by Satan in the desert of the Holy Land, they faced their demons and did not succumb. But Hattie suspected that some of those men did not actually defeat their devils. She saw a guilty look on some of their faces, and also on the faces of the men who clapped them on their backs and praised them for their courage against temptation.

"It was awful," Eudora said in her light, child-like voice. "But I got away."

"How?"

"The Indian took me. But not before I nearly froze to death. This horrible, disgusting man kept me naked in the cold on the floor of a jail cell, if you can believe that. Me, of all people. My father was the governor of Memphis and he kept me cold and naked like an animal. I hope somebody puts a bullet in his belly someday."

"I used to think that men like that would eventually get what's coming to them, that the Lord would get His vengeance on the wicked. But my own father's been on this Earth for far too long for that to be true."

"Mine got what was coming to him, I guess. I heard he did some bad things and now he's gone."

"I'm sorry."

"He was good to me. I wasn't so good to him sometimes, I guess. But he loved me more than I thought he did."

"You were fortunate, then."

Eudora nodded. "After Bolivar, I traveled with Horsethief until I got here. We crossed the big Mississippi River and rode for days and days. Now he's gone and I'm here."

"Where did he go?"

"I don't know. Maybe ask your husband, I suppose. He took him. Shot him and took him and he took me, too."

"I'm not so sure he's my lawful husband, to tell the truth. Lawful in the eyes of the Lord at least. My father spoke the vows in my stead. I was in too much shock to say anything myself. That was good enough for them, though. My father professes to speak from the right hand of God, and the people listen. So I suppose it don't matter a bit if I think he's not my rightful husband. Makes no difference. But enough about my troubles. You've had quite a journey."

Eudora shrugged. "The worst part of it all was the cold. No matter what I did, I was always cold. I can't get away from it. I hear it's warm in California."

"I've heard that too. My father says it's a rumor designed to lure people away from the truth and into the hands of the Devil."

"That's silly."

"Yes, I think so too."

"It might not be the truth, but it ain't that devil nonsense neither."

"So, you're still determined to go?"

The wind outside gusted and rattled the window. "I am. Even if I have to go the rest of the way by myself."

Hattie listened to the house creak and groan in the gale. This delicate little pampered waif of a girl traveled hundreds of miles from Tennessee to her home in Texas. She faced the burning cold and hunger of the plains and the barbarism of men. Escape had been possible for Hattie, too, yet she hadn't the nerve for it. She hadn't thought escape was possible before, but maybe now there was hope.

"I'm awfully tired," Eudora said. "If your husband comes back, please remind him he said he would bring me my things. My saddlebag. He also promised not to pry. A girl has a right to her little secrets. And that goes for you, too. My personal things are my own."

"Fair enough, Eudora."

"You can call me Dora. I like you, Harriett. You've been good to me."

"I like you too, Dora. And you can call me Hattie."

Eudora closed her eyes and soon her breathing became heavy and rhythmic. Hattie watched her chest rise and fall and she wondered if she had the strength to do what this girl had done. She imagined them leaving together, sneaking out of the house under the cover of dust and darkness with an oil lamp trailing a line of black smoke behind them. Erasmus and Lupe would meet them out by the stables with four horses saddled and stocked with supplies and they would, all four of them, ride hard and fast towards the setting sun.

Sometime later, Ransom returned. He saw Eudora asleep by the window, so he pushed Hattie onto the bed and lifted her dress and took her from behind. It was more painful this time, but the shame outweighed the pangs, and spasms, and the tearing of flesh. She would not wake Eudora by crying out. She grit her teeth and clung to the iron bed frame with an equally iron grip. She cried noiselessly into the quilted blanket she kept on her bed, the same one she had cried into as a child when her mother rapped her knuckles with a birch wood cane when she lied or laughed or wept too loud.

When he finished, he told her to clean herself up and he left. Hattie kept her head down until she was sure that Ransom was gone. She looked over to Eudora, who lay still on the sofa, her head turned away and her breath not as deep and rhythmic as before. She stood up and her head swam but she had no time for sleep. She had to fetch water and a rag and clean herself up. Then she would have to check on her mother and give her medicine, clean her sheets, and wash her. She would have to see about Eudora's saddlebag and get her something to eat when the girl decides she's waited long enough and can pretend to wake up.

Once she had taken care of everything else, then she could sneak out and find Erasmus.

Chapter 39

Serpent's Bluff, Texas (November, 1881)

Nikki Free

Nikki and Conny woke the next morning to the scent of meat cooking over an open fire. Deliverance had given them a room upstairs and Nikki found the bed soft and cleaner than anything she had slept in for years, but the smell of the savory meat coaxed her out of it earlier than she would have on her own.

They got dressed and knocked on Farhad's door. When there was no answer, they tried to open the door but found it locked. The Bedouin had been known to sleep in after a night of heavy drinking, so they followed their noses down the stairs and out the front door. Several fires had been set up down the middle of the street, and all of them had several thick slabs of meat skewered onto sticks and placed over the open flames. The marbled flesh sizzled and steamed, and the fires below sputtered and flared. Some of the fires had large pots with organs, entrails, and bones of various kinds bubbling in water, and in one fire at the end boiled a whole horse head.

"Conny?" A dread rose in her heart.

"You stay here, I'll go check on the horses." He hurried off in a run. The once sweet aroma now smelled sick and the bile rose in her throat. She returned to the lodge, unable to stomach what she saw.

Deliverance sat at the same table they shared with her last night. Nikki crossed the main floor, now empty like the husk of a great locust half buried in the dust. She took a seat opposite the young woman.

"Those my horses out there?" she demanded.

"Most like."

"You tricked us. You fed us whiskey and tobacco and all the while your people were butchering our horses."

"I did no such thing, Nikki Free. I don't run these folk. I run my lodge and that's it. What they do outside these walls is not in my domain. I didn't know nothing about it until this morning, same as you." She said it with certainty, but Nikki believed it wasn't quite the truth. Her heart sank.

"Goddammit. They were my way out of this. Now I've got to go the rest of the way to California on foot? Sling all my supplies on my back? I don't got the strength for that."

"Paluxy Boys got horses. You could thieve a couple from them. I wouldn't shed a tear over that."

"Wouldn't they blame you for it?"

"Maybe. Can't say I ain't itching for a fight."

"Shit." Nikki buried her face in her hands. "Conny's gonna want blood."

"He can't blame them. They're hungry. What's he gonna do? Shoot up a bunch of starving men and women over some horses?"

"Might be just what he does, and I can't say I'd stop him if he did."

"Well, to tell you the truth, I'd say with the horses they took, that about makes us even."

"Even? You didn't tell us there was a price for any of that last night."

"That's not what I mean. I gave that freely. I'm talking about Wu."

"The Chinese girl?"

"That's the one. Your friend took off with her. And, truth be told, four horses for Wu is quite a bargain. She was worth more than that." Deliverance thrust a folded letter at her.

Nikki tried for a moment not to believe but in her heart, she knew it was the truth. Farhad had left. The Bedouin wanted to see California, but he also didn't want Conny to have to watch him die. He could seem prudent at times, but she also knew him to be impulsive and reckless. She took the letter and read.

"Wu left one for me, too. When I got mine, I checked their room to see if I could catch them before they left, but it was empty save that note."

"Did you send anyone after them?"

"No. There's no point in it. They know how to not be found. If they don't stay to the road, then finding someone out there in all that dust just ain't possible."

"Shit. Shit, shit, shit." She couldn't decide what was worse. That Farhad had left them, or that she would have to tell Conny.

"Can I ask you something, Nikki?"

"Why not?"

"What's in California for you? Why are you following a white man across the Wastelands to find some paradise that don't exist?"

"I don't follow Conny. We go together."

"Do you? Let's say California is a new Eden and you find civilized people and fertile soil to grow food and not just more dust and death, do you think these civilized people won't put you in irons again? And what do you think your white master out there is going to do when you get there? Put you to work on those fertile fields, maybe? Or if you ain't obstinate enough, maybe he'll let you clean his house and do his chores, and nurse his little white babies from his new pretty little white wife?"

"You go too far. You don't know him."

"You've asked yourself those same questions, Nikki. Don't tell me you haven't. White man's civilization ain't for us, and you know it."

"It can change, I've seen it myself."

"Can it? Maybe for a time. How are those holes in your hands healing?"

Nikki rubbed her palms with her thumbs.

"White man's civilization." Deliverance said in a mocking tone. "That's what white man's civilization gets you. Nailed to a goddamn cross or hung from a tree or even flayed alive. But why don't you stay here? I need a few good gunfighters. These people were slaves, not soldiers. They can't defend themselves for shit. I'll even let you keep your white savior. A man so white it's his goddamn name."

Nikki laughed despite her anger and indignation. She trusted Conny. She trusted him with her life, and with her freedom. She understood why Deliverance, herself the daughter of slaves, would not. She knew the hatred, the frustration, the inhumanity. Deliverance had never lived a life where she was treated like an animal, but if this gang she called the Paluxy Boys got their way, she someday might.

But then there was Farhad. She could still find him. They could leave as soon as Conny got back, and with any luck, there might still be some vague trail. They may find a hint of his passing in the falling dust, fading like a forgotten dream. She loved the Bedouin. She had enjoyed his company more than anyone else's for as long as she could remember. She loved Conny too, but her love for him was a love of safety, of comfort, the love of a man who loves you back more than he loves any other woman. Her love for Farhad was immaterial, ethereal, something she couldn't explain but a primal attraction to his confidence. She didn't want to lose him to the Wastelands like she lost so many others. She held his face in her mind for a moment and wept.

It took Conny a little more than an hour to return. The folks in town had taken everything from them, all of the horses as well as the gear. He said he left most of his anger on the lifeless plains, but it returned with vigor when he smelled the still-cooking horse meat. He looked around, suspicious of everyone, and thought that every article of clothing he saw on a man, every blanket or canteen slung over a strange shoulder, belonged to them.

He told Nikki as much, and he became cross when she didn't share in his anger. Deliverance's warning about him burned in the back of her mind and she was shamed for thinking it. Conny would never make her a slave and he would put a bullet in any man who tried to do the same.

But what if they arrive in California and the white men there are building their paradise off of the backs of people like her? Unwelcome visions invaded her thoughts. Visions of a mob of pale men who reached out for her and dragged her away from Conny and set on her with irons, of mothers crying for their children who were ripped from their arms, of men toiling in fields with echoes of the whip on their backs, and the disgust and contempt cast on the pallid faces that peered out of carriage windows that passed them by.

When she told him of Farhad and gave him the man's letter, he wanted to set out immediately to find him.

"He doesn't want to be found, Conny." She put her hands on his chest. "He says it right in his note."

"I don't right care what he wants, I ain't gonna let him run off like that. What in God's name was he thinking? He found hisself a woman he likes and so he don't need us no more? To hell with Conny and Nikki?"

"Not at all, Conny. He just wants you to be free of him."

"What the hell does that mean?"

"I don't know, it means he's getting worse, maybe? He wants to go to California, but he doesn't want to be a burden to you. And he doesn't want you to have to watch him die."

"Once again, I don't right care what the good goddamn he wants. He's a fool. A goddamn fool. Heading out for California without us, of all the—" His anger choked the words out of his throat, but it was tears that stood in his eyes. "He had no right."

"To be fair, we did once try to tell him he needed to go to Mexico and let us carry on without him."

"I only went along with that because I knew he wouldn't do it. Son of a bitch." Conny paced the floor of the empty saloon and kicked a chair across the dance hall. "I raised that boy. I raised him. It's my right to see him to the end, goddammit. And it was his right to have me there." Conny's face reddened and he took deep, choking breaths. "He needs me there. He needs me."

Nikki took him in her arms. His chest heaved and sputtered, and he held her tight. "I know, I know. But he's made this choice and we can't do nothing to stop it."

"I have to go after him."

"And what about your other friend? What about Crowkiller? The Paluxy Boys got him, and he needs you, too."

"The hell with him. He can take care of hisself."

"And then what about me? To hell with me, too? Because I need you."

Conny pulled up a chair and sat down, agitated still. Conny was right, he had raised Farhad. Nikki traveled with him, and even loved him, but Conny raised the man, and she couldn't fault him for wanting to charge off into the Wastelands to look for him. He had lost so much already.

But so had everyone else. There was no one alive who hadn't. Grief was so common that she hardly thought of it anymore. How long had it been since she had given a single thought to people long gone, people like Fanny Boone? She had stayed up with her all night on December 31st and into the early morning hours of January 1st, back in 1859, Heartbreak Day. The day contracts were signed to rent out men and women to work for other masters and Fanny was certain that their master, Nikki's father, would rent out her son's services. The railroad had charged him too much to haul his grain and he lost a good deal of money that year, so everyone had been saying he might sell a Negro to work on someone else's farm and Fanny was sure it would be her boy Clem. Clem could be difficult at times and had a bit of a rebellious nature, so it stood to reason that he would be the one to go. That morning, they clapped Clem in the irons and sent him down to Natchez. They locked Fanny in the slave's quarters until she could look at the sun again without wailing. Everyone had lost people. Even before the Calamity, heartbreak was the rule, not the exception.

"I think your best course of action is to go after the Indian," Deliverance said. "He could track your friend better than you can, Mr. White."

Nikki didn't trust Deliverance, the girl certainly spoke up now for her own gain, but she also couldn't disagree with what she said.

"I would need Farhad to even think about pulling off some kind of rescue. We might be decent gunfighters, but Nikki's only been in a couple of scrapes and I'm out of practice, so to speak. Crowkiller's gonna have to get hisself out. He's a capable man."

Even for Nikki, Conny was not easily swayed sometimes. "How many of our horses did your people take?" Nikki asked.

"Three."

"And they've butchered all three?"

"Yes. For what it's worth, I asked them not to. I thought they'd be put to better use against the Paluxy Boys, but hunger rules men's minds sometimes."

"That means Farhad likely took one," Nikki reasoned.

"And he also likely led someone right to them while he was at it," Conny said.

"He didn't know."

"He should have known better."

"Well, we can't go after him on foot when he's riding a horse."

"We damn sure can. That horse will be easier to follow. I hear the wind ain't so bad west of here. We pick up his trail and we follow it. All the way to California if we have to."

"I don't know who told you about the wind," Deliverance said. "But they were dead wrong. The wind is bad all the way up to the mountains."

"What mountains?" asked Conny.

"I don't know the name of it. We don't have much need for names of far-off mountains, gringo."

"Then you don't know any more than I do."

"My people ain't wrong."

"I'll take my chances." Conny stood up. "Nikki, we're wasting time. Farhad has a head start. We need to get some supplies and head out."

"I can give you some supplies, Mr. White," Deliverance said. "It's the least I can do, seeing as how they ate what rightfully belonged to you and all."

Conny nodded. "I'm obliged then."

Deliverance left and Nikki and Conny stood face to face, alone. "It'll be fine," Conny told her. "We'll leave as soon as she gets us our supplies. We'll get to California and things will be fine, just like we planned."

"Conny. What if California isn't what we think."

"Nonsense. Crowkiller says he saw the money, and so did Becker. Rumors are rumors, but there's proof enough. Things in California are better. Like they used to be."

"But things for me weren't better, Conny. That's the problem. And now I'm starting to worry that we get to California and things go back to how they used to be. For me, for you...for us."

Conny took a labored breath. "I have to find him. Me, him, and you in California, it's been our plan this whole time and that son of a bitch betrayed me."

"Is that what you think he did? Betrayed you?"

"He was always loyal to me. Now he's turned his back on me, Betrayed me, like everyone else."

"Conny, he didn't betray you. This wasn't about you, it was about him being the master of his own life. About him deciding on his own terms how he's gonna go out. How he's gonna live before he goes out."

"I got to hear him say that. I've put too much of my life into him. Please." He took her hands in his. "Please come with me."

"Please don't ask this of me. I won't say no, but please just don't ask it of me. Please stay." Her voice broke.

"It's this place, that it? You'd trade paradise for a saloon in the middle of the Wastelands? You'd give up Farhad? Me?"

"A paradise for you might not be a paradise for me. Conny, I trust you, I do. And I love you. But I do not trust and love your people. Any paradise your people are making is not likely to include an equal place for people like me."

"You don't know that. People forget. People move on from those kinds of ideas."

"Did your friend Becker move on? Have these Paluxy Boys moved on? People don't move on, Conny. And if they do it's only once they've become old. Old enough to realize they were wrong but too old to convince the young not to make the same mistakes. It ain't this place, Conny. I'm afraid. Now you'd do your best to protect me, I know that, but against a whole nation, those guns ain't gonna be worth scratch."

"Nikki, I don't give a good goddamn about California. If you don't want to go, that's fine. That's all right with me. If you're afraid, I understand. But I have to go after him. I have to give him a thrashing for leaving and I have to say my goodbyes."

"Then we go quickly and we come back after you have your words, then?"

"No. You'll stay here. I'll move faster if I don't have to worry about your survival every step of the way. You stay here. I'll find him, say my peace, and come back to you."

"Are you sure this is worth it? You're risking an awful lot on running off just to berate the man. Your life, my happiness, our future together."

"I'll be alright. And I have to do this. I don't want to feel the same pain every time I think about him that I do when I think about Elizabeth. If he's leaving for good, I need to be able to close that door. I need that for me."

Nikki felt that her whole life had been nothing but an endless string of betrayals, one after the other, but in a way she understood. Of all the people in her life who had come and gone, Farhad had somehow meant the most to her.

"I'd just love to see the look on his face when you come strolling in from out of the dust." Pain tightened her chest and throat and tears fell in great drops from her tattooed eyes. "Tell him I'll miss him and I love him."

"I will. Nikki I—"

"Just kiss me and leave. The sooner you leave the sooner you'll be back."

Chapter 40

Sorrow Draw, North Texas (November, 1881)

Eudora Becker

Everything had been going very well for Eudora until the morning that Ransom fetched her to go see Reverend Mothershed.

About the worst she had to endure in the few days she was kept locked in that room were the nightly visits by Ransom when he would take Hattie to her bed. Eudora pretended to be asleep, but she suspected that Ransom saw through it and took a great deal of satisfaction in imagining she was awake and listening. Ransom was the kind of man who was possessed of a beautiful face, but an ugly soul. Now, she liked a man who could be mean and violent just as much as the next girl, but that kind of depravity in the bedroom showed her a wickedness that couldn't be washed away through a few batted eyelashes or an exposed white neck. It was something deep and primal and made her bile rise at the thought.

Still, he had power around here. And it never hurt to have influential men wrapped around her finger. And so she threw a few sidelong glances his way and more than a couple of knowing smiles when she saw him. As long as Hattie stayed with her, Ransom should keep his hands, and other parts, off of her. Still, it was a fine line she walked, like skirting the edge of the fog of dust, one wrong move and she could slip from the light and Ransom would throw decorum out the window and she could end up on the bed rather than Hattie.

Hattie had become something that Eudora never knew had been missing from her life. She had always assumed that her little charms worked only on men (and certain women who enjoyed the company of other women), but she didn't know they could be used on motherly types. Hattie fed her, made sure she kept warm, brought her new clothes to wear, and even combed her hair for her with a heavy ivory comb. She showed her a warmth and tenderness that, unlike the men, required no promises of future pleasures, or hints at what might be. She simply did these things for her because she wanted to do them.

After a few days locked inside the room, Eudora got what her father called "her shakes." Frustration and boredom settled in, and she shook her leg furiously and moved from sofa to bed to floor in an endless rotation. Hattie read to her since she never had the patience to learn to read herself, but the books she read failed to keep her interest.

Hattie started by reading the Bible to her, but Eudora let her know straight away that she loathed the boring old thing. She didn't understand half of the words they used, and she wouldn't likely care for the story even if she could follow it. Eudora had never seen someone so taken aback before and she laughed and had to tell her that it was alright. The God of her Bible didn't care for the affairs of Men, if he had ever at all. She told Hattie that most people where she came from had concluded that they had little use for the Bible anymore. If it couldn't even have warned them about the Calamity, then what good had it been?

Hattie had just stared outside the window for a good bit, then took a different book off the shelf. The Cabinet Minister, a novel that was somehow even more dull than the Bible had been. Eudora let Hattie read though, as it seemed to give the woman some pleasure.

And so, although it made her a trifle nervous when Ransom arrived and told her he was going to take her to see the Reverend Mothershed, it was still an escape from that room, and from the rattling window, and that insipid book.

Ransom led her down a long and dark hallway that seemed all the more ominous for the sound of his heavy footsteps and his jingling spurs. She was struck by how similar it was to her father's office in Memphis. Both places still had paintings hung on the walls, still had their wainscoting and other remnants of the decadence of the past. The memory brought sudden tears that she had to fight back.

She thought instead about Horsethief and how he promised to protect her. She thought about how Ransom had never brought her saddlebags. She thought about things that made her angry and her tears retreated.

Mothershed's office was smaller than her father's. Like his, there smoked an old iron stove in the corner, but there were no flags or maps, no military books on the shelves. No seals or insignia. A severe old man sat at a plain desk. He had an enormous Bible in front of him, and a stack of papers. Ink wells, both empty and full, scattered about the desk and littered the floor. His fingers stained black and purple from what appeared to Eudora to be frenzied writing. She didn't know how to read or write, but the writings she had seen made by people had always been soft and flowing, they reminded her of flowers and water, of gentle wind and long-stemmed grasses. This writing was more like teeth and knives, the marks thick and angry.

"Reverend, this is the girl." Ransom pushed her forward to stand in front of the desk.

The thin old man smiled a closed-mouthed smile. It looked uncomfortable, somehow, as if the expression was foreign to him. "Good evening...Eudora, is it?"

"Yes sir," she said. She didn't want to sound frightened, but she didn't know how not to in his presence. This was a man she knew she could not bat her eyes at. There was no amount of skin she could let slip to make him soften to her.

"Reverend. I am a man of God, girl." His voice was high and sharp, like a bow drawn wrong across a fiddle.

"Reverend," she said by means of apology.

"Eudora. Ransom here has told me your story. Where you came from, how you got here, why you were traveling with the heathen savage. He told me all as you told him. If there was a lie in his words I don't hold him at fault, he simply relayed the information you gave to him."

She felt Ransom tense beside her. "Reverend, I didn't lie to him if that's what you're suggesting."

"A lie of omission is just as much a lie. 'Therefore to him that knoweth to do good, and doeth it not, to him it is sin.' You knew more than you told, yet you kept silent. That is a sin, child." The old man stood. He was small, still taller than Eudora, but not as tall as Ransom or any other man she had seen here. Yet clearly Ransom feared him. But why? She feared him, for sure, but much of that had to do with the importance everyone here placed on him.

"I don't understand." Did Horsethief tell them that they had shared so many cold nights together? Did they know about Jeremiah and the meat the Magistrate fed her?

The Reverend dropped a burlap sack on the desk and opened it up. Eudora didn't have to look in it to know what it contained.

"I think that this might have had something to do with why you were making your way west when my boys found you." He spilled the stacks of money onto the desk. They were just as she had seen them last. Thick stacks swollen from river water, the edges rough and dirty from five hundred miles of travel through the Wastelands.

They looked beautiful. Eudora resisted the urge to grab them and run. It would do no good. The stacks were so large she could only hold one at a time in each hand, and Ransom would cuff her on the head before she could take more than two steps towards the door.

But she had been beaten before and still she made it out the other side. She could beat them, somehow. Horsethief would come and he would put a bullet in Ransom and grab her money and they would ride out together again. She tried to blink away tears, but they were not the tears that she could call at will and turn off whenever they no longer served her.

"So, girl. Tell me about these banknotes here. Who are you, why do you have them, and where are you going with them?" The reverend put his knuckles on the table. They were old, pale white, and twisted like knots in the dead trees.

"They belonged to my father," she whispered.

"Who is your father?"

She told him about her father, the great Samuel Becker, governor of Memphis. She told him about her plan to take the money and run to California because it was the new Eden, a paradise unlike anywhere else on Earth.

"A new Eden?" he asked. "You aren't the first to come through here with talk about California being a paradise, girl. No, there have been others. Some even had money like this. One thing I always asked them, though is this: if California is such a paradise, then why didn't they stay there? No one ever gave me a good enough answer."

Eudora had asked the same question once of Jeremiah. If the people with the money had it so good out west, why did it end up all the way in Tennessee? She didn't remember what he said to that, but she did recall that also hadn't been a good enough answer.

"I'll tell you what I do know, girl. There's no new Eden out west. It's a new Sodom. God is drawing all the unbelievers out to California, to Satan's new den of iniquity, so he can destroy it and extinguish them all in one righteous and glorious strike."

She had one hope and one hope only. She could play the obedient and docile girl. The one who was full of contrition and who yearned, above all else, to please. She would humble herself, show a great deal of remorse, and then figure out a way to get her money and make her escape. If Horsethief didn't come to rescue her, Hattie could be persuaded to run away with her.

"I don't believe things occur by happenstance," Reverend Mothershed said. "I believe the Lord puts people in our paths for a reason. And therefore, I know you are here for a purpose. The Lord has sought to spare you from the wickedness of Sodom. You are still redeemable, as He wills it. So, I have decided that I think you will stay here with us."

"Thank you, Father." Eudora bowed her head.

"Reverend is fine, girl. We're no Catholics here. We do not wrest that title away from God the Father. I am merely His earthly servant, honored though I am to be His Final Prophet and the Deliverer of the last of his children."

"Of course, Reverend. Thank you," she said. The words felt dead in her ears.

"I do need to know something before I make a final decision on the matter."

"Yes, Reverend?"

"Did that heathen savage take your honor before we caught him?"

"I beg your pardon, I don't understand?"

"Did the Indian take your virginity, girl? Did he violate you?"

"No Reverend." She didn't lie. Horsethief had been her lover, but she had not been a virgin. The old man had asked the question with intensity, and she felt that the correct answer, that is, the answer he wanted to hear, was "no," though she couldn't be sure exactly why. Women in Memphis were expected to lie with men when they were able, so most left their virginity behind as soon as they could. The less experience a woman had, the less desirable she was as they believed a woman who laid with more men could have more children. But one thing she learned on her long journey was that the farther she was from home, the stranger the people's beliefs became.

Mothershed took his seat. "Good, good. I hear," he said, softening his tone, "that my daughter has been tending to you these last few days, is that true?"

"It is, yes."

"And how is that arrangement? Do you two get on well together?"

"We do, Reverend. Hattie has been good to me. Perhaps better than I deserve."

Mothershed smiled at that. For a moment, he appeared as just a kind old man, someone who Eudora would shower with affection and kiss on the head before she ran off to meet a boy behind the stables for a roll in the dust.

"Well, then there is no need to separate the two of you. But there is one more thing we must do before I let you go back to your room." The old man rose and opened the door to the iron stove. "We must rid you of any temptation. We wouldn't want you to fall back into sin and fail to make the coming Kingdom."

He took two stacks of banknotes and threw them onto the smoldering coals.

Eudora screamed. Thick hands grabbed her arms before she could lunge at him. She struggled against the iron grip that held her fast, but they might as well have been shackles and chains that held her down.

SORROW DRAW

The old preacher took the money, one stack at a time, and threw them in the furnace. The fire blazed hot and red and Eudora felt its heat on her face and her tears fell like rain in the desert and she screamed until she tasted blood, and she kept screaming.

It was all gone. Everything she had worked for. Five hundred miles of agony. Her father, Jeremiah, Horsethief. Every sacrifice, every death, every frozen sleepless night, every pang of hunger, every locust she ate, every weevil-filled piece of hardtack, every slow mile upon endless mile, all for nothing. All ended here.

Ransom let her fall to the ground when her legs could no longer hold her up.

"This rebellious behavior of yours is something we will have to stamp out. The Lord tells us that the rebellious dwell in a dry land. Perhaps a few days of exile in the wilderness will drive that demon out of you. The wilderness is very dry, child."

Eudora lunged at Mothershed, but Ransom was faster. He spun her around and he punched her hard in her belly. Pain shot everywhere and again her legs failed her and she collapsed. She clutched her knees to her chest and lay on the floor, her face a mess of tears and vomit and blood. She didn't want to get up. She wanted to lay on the floor and let the boards swallow her body whole so she could sleep and wake back up in Memphis, in her old room. She would run down the big street, past the barber's, past the bank and the lawyer's buildings, up the hill to her father's office, kicking dust up her dress as she ran. She would jump in his arms and tell him she loved him. She would see the money on his desk but this time she would walk away and let her father take her by the hand to the mess hall to eat a boiled egg and, if she was good, a scoop of butter from a penny lick.

And she was always good.

Chapter 41

Sorrow Draw, North Texas (November, 1881)

Cornelius White

THE WILDERNESS WAS STILL and quiet and Conny had little trouble following Farhad's tracks. He stopped to smoke some tobacco that Deliverance had left in his pack of supplies. He had been on the move for a few hours and his body ached and hunger overwhelmed him, but the weed would have to suffice. Soon the winds would pick up and he would lose the trail.

But it came to pass, when Ahab was dead, that the king of Moab rebelled against the king of Israel.

Another meaningless verse, Farhad would have said. The Bedouin's departure weighed on his mind. Nikki told him that it wasn't a betrayal, but it felt the same as one regardless. Conny found him wandering the streets of New York City. Alone and starving, living among the rotting corpses of fish and people and it was Conny who had raised him and cared for him.

Conny, too, had been lost. He had wandered south in a daze after he found the mummified bodies of his wife and children. He could never quite recall why he went south, or why he traveled at all. A part of him wanted to stay in Vermont, to bury himself alongside his family, to lie down next to the remains of his children, but in a cruel twist of fate, the Calamity had preserved his wife's body so well, the last memory he had of her was her withered arms cradling a swollen belly. She had been with child. Conny hadn't seen her in nearly a year. In that moment, standing in front of her withered corpse, she had died twice. Her body, mind, and spirit had been taken by the Calamity, but her betrayal had murdered the woman he had always believed she was. And so he wept, and he buried them all together in the dirt, but he didn't belong with them.

Then he left Vermont and he wandered. It didn't take long for the people to turn on each other, and so he walked, and he fought. He stole when he was hungry, and he killed when he needed to kill. To this day he couldn't tell a single soul exactly why he took Farhad in. He had met many other orphaned children before he found himself wandering through New York, and most of them he simply walked right past. There were so many like him who walked that new land in a fog, without direction, without care about life or death. When he found Farhad, the boy latched on to him, learned his language in a matter of days, and he had pulled Conny out of the abyss, and given his life a purpose.

He ran on and continued to follow the trail the horse cut through the dust. The dead trees were tall and wide, their trunks worn smooth from years of sandstorms. He fell more than once on a stone or a half-buried root. He battled the pain and exhaustion that threatened to put an end to his chase. Every breath was a struggle, and the icy air stung his throat and burned his chest. Blisters on his heels popped and the serum-soaked stockings froze inside his boots, but he pressed on. He knew nothing but the trail on the ground in front of him and the need to keep moving.

The wind picked up like the awakening of a great beast, not slow and gradual, but nearly all at once. Within minutes the trail he followed had disappeared, vanished like drops of blood in the rain.

Conny fell to the ground. He gave in to the pain, to the anguish, to his body screaming at him to stop. He knew the direction, he could still make his way west, but Farhad had already taken a few twists and turns, as if he knew Conny would come after him and he had done his best to keep him at bay.

If that was Farhad's wish, he now had little choice but to honor it. Rest was his only thought now. He had lost. Farhad had beaten him. He closed his eyes and the tension in his muscles released and he melted into the ground.

Then came the shakes. He spasmed and shook in the cold, and he would have to get up and walk back to the saloon. He made a promise to Nikki that he would return and if he didn't, she might come looking for him and meet the same fate. In his mind, he saw an image of Nikki's twisted body lying in the Wastelands, unmoving and slowly shrouded in dust.

A gunshot pierced the air behind him. There was no more potent drug to awaken a gunfighter than the report of a revolver. Wracked with pain, he jumped up, and raced towards it, somewhere beyond the edge of the fog of dust, but near enough that the wind hadn't swallowed the sound.

There were more gunshots. Two, three, four... Conny lost count. Rifles and revolvers, shots fired on top of each other. At the bottom of a small hill, he counted ten men on horses. He moved closer and five bodies lay twisted on the ruddy ground, their riderless horses bolted in panic.

It could not be happenstance that these men were here, right where Farhad's trail had led him. If these men were the Paluxy Boys that Deliverance warned them about, they would likely do savage and brutal things to Farhad and Wu.

Conny ran around their flank to see what the men were shooting at and what shot back. He moved as quiet as he could, the wind doing most of the work to mask the noise, and the dust that covered him from head to toe kept him relatively obscured. He took cover behind a rock and pulled out his Henry Repeater.

"I wouldn't come any closer if I was you." He recognized Farhad's voice shouting above the wind.

The men had dismounted and most took positions behind rocks or large trees. "Nonsense," an unfamiliar voice shouted. "We got you dead to rights."

"Dead to rights? Now what crime could I have committed against you gentlemen?"

"The crime of trespassing. You're on Paluxy Boys land."

"Trespassing? You hear that, darling? These men own this parcel of shit."

"Come on out, friend, and we might let your woman live."

"Friend? Why you gentlemen ain't behaved yourselves in a very friendly manner, now have you? In fact, you've been so disagreeable that you've gone and made me shoot a whole number of you." Farhad was stalling. One of his greatest strengths outside of his dead aim was his ability to keep his quarry talking when he ran out of shots so he could reload.

"Shut up," the man yelled. "We got you outgunned and you're in for it. Come on out, now and we'll be fair with you."

"Your 'fair' comes with me and my lady friend swinging from one of these trees, I reckon." Farhad fired a shot and the back of a man's head exploded in a cloud of red mist.

The air between them erupted in a cloud of gunfire. Conny leaned out of cover and fired several rounds. From his position, he had a much cleaner shot and two more men fell.

The remaining Paluxy Boys scrambled like barn rats for better cover, their faces registered their confusion at a new enemy shooting at them. A moment later they fired another volley, splitting their shots between Farhad and Conny. The dust and rock around him exploded.

He glanced down at Farhad who had his back against a big wind-worn oak, Wu's head in his lap. Farhad looked over and the two locked eyes. The Bedouin smiled, then gave the signal that he was out of lead.

Conny peered out from behind cover and counted. Six men left, as far as he could make out.

"I don't know who you are, but you picked the wrong fight, *cabrón*," the man yelled.

"Funny," Conny replied. "I was about to say the same thing. The name's Cornelius White. And that down there's my friend. I suggest you get on your horses and go back to whatever cleaned out, dust-taken town you rode in here from, else you'll all end up like your friends there."

"The only ones not walking away from this now are you."

"Pretty bold talk, seeing as how half your men are bleeding from holes in their heads and we ain't lost one yet." Conny put down his rifle and skinned his six-shooters. "Farhad," he shouted. "*Yarkab! Hisan!*"

That was their code phrase to run. Flee. Conny was pretty sure he had spoken it properly, but they had never before used it in a fight. Farhad didn't often back down easy.

Farhad shook his head.

"*Yarkab*! *Hisan*!" he shouted again.

Farhad stared long at him and Conny wept for his friend. For his brother.

"Allah yakon moakem, my friend." The Bedouin said. "Ahbak ya akhi!"

Conny jumped up and fired, a revolver in each hand. An answering hail of gunfire exploded around him.

Farhad cursed and pulled Wu up and they climbed onto the nearest horse. Within seconds they had disappeared into the haze of dust.

The Paluxy Boys fired after him and then turned their lead back onto Conny. A bullet ripped through his knee, and he collapsed. He rolled back behind cover, the pain burned, and his blood cooled fast around his leg. He had two shots left in one revolver and three in the other. His only hope was that he could pick off another couple of men and the rest might run. They would have to come to him, though. He lay on his back and looked up at the falling snow. Somewhere the caw of a crow cut through the stillness, and Cornelius White waited for his death.

The cry of warriors, like the howls of coyotes, echoed through the dead woods. Conny had heard Crowkiller use the same war cry when they fought together, but now there were many of them, and their cries were like a chorus that breached the silence and descended on them all with a wild and pure fury. Conny peered from behind cover again. A dozen Indians charged the Paluxy Boys, some shot rifles, and others fired arrows from short bows. The white men screamed and ran, but none of them made it very far before they fell.

Conny hid behind the rock and closed his eyes. They were near the Red River, and their little gunfight must have alerted an Indian patrol. Men screamed wicked, primal screams, and he could hear the familiar sound of heads getting scalped. Conny slowed his breathing and clenched his fists to distract from the pain in his knee. If the Indians found him, he would be scalped like the Paluxy Boys who lay bleeding not more than thirty feet away.

It always somehow surprised him how quickly gunfights were over. A game of cards, a hot meal, bedding a woman: all these things could take up more time from a man's day than killing a bunch of other men. The Indians were fast and efficient. Within minutes they had taken the horses, the guns, and stripped most of the men bare. They left the way they came, back to the Red River Conny supposed, shouting their war cries until they vanished in the wind.

Chapter 42

Sorrow Draw, North Texas (November, 1881)

Erasmus Mothershed

ERASMUS'S EYE ACHED. Or, rather the hole in his face where his eye had once been, before Ransom Eisenhardt cut it out of his head, ached. He had spent the first night after that Sunday in the grocer's old store where he had often met with Lupe, but Lupe lived in Serpent's Bluff now, away from the threat of his father. At least for now.

He had spent that first night crying in anguish and humiliation. His left eye still produced tears and they would pool in his empty socket until he leaned his head forward to drain them out into the rag he kept over it.

Laudanum had been stored in the back under one of the floorboards for future emergencies and Erasmus felt that this fit that description well. He drank liberally from more than one bottle throughout the night, daring the morning not to come, tempting fate to close his other eye forever.

Time ceased all meaning. Night and day bled into one, aided by the fact that there was presently little difference between the two anyway. True despair cared nothing for the time of day.

He awoke to Maria standing over him. He had been laid on a bed. He was naked and washed and a warm fire roared in the stove, and she had properly bandaged his head.

"That dirty rag you were using had started to stink," Lupe said when Erasmus touched the bandages.

Of all the people to find him here, Lupe was the last he wanted to see, but there was also no one he wanted to see more. He had tried to slip away into the abyss of death with opium, and if that didn't work, he had hoped to turn into a frozen corpse before anyone found him.

"What are you doing here?" he asked.

"Making sure you live. For a time, we no sure about it."

"I didn't want to live."

"Didn't want to live? Because of your eye?"

"Yes."

"Why?"

"Because it's hideous. Have you seen it? There's a gaping hole in my fucking head where my eye used to be."

"A bit hideous at the moment. But it will heal."

"Get out."

Lupe sat on the bed beside him. "It will heal. And then you will look dashing again, my love."

"Dashing? With a scarred hole in my face?"

"With an eye patch, yes. And you are more to me than your eye."

Maria clicked her tongue and waved Lupe out of the way. She brought a bowl of hot water and a rag and she cleaned his wound.

"It was my father," Erasmus said. "He pulled me up to the altar in the middle of his sermon on Sunday and had them cut my eye out in front of the entire town."

"I know."

"You know?"

"Yes, Rasmus. I know more people here than just you. Everyone talk about it. The Father bring you up front, then some men hold you down and Ransom cut the eye out. Yes, I know. Whole place talk about it."

"Of course they are. They must have gotten a really good show. Very entertaining, I'm sure."

"Not everyone believes your father, or want to follow him."

"Well, they sure sat idly by and watched. No one stood up for me. Not a single damned one."

"Of course not. They afraid."

"Some of them, maybe. And they should be. The rest of them enjoyed it, I'm sure. 'The Sodomite finally got what was coming to him, eh?' Yeah, they felt the righteous hand of God there, no doubt. But they aren't safe either. My father won't be satisfied with this." He pointed to his bandaged and bloodied eye.

"How much from Sunday you remember?" Lupe asked.

"Well let's see, I seem to recall a knife carving my fucking eye out of my head, the rest is a bit of a blur, if you pardon the pun."

"That it?"

"What else is there?"

"Did you see what happened to your sister?"

All thoughts about his eye were swept aside. What could his father have done to Hattie? She had committed no sin. She was humble and mild, obedient to a fault, the ideal daughter, much better than the crooked old man deserved.

"What did he do to her?"

Lupe put a hand on his chest. "After they…punish you, they take her to the altar and marry her to Ransom Eisenhardt."

He had dreams in his long, drug-fueled sleep, dreams where Hattie was forced to kneel before the altar and their father, Ransom at her side. He had hoped they were only dreams.

"Someone reliable told you this?"

"A few someones told me."

Erasmus didn't doubt it. This is the exact kind of cruelty he could expect from his father. This game was a long time coming, but Erasmus made the mistake of thinking that Reverend Mothershed would ease into it, that the old man would open with a safer move, but he didn't. He attacked right away, and Erasmus had to plan an equally bold move in retaliation, or the game would be over before it had hardly begun.

"What day is it?"

"Tuesday."

"Shit." He sat up. "Help me get dressed. I have to go."

"No, you have to stay here and heal."

"I have to go to her, she'll need me." Ransom wouldn't wait for Hattie to come around. He's already bedded her, and she needed someone to help comfort her. It should have been him. He should have known that father wouldn't be satisfied with a single eye. Marrying off Hattie while Erasmus licked his own wounds ensured that neither of them had the other for comfort. "Where are they keeping her?"

"She in Mothershed house. Paluxy Boys find a couple wanderers in the Wastes. An Indian and a white girl. They have Hattie looking after her. They say the girl is a delicate thing."

"What about Ransom? I'm sure he comes calling, right?"

"He stays there, too."

"In my house?"

"So I've heard. Your father has brought in a few Paluxy Boys to be guards, I think. He's getting…aggressive."

"I know." Erasmus said dryly. "How could so much change in so little time?"

"Lay back down." Lupe pushed him into the bed.

"No, I told you to help me up, I have things to do."

"Yes. You have to rest and recover your strength, so you are well enough to travel."

"I'm not going anywhere."

"Yes, you are. I can convince the 65ers to take us in. Henri knows my mother. You can hide out there, and we can be together."

"The 65ers might take you in, but they would never let me anywhere near their caravan. And you know it." The 65ers might not have the largest caravan of junk dealers in Texas, but they had the oldest. And they didn't get to be the oldest by letting everyone in. They were secretive and always on the move. And if they knew he was a Mothershed, they might just bury him in the dusty Wastes and be rid of him.

"I can be very persuasive."

"And what about Hattie? Should I just leave her to face a lifetime of indignity under Ransom? She needs me now more than ever."

"And so do I."

"You don't understand, do you?" He didn't mean to yell, but it came out and once it came out, he couldn't take it back. "This doesn't end well for me. It was never going to. I was an idiot for ever thinking it would. I don't get a happily ever after. I am the son of the Devil himself and I don't deserve one."

"I do."

"I'm sorry, Guadalupe. I guess you and Hattie both bet on the wrong man. Our story was only ever going to end in tragedy."

Erasmus slipped into his house unnoticed. Darkness fell and, though the distinction between night and day had diminished, most men retained that natural tendency to wake when they knew the sun had come up, and sleep when the gloom of night shrouded the world, so his passage through the hallways had gone unnoticed by any of the Paluxy Boys his father might have made into new residents. He paused a moment at Hattie's room and peered inside. There were two sleeping forms on Hattie's bed. It must have been Hattie and the new girl that Lupe had mentioned because neither form looked large enough to have been Ransom.

He made his way down the hall, more by feeling than by sight. He had difficulty adjusting to his new vision. He learned quickly to turn his head to his left side to compensate for his blindness, but still, even alone in the darkness his face burned with humiliation. He would have to walk this way for the rest of his life. He knew plenty of people who weren't whole. Missing limbs and eyes were fairly common. The world tried to take all it could from people and still, they clung to it with an iron grip. But he had enjoyed his vanity for too long. He had been complete. Unmarred. Perfect. Reverend Mothershed had known just how to cripple him. He almost admired it.

As foreign as everything felt to Erasmus now, he half expected his mother's room to have also undergone some fundamental alteration since he last set foot in it. The gossamer curtains in the large window undulated slowly in the cold draft. The iron stove in the corner burned hot—someone had been here recently to add coal to it. Good. He didn't have to worry much about being disturbed.

The slender figure of his mother languished in the center of the large bed, the linen sheets stained shades of brown from all manner of her bodily fluids. A single candle on her bedside table gave off a wan light and Erasmus walked, by memory, to the wooden chest that held her medicine. He took out two small bottles—he knew them by touch. Amber-hued ribbed glass with a cork stopper. He had often sat in this room and held those bottles, daring himself to have the courage to give them to her.

He pulled up a velvet chair of deep burgundy and sat in it at the foot of his mother's bed.

"Where have you been?" she asked in a strained voice.

"Sorry, mother. I've been...delayed."

"These men they have here...they don't know what I need. They don't give me the right medicine."

"Don't worry, I've got the right medicine for you."

"What...happened?"

Erasmus put a hand to the bandage on his head. "Just a little accident, is all."

"You get in a fight with one of these boys? They pop your eye out, or will it heal?"

"It won't heal, mother. It won't ever heal."

"Oh. I'm sorry. It'll be a hell of a thing for you to have to live like that."

"You aren't making this any easier today, are you?" he whispered so she could not hear him. He put his hand over hers and she did not recoil. "Ma. Do you want me to help you?"

Eula Mothershed smiled a thin, frail smile. Her pallid skin took on a blue cast in the dim light. "I've already helped myself."

Erasmus frowned.

"They left me alone too long, and I found your box. I needed my medicine. Hattie hasn't come to help me, and you were gone. So I took care of it myself."

On the bed beside her laid a bottle of laudanum. "Ma, how full was that bottle?"

"The hardest part wasn't even the walking. The hardest part was getting that stopper off the bottle. It was new. Or, as new as anything can be these days."

"You drank the whole thing?"

"I could swallow today."

"You drank the whole thing?"

"I think I've been punished enough, Erasmus."

"Have you?"

"I think so."

Erasmus wasn't sure. What he did know, is that she had robbed him. After everything he endured, she stole his climax, his coup de grace. He had been her angel of both life and death and she had denied him his benevolence and his malice. It was not for her to decide whether or not she had suffered enough, he had appointed himself judge and jury, and she usurped him as executioner.

But perhaps she had also saved him. He would not be a murderer. He may not have been completely guiltless, but he did not pull the trigger. He didn't wield the knife of matricide that would sever her mortal strand, she had given herself the fatal blow.

"I dreamed about Susan the other night. I can barely recall what she looked like, but she had been so vivid in my dream, so alive. Alive, that is, until you had her hanged. Mother, did you kill Susan? Or is that something that only happens in my dreams?"

"That old Negress? I didn't kill her. The Boys did. Your father was furious because they cost so much money, I lost him a thousand dollars he said. That made it all the worth it to me. Ugly bastard. Both of them, I guess. It was Susan, it was her fault. The Boys knew it as well as I did. It was all on account of your brother. He died when he was only a few months old."

"I think I remember him a little bit. He had colic." He tried to pull out the memory of his infant brother, but it was like fumbling for a match in the dark.

"The thing never could be quiet. I hated that sound. You and Hattie didn't cry so much, and when you did you had the wits enough to stop when I thumped you for it."

"He was a baby, mother."

Eula rolled her eyes.

"He wasn't sick, was he?" Erasmus asked.

"He was weak. Frail. And he would never stop wailing. That old Negress could always get him to quiet down and suck, he wouldn't take the tit from me."

"So you had her killed out of petty jealousy?"

"Jealousy? Have you lost your damn mind? I didn't have her killed out of jealousy. She killed my baby, that's what she did. Smothered him and tried to blame me for it."

"You know I don't believe that. You're going to take that lie to the grave though, aren't you?"

"You believe what you want."

"All right, mother," he said. "What do you want me to do?"

"Just sit with me for a spell. Just a little spell. It'll all be over soon."

For Eula Mothershed, it would be. Her words came out in barely more than a whisper now, as if she just breathed them out, rather than gave voice to them.

"I suppose it will be. You know mother, I should leave you here to die alone. It would be the last bit of justice I have left to give."

Eula's breath slowed and her pupils shrank, and to Erasmus, it appeared as if she stared at something far off in the distance.

He leaned in close to her face and whispered, "It was me, you know. Not at first, I admit. You really were sick to begin with. How many years did you lie here? Stinking up this bed, shitting yourself? Hattie was scarcely fifteen. She's a grown woman now. Father forced her to marry someone she hates. I guess you finally have something in common with her after all."

With each shallow breath, Eula's throat gurgled, and saliva boiled from her open mouth.

"I don't know when it turned from medicine to murder, if you can call it that. I prefer to think of it as justice, of course. You were a wicked woman, mother. And maybe I didn't deserve better than you, but Hattie did."

When she took her final breath, Erasmus held his own. He waited for the next breath to come for a long time, and when it didn't, he exhaled a great explosion of air, the weight of years gone at last.

Chapter 43

Sorrow Draw, North Texas (November, 1881)

Hattie Mothershed

Eula Mothershed passed away on November 21st, 1881. Hattie would never forget where she was and what she was doing when she heard the news. She sat on a large hooked rug in front of the fire and cradled Eudora's head in her lap. She read from a book, *The Apology of an Officer*, and did her best to sound lively and entertaining. Eudora could be difficult to keep happy, and her moods were something that Hattie couldn't quite anticipate yet. Sometimes she would be content to lie in her lap and listen to a book, no matter how dreadfully dull, and other times she would stand up, furious and frustrated during the most exciting part of a story, because she felt too confined in their room, or she tired of salted meats, or she had decided that she didn't like the sound of her own voice and she blamed Hattie for not telling her how irritating it could be.

The girl's mood had darkened since she returned from her visit to see the Reverend. She wouldn't talk about it, but it was clear that Ransom had roughed her up. Her swollen eyes had turned a bright red, the face of a woman who wept without apology, and she clutched her stomach and squirmed on the floor for more than half a day. At first, she simply cried and said, "They burned it, it's gone," over and over again. When she had regained her wits, she refused to elaborate and she told Hattie that it no longer mattered anymore and furthermore, *nothing* mattered anymore if she were to be completely honest. Even drawing now held no interest for her, though she had earlier squealed with delight when Hattie brought out paper and pencils of various shades and hues.

This particular book she currently read seemed to be of the 'dreadfully dull' variety for Eudora, and the girl would likely not tolerate it for long. Sure enough, Eudora had just finished her third drawn-out sigh in as many minutes and Hattie resolved to finish the book on her own when she had the opportunity. It had never caught her attention before, though she had seen it on the bookshelf many times growing up. The book spoke about the minds of men and the reasons they waged war on each other. The inscription on the inside suggested it had been given to her father as a gift by a gentleman from England who had been a part of the church before the Calamity.

"Careful. You'll bore the poor girl to tears reading that," spoke a voice Hattie could recognize anywhere.

She bolted up and ran to him. Behind her, Eudora yelled in protest, but Hattie ignored her. She put her arms around Erasmus and cried. She held on so tight her arms ached when he had to push her back.

"It's good to see you, too Hattie."

His skin had grown paler since she saw him last, and his thin frame somehow appeared even more skeletal, and he wavered on his feet like a reed blowing on the riverbank. His bandaged face bore a haggard countenance that his weak smile did little to dissolve. He had been so beautiful, with a face that the Romans would have chiseled into marble. By marring his flawless face, their father had taken from him the one sin he truly was guilty of. His vanity.

"Rasmus, I'm sorry," she cried. "I tried. Believe me, I tried but no one listened to me."

"I know Hattie," he said. He cradled her face in his hands. "I know. I think you screamed louder than me."

"I can't believe he did something so awful. I know he's a wicked man but to his own son? Oh, Erasmus, I just can't believe it."

"Hattie, is it true? Did he force you to marry Ransom?"

"He did." Her face burned and she had trouble meeting his eyes.

"Did you agree to it?"

"Of course not. But they didn't give me the opportunity to disagree."

Erasmus embraced her. He smelled of whiskey and sweat. "Well, just so you know, if you didn't give your consent to the marriage, then you have a strong case for your marriage being forfeit."

"Forfeit? By what law?"

"By the laws of all decent and honorable men."

"Oh, Rasmus. If there were only such decent and honorable men among us, then that might mean something. But I suppose it doesn't mean I'm married in the eyes of God, right?"

"Hattie, if you don't think that God doesn't condone forced marriage, you really haven't read the scriptures well, have you?"

"I read them all, many times, Erasmus Mothershed."

"Well then, you only remember the ones you agreed with, I guess."

"So do all the pious people I know. Don't matter anyway. Ransom took his husband's entitlement from me regardless. Maybe I should have spent the night with that man from the Lodge, after all. At least I'd have that."

He held her close and kissed the top of her head. "We'll get out of this somehow. But Hattie, listen to me. Things might get bad very soon."

She pulled away and smoothed the front of her dress. "Aren't they very bad right now?"

"I mean worse, maybe. Mother is dead."

This shouldn't have been shocking news. Mother had been so ill that every day her death had been a possibility. But she held on to life for so long that it seemed she had defeated death, or perhaps it had lost interest in coming for her entirely, and she might have lived forever in a constant state of expiration, a barely alive corpse that knocked on Hell's door but found no one home.

"Are you sure?"

"I was there when it happened."

"Did you…" She let her question trail off.

"No. I was going to. I wanted to. I had hoped to punish Father for what he did to me. You know, take away the only thing he had ever loved, but she had already drunk a bottle of laudanum before I got there."

"Erasmus, I'm glad it wasn't you."

"I'm not. She deserved a worse death."

"There are a lot of people around here who deserve a horrible death. Doesn't mean I want it for them."

"As always, you're a better person than me. But Hattie, father will find out soon. Now is going to be the time to pretend to mourn. Shed tears, wear black if you have it, and keep away from him at all costs."

It was good advice, and she worried more for Erasmus than for herself. She served as a useful commodity for her father, not as a source of shame and disappointment. She could become invisible to the old man if she wanted to, but Erasmus shined like a beacon, He was a lighthouse that pierced the perpetual fog of reverend Mothershed's temper, and the priest could follow it like a lost ship.

"What are you going to do?"

"Find a safe place for myself, I guess. Father would likely not want me anywhere near the funeral service. What about you?"

"I'll be the good daughter, I suppose. When they announce it, I'll feign shock and sorrow. Then I'll go and wash her body and dress her in her fine clothes. We should lie her outside. It would be the best way to preserve her until she's buried."

"What about her?" Erasmus pointed behind her.

Eudora sat half in the dark, frozen as if she had been caught trying to hide. She looked at them and although she had no stakes in any of this, she had the face of one who had been eavesdropping with great interest.

"Her name is Eudora. Ransom found her wandering around as he says."

"I heard. Is she trustworthy?"

"I think she's partial to me, but no one else here has really given her much kindness, so yes. I'd say she is."

He stayed for several more hours before Hattie had to force him to leave. He played a dangerous game. There was no prohibition against him being here, and she told him that their father sounded as if he wanted Erasmus to stay, just a more humbled version of himself. He gave a short laugh and maintained that he could not possibly ever humble himself. "Truth be told," he said, "if I were to ever be successful at humbling myself and eliminating my own pride, I'd end up exceedingly proud of myself for it."

They read from *The Apology of an Officer*, and Erasmus regained a small portion of his old charm. He read from the book in a mocking tone, he joked about the logic and the tales the officer told, and then, at times, he nodded his head fiercely and said, in a solemn tone, something like, "This...this I can agree with."

No more than an hour after Erasmus left, the church bell rang. The church had been topped with a single, massive bronze bell that rang once every day at seven o'clock, or as near as anyone could tell, to wake the town and call them to service. There wasn't always a sermon, but often there was, and reverend Mothershed believed that the townsfolk should start every day with a communal prayer. Then some time to sort out the day's business, and to the censures, and any judgments to be rendered. The bell had been nicknamed Old Weaver because the first time it rang was for Thomas Weaver's funeral. Mothershed had bought the bell with money from his properties in Auburn and had it shipped by steamer from the manufacturer in New York in 1850. A real American enterprise, it was. "Only in America," he had often said. "Just try doing that anywhere else."

It rang deep and somehow somber this morning, and Hattie realized it wasn't 7 o'clock, but much earlier still.

It peeled for Mother. Eula Mothershed's body had been found.

The bell continued to toll. Sometime later, Ransom arrived, dressed in clean clothes, his hair combed back.

"Have you heard?" he asked her.

Hattie shook her head 'no,' not trusting herself to speak.

"I'm terribly sorry to be the one to break the news to you, Hattie. Your mother passed away last night. I know it ain't unexpected, but I also know you did your best to take care of her and make sure she was comfortable these last few years."

Hattie picked up a subtle tremble in his voice. She tried to appear shocked at the news. "I assume my father knows by now?" she asked in a small voice.

"He does. He put us on a special mission. Put the fear of God in us about it, too. He's got a fire in him now. I feel things he's been talking about are coming to take shape soon. First us, our marriage, now this." He struggled to hide what looked to Hattie like a wide-eyed excitement.

"Do you believe my father? Do you think his prophecies are true?" She never thought Ransom to be the kind of man who took those things to heart.

"I didn't use to but...I don't know. It's hard to argue now. He believes, and it makes me want to believe, too. It does kind of make sense. If he really is fulfilling scripture and all. I don't know. It's exciting to think about, though. He does have a lot of the answers when nobody else does. I'm sure you must believe him, right?"

"Oh of course," she lied. "I've always believed. I'm just used to other people thinking he's crazy, that's all."

"I think a lot of did at first. Now, I know more people who believe than who don't. Whether he's true or not, these are exciting times and exciting things are coming."

The bell continued to toll.

"I'm real sorry your ma won't be around to see them, though," he added. "These exciting times, I mean."

Hattie nodded. "Thank you, I'm obliged. I suppose I need to tend to my mother now. I have to wash and dress her and get her ready for her burial."

"That's the business I have to attend to as well."

"What do you mean?"

"Your father has...orders." He came further inside the room and closed the door behind him. "I don't know how much I'm supposed to tell, but you are my wife, and keeping secrets from each other right from the start don't sit too well with me, so here it is. Reverend Mothershed has orders for me to ride for Serpent's Bluff. We're to round up your mother's old slaves and bring 'em back here. He wants to send her to the afterlife with her servants to help her prepare a place for him. For him and for the rest of us when the time comes."

Hattie put her hand on the iron bed to steady herself. "And you think this is necessary?"

"I don't know if it is or if it ain't, but I know your father says it is. I'll do my duty, Hattie. Just as you'll do yours. Get your mother ready. Me and the Boys ride soon. We've got men digging her grave right now. Once this is all over, all Hell's gonna break loose, you can bet on that. First, we'll wipe out them Negroes and that saloon and all the degenerates there, then we shore up our numbers and ride for the Indian Territories."

"Praise the Lord," Hattie said.

"And your father. He deserves a good deal of the praise, too." He took her by the neck and kissed her lips. "I'll see you at the funeral, God willing. I don't expect the Negroes to put up much of a fight, but anything is possible, I suppose."

"Farewell, my husband." Hattie didn't trust herself to say anymore.

When he had left, she turned to Eudora who still hid in the shadows. "I have to go. You should stay here. Don't wander off, and don't go to the funeral. Just stay here."

"Are you going to dress the body?" she asked. "I can come and help."

"No. I mean, yes. Well, yes and no. There's something I have to do first."

"What's happening, Hattie? You look frightened and I don't like it. It makes me frightened."

"Nothing, dear. It's just something I have to take care of." She needed to find Erasmus and she needed to do it quick. Someone had to warn the Lodge before Ransom got to it first.

Chapter 44

Serpent's Bluff, North Texas (November, 1881)

Cornelius White

The Indians hadn't rounded up all of the horses. During the gunfight, several had bolted but at least one returned. Conny lost all reckoning of time on the frozen ground. If he cared enough to live, he would have to get up and walk. A difficult task considering a bullet had passed through his knee.

Farhad was safe. He had ridden off and escaped and all of the raiders who had tried to take the life of his friend lie all about, their lifeless bodies twisted in grotesque displays of gore and inhumanity. He felt nothing for them but relief that they were dead.

He resigned to pass away on the floor of the dead forest, to let the Calamity claim him as it will eventually claim everyone. He floated above the ground. Death, like cloudy black tendrils, pulled at him and his will faltered. But before sleep took hold, he thought of Nikki Free. He thought of how she would do fine without him. That she was safe with her people, she had the Lodge now, and they would take care of her.

But they would do it without him. His part in her story would come to an end and she would live on with the memory of a man who came into her life for a short time and left. Eventually, he would pass from her memory and become another nameless soul who had lived and died in the ruins of mankind.

That might still be his fate, but he had not yet had his fill of Nikki Free. He had to see her again, to hold her in his hands and to fill his head with the scent of her body.

If he died, he resolved to die fighting his way back to her.

Howling wind blistered his face and he opened his eyes to the sky. The limbs of the dead trees crossed the heavens like cracks in the ice. He rose with some effort. The cold helped to numb his leg but as soon as he warmed himself by a fire, the pain would overwhelm him.

He found a horse on the edge of his vision and pulled himself into the saddle. He rode back to the saloon through the falling snow and dust. Several hours later, he arrived slumped in his saddle, his grip on the reins slack. Men and women pulled him down and brought him to a room and laid him on a bed. Nikki's voice gave orders, and a warm hand gripped his own. Someone removed his clothing and washed him, dressed his wounds, and covered him with a wool blanket.

When the room emptied and only Nikki remained, he told her about Farhad and the Paluxy Boys, about how the Indians killed them, and how he kept himself hidden. Nikki listened and cradled his head in her lap. She gave him laudanum and his head swam.

Deliverance came to see him, and she let him know that she had personally seen to his horse and that no harm would come to it. She said it was the least she could do for him killing so many Paluxy Boys. Conny thanked her and resolved to put aside his anger at the earlier loss of his horses. The people at the Lodge had their own code, their own sense of honor and justice and it would do little good to bring the attitudes they had cultivated in Memphis over here. Memphis had been ripe for conquest, its people shiftless and without direction. They had succumbed to the Calamity and the despair that it brought. These people thrived in it.

This is where Nikki belonged, and it was unfair for him to demand she stay true to a promise she made before she knew of the Lodge and the safety and peace that it gave her. She wanted him to stay with her, and he would.

The door opened abruptly, and a man came in. He had a maimed right hand the same side of his face sagged like a melted candle. "Deliverance," he said. "Someone's here to see you. He says it's urgent."

Another man pushed his way through. Even in an age of famine, he was tall and lean. A bandage had been wrapped around his head; a great brown disk of dried blood sat over his eye like a coin for the ferryman.

"Mothershed?" Deliverance said in a tone that told Conny she had not expected this man.

"Erasmus, please. I think I'll leave the name of Mothershed behind me for good," he told her.

"What happened to you?"

"My father. He plucked my wandering eye in front of God and the whole town. Well, he had his men do the plucking. He lacked the strength or courage to do it himself."

"To his own son? That's cold, even for him."

"Well, he's saving his best for the next act. Deliverance, they're coming for this place. And they'll be here soon."

"Who?"

"The Paluxy Boys."

"The Paluxy Boys?" asked Conny. "I don't know if that'll be much of a problem. I killed quite a few of them myself today, and some Indians got the rest."

The man turned to face him. "Who are you?"

"Name's Cornelius."

"How many did you kill?"

"Ten."

"Well Cornelius, I'm happy to hear that, but it isn't nearly enough."

"You've been playing both sides of this for a long time," Deliverance said. "Now I think it's about time you got straight with me. I want some answers. You can start by telling me exactly how many men those Paluxy Boys got."

"I haven't been playing both sides," Erasmus replied. "I've been playing my own side. But it appears our sides have joined together. So, to answer your question, I don't know exactly how many men they have, but it has to be well over three hundred."

"Three hundred? Jesus Christ." Deliverance asked. "How the hell did that old codger get three hundred men? There weren't even half that many men in the whole town when the Calamity hit."

"That was eighteen years ago, Deliverance. He's been collecting people for a long time. Travelers just passing through get caught up and find they can't leave, promises of food and safety bring people to him. He's absorbed whole groups of scavengers who take up his cause. Believe me, there's more men under his influence than you know. Three hundred is a guess, and I'm being a bit conservative, truth be told. And they're coming."

"How many are coming? All of them?"

"I don't know how many, but I'm sure it isn't all of them. They aren't planning an assault or a massacre yet, but..." He shifted his weight from foot to foot. "Look, my mother's finally gone. She died late last night. Reverend Mothershed, my father, he's beside himself with grief. She was the only thing in all the world that he truly loved, and I think he believed God would save her. But He didn't. Now he's finally snapped, so to speak. He's going to bury her tonight. He said he can't stand the thought of her in Heaven taking care of herself, so he's sending her there with some...slaves...to serve her in the afterlife."

"What in the fuck's he doing?" Deliverance straightened up and took a step towards the lanky young man, who recoiled.

"He plans to raid the Lodge and take some of you back to bury with her. Deliverance, I came here as fast as I could to warn you. They're on their way."

Deliverance pushed past him and out the door. She gave orders to round up all the fighting people, men and women, and told them to arm themselves. "I need your help," she said when she came back. "These people can't shoot guns for shit. I need a few gunfighters on my side. Please."

"Now wait," said Conny. "We know these Paluxy Boys are coming here, and we know why. There's no need to stay and fight. Tell everyone to run for the hills and hide out. They'll find this place abandoned and have to leave."

"No, then they'll head into town and get what they want there," Deliverance said. "I got my ma and my pa there, and so do a lot of others. That's where our kids are at, too. If we run for the hills, the Paluxy Boys will burn this place to the ground and take what they want in town."

"Then we ride for town and move everyone out of there, too."

"Not enough time," Erasmus said. "We're wasting time as it is. They are coming and fast."

When Conny sat up and swung his legs over the side of the bed, Nikki put her hand on his chest.

"No you don't gunfighter. Not so fast. You've already killed enough of them today and you got yourself shot up pretty good in the process. You need to stay here."

"The hell I am. You honestly think that's gonna keep me in bed?"

"It was worth a try." She moved to the window and peered out through the curtains. "I got an idea, though. Why don't you stay here? You got your rifle. Take a position by the window. You can pick those sons of bitches off from right here."

Though it did seem a bit cowardly to him, as far as plans go it was solid. He couldn't run or dodge gunfire with his leg shot up and the window did give him a good position to rain down lead on the Paluxy Boys.

Nikki fetched his rifle and a wooden box of lead. She left him two powder horns that she got from Deliverance with the promise that Conny was worth more with those than half a dozen of her own men. She kissed him and left to help the Lodge prepare for the coming fight.

The man named Erasmus remained near the door, motionless since the two women had left. Conny did his best to ignore him, but the silence pecked at him like a horsefly. "You ain't got nothing better to do right now than just stand there?" he demanded.

"I'm not sure what I can do, to be honest. I can't shoot a gun. I was never very good at it, and I imagine the loss of my eye won't have improved my performance any."

"Maybe you can help the women and children downstairs. There's gonna be more to this fight than just the gunfire. That's only part of it."

"I'll just be in the way. To be honest I feel wretched, like this whole thing is somehow my fault. I know it isn't, but it feels it all the same."

The young man stood holding his own hands in front of him and stared at the ground with a timidness that set Conny's teeth on edge. "Alright fella, but you'd better find a spot to hide yourself. Once I start shooting, they're gonna know where I'm at and they'll start slinging lead right into this room."

Erasmus had a quick eye, and Conny suspected a sharp mind as well and he allowed that he hadn't exactly met the man at the best of times. The young man sat in a corner of the room, the farthest from the open window.

"Your pa really do that to you? Cut out your eye?"

"As I said."

"That's a hell of a thing to do. I imagine you and your pa don't along right well, then."

"Not at all. He has some religious beliefs that I don't cotton to, and he doesn't appreciate my little…indiscretions."

"Your what?"

"I like to fuck men. Well, one man at the moment at least."

"Oh, I see." It had been some time since Conny had given any thought to the sin of sodomy. In Memphis it was tolerated, so long as an effort was made to bed a woman when your time had come, it made no difference to anyone who you buggered on your own. Sins stay hidden in the dust was a saying that the people were fond of, and for the crimes that had once been called sexual perversions, that was mostly true. "So your father's still one of them old preachers, eh? The old fire and brimstone kind? God doesn't change no matter how much the world does?"

"That's him all right. I'm sure you know the type well."

"I used to."

"Not anymore?"

"Nope, not anymore."

"Aren't there any of those kinds of ministers where you're from?"

"Not in Memphis, no. We killed 'em all there."

"I see," Erasmus whispered. "Well, maybe you'll get the chance to do the same here."

Chapter 45

Serpent's Bluff, North Texas (November, 1881)

Deliverance Hill

The Paluxy Boys came on them fast. Some of the people had armed themselves and prepared to make a stand at the Lodge. Some of them hid among the dust and debris of Serpent's Bluff. There were no accusations, no sidelong glances at those who fled. Nikki Free's help and advice had been invaluable to Deliverance, who commanded the people of the Lodge with a counterfeit kind of confidence, one that stemmed wholly from the trust she had in those around her.

If only she had more time. The people still scuttled about, disorganized and panicked, when the Paluxy Boys arrived. When they came, they circled about the Lodge and rode around on the edge of the haze. They yipped and yelled, they shot their revolvers in the air and stirred up a cloud of dust around them. It was as if they were inside the eye of a hurricane, the circle of dust rose high into the air until it obscured what little sun still showed.

Deliverance fought the panic that rose inside and looked about for Nikki, for some reassurance that she was still with her. Nikki stood unflinching with a revolver in one hand, and another in her gun belt. She wore an old military coat and hat, men's breeches, and a large scarf she called a keffiyeh wrapped tight around her face. Despite wearing only her white brothel gown and rifle, Deliverance found comfort in the sight of this woman.

The riders pulled their horses in with each pass and the circle grew smaller. Nikki lifted her revolver and took aim, but she waited. A gunshot echoed directly above them, and a man tumbled off his horse. Deliverance flinched and ducked. The sound of gunfire almost always startled her. No matter how many times she heard it, it always seemed louder than the last.

As soon as the shot was fired from above, Nikki Free fired her revolver into the circle of horses and felled a man. The circle broke and the horses scattered like leaves in the wind. The yips and yells turned to barked orders and more gunfire fell on them. They hadn't expected to find resistance, and their circle crumbled to the hail of smoke and lead.

The haze and dust shrouded the men and Deliverance lost all sight of them. Still, she emptied her rifle into the ruddy cloud and heard the screams of horses and men. There was no longer anything to aim for, she fired and cocked, fired and cocked until her rifle was spent and her ears rang and felt as if they were underwater, and all sound was far away and muffled.

On her right, Nikki kneeled, reloading her revolvers. Gunfire faded away and Deliverance heard a woman scream. She threw her spent rifle on the ground. Her hands shook and she wrapped them around her chest, suddenly aware of the biting cold.

If only Wu could see her now, her disappointment would be complete. Deliverance had always thought she would die in a gunfight, but her first time shooting at real men hadn't turned out well for her. The rifle lay on the ground, spent. Dust was all she could see in every direction, and she no longer knew which way to run, if running was what she wanted to do. Nikki Free put a revolver in her hand and shouted in her ear, yet she still sounded far away, distant and somehow unimportant. Her enemies had become phantoms in the smoke and haze of Calamity. She spun about, searching for something, anything. A shadow, a silhouette against the rust-colored world, but she saw nothing.

The roar in her ears began to fade, and there were more screams, but they didn't come from the mouths of men. Deliverance spun about, but she couldn't tell what had happened to her Lodge or her people. The thick dust enveloped everything, and she screamed and cursed it. A man on a horse rode out of the dust in front of her, like a creature of the deep rising to the surface, and he threw a rope around her. She was pulled from her feet and she hit the ground and darkness took her.

Chapter 46

Serpent's Bluff, North Texas (November, 1881)

Nikki Free

WHEN THE DUST FINALLY cleared enough, Nikki looked for Deliverance among the wounded and dead. There were very few. The Paluxy Boys hadn't come for a fight, but to round up women like cattle and take them back to Sorrow Draw. Conny and the lanky white boy had come down from the room they were holed up in and Nikki chided Conny for walking on his bad knee.

As near as Nikki could figure, five women had been taken, including Deliverance. "I saw her get taken," she told Conny. "I hoped maybe she fought them off, but she ain't around here. She's gone, Conny."

He took her in his arms and held her tight. "You did everything you could, you know that. I was up there, I saw it all. Must have been fifty men, all told. There wasn't no way of winning this, not unless we had more warning."

"I came here as fast as I could, I promise you that." Erasmus held his hands up in front of him.

"And I thank you. Really, I do," Nikki said. "They may have gotten what they came for, but with your warning, we at least were able to put up a fight."

"It was a hell of a fight, too," Conny said. "How many of those Boys we get?"

"Looks like nine, near as I can tell. The dust is still pretty bad, but I think we got all of their bodies accounted for."

"I don't think they expected to lose anyone today, I reckon we can call that a victory."

Nikki shook her head. "I don't know if this is what you'd call a victory, Conny."

They walked around the Lodge and gave help as it was needed. Some wanted food, others water. One man with gout in his hands had a bullet take off his ear. Nikki wrapped his head and gave him a pull of whiskey for the pain.

When there was nothing more to do, they sat and drank from a whiskey bottle.

"Now what are you going to do, Erasmus?" asked Nikki. "Going to stay here and help out?"

The pale man shook his head. "No. I'm going to go back to Sorrow Draw and act like I didn't see any of this. I'm going to attend my mother's funeral and see what I can do to help those women that were taken. I don't know what I can do, but I have to try to do something, I suppose."

"Is there an Indian man there?" asked Conny. "Someone the Paluxy boys found, and a young girl with blond hair?"

"Yeah, I've met the girl. She's sweet enough. I heard the Indian is being kept in town somewhere. You know them?"

"We do. Keep an eye on the girl, don't trust her. But find the Indian. Or find where he's being held. Tell him you know me and you're a friend. He can help."

"What do they want him for?" Why they had decided to keep Crowkiller alive and not kill him concerned Nikki. Men like this Mothershed and the Paluxy Boys would, more often than not, use the capture of someone like Crowkiller as a celebration. They should have paraded his body through the streets and flayed him alive or hung him from a tree…or crucified him…in front of the townsfolk already. But they hadn't.

"I'm not sure," Erasmus replied. "I think my father suspects he's an important person of some kind and he might know something about the Indian

SORROW DRAW

Territories. My father is after them next. I think he has some plan to grow his numbers and launch some kind of assault."

Conny laughed. "Assault? On the Indian Territories? I would love to see them try."

"My father is many things, Cornelius, but unfortunately one thing he is not is a fool. If he thinks he has a chance of succeeding at it, then believe me when I tell you that he does."

"I don't believe that. No one left on this Earth has an army big enough to do that."

"Then he has some other plan that doesn't require an army. Maybe this Indian is a part of that. I don't know." Erasmus stood up. "I have to leave. I hope to see you two soon. I hope you plan to stay and help."

Nikki drew out a large piece of paper and burned a stick over the flame of a candle. "Before you go," she said. "Make us a map."

She told him to mark down the important places, where he lived, where Eudora was, and any possible place that Crowkiller might be held.

When he finished, he handed it back to Nikki. "That should be most everything," he said. "Listen. Whatever you do, do not underestimate my father. I did once, and look what it cost me. Half of my sight and all of my beauty. If you underestimate him, the cost will be far worse."

"What are you thinking?" she asked Conny once Erasmus had left.

Conny stayed silent for a while. "I think," he said at last. "That you want to get the girl back, don't you?"

"I can't just leave."

"That didn't answer my question. You want to try and save the girl? Deliverance, I mean?"

"Well, she's been good to us."

"Nikki, just tell me you want us to stay. Is that so hard?"

"I hardly know her, really. We could just leave now. Put this behind us. This shit...this could get us killed. I could lose you. And for what? We don't owe these people anything. Even Crowkiller and the girl. What do we owe them? We can take our chances in the Wastelands."

She held back tears, but her voice strained.

"But," she said. "I've been holding this inside me for so long. This need to make amends. I failed so many people in Commerce what if I'm here now to make up for it?"

"What happened in Commerce wasn't your fault."

"No, but what is my fault is not doing nothing about it. I was afraid. After I saw what happened to Augusta, I was terrified of that happening to me, so I kept quiet. Even as the people started to disappear, and the crosses started to fill the riverbank, I hid and did nothing. This is my chance to help to make up for not helping before."

Conny slid his chair next to hers and took her hand in his. It was rough and large and painfully white. But it was warm and comforting. "The more I've been thinking about it, the more I think that California ain't likely all they say it is, don't you think? A fool's dream more like."

He kissed her on the mouth, soft and slow. His beard scratched at her face, but his lips were soft and warm.

"I think I just might love you, Conny White."

"I hope so."

Chapter 47

The Wastelands, Somewhere in West Texas (November, 1881)

Epilogue

The horse walked slow over the dust-covered rocks, each step it took unsure of what lay beneath the blanket of powdered earth. The two figures rode hunched over, the man behind, shielding the woman from the bitter wind. The landscape had become a monotony of dunes and hills, plains and rocks, all bled one into another like wet paint mixed on a canvas.

They stopped for food when they were hungry. They ate crickets and salted meat and watered their horse. They moved on. When they tired, they stopped and slept, and one night the man woke the woman and showed her the most amazing thing. The moon made no glow that night, and high above them, through the fog of dust, they could see a star. First Rigel, then Betelgeuse. Two stars of the giant, Al-Jabbar. They watched the stars until the dust returned and blanketed them again.

They made love amid the dust and ruin, life among the lifeless. They slept without fear. When they awoke, they got back on their horse and returned to their travels.

Neither worried about the direction they moved, both content to be where they were, in that moment, with each other. The woman spoke to the man in Cantonese, the language of her people, and he spoke back to her in her tongue. She laughed when he said something wrong, and laughed when he said something right. He picked up her language faster than she thought possible, and he seemed to delight in learning it, though she almost hated to hear it come from his mouth. She had once despised the sound of her language coming from a man's voice, but this man made her forget about who she had been and what she had once hated.

For his part, he loved to listen to her speak and he encouraged her to do it as much as possible. The language of her kind was unlike anything he had heard before, lilting and musical, and he felt like an explorer who had just discovered a strange new land.

And so they spoke to each other as they traveled across the barren Wastelands, two figures adrift on a sea of dust.

End of Book One.

Acknowledgements

There are a great many people who contributed to the creation of this book, whether they are aware of it or not. While it might be impossible to acknowledge all of them, I'll certainly give it my best shot. And if I forget anyone, you have my deepest apology, and I will make an effort to correct that oversight in my next book.

First, to my alpha readers: my wife, my dad, and my sister. Your advice and encouragement meant the world to me. Special shout-out to Dawn for sticking through with it until the end.

I would like to thank Jeremy Agnew for his wonderful books about life in the Old West, especially *Alcohol and Opium in the Old West: Use, Abuse, and Influence.* My research was made infinitely easier by reading yours.

Finally, I'd like to thank all of the men and women who have contributed to my love of stories and all of the characters who have had to navigate through them. George Lucas, Larry McMurtry, James Cameron, David and Leigh Eddings, Margaret Weiss, Tracy Hickman, Steven Spielberg, Ursula K. Le Guin, J.R.R. Tolkien, Robert E. Howard, Cormac McCarthy, Charles Dickens, Jean Auel, Carl Sagan, Walt Whitman, Val Kilmer for portraying the coolest Doc Holliday ever burned onto film, Seth MacFarlane, Drew Karpyshyn, Madeline Miller, Libby Hawker, Shigeru Miyamoto, William Shakespeare, the first three seasons of LOST, Oscar Wilde, Jim Carrey, and so many, many more.

You are all a part of me. I contain multitudes.

About the author

TIM BRUMBAUGH HAS NEVER really had what people call a "hometown." He spent most of his young life moving around the country with his unbelievably strange and eccentric family, from California (where he was born) to Maine, and a dozen states in between. He grew up on the NES, Genesis, and SNES, and he's still an avid gamer and can spend way too much time on Steam or the Xbox, and not enough time writing. He also enjoys doing a bit of astrophotography, dressing up as Star Wars characters, and collecting fossils. After a fifteen-year stint in Texas, he now lives in central Pennsylvania with his wife and kids.

His debut novel, *Sorrow Draw*, is a dark Historical Fiction novel set in a post-apocalyptic America of the 1880s. *The Last Goblin Shaman* takes an abrupt turn from the apocalypse to low-stakes fantasy. It is his second novel.

Made in the USA
Middletown, DE
26 July 2024

57942885R00262